Children of Secrets

— A Novel —

Lander Duncan

iUniverse, Inc.
New York   Bloomington

Children of Secrets
A Novel

iUniverse books may be ordered through booksellers or by contacting:

iUniverse
1663 Liberty Drive
Bloomington, IN 47403
www.iuniverse.com
1-800-Authors (1-800-288-4677)

ISBN: 978-1-4401-8351-5 (pbk)
ISBN: 978-1-4401-8353-9 (cloth)
ISBN: 978-1-4401-8352-2 (ebook)

Printed in the United States of America

iUniverse rev. date: 4/26/10

Children of Secrets

— A Novel —

Lander Duncan

iUniverse, Inc.
New York   Bloomington

Children of Secrets
A Novel

iUniverse books may be ordered through booksellers or by contacting:

iUniverse
1663 Liberty Drive
Bloomington, IN 47403
www.iuniverse.com
1-800-Authors (1-800-288-4677)

ISBN: 978-1-4401-8351-5 (pbk)
ISBN: 978-1-4401-8353-9 (cloth)
ISBN: 978-1-4401-8352-2 (ebook)

Printed in the United States of America

iUniverse rev. date: 4/26/10

— Dedication —

Nancy Duncan, my remarkable wife of forty years, embraced the lengthy life cycle of this manuscript with her love, determination, and sacrifice. Her diligent research; unflinching, skillful editing; efficient and unfailing manuscript management and production; and meticulous proofing made her a brilliant collaborator.

She suffered with me during some rather bleak times when I struggled with only a mere approximation of the story in my mind. We often picked up those broken fragments of ideas and, during our hundreds of long walks, glued them together with her fresh insights.

I have relied on Nancy's courage and deep devotion. Just looking at her brings me joy.

— Prologue —

It has always been difficult for me to face the truth about my childhood because it requires a commitment to explore the lineaments and features of a history I would prefer to forget. Childhood produces no verdicts— only consequences and the freight of memory. My brothers shared with me those deeply lived days of growing up amidst frayed seams and spilling pockets, conflicts of race and identity, anguish and betrayal, deprivation and abandonment, and a scuffle to survive. Etched in our common destiny are those excesses and ambiguities—sometimes heart-shattering and imprisoning, sometimes ignoble—that resulted from being the sons of a father whose violent and untimely death left us to be raised by a badly damaged, complex mother.

I wish I had no history to report. I've pretended for so long that my childhood did not happen. I had to keep it tight, up near my chest. I could not let it out and have to contend with memories overwhelmed by the dominance of fear. My childhood tasted of fear; I breathed it in like air.

At the age of seven, I learned of fear from perverse and imaginative teachers who knew well how to instruct children about its dark, twisted, and virulent roots. My perfect teachers came in hoods and robes and perpetrated a night of horror that still hides in my head somewhere.

I was vulnerable to the overpowering terrors and deeply buried anxieties that accompanied the nightmarish nature of the brutality of that experience. Prone to panic attacks, hallucinations, and night terrors, for more than a year I endured intermittent hospitalizations. Those night terrors defined my beginnings in the small town among the foothills of the Allegheny Mountains in southwestern Pennsylvania, where we sought refuge from the wrath of the Arkansas Delta.

There was one place that I had something resembling peace of mind—my front porch that sat pooled in the coolest shade. Although the porch was dilapidated like the rest of the house, it was the central part of my daily routine, my command post, my hiding place. I could observe my limited world passing by without feeling in danger. In dramatic contrast to the decaying, ruinous condition of the porch with its scaly railing and splintering floorboards, a profusion of morning glories climbed in all directions and created a fortress of funnel-shaped flowers, a mixture of red, blue, pink, purple, and white. They were fragrant and had large, dark green, heart-shaped leaves that provided a measure of privacy with their density. I could push the leaves aside to look out without being noticed.

There were times that I summoned the courage to leave the security of the porch and venture to the end of the street. But inevitably, I raced back to my house and cowered in the corner of the porch in panic and terror that I would be discovered—by a ghost, a phantom, an apparition, a boogeyman.

My porch gave me a deep sense of serenity, a feeling of warmth and safety. Like those morning glories whose flowers open in the morning and close in the sunlight later in the day, I knew that those fits and voices and imaginary things would one day close and go away. And they did as I approached my eighth year. It all just lifted and slinked away, as though I had been pardoned for a crime I did not commit. I came back to my childhood but had lost a great innocence. I understood even then that my mind and I were not going to be on good terms for the rest of my life.

Edna St. Vincent Millay said "… childhood is the kingdom where nobody dies. Nobody that matters, that is." And I did matter; I had to believe that.

I betray the integrity of my childhood history by turning everything, even sadness, into romance. There was no romance in that hideous period of my life. The fears continued: of neighbors, preachers, teachers, God; of being abused and insulted; of being discovered, castigated, haunted, beaten up, chased, ignored, locked in, locked out, abandoned. I had every reason to hold on to these fears as it turned out.

Our mother huddled us boys together and compelled a promise from each of us that we would never tell a living soul what happened to us in Arkansas. The subject or mention of our father became taboo. That binding covenant we entered into was an unbearable weight our mother placed on our fragile and ravaged childhood existence. To be forced to suddenly erase him from our lives with no trace or way to register or mourn his loss was damaging and difficult to grasp. The emptiness and sadness was distorted and turned into something shameful by our mother.

We endured a vast emotional terrain of uncertainty, rituals, and ordeals, and the ever-present struggles to grasp the confusion resulting from our sense of identity shifting beneath our feet or the doors of self-perception slamming in our face. Against the agonies of a brutal life, our mother struggled to preserve for us the multiform appearance of our life as children. The portraitures and still lifes visible through the blooming window of time evidence the courage and resilience of my brothers who give testament to the ability of children to outlive their suffering—if given the chance.

But I will praise her for teaching me to seek out the beauty of nature in all its shapes and intricate designs, to see the world through a dazzling prism of authentic wonder and imagination, and to want to be extraordinary. I cannot watch a sunset without thinking of her.

I wanted to love my mother in all her flawed, outrageous humanity. But I lost the opportunity to address her directly about the felonies committed against all of us. She was remarkable in so many ways that the gifts she bestowed almost equaled the havoc she so thoughtlessly wrecked. I could not hold her accountable or indict her for crimes she could not help—ones that I remember with both tenderness and pain, ones that made me forgive her transgressions against her own children. In families, there are no crimes or sins beyond forgiveness.

Although I managed to elude the demonology of my youth by following my mother's redoubtable habit of keeping secrets and hiding things, the accumulation of so much emotional pain and the discovery of that final, shattering confession sent me into seclusion from my family these past forty years.

Too long estranged from my family, I feel compelled to confront the past and be freed of the chronic guilt and regret that has burdened me. Wading along the shallow shores of my history, it has taken me nearly a decade to muster the courage to head out toward the deeper waters where all the bones, wreckage, and black hulk await my hesitant inspection.

Children of Secrets was written largely from memory and what I was able to unearth from my research. Truth is always an elusive science, and too much concern with the specificity of available information could undermine those truths enlivened by the imagination. Without beauty, there is no pleasure in written truth; yet, ecstasy and woe lie within the pursuit of beauty.

The truths of *Children of Secrets* became a reconstruction, a product of a reshuffling process I used in an effort to extract appropriate scenes and events from the limitless and extravagant images and remembrances of the first two decades of my life. As a powerful chronicle of a time, the historical backdrop remains intact. Liberties were taken as I imagined some of the dialogue, smoothed a few narrative corners, and invented scenes and geographies with no real-life, real-world counterparts or truths.

Physicist Leo Szilard appreciated my dilemma well. Szilard once told his fellow physicist Hans Bethe that he had no intention of ever turning the diary he was keeping into something publishable; he was simply recording the facts of his life "for the information of God."

"Don't you think God knows the facts?" Bethe countered.

"He knows the facts," said Szilard, "but he does not know this version of the facts."

Part One

Fall 1939

— Chapter One —

Fall 1939 is remembered as one of exquisite warmth and sunshine in Tuskegee, Alabama. Abigail Louise, the middle child and far and away the most notorious and bumptious of the Bryant clan, was at the center of a crisis that presented itself out of nowhere. I must open some doors to the past to narrate my understanding of how the calamity unfolded, took shape, and formed the potential to cause humiliation and disgrace to our family.

Possessing straight black hair, which she usually wore in a long, braided ponytail, smoldering and expressive light hazel eyes, and a slightly olive complexion complemented by a few scattered freckles on her face, Abigail could pass for white. And she often did by ignoring the segregated seating in the movie house. She was quick-witted and funny but harbored a dark side that kept her a bit of a mystery to her family. At the age of fifteen, she had a pensive, melancholy demeanor, shadowed by a rare but majestic smile. At five foot nine, Abigail was a young woman of diabolical beauty. She used her looks as a lure and as a weapon. She bartered it and flaunted it. Keenly aware of the hypnotic effect it had on people, she played it for all it was worth.

As she walked across the Tuskegee College campus that fall, the young men lined the walks like crows on a wire to admire the soft, newly sculpted curves that had appeared so recently on her thin, girlish body. Her ripening that year was so sudden and lush that she, along with her seventeen-year-old sister Margaret, became a topic of conversation among the Tuskegee men.

Margaret had soft, luminous features and a doe-eyed self-conscious beauty. Abigail's attractiveness was edgy and explosive. Margaret's beauty held its breath more often than not. In those rare instances when she chose not to withhold it, her beauty tiptoed into view and took her audience by surprise. She was reluctant to accept the responsibility that beauty asked of her. Being pretty was trying; being found sexy was unbearable. Nothing discomfited her more than the unwanted attention of the young Tuskegee men. But what should she have expected with the high carriage of her walk, her beautiful legs, and her effortless elegance? Margaret and Abigail were commonly spoken of as "The Chaplain's Daughters."

Dr. Bryant, Chaplain Bryant—and "Papa" to his children—was outgoing and sharp-witted. An enterprising and pragmatic wheeler-dealer, he was hardly the austere, pious, prototypical theologian and chaplain. His most hard-line critics sometimes referred to him as a cunning and ruthless strategist. He projected an aura of power, more than merited as the Dean of the Tuskegee faculty. A little over six foot four, he was always darting, dashing, rushing—even when there was no urgency—with quickness and enthusiasm, spiritual abundance, and an urge to action. Papa had pale, greenish-grey eyes and a translucently caramel, northern European pigmentation that could be taken for just about any race. He remained in possession of a full head of wavy, black hair, which he parted in the middle similar to the characters in an Ingmar Bergman film.

Abigail's father had no illusions about who had the ultimate authority inside and outside Tuskegee. With a curriculum vitae of considerable distinction, he was among the first Negroes to be awarded a doctorate in philosophy from Yale University and earn a doctorate in divinity and religious studies from Howard University. He also enjoyed a successful tenure as the Chairman of the School of Theology and Graduate Studies at Oberlin College in Ohio. However, in nearby Montgomery, he was not allowed to enter the public library. He had to use the freight elevator in hotels when a white colleague from another university or seminary would visit. At the bus and train terminal, he was required to use the "colored" toilet and drink from a separate water fountain. He stood in a different line at post office windows and Western Union counters. He was expected to give the right of way to whites on the sidewalk. He could not try on a hat or a pair of gloves in a white store. He drove his green Model A to the edge of Montgomery in the Negro section of town to find a gas station that would serve him. And under no circumstances could he eat in a restaurant or at a lunch counter that had a strict policy of isolation from white patrons. In spite of a reputation for being a venerable leader in his field, no state university in the entire South would receive any of his children when they reached college age.

Abigail's father understood the nature of prejudice and knew that its most volatile form—creeping, insidious, and not easily recognized— presented the greatest challenge in raising his children, especially the headstrong, defiant Abigail. The warnings she received at home from her mother were relentless: "Everything you do is dangerous. Everything. The smallest, most inconsequential act can be the thing that brings you crashing to earth." But like her father, Abigail was not easily intimidated.

Papa openly referred to Abigail as "the prize" of the Bryant brood. She disarmed him and kept him off balance with her irreverent, playful manner. She was the only one of his children from whom he would allow banter and repartee, much to the chagrin and disapproval of his wife.

Abigail's mother, Elizabeth, was a diabetic. Her pregnancies had been difficult and resulted in complicated and premature deliveries that the small, local hospital in Montgomery was ill-equipped to manage. Less than ten years separated the five children. Welcome was born in 1917, followed by Margaret in 1921, Abigail in 1923, Ann in 1925, and a boy they prayed for, Fletcher, in 1927.

They were raised Evangelical Methodist southerners through and through. They couldn't play cards—they were tools of the devil—or games with dice. They could not accuse anyone of lying, instead they were telling a story. Anyone born into a generation before theirs was *ma'am* or *sir*—whites earned that right regardless of age. If the girls could be heard through the open windows, loud enough for their mother to discern their voices among all the other children, they were summoned in from play and had to sit quietly like ladies.

Rather than jealousy or rivalry, Abigail's brothers and sisters were taken with her piano virtuosity and vocal gifts, her beauty, and even her strength and willfulness. Like young lions and lionesses, they tried to shield their sister from their mother's harsh words. Whenever the considerable anger for tripping over family protocol and regimentation was directed toward Abigail, they surrounded her in a protective circle, their voices in respectful objection to their outnumbered mother. As though he was watching a stage comedy, Papa was usually amused.

Papa never lost his temper. He dealt with his children with words, with speech. His language carried great fullness, clarity, and bravado as though, even in ordinary conversation, he was reciting Marc Anthony's speech over the body of Caesar. He spoke with deliberateness, precision, and directness. With the exception of Abigail, he could wither his brood with words. But it was important to him that the Bryant children speak properly, and he scrutinized their every word, it seemed, by pouncing upon them to correct their diction. A path was worn to the shelf that contained the great, unabridged Webster's dictionary that Papa's father had left to him. They turned the thin pages, brittle with age, to the entry he requested and often had them read aloud. The definition often went on into Greek and Egyptian conceptions, but Papa had them stop short on the treacherous edge of antiquity.

The Bryant children accepted Papa as someone capable of transforming them into whatever they wanted to be. In the Philippines, during the First World War, he had survived a bullet and had the scar to prove it. "If my heart had been going this way instead of that," he announced once, while arbitrating a dinner fracas, "none of you would be here today." It was a joke, of course, but it was also a message that seemed to prevail in the household. Papa had supernatural powers. His fate had determined their existence. While they became too old to hold his hand, too big to ride on his shoulders, there was no escaping the enchantment he held over them.

Despite her struggle with diabetes and heart disease, Elizabeth was an energetic woman of commanding presence who autocratically administered to the household. She was opinionated, unyielding, and impolitic. This imperious whirlwind of a woman was recognizable a hundred yards away by her great, tangled wreath of wiry black hair sprinkled with white. Thin, tall, and angular with the severely sculpted features that automatically were associated with highbrow women, she discouraged the children at an early age from calling her mama, mommy, mom, and other such familiar maternal titles. She simply preferred *mother*.

Abigail's strong-minded individualism clashed with her strait-laced, self-righteous, and possessive mother. She was intolerant of her mother's relentless judgments and moral opinions. There was a certain tone that Elizabeth used when she disapproved of something Abigail did; it was as if she drew on a private source of wisdom that was unassailable and almost sacred. It was when she reached for this tone, and the expression of listening to inner voices that accompanied it, that Abigail particularly disliked her. It was not often that they laid aside their maneuvers, rivalries, power struggles, and surrenders. Their mode of communication seemed like sonar, each bouncing pulsations off the other and listening for an echo, which produced baffling moments of tears, anxieties, and raging frustrations.

Abigail's room adjoined her parents' bedroom, and she often heard them talk at night. Even when the words were indistinct, the hiss of her mother's unhappiness with her came through the walls, "She won't listen to me and challenges everything I say." Papa tried to seal over the wound or whatever it was that she inflicted on her mother that day.

Papa and Elizabeth seemed mismatched. Yet, when they spoke to each other it was with the deepest civility. There were no light bantering moments, no hints of flirtation. Nothing interfered with their unexamined affection for each other. Love could be felt between them, but it was a love without flame or passion. There was occasional rancor about the children. But there were no fevers, no rising and ebbing of the spirit to chart. It was a marriage without weather; only Abigail disturbed the windless days in the Bryant home.

Perhaps Abigail's strongest ally was Aunt Arnetta. Their unique relationship began when Elizabeth's delivery complications and an extended hospitalization brought Arnetta to Tuskegee to help care for the newborn Abigail. Arnetta had never conceived, and it left her unfulfilled and discontent because of her remarkable love for children. Over the years, she overwhelmed Abigail with attention on her frequent visits from her home in New York. Arnetta's devotion to Abigail sometimes caused bitter disagreements with her younger sister, Elizabeth. She was accused of pampering and spoiling Abigail at the expense of her other nieces and nephews. Elizabeth took inexhaustible pleasure in demeaning her sister with occasional torrents of self-righteous denunciation.

Arnetta was a bit of a character—a blend of an iconoclast and a Renaissance dilettante. Her allure was offbeat, indefinable, and original. There were rumors about affairs and infidelities. She was a well-known gifted classical pianist who had been held back by her color. Her energies went into her music studio in Harlem, which became a foundation and launched young Negroes seeking the future she felt had been denied to her. Arnetta's storied recitals and extravaganzas, as well as her own performances accompanying a jazz ensemble at clubs around town, gave her a devoted following and reputation.

Arnetta had three-year-old Abigail mastering the grammar of scales. Throughout Abigail's childhood, Arnetta was always there, trying to convince Abigail that she had the talent to reach a high level of competence. Abigail spent entire summers in New York City studying voice and piano, reading and writing poetry, and having social grace and etiquette foisted upon her. She reveled in the freedom of being away from her mother. An ambivalent Elizabeth reluctantly gave in to her daughter's extended visits to New York. The realization that each trip took Abigail a little further emotionally from the family did not escape her. She consoled herself knowing that New York was a city that could extend Abigail's talents and was worthy of her gifts.

Two places served as a common ground between Abigail and Elizabeth. The garden in the backyard—where Elizabeth grew flowers that captured notoriety throughout Tuskegee—was a place they worked quietly together for hours with the seedlings, cuttings, bulbs, and blooms. The flowers seemed to signify a truce between them and a potential for a relationship of sanity, order, and even beauty.

Abigail found pleasure in the rejuvenating rites of spring, even the nuisance of extracting dirt from under her fingernails after hours in the garden. She lopped, lifted, dug, and planted the seed packets her mother gave her—nasturtiums, poppies, sweet peas, petunias. Abigail loved the feel of the hoe handle in her palm as she folded the ridge of soil over the seeds. Sealed, they ceased to be hers. There was simplicity in getting rid of something by giving it to itself, destined for a succession of explosions of color. People came from all over Tuskegee to see Elizabeth's Acres, as it was called, at blooming time.

The other site where they enjoyed brief periods of harmony was in a nook upstairs. They shared poems at a little desk with wicker sides. Elizabeth had published a couple of small books of poetry and was successful in having poems published in periodicals and literary magazines.

Whether they were in the garden or the upstairs nook, those were times of tranquil standoffs. They required no discussion about their conflicts or needed any reassurance. Maybe there was just the want for an unquestioning presence that existed, regardless of the discord between them. However, efforts to alter the course of their relationship could not surmount the things they had said that wounded, damaged, or destroyed them and left each with blood on her hands.

Abigail sought refuge from Elizabeth on campus where Papa spent most of his time. The stone chapel with the rectory and classrooms attached was the most impressive building on the horizon. It was the center of the universe to Abigail. The end of Sunday service bestowed a moving experience that consumed her with awe: the darkness of the chapel, the singing of the men's choir soaring in descant, the lofty, spiraled ceiling multiplying the clamor. Suddenly, as if a great storm had ceased, there was no music. The silence held by the student worshippers and the townspeople was broken by the resounding chimes from Booker T. Washington Hall signaling the noon hour and the end of the service. As the impressive carved wooden doors were opened, an ethereal shaft of sunlight flooded the dark, and the noise of the campus broke the quiet. Papa stood at the far end of the front aisle. Dressed in a blend of academic and theological robes and brocades, he prepared to lead the congregation out of the chapel. Abigail was proud of her father. She, and the rest of her family, enjoyed the gleams of recognition that fell onto them due to Papa's high visibility.

Lately, the courtesies of the day to the Bryant family members on the campus and around town were lukewarm and reflected a growing dissent from various pockets of the community. Commissioned in 1916 as an army lieutenant chaplain, now with the rank of captain to go along with his academic credentials and status, Papa was the architect in bringing the Army Officer Training Corps (OTC) into existence at Tuskegee. A furor and challenge to the growing presence of the program and its cadre of white training officers was building and taking aim at Papa. Some complained that on the days when dress uniforms were required to be worn by student cadets, the campus looked like a military academy with all the pomp, pageantry, and protocol.

One group of faculty representatives delivered a strongly worded memorandum to the president of the college:

> *Why should our young Tuskegee sons and students be trained on this campus in an endeavor that might mean being called upon to shed their blood for Roosevelt's America, or Cotton Ed Smith and Senator Bilbo, for the whole Jim Crow, Negro-hating South, for the low-paid, dirty jobs for which Negroes have to fight, for the few dollars of relief and the insults, discrimination, police brutality, and perpetual poverty to which Negroes are condemned even after obtaining training and a degree from our College? When our students ask this question of our government, of this country, of us, what can be answered? Nothing. Nothing but lies and empty promises of better treatment in the future. Why must they risk dying for this? They are not afraid to serve and to fight. Negroes have been some of the greatest fighters in history. But the democracy that our sons and students might be called upon to fight for, foreign leaders and countries are not depriving them of....*

The letter went on to accuse Papa of violating the charter and underpinnings of Tuskegee's mission. The closing paragraph delivered a threat to boycott classes until OTC was banned from the campus. The letter was released to the local and national media. Several prominent Negro leaders fueled the faculty resistance by arguing, in the press and at meetings and demonstrations, that the fight for democracy at home was where the preparation of students should be. As the faculty executive to the commandant of the OTC program, Papa was thrust into the national spotlight as the spokesperson in defending the Tuskegee OTC as "a program that would bring enhanced citizenship rights to Negro Americans and develop a new generation of leaders."

Papa held his ground against the controversy swirling around the campus. With the support of the president, Papa informed faculty dissidents that OTC would stay. Anyone who was unhappy about this, or failed to teach their classes, should think about leaving or taking early retirement. Days later, he announced the establishment of a formal military science department in hopes of enticing the Army Air Corps and U.S. Navy to set up officer training programs on campus. He was met with resentment from a healthy contingent of Tuskegee faculty who had no tolerance for what they described as Papa's bulldozing conceit, authoritative ego, imperiousness, and obstinate autonomy.

In spite of his importance to the revitalization of Tuskegee, which brought national media attention to the school, badly needed federal dollars, and a twentieth-century curriculum, Papa was not immune from campus politics that could place him and his family in jeopardy.

Abigail spent vast amounts of time on the Tuskegee campus. Aside from routinely visiting her father's office, she attended formal and informal events and gatherings. She used the main library, attended chapel services conducted by her father, and took piano and voice lessons from the director of the famed Tuskegee Men's Choir—all for no reason other than to prance and charm her way into forbidden contact with the Tuskegee men. Most of the young men resisted her, knowing how dangerous such a liaison would be.

Often, Abigail talked Margaret into her conniving and girlish silliness and teasing by vying for attention during their walks on campus. There was one student that Abigail and Margaret had swooned over for two years. They saw him at chapel, around Papa's office, at the Tuskegee Men's Choir practices in the music auditorium, and at other chance sightings around campus and in town. In a student body of approximately 1,700 Negro men, this six-foot-three, sleek-framed young man with dark brown eyes, ruddy complexion, and a mustache reminiscent of Clark Gable stood out like a Greek god. Abigail romanticized and fantasized about him.

When Papa introduced Abigail to Greek classics, she consumed them like cheap romance novels. Gods, heroes, and myths intrigued her. She read the *Iliad* that summer and teased with Margaret that the

Tuskegee man, whose name was CJ Duncan, was her heroic Achilles. Abigail proceeded to tell her sister the story of the brutal quarrel over a young girl and her young body and the sexual delights between Agamemnon and Achilles. Abigail spiced up the myth with words such as *appetite, honor, alienation, estrangement, phallus,* and referred to herself as the young girl in the *Iliad* who had been stolen from her father. Thereafter, whenever they saw him, Margaret said to a blushing Abigail, "There goes your Achilles."

CJ was selected as the senior cadet-commander of the Tuskegee OTC brigade and accorded the distinguished military student prize for the 1940 commission class. Papa knew CJ well, but did not cave in to Abigail and Margaret's repeated probing for information about him. An honor student in biology, captain of the boxing team, tenor in the men's choir, a member of the debate team—was all Papa would reveal.

Infatuation was a dangerous possession in the heart of the fifteen-year-old Abigail. She looked for opportunities to run into CJ, confident that her free-spirited demeanor and coquettish teasing would provoke him into some innocent flirtation. One day, she cornered CJ in the library—no introductions were necessary. He was gentlemanly and appreciative of the attention she paid him and accepted an invitation from Abigail to meet after her piano practice. She danced away mentioning that she had to be home by dinnertime. Their meetings became more frequent and longer. Abigail poured out her life and dreams. CJ was overwhelmed by the trust she bestowed upon him with such intimate details. She gushed as if she had been saving up her memoir and had to surrender it or be consumed in its untelling. She felt herself saying too much, explaining too much, and overexcited.

Drawn by a force that was too irresistible to question, CJ fell into a serious friendship with Abigail. For nearly four years, he managed to stay away from agitating entanglements. CJ was skillful at carving up his days so that there was a minimum of clutter to distract him from his objective to excel. But he longed for Abigail when more than a day or two passed without seeing her. She was intoxicating. His carefully constructed defenses began to slowly crumble—but not without great difficulty.

It was hard for Abigail to ask CJ even the most innocuous questions about his past. Everything was painful. Everything was pungent. CJ's past, the good and bad, was always delivered in fragments. Even with a fertile imagination, Abigail found it almost impossible to piece together the missing parts of his history. Any question could sound the alarm for a silent retreat.

Abigail was drawn to the mystery of CJ. She gently prodded him for information, "I don't need to know everything. I just want to know a few things. Sometimes, it seems to me that you don't want to tell me anything. It almost seems secretive as though you don't want me to know. I'm not asking you to explain, justify, or apologize for anything in your life."

Abigail managed to take the facts in the unsorted and ill-fitting increments given and put together something that she concluded might be part fiction. He had arrived at Tuskegee from a farm in the Arkansas Delta with his father's first and middle initials for a name. It was on his birth certificate that way. His father promised him the remainder of the letters to his name if he amounted to something and earned them.

CJ's biography of his father, Christian James, was one of uncomplicated craziness and a disaster as a father and husband. CJ cynically called his father a gypsy-blooded wanderer because he did not put that much imagination into his travels. He just liked the feeling of being on the road, and it did not matter much to him where he was going. The summons would strike him without warning, and he would leave the farm straightaway. Even in repose, he had a distracting nervous mannerism. His right leg would shake and jiggle as if there were an engine idling beneath his knee. That vibrating leg was always a reminder to CJ that his father could be gone the next day. To his credit, he never left during the cotton-harvesting season. During his frequent absences, CJ and his mother had the daunting task of keeping the farm going. For some reason, CJ's father never got around to the fundamental business of cotton farming or raising his only child.

For months at a time, his father left him, his mother, and the farm while he drifted around the south selling Bibles, cutting hair, and spreading the word of the Gospel as he sprinkled talcum on freshly barbered necks. He deposited the Lord's word like pollen on every Negro soul he drifted upon in his errant, unpremeditated ministry. Along the back roads of the Negro rural South, he carried one suitcase filled with his clothing and barbering tools and another larger one brimming with Bibles of all shapes and sizes. The least expensive Bibles were black, utilitarian, and the size of a child's shoe. But the print was small and could induce myopia if read too fervently in bad light.

Christian James considered it his duty to push the showier lines. The elite Naugahyde Bibles were dyed milky white and had gold tassels to use as page markers. The spoken words of Jesus of Nazareth were printed in vivid red ink. The poor Negro sharecropper and tenant farmer families invariably snatched these most expensive Bibles up and purchased them on a generous payment plan.

In Christian's wake, these people often had to make the difficult choice between paying the monthly installment or putting food on their table. His pious and God-struck presence certainly must have made the choice more difficult than it should have been. He equated not making a payment on a Bible with grievous, unspeakable sin. But to his credit, he never brought himself to repossess a Bible once he had filled out the family chronology in the middle of the book. He believed that no Negro family could feel truly secure or free until they were all "named-up" in a decent Bible where Jesus spoke in red. Though it sometimes strained his relationship with the company that supplied him with the Bibles, he refused to take the word of God from a poor Negro man's house. The Bible company sent other men to repossess the Bibles or collect the money due. But Christian James sold more white Bibles than even the white salesmen did and that was where the real money was made.

As a salesman, Christian became something of a legend. He went door to door and hit small towns and farming areas dominated by Negroes. If a family was not in need of a Bible, then someone in that family was probably in need of a haircut. He cut hair for a whole family at a group rate. Above the razor's hum and a dense cloud of talcum, he brushed the falling hair from the necks of squirming boys and girls while he spoke of the life of Christ.

During the height of the Depression, Christian quit his job as a barber and Bible salesman. Under the belief that the Depression was a celestial sign of the imminence of the Second Coming of Christ, he wanted to be close to home. He focused his energy on the farm and took a job at the nearby sawmill.

CJ's great grandfather, born into slavery, was given a sixty-acre plot of land at the end of the Civil War. CJ's grandfather, born a free slave, farmed the land and purchased an adjacent forty-acre parcel from a pauper in the Confederate Soldier's Home in Little Rock. The purchase price was the payment of the taxes to keep it out of the government's hands. That pauper's great grandfather had commanded a battery under Brigadier General Beauregard that fired on Fort Sumter. It was said that Beauregard refused to speak to a Yankee or a Negro, male or female, until the day he died.

The Duncan farm, all one hundred acres, was surrounded on three sides by the Arkansas River and creeks and was part of the Marlcrest plantation. It had been a tenacious struggle for those who farmed the land to survive the floods and droughts that resulted in fields plowed under and crops destroyed. On more than one occasion, they nearly lost the farm.

Most of the hundred acres was dedicated to cotton. Early every spring, Christian got a crop loan from the owner of the cotton gin. The money was spent on seed, fertilizer, labor, and other expenses. A bale of cotton was worth $150 give or take, depending on the market. If the weather was perfect, particularly through the picking process, a good crop could produce a bale an acre. Inevitably, something went wrong and the farming operation lost money. Debt was carried from the previous year. After several years, the farm was deep in debt.

Christian finally conceded the farming to a family of Negro sharecroppers, the Meriweathers, who also farmed their own ten acres on the low side of the river, no more than a half mile away. The Meriweathers, who appeared to be doomed to eternal poverty before the relationship commenced, had seven offspring—six of whom were boys—and the children's grandmother, Hatti Mae. Everyone picked cotton. They managed to bring in profitable crops that helped get the farm out of debt.

The Duncan farmhouse was situated to provide a view of the river and benefit from the river breezes. The Marlcrest cemetery was adjacent to the farm. The tombs and graves housed the bodies of the plantation families, children who'd died at birth, those who had been felled or trampled by horses, and those who died from cholera or yellow fever during the 200 years that Marlcrest had been in existence.

Before the Civil War, slaves hauled muck, called marl, up from the river. This earthy deposit was used as a fertilizer for soils deficient in lime. It was spread on the fields—hence the family crest. Smothered in the mud, collapsed in the heat, snake bitten, or drowned, many died there. They were buried in a corner of a distant field that the pinewoods had taken back years before CJ's father was born. Duncans were buried on that plot of land.

CJ told the story of his mother in the manner of a confession and apology. A Cherokee Indian girl with the unlikely name of Hallie was an annual visitor to the Duncan farm beginning when she was only eight. Like the Mexicans and hill people from the Ozarks, her sizeable family and extended family showed up in the Delta during the cotton-harvesting season. After six seasons, they inexplicably stopped coming and left Christian in a scramble to hire workers to bring in his crop. Hallie ran away from physical and sexual abuse within her family and appeared three years later at the Duncan farm doorstep—barefoot, tattered, beaten, hungry, and blind in one eye from a degenerative eye disease. She was a distracted, incoherent, almost wordless, illiterate seventeen-year-old girl.

Christian took her in as an itinerant to help around the farm under the assumption she would leave on her own accord or someone would come to claim her. No one knew the world she had come from that shaped her, squashed her, and left its permanent imprint. When she arrived, Hallie had the look of someone for whom family betrayal was as basic as bread. She had the look of a runaway who had suffered from the galling monotony of abuse. She never cried. The disaster of growing up had squeezed Hallie dry of even her tears.

She was the consummate farm laborer in duties that included cooking, cleaning, and taking care of the livestock and a sizeable vegetable garden. Strong and lean, work was what she did best. She possessed a toughness; there was something vigorous and implacable about her. For someone who seemed to have lived entirely without good fortune, she never lamented her circumstance to anyone. She did have a certain shrewdness about her, but it was narrow and antisocial, negative and pessimistic. It was the shrewdness of somebody who expected nothing and carried with it a fatalistic message: *keep your head and expectations down, and you might slip by unnoticed. Don't say things can't get worse—pray they don't get worse.* She was convinced that hope created disappointment. This was an adolescent girl whose life had been beating her down almost as long as she had lived. Whatever Hallie learned came from that.

The age disparity aside, Christian and Hallie had little in common. But they managed to distill the essence of everything reconcilable, including the discrepancies that existed between them, into a relationship that produced a son three years after she arrived on the farm. The relationship was described as a common law marriage. It was a relationship devoid of much affection and left Hallie seeking to fill her immense loneliness through an uncommon closeness with her son. CJ never felt a maternal bond, only a dependency he blamed on his father. Sometimes, Hallie tried to treat CJ as an equal, and in so doing, robbed him of any chance of being a child. Worse, she allowed him to parent her, stealing from a generous, eager child what she had been denied by her own family. She let CJ carry her inexorable unhappiness and turned his childhood into a duty.

* * * * * * * * *

Papa's notoriety earned him an appointment in the Roosevelt administration as advisor on Negro Affairs, consulting to the office of the secretary of war. Papa's eldest son, Welcome, was part of the first graduating class of Tuskegee officers. Papa took full advantage of the voice he earned in the national debate regarding the nature of the participation of Negro Americans within the armed forces. Welcome was serving with the Negro Twenty-fifth Division somewhere in southern Louisiana. He bombarded Papa with dramatic stories about the daily conflicts and explosive conditions created by the practices and thinking of his military superiors and senior command. Papa was relentless in his recommendation for the military to abandon its "segregation without discrimination" policy that created separate and unequal conditions.

With the ominous Pacific threat, European countries on the verge of being overrun, and the likelihood of the United States being drawn into a war, Papa waged his own war. His major hope of turning the tide of animus on campus and rescuing some redemption resided in Washington, D.C. The Selective Service bill being debated in Congress would give Roosevelt the authority to bring Negro men into every branch of the military. If passed, rather than simply the all-Negro regular army units, this bill would allow Negroes to serve in the military in numbers disproportionate to their percentage of the population. It would also ban discrimination in the recruitment of Negroes, afford the opportunity for Negroes to volunteer for induction, eliminate discrimination in the training or selection of men, and allow the assignment of Negro soldiers to both combat and service units. Papa worked diligently in Washington on behalf of this bill. The passing of any parts of the legislation would place Tuskegee in the national spotlight because of its leadership in the training of Negro officers and greatly expand the flow of federal dollars to build existing and new programs in other departments. Papa's role in the military presence on campus gave his enemies an easy target. The OTC and military science program could easily be dismantled should the bill be defeated.

During this time, Papa was embattled and preoccupied. Much was left unattended at home, particularly Abigail's comings and goings. Elizabeth's diabetes and heart problems had her in and out of the hospital. Abigail's room on the first floor opened to the backyard. This made it easy for her to sneak out to meet CJ, who was breaking curfew and student conduct rules that could result in probation or even dismissal. CJ disregarded the warnings from fellow students. He engaged in a heated exchange with Clancy, his roommate and closest friend, which turned into a scuffle. Clancy, a lean, malt-pale colored farm boy from North Carolina, pounced on CJ in a final gesture to rescue him. He had exhausted all attempts at reasoning. In desperation, he tried to prevent CJ from another late-night caper with Abigail.

"CJ, you're *seeing* her tonight?" Clancy quizzed in his contemptible squeaky voice. Clancy got to his feet and challenged CJ, "You give this up or we'll both be kicked outta here, our futures destroyed and disgraced in the process. This isn't right; she's just a little girl, not more than fourteen or fifteen."

CJ turned serenely, "If you were in love, you'd understand."

As CJ was about to leave, Clancy came up behind him and caught him around the neck with one arm. CJ's body stiffened as he spun around. In a matter of seconds, Clancy found himself lying on the floor, looking up at CJ's face, which was upside down in his vision.

Angered, Clancy got to his feet and would have gone for CJ again, but fellow students who were drawn by the ruckus grabbed his arms and held him. He shook them off and without a word returned to his desk. Everyone in the room seemed to know what the skirmish was about. CJ left the room and slammed the door; he didn't return until midnight. He was incapable of holding back the weight and magnitude of his wanting and could not resist Abigail's innocently seductive advances.

A passion between CJ and Abigail developed and burned for two months—like a brief spark in the night. As the student-commandant of the OTC brigade, CJ had keys to training offices and classrooms. He took advantage of the opportunity this presented for their rendezvous. Experiencing the strength of a first love that had not been jaded and disillusioned, they did not need a subtle prod. The intense physical insistence and urge was present. Excited and full of fear, CJ put his hands on Abigail's shoulders. Her bare skin was cool to the touch. As their faces drew closer, CJ was uncertain enough to think she might spring away. Her mouth tasted of the forbidden lipstick—given to her by Arnetta—and salt. They drew away for a second. He put his arms around her; this time they kissed with greater confidence. Daringly, they touched the tips of their tongues. It was then that she made a deep, sighing sound which, he realized later, marked a transformation.

Until that moment, there was still something uncomfortable about having Abigail's face so close to his. He felt watched. But the contact of tongues, alive, moist flesh-on-flesh, and the strange sound it drew from her, changed that. This sound seemed to enter him, pierce him down his length so that his whole body opened up, and he was able to step out of himself and kiss her freely. The self-conscious and secretive CJ seemed to disappear. The sighing noise that Abigail made was greedy and made him greedy, too. He pushed her hard into the corner, between the shelves of books. As they kissed, she was pulling at his clothes, plucking ineffectually at his shirt. Their heads rolled and turned against one another as their kissing became a gnawing. She bit his lower lip. He pulled away and then moved back and kissed her throat, forcing her head against the shelves.

She pulled his hair and pushed his face down against her breasts. He noticed she was wearing a little silver cross. There was some inexpert fumbling until he found her nipple, tiny and hard, and put his mouth around it. Her spine went rigid, and then she shuddered along its length. He trapped her nipple between his teeth; the sensation was unbearable. Tilting her face slightly, CJ kissed her eyes before parting her lips with his tongue. For both, there was nothing but obliterating sensation, thrilling and swelling and the sound of fabric-on-fabric and skin-on-fabric as their limbs slid across each other in this restless, sensuous wrestling. A button pinged against the floor and rolled out of sight.

CJ's experience was limited. However, he knew they need not lie down. As for Abigail, beyond the fantasy, the novels and poems she had read, and the teasing with Margaret, she had no experience at all. Despite these limitations, it did not surprise them how clearly they knew their own needs. They were kissing again; Abigail's arms were clasped behind CJ's head. She was licking his ear and then biting his earlobe. Cumulatively, these bites aroused and goaded him. Under her dress, he felt for her buttocks and squeezed hard. Keeping her eyes fixed on his, she reached down to remove her shoes. There was more fumbling now with buttons and positioning of legs and arms. Without speaking, he guided her foot onto the lowest shelf. They were clumsy, but too selfless now to be embarrassed. When he lifted the dress again, he thought her look of uncertainty mirrored his own. But there was only one inevitable end, and there was nothing they could do but go toward it.

Supported against the corner by his weight, she once again clasped her hands behind his neck, and rested her elbows on his shoulder and continued to kiss his face. The moment itself was easy. They held their breath before the membrane parted. When it did, she turned away quickly, but made no sound. They moved closer, deeper and then, for seconds on end, everything stopped. Instead of an ecstatic frenzy, there was stillness. Abigail whispered his name—those two initials—with the deliberation of a child trying out the distinct sounds. When he replied with her name, it sounded like a new word; the syllables remained the same, but the meaning was different. Finally, he spoke the three simple words that nothing can ever quite cheapen. She repeated them, with exactly the same slight emphasis on the second word—love—as though she had been the one to say them first. CJ's religious beliefs had wavered, but it was impossible not to think of an invisible presence or witness in the room. These words, spoken aloud, were like signatures on a contract.

Motionless for perhaps as long as half a minute, they began to make love against the bookshelves that creaked with their movement. That night blazed. They could not get enough of each other and were unable to stop. Their exhausted greedy arms reached for each other again and again. They sank into the familiarity of each other. Many nights thereafter, there ensued clandestine meetings. They experienced moments of unbreakable tenderness, reckless and clumsy fondling, frenzy and craving, lightning looking for a place to strike, a thunderstorm of emotion, an exquisite sweetness and lust, lovemaking at every stolen opportunity, and a pregnancy!

Abigail became isolated and withdrawn from her family. No one seemed to notice her loss of appetite, nausea, and fatigue. After a missed second period, Abigail *knew*. It took her weeks to surrender the news to CJ. She fell upon him the night of her telling with brusque hugs, cannonades of kisses and caresses, and torrents of tears. CJ reeled from the shocking revelation, but he quickly regained his composure out of concern for Abigail and the loving reassurance he wanted to express. That night, there was a proposal of marriage and talk of running away to the Duncan farm in the Delta. There were pledges of eternal love and promises of not letting anything stand between them and having their baby.

Briefly carried away with the emotion of the moment, they soon were harkened back to face the reality and consequences of the pregnancy. Their lives had suddenly been altered; certainty about anything disappeared. It was a tragedy suddenly unfolding with pervasive, destructive potential. They huddled together for hours shivering with trepidation, trying to formulate a way of telling her family. They talked each night with their attention funneled down the narrow track of the pregnancy. They fluctuated wildly between clear, focused, and deeply connected to exhausted, flattened, tearful, and bereft. The decision to deliver the news at dinner on Friday, Bryant family night, was as far as they got.

* * * * * * * * *

Family night was always much anticipated. Replete with tablecloth and china, several courses of family favorites were followed by Bible study and prayer. The family gathering took on additional significance when Welcome sent word that he had been granted a three-day leave from Fort McClelland and would arrive on Friday afternoon.

Over the years, the Friday repast was an opportunity for a higher level of dialogue. There was a reverence about these gatherings that took them into weekends of church activities, culminating in Sunday services that extended to midday. When she was younger, Abigail loved the part of the Friday dinner of going around the table and each person reciting a Bible verse. She spent hours with the Bible before dinner, finding long, twisting, complex verses full of archaic language. Then she'd recite them when it was her turn. No one would dare interrupt a recitation from the Bible, although there were growling stomachs and much kicking under the table. She always included a question in her discourse. When the theme of her verse came from the Apostles' Creed, Abigail blushed and asked, "About the Resurrection of the Body, are we conscious between the time when we die and the Day of Judgment?" Her reply came in the form of a lot of blinking and pursing of mouths around the table. The faces of her brothers and sisters usually went blank, as if an indiscretion had been committed.

As a rule, Papa's answers always tried to find their way back to his favorite query, "And how does that scripture inform the way we should live our lives?" On occasion, Welcome or Margaret joined the skirmish and a full-scale debate ensued. Sometimes, Abigail would pick up on the awkward current running around the table and shut up, relishing that she had astonished and thwarted everyone. Other times, Papa had to rebuke and put her in her place with a gentle reproof for what he scolded as *being smart*. Elizabeth usually expressed a mild look of disbelief, a look that was delicately disquieting, and then shook her head, pursed her lips together, and smiled wryly in obvious disapproval at Abigail. The word *smart*, when it was applied to Abigail, meant attention seeking and obnoxious. She did love being the center of attention and flourished under the influence of that perception.

For the first time, Abigail dreaded Friday to come. Welcome entertained everyone at dinner with his stories about camping in the swampy backwoods of Western Louisiana. He mentioned the number of critters that crawled out of the swamps and into their encampments to share their tents. He had anecdotes about feral pigs, armadillos, swamp rats, raccoons, chiggers, and snakes.

But he saved his best for the razorback hogs that constantly ran through the camp, "Louisiana's overrun with hogs, razorback hogs. They have sharp spines and long, skinny legs. The males have tusks. Let me tell you, this is one ugly animal. They'd run wild and just tear through the camp in passels. The male would lead, and the female with her little ones followed behind, looking for the food waste from the kitchen.

"One time, I tried to shoo them away, but they refused to budge. I tried to maneuver my way around them, but fell backward onto the ground. One of the hogs straddled me, and I found myself pinned under a 400-pound razorback. There he stood, right atop of me. I don't mind telling you I was plenty scared. My men were whooping and hollering; I was panicked and petrified to make any movement at all for fear of being sat on. It was only a matter of seconds. But the hog moved on, and I was spared. The men quickly took matters into their own hands. They killed the hogs and barbecued them. Those hogs made for some mighty good eating."

Margaret's news that she had received acceptances to Spelman College and Howard University turned the conversation away from hogs, the inhospitable terrain of the bayou, and how bad things were for Negro soldiers, not only in the Southern countryside, but also on Southern military bases. Margaret seemed to be leaning toward the all-Negro women's college in Atlanta. She had not bought into Elizabeth's vision for her: attending Howard to get a degree, any degree; meeting a light-skinned boy studying to be a doctor, from a good Negro family; getting married, settling down, raising children, and participating in cotillions and other events as part of the topmost ranks of Negro society.

Just as everyone headed toward the living room for Bible study, a knock on the door made Abigail's heart jump. The sound of her heart thumping almost drowned out all other sounds. Welcome greeted CJ cordially. He was an underclassman and cadet at Tuskegee when Welcome graduated. Welcome was left with the impression that CJ was angry, petulant, and arrogant; had a chip on his shoulder; and was too eager for confrontation. The only thing he found to his liking about CJ was his work ethic and passion to succeed.

Abigail went to the door, led CJ by his hand into the living room where everyone had settled. Guilt and responsibility slid together like two substantial shadows inside his chest. CJ was conscious of the effort of breathing. Every action—taking one step after another into the living room—felt like a precarious extension of a long, mechanical sequence insecurely linked to his heart. No one came to the Bryant home unannounced, and an immediate attitude of indignation took control of Elizabeth. Papa knew that CJ had learned protocol, etiquette, and social grace from the military manuals and classroom discussions about officer conduct. Aware that CJ's father was gravely ill, he was concerned that his condition had further eroded.

Before any inquiries could be made of CJ, the words, "I'm pregnant" came out of Abigail's trembling mouth. These weren't the words she wanted. They were not large enough; they were too tidy. Even a string of the most potent and hefty words would not have resonated the awful consequence of her condition. Their secret was out. But it was childish sentimentality to suddenly think that their difficulties had come to an end with the words, "I'm pregnant" and that all complications ceased to be, their battle somehow abjured.

For an eternity of just seconds, there was raging silence and expressions of shock and disbelief. Papa's face contorted, his body language twisted in agony, and his mouth trembled as the words, "You're what?" exploded through the room.

Abigail got as far as, "I'm preg…" before he repeated the question in several more bursts. The intonation moved from disbelief to outrage. CJ tried to interrupt, but Papa stopped him cold and delivered a scathing, stinging invective in which he accused CJ of a betrayal of trust that robbed their daughter of her innocence and her future, destroyed and brought dishonor on two lives and two families, and broke a moral covenant with God. Pledging to take action to have him dismissed from the OTC program and expelled from Tuskegee, Papa ordered CJ to leave.

With a suppliant humility, CJ refused Papa's command and stood fast. He expressed his love, respect, and marriage intention over Papa's boisterous, "I don't want to hear it." He apologized for the harm and pain he had inflicted and promised to immediately withdraw from Tuskegee to spare the family the public embarrassment of a formal expulsion proceeding. Papa repeated his demand for him to leave. As he turned to depart, CJ kissed Abigail tenderly and told her he would abide by her wishes—but could not bear losing her.

It was now Abigail's turn. Her sisters huddled around her as they usually did when she was in trouble, trying to absorb some of the pain. Abigail cried hysterically. Papa just looked at her and shook his head, "You break my heart, Abigail." Trying to hold back the visible tears, he walked away and headed for his study. Abigail followed him and begged for forgiveness and mercy for CJ. He tersely stated, "I need to be alone. Go talk to your mother. I have nothing to say to you right now."

Elizabeth responded with no display of shock or disbelief. There was no convulsed, uncontrollable crying, not even a tear. There was no rage or hostility, no blame, no chastisement, or threats. There was also no affection, tenderness, or reassurance. There was no maternal comfort and understanding or effort to lessen the pain. Elizabeth had a habit of wrinkling her brow about what was said in judicious silence. If she decided that indeed a response was warranted, one would be forthcoming after considered opportunity to weigh her words. Elizabeth's primary concern was not Abigail, but containing this front-page news from becoming gossip.

Elizabeth knew the basic laws about gossip in the Tuskegee campus faculty and social neighborhood circles. She stayed abreast of it and tried to keep her family free of it. She understood that you never knew how many people were talking about you behind your back. And most importantly, she knew that gossip spread from friends to acquaintances to people you'd never met. Out of garbled, vivid, and definitive conjectures, stray tidbits and guesses, a hard mass of what everyone "knew to be true" emerged. Repetitions and retelling turned all the little pieces into facts.

She knew and had been witness to the fact that elaborate stories about someone were told by perfect strangers. Elizabeth knew that however they tried to handle the situation, gossip would inevitably follow. So it was the shape and amplitude the gossip would achieve that was her primary concern. Going against her faith, she made the decision that honesty would not serve the family well in this situation. Elizabeth gathered the children together and extracted a solemn oath, "You must keep Abigail's pregnancy a secret. This one time, I am asking you to put aside the family rule. Family respect and honor are at stake and possibly Papa's position at the college." Without so much as a word to Abigail, an inconsolable and brooding Elizabeth joined Papa in his study.

No one slept that Friday night. Whispers, quarreling, stifled sobs, and occasional percussive rumblings kept a constant murmuring undertone cutting the hush of the darkness. Abigail joined Margaret in her bed and willingly shared the details of her clandestine affair with CJ. Margaret derived great pleasure in hearing the saga—as though she were listening to a romance novel or, better yet, a contemporary Greek Classic. Abigail even kidded, "I suppose I'm living out the drama of the Iliad; CJ is my Achilles."

But there was nothing mythical or cavalier about Margaret's great distress or the misery she felt. She ached from her powerlessness in the situation. Margaret shared her feelings of guilt with her sister, "I encouraged you with CJ. I overdid the kidding and flirtation, provoking you, even participating in the curiosity." As the eldest sister, Margaret felt responsible by being so self-absorbed that she had not looked out for Abigail. Margaret knew her mother would hand some of the blame to her.

Everyone gathered for Saturday morning breakfast as was the custom of the house. Before the blessing was offered, Elizabeth startled Abigail with an ultimatum. She and Papa had spoken with Arnetta at the crack of dawn. Arnetta was disturbed and overwrought by the news. However, she had agreed to their request to let Abigail live in New York with her until the delivery. Elizabeth issued the conditions of the relocation in a stark and biting recitation. Abigail was never to see CJ again; the baby was to be given up through adoption to Arnetta; Abigail would attend a private boarding school after the birth of the child.

To everyone's chagrin, exasperation, and even anger, Abigail bitterly refused the offer. She threatened to run away to live with CJ in Arkansas if she were forced to move to New York. They tried to frighten Abigail with warnings about the dreadful living conditions in the Arkansas

Delta and reminded her what she was giving up in favor of a life with dirt-poor, illiterate, cotton-farming sharecroppers and hillbillies. There ensued a brutal, bitter exchange. Her mother vowed to never forgive her for bringing shame on herself and the family, for slapping her Aunt Arnetta in the face with her juvenile selfishness and insolence, for persisting with a mistake that would surely beget others, and for turning her back on her family to pursue an adolescent infatuation. Abigail would not budge and sequestered herself in her room for the remainder of the day, refusing to eat or talk to anyone.

The family went to church on Sunday morning without Abigail. Elizabeth had a cold, bare space inside where she could live by the absolutes she declared. But Papa was not willing to gamble on losing Abigail. On the way home, he announced, without Elizabeth's blessing, that the family would support Abigail's decision to marry CJ, have his baby, and move to the Arkansas Delta.

Despite what it might cost him for breaking university and army code of conduct rules in allowing CJ's infractions to go unreported, Papa let it be known that CJ would graduate from Tuskegee and receive his lieutenant bars. He could not bring himself to destroy CJ's future—only four weeks away from graduation. CJ had worked too hard and come too far. Papa said he would rather look for another career than lose his daughter. Having breached his faith by not standing up to temptation when tested with a moral dilemma of great consequence, Papa felt demoralized and hypocritical.

Papa outlined his expectations with CJ and let him know, "I will be a constant, sometimes annoying presence in your lives."

On the day of graduation, CJ's father lost his battle with pneumonia and passed away. Papa attended the funeral in Little Rock with CJ and was unnerved by the living conditions to which his daughter would be exposed. He instantly regretted his decision to acquiesce to Abigail's wishes and returned to Tuskegee with a sense of dread and torment. Keeping his shock and guilt to himself, he began to prepare for consequences that could bring his daughter great suffering.

Abigail completed her tenth year of school. Papa gave them their wedding vows in the Bryant home. With the exception of Arnetta, only the immediate Bryant family was in attendance. Arnetta put aside her disappointment and arrived loaded with wedding gifts for

Abigail. There was no reception, no honeymoon, only a formal dinner reluctantly prepared by Elizabeth. Abigail received a bouquet of flowers from CJ and a deed of trust to the Duncan farm that had her name added to it. Christian had deeded the property to his son years earlier. Hallie never shared in the title to the property. From her family, Abigail received a white Bible and one hundred dollars.

CJ had only one week before reporting for military duty. He brought his father's truck back with him after the funeral, and they loaded Abigail's few belongings. As she headed off to her new life, Margaret and Ann fumbled with their good-byes, beginning sentences, but not finishing them, "Well, if you're planning to … and "I just thought you might …. They were trying to say something that refused to be said. For Abigail, she had an anxious feeling that the meaning of her life was about to become clear and that it would be dreadful. She struggled to gain some emotional balance over the separation and could not resolve the heartache over leaving. Elizabeth could not bear to see her fifteen-year-old daughter leave and remained cloistered in her room as Abigail and CJ pulled away.

— Chapter Two —

About a half mile from the farm, where the gravel thinned and eventually surrendered to dirt, the road over the Arkansas River became a one-lane, wooden bridge. The bridge had been built in the late twenties as a WPA project and was sturdy enough to withstand the weight of tractors with loaded cotton trailers. But the thick planks popped and creaked every time it was driven over. As Abigail would experience many times, if she looked at the brown water directly below, she'd swear the bridge was swaying.

As they passed the outer perimeter of the farm, neat rows of green stalks stretched to the tree lines that bordered the Duncan land. It was the growing season. The cotton was coming to life by the minute. CJ gently enlightened Abigail, "In two months time, the fields will be awash with a sea of white. The end of August marks the beginning of harvest season and nearly a hundred acres of cotton will have to be picked around here by the beginning of October."

As they drove farther down the dirt road, the farm came into view. The house looked like it had been recently painted off-white with forest green shutters. Blissfully ignorant, it looked to Abigail like a postcard of a picturesque farm scene. CJ drove past the house that had three pin oaks—each more than seventy years old—shading the house and yard. Continuing, they passed two chicken coops, the water pump, a clothesline, the tool shed, and sugar maples that turned bright red in October.

They parked near the barn and silo, which were exactly one hundred yards from the back porch steps. The Duncan farm owned a cow named Isabel, chickens, two mules, a seed planter, a cotton trailer, a flatbed trailer, a wagon, and a John Deere tractor that was visible near the rear of the silo. An extensive vegetable garden was located on the east side of the house. This was the quiet side away from the kitchen door, the barnyard, the chicken coop, and the small dirt drive. The garden was enclosed in a wire fence four feet tall to keep out the deer and vermin. Corn was planted around the fence so that once the rickety gate with the leather latch was closed; it was like stepping into a secret world hidden by stalks.

Five wooden steps ascended to the front porch; a creaking swing sat on one side and two padded wooden chairs sat on the other. The house was not large with three bedrooms, a kitchen, and a living room. It was so old that the plank floors under the multicolored braided rugs sagged in places. The kitchen was small and hot. A round, oscillating fan rattled away on top of the icebox and tried to keep the air circulating. In the living room, a box fan only worked about half the time. A door inadvertently closed or blown shut would disrupt the movement of air, and the house became unbearable. At times, wind would compete with the box fan, and the hot air would gather in the living room before making its sweltering way through the house.

Abigail was charmed by the interior of the barn. Some high, small windows and the gaps between the slats admitted shafts of light that reminded her of the light in a cathedral she had seen on one of her trips to New York. The light revealed an atmosphere glittering with dust from the hay stacked in staircases of bales at one end. Abigail felt deep in the sea of time. There were elements of old farm machinery rusting away in the corners and pieces of lumber, ten-gallon milk cans, boxes to hold berries, and empty barrels here and there. But her fascination with the farm began to dwindle.

Abigail's delight quickly faded when she could not find the bathroom anywhere. "Where's the bathroom?" she reluctantly inquired.

CJ took her hand and led her to the back porch. He pointed in the direction of the barn, "The outhouse is right over there." This was the first of several shocks delivered within minutes of their arrival.

There was no indoor plumbing. The outhouse, a small wooden closet sitting on a deep hole hidden behind the tool shed, was stifling with humidity. It was dark; the only light came from the tiny cracks between the planks.

On one of her first experiences, Abigail took a flashlight with her as she walked through the wet grass to the outhouse. She set the flashlight, burning, beside her. An insect alighted on the lens, projecting onto the wallboards the faint rim of its wing, its long, hinged legs, and the dark cone at the heart of its anatomy. Abigail's enveloping fear was dense, internal, and all around her. When she stood up, automatically hunching her shoulders to keep her head away from the spider webs, it was with a numb sense of being cramped.

Out in the open again, as the beam of the flashlight skidded with frightening quickness across the remote surfaces of the barn, the tool shed, and the giant pine that stood by the path to the woods, the terror descended. Abigail raced up through the clinging grass, pursued not by one of the wild animals the woods might hold or one of the goblins her superstitious aunt had communicated to her in childhood, but by specters of her imagination. In the momentum of her terror, her overactive imagination provided hideous possibilities that added their weight to her impeding oblivion. Abigail never found the outhouse congenial, considered it an indignity, and bore a grudge against it.

Four days stood between CJ and his departure. "Deliverance to the demons that harken" was the catch phrase Abigail used when referring to CJ's mustering for military duty. During these precious few days, they focused on the cleanup and repairs around the badly neglected farm and managed to keep the terror of CJ's leaving perpetually at bay. Staying busy freed them. It was only in the quiet hours that they felt the enormous dread.

On the eve of the third day, Abigail lost her self-control. Returning from the outhouse, she inadvertently squashed one of the huge brown Delta snails, the ones with a shell the size of a large marble that seemed to slide all over certain areas of the farm. The popping sound, like the cracking of walnuts, frightened her, and she let out a scream. CJ ran to her and found Abigail holding a slipper dripping with the viscous glob of the snail's remains. Standing on one leg, she released all her pent-up tears and sobbed, "I can't do this alone CJ, I need you here with me." CJ looked at Abigail with remorse and sadness. His lips parted to say something, but before he could speak, Abigail crumbled into his arms. He picked her up tenderly and carried her to the house.

Their lovemaking had been vigorous, even desperate on that last night together. But afterward, in the early hours of the morning, Abigail was unable to sleep. She lay in bed staring at the beams on the ceiling, listening to the big spooky moths that every now and then bumped with a flicker of soft wings against the torn screen on the bedroom window. Close by, a bird that Abigail could not identify kept up a disturbance of flirtatious twitters. Closer still, under the house, beneath them, small rodents made clumsy, scuffling sounds. Abigail focused on these sounds one by one. By distracting herself long enough, she might avoid being pulled down the tributaries of despairing thoughts that could mire her in absolute dread.

Abigail could tell from CJ's breathing that he was deep in slumber. She wondered, *How can he sleep?* Upset with herself for being so demoralized, she could do nothing to avoid the mudslide that enveloped her. Abigail couldn't fight the fatigue any longer and drifted off into a shadowland where fantasy mingles with dreams.

Upon awakening, her heart pounding with joy, she could not recall the pleasurable contents of her dream with the exception that CJ received orders from the army that delayed his reporting for duty. CJ continued to sleep. *Get a hold of yourself,* Abigail reprimanded herself. She recalled the promise she made to CJ on the trip from Tuskegee, "I won't turn your leaving into a drama, soldier boy."

Until this very moment, Abigail hadn't rehearsed how she was going to say goodbye. But for now …. She spooned close to CJ and caressed one side of his chest and nipples. CJ rolled slightly taking Abigail with him. Her warmth was waiting to receive him. They made love as though touch and passion in itself was reassurance and consolation. CJ shuddered from a powerful orgasm; Abigail moaned breathlessly. That moment filled Abigail's mind like an ecstatic heartbeat.

Before noon, a uniformed CJ climbed aboard military transport in Little Rock while Abigail tried to sort out the mechanics of getting a bath.

Bathing was a primitive experience for Abigail. During the week, she filled a washtub with water and left it in the sun all day so that there would be warm water in the late afternoon, early evening to wash up. On Saturdays, before going to town, she concocted a bath ritual on the back porch, shielding herself with an old bath sheet. It took her eight trips hauling the water from the pump with a bucket to get the tub a third full. She kept one bucket full to pour over her head to rinse the soap. She flatly refused homemade soap from the Meriweathers that smelled of lye and turpentine. After finishing her bath, usually in cold water, she pulled the plug from the tub and watched the water seep through the cracks of the porch. How she missed the oversized bathtub and hot tap water in her parents' home.

A far cry from the pampering she received growing up in the Bryant home, the culture shock was daunting, overwhelming, alienating, and harsh. But more than anything else, it was frightening to the point of wanting to call an end to what seemed a blending of dream and nightmare. She was grossly unprepared and collided with it in dramatic fashion.

The melancholy and discontent slipped into Abigail's letters to CJ: "I did not understand when I left how hard it would be. I am so confused at times. I feel lonely and cut off from all that is important to me. My past life seems to be disappearing and my memories grow jumbled. It's as if I am dissolving and reforming. I am turning into something I don't recognize. I lay awake and my life in Tuskegee—my childhood, even my brief time with you pass—pass by my eyes as if it had been lived by someone else. Please forgive my wonderings, but I feel so lost here."

CJ was dealing with a different type of isolation and separation, and managed only morose, maudlin, and self-pitying letters to Abigail. Stationed at Fort Huachuca, located at the far reaches of Arizona at the very edge of the state (seventy miles southeast of Tucson and twenty miles north of the Mexican border town of Nogales), CJ complained of being as far away from any American city as you could get and still be within the borders of the continental United States. "Smack dab in the middle of nowhere" is how the soldiers described their segregated and isolated geography. "The racial snubs and indignities of Fort Huachuca," he wrote, "would take too much energy and endurance to record the infinite number of ways that it offends me." The daily grind of training was carried on in the extreme heat and freezing temperatures that frequently occurred on the same day. Fast-moving thunderstorms, snowstorms, and sandstorms blasted during field exercises. CJ's letters carried constant reminders of the harsh conditions: "… hailstorms and lightning storms accompany the thunder every day; they are terrifying. The lightning came so close to me that sparks leaped about the rocks at my feet and my hair seemed to bristle and crackle."

Abigail was not one to retreat for very long. Her stubbornness began to pour itself into the transformational duties of preparing for motherhood in the deep, rich center of rural Arkansas. She began mastering and taming Delta life into something personal and not quite so forbidding.

Abigail was left with Hallie, her mother-in-law, who was in failing health. There were rumors that she was in an advanced stage of syphilis. She appeared veiled in a shroud of precocious senility. Her blind eye gave her a proud, divided look, as though half her face slept while the other side stayed fiercely alert. Disfigured, she looked like a woman sentenced not just to imprisonment at the farm but condemned to some even greater anguish for the rest of her days. Hallie had the profile of a horse: a long face, big teeth, lank hair, and one eye that shone with dark, equine clarity. The most perplexing part of sharing residency with Hallie was that her mind wandered. Seldom were there instances of perfect clarity when Abigail could glimpse any sense of her. There were moments when she was a child asking her mother for favors. In the next instant, she was a farmer's wife concerned over the cotton crop or a mother complaining that her son never leaves school long enough for a good visit with her. She had mistaken Abigail for her mother, a neighbor who moved away years ago, and other assorted people from her past.

There were times when Abigail helped Hallie bathe and felt the terrifying fragility of her bones. Hallie wasted to nothing, hardly seventy pounds. She was dying as much from humiliation and loneliness for her husband and son as she was from her substantial physical ailments.

When Hallie's veil lifted, Abigail pulled from her the secrets, mysteries, and rhythms of the farm, survival in the Delta, and her reminiscences about CJ growing up. Information came out of Hallie in bits and pieces. It was an awkward and difficult task. Some information revealed unasked-for snippets. Sometimes, wisps flew inadvertently out of Hallie's mouth. Sometimes crucial facts had to be extricated.

The information revealed was never orderly. Each of the fragments seemed independent and unrelated to anything else. They were compact, self-centered, and at times, contradicted what CJ had told her. Abigail realized that part of this Duncan family would be in her baby. "Who are these people?" she sullenly posed to no one. She felt their presence. It was a nameless, faceless, invisible presence. There would be no answer to her questions.

Before CJ had left the farm to begin his active duty in the military, Hallie clutched his hand in a hard, blue-veined grip and pleaded, "Take me with you, son. I refuse to die with this stranger you have brought to my house. Please son." CJ's departure killed her a little bit more.

It nagged at Abigail that Hallie stole her goodbye from CJ. Hallie considered Abigail an outsider and that never changed even after months of feeding her, cleaning her feces, keeping her washed and free of bed sores, and trying to ease her pain. Abigail struggled to assuage the abysmal depths of her loneliness. She let CJ know his mother was failing and begged him to take a leave and come home. But his furlough requests were repeatedly denied and the three-day passes offered were hardly adequate to reach Arkansas. Mercifully, Hallie died six months after Abigail arrived.

CJ sent Abigail instructions for Hallie's burial in a grave site overlooking the river next to Christian. There was to be no memorial service, no prayers. Abigail and the Meriweathers were the only ones in attendance. When Abigail returned to the empty house after the burial, she realized that Hallie had left no heirlooms, no legacy, no family recipes, and no words of advice or pieces of wisdom—no testament that she ever existed. She shuddered and recoiled, her head scrambled with random thoughts and images of Hallie that were unarranged, unsorted, ungraded, and anxiety provoking.

The Meriweather family's ten acres were within walking distance— across the bridge and up river—from the Duncan farm. One or more of the six Meriweather boys was always around the farm either in the fields or doing maintenance chores. They had promised CJ that Abigail would be treated like family, and they kept their word. Hatti Mae, the eighty-five-year-old matriarch of the family, with some sixty years of midwifing, kept constant vigilance over Abigail's pregnancy.

The most important Meriweather in Abigail's life was Doretha, who contrasted with Abigail sharply. Ebony skin, dark almond eyes, a soft, black cloche of kinky hair, and dimpled cheeks produced an appearance just crossing the dividing line between adolescence and womanhood. Petite, her shape lost to her pregnancy, she had a habit of holding a loose fist to her face to cover her defective mouth. She had apparently learned it early and practiced it all her young life: hiding her cleft lip with her right fist was her perpetual apology to the world for a birth defect over which she'd had no control. The lip, split just to the left of her front teeth, exposed a quarter-inch gash of gum and gave the illusion that she was sneering. But Doretha never sneered. She apologized. She put her fist to her mouth for neighbors and friends, for the reverend of the church, for her husband, and even, sometimes, for herself when she caught her image in a reflection. She rarely talked about her harelip, and on those infrequent occasions when she did, it hit like a snowball in the eye.

Their first attempts to get to know each other were not promising and reflected the disparities in appearance and upbringing. Abigail had no real consciousness about being a Negro, which hardly seemed possible in a place where color was a common denominator for just about everything. She was frequently mistaken for white and employed it only as a convenience. She figured out early in her childhood that her color gave her special privilege.

And it wasn't just her talent that brought her attention from her Aunt Arnetta, who loved to comb her hair, dress her up, and show her off. Negro boys fawned over her and treated her like a princess. She liked the independence and agility her appearance gave her, a sliding relationship to everything. There was nothing insolent or arrogant about it—reckless, naïve, and misunderstood, perhaps.

In Doretha's circumstances, her color was like a phobia that imposed its own bigotry and she immediately attacked Abigail in an attempt to suck her into the inescapable reality of the Delta. Doretha let Abigail know, "Your light skin, good hair, and funny cat eyes don't make you no better—you just be different. You ain't gonna *pass* 'round here, you no better than anybody else, you's a *nigger* just like the rest of us, and you gonna hafta work just as hard." Abigail had heard all of this before in Tuskegee, even from her teachers and just shook off the outburst as jealousy and bad manners.

They were just a year apart in age; both were expecting their first babies a month apart; both had husbands serving in the army; both possessed common individual characteristics, such as a naturalness, ease, and lively innocence; both had been spoiled and pampered—Doretha by her six older brothers and grandmother. A close relationship was inevitable. How could it be otherwise?

Their dissimilarities disappeared into the fabric of daily life as Doretha nudged Abigail into the rhythm of farm life. Abigail learned how to milk Isabel and take care of a garden that supplied fresh vegetables during the summer and enough left over for canning to sustain both families through the winter. She learned the art of making biscuits and how to gather eggs without stepping on huge rat snakes that inevitably left her crying for two days. She also learned how to keep grits from being mealy and how to cook greens to avoid the swampy odor if they were boiled too long.

Doretha's father, Stuart, felt strangely territorial and threatened by Abigail. He struggled with her presence and constant pestering about the operation of the farm. At harvest time, he was hardly subtle in letting her know that CJ worked the fields whenever he could and reluctantly allowed Abigail to try her hand at picking. There were trips to the cotton gin where Abigail watched in awe as the freshly picked cotton was sucked from the trailer, disappeared into a building, and emerged at the other end in neat square bales to be loaded into trailers headed for the Carolinas.

Stuart's stern demeanor softened with the closeness of his daughter's relationship with Abigail. He slouched, a posture that was the product of a life of hard labor and picking cotton. All semblance of a neck had been lost, and his swollen middle resembled an old-fashioned clay jug. His voice was reedy and faint, producing its sound on the intake of his breath. Socially, he was more intake than output, though an occasional chuckle could be taken as an agreeable signal. He never quite became comfortable with Abigail and acted bemused by her appearance on the Duncan farm and at their dinner table. He even made a point of this bemusement, demonstrating a preoccupation with activities around the farm when she was around.

Mildred Meriweather treated Abigail like a daughter and pampered her. She swept Abigail into the fold with a voice full of breathy enthusiasm about her family, the seasons, the cotton crop, and especially about the church and her religion. There was no mistaking the content of her life as she matter-of-factly ran a household, basking in her gravity, with an unquestioned competence capable of facing up to anyone or anything. Approaching forty, she had gone through her share of life's tests. She remained relatively selfless, as if her self were something she had absentmindedly left in another room, like a pair of reading glasses. Her bearing was so nicely honed in all her doings around the farm that even mothering six sons could not crack her composure.

Mildred was shoe-colored black that had a healthy glow, as if her darkness had been rubbed deep into her skin. Her soft black hair, scarcely touched by gray, was abundant and wiry. It was usually braided and pinned up in the familiar farmer's wife style. Sometimes, Mildred was almost inconspicuous by being drab and brisk, reserved and tense, and a bit aloof in her usual attire of a man's checked lumberjack shirt that hung over her belt like a maternity blouse. Wearing baggy clothes concealed an oddly good figure for a woman who had taken seven pregnancies to full term. Her slight spread was that of a woman who had fulfilled her duties and knew herself to be, whatever shape the future would bring, basically an attractive woman. It was Mildred who led the active role of the Meriweathers in the life of the church. She sang in the choir, taught Sunday school, and was a deaconess. It was like an extension of the farm and her family; there was always some practical reason for her to be at the church.

The Meriweather house felt like a ship underway; it shook and trembled with the perpetual passage of feet and activity. And Abigail jumped on board as a grateful passenger.

Abigail could not develop a taste for chitlins, buttermilk, okra, green beans boiled in fatback, squirrel, and sweet sunfish cooked into potpies, venison, and whistle pigs, better known as groundhogs. Doretha was as good-natured about Abigail's cooking and eating habits as Abigail was toward Doretha's Delta language and the way she spoke.

Abigail's southern accent was significantly patrician. She refused to slip into the language of the Delta that she kindly called colorful. The Meriweathers had resisted any homogenizing influence of speech from the rest of the South and kept a distinctive accent and used words that were unrecognizable to Abigail. By placing sounds before verbs to keep the rhythm alive, Doretha spoke in a highly inflected style; her speech rose and fell like spoken poetry. Abigail made it her mission to teach Doretha Standard English. With only a sixth grade education, Doretha good-naturedly accepted the grammar lessons. Abigail was both surprised and embarrassed when she caught herself proofreading Doretha's sentences as she spoke them by adding a "*g*" to the end of participles. She scanned Doretha's clauses to make sure they "*ain't got no double negatives,*" or clipping long vowels, and making sure she used *lay* and *lie* and *brought* and *bought* in a manner that wouldn't embarrass her. It was confirmed: she was still a Bryant.

Doretha was not illiterate, but had great difficulty reading. Most days, Abigail found time to teach her things. Doretha took a great liking to language. She spread the *Little Rock Gazette* on the table and asked Abigail to listen as she tried to read. When she came across a sentence containing a new word, Abigail helped her sound it out and would ask, "What does it mean, you think?" After a few wild guesses, if she didn't know the meaning, Abigail got the battered, coverless dictionary from the closet floor. The type was so small she had to slide a magnifying glass down the page. When she found the word, she let Doretha take a look, and there it was—huge, inky-black letters bleeding off in rainbows under the fractured light. They both learned not just new words, but the names of flowers, small towns, and rivers. Listening to Doretha repeat a word she had fallen in love with was like watching her stick a finger into Abigail's mixing bowl, swirl it around, and extract the unfamiliar brandy sauce that Abigail had learned to make from her mother to pour over bread pudding; she savored the taste and feel of it on her tongue.

A deep bond, uncommon closeness, and intense attachment developed between these two girls who were becoming women together. They teased each other about how fat they were getting and shared the disappointment of their husband's absence due to military duty during holidays and special events. Huddled around a radio barely audible from so much static, they listened to *Amos 'n Andy, Fibber McGee and Molly, The Great Gildersleeve,* and Jack Benny cracking his jokes and suffering his embarrassments. The old radio brought them the voices of the famous gospel singers Lula Bell and Scott as well as Bing Crosby, Lowell Thomas, and Kate Smith.

On weekends, Doretha and Abigail fished and cooked their catch of perch, pike, bass, catfish, and sunfish on an open fire; they baked cobblers from dewberries and blackberries gathered from their secret places on the bluffs above the Arkansas River. They relished those Saturdays together in Walnut Grove, a little town three miles from the farm, down Highway 218.

The highway became Main Street for the short stretch it took to negotiate Walnut Grove. Past the Walnut Grove Methodist Church, every store, shop, business, and even the school, faced Main Street. On Saturdays, the traffic inched along, bumper to bumper, as the country folk flocked to town for their weekly shopping. It was a much-anticipated Saturday ritual. The basics were purchased at Pop and Pearl Johnson's grocery store. During picking season, the shelves burst with fresh produce and canning supplies. The first couple of hours in town were spent in crowded aisles with clutches of Negro women more concerned with saying hello than buying food and waiting in line to be checked out. There were separate lines for Negroes and whites. As long as someone white was waiting, Pearl, who usually handled the register, ignored Negroes. It was her calling in life to monitor the movements of the town population, so any question was answered with a question—which slowed her down. With glasses on a cord around her enlarged neck, she controlled the volume of the conversation and the gossip network. A long line at the register resulted for the Negro women. Good-naturedly, they talked about gardens and weather and church, who was having a baby, and who might be. They prattled on about a funeral here, a revival there, and an upcoming marriage. There was no mention of poets, writers, classical music; there was no flow of ideas. And for brief periods, Abigail felt herself adrift. A feeling of displacement—profound and enervating—overtook her.

After the grocery shopping, Abigail and Doretha roamed Main Street and moved with the languid foot traffic toward the north end of Walnut Grove. It registered with Abigail that the white ladies she passed were the homeliest looking women she had ever laid eyes on—shapeless figures, plain, manly faces, and heads full of thin, brown hair drawn back into tight buns, as plain and simple as a bar of soap. They went to the drug store and fingered through the shiny magazines, *Life* and *Liberty* and *Collier's* and the *Saturday Evening Post*, on the upright wooden rack.

With ice cream cone in hand and fresh with the images of the tweedy pipe-smoking writers, bespectacled lab coat inventors, and slick-haired café-society people from the magazines, they headed toward the hardware store and the co-op. The co-op offered items such as bullets, hunting rifles, and shotguns that could be bought, sold, or traded. Occasionally, men walked into the store with some wild game slung over their shoulders. For those who fished, there was an assortment of rods, flies, plugs, and spinners. Out back, a tank, with a garden hose stuck in it, harbored night crawlers, mealworms, and minnows. This emporium of goods also sold three kinds of snuff and a bewildering number of pocketknives. One old gas pump sat in the rear of the building where gas and oil could be bought for vehicles and boats. You could even get a sandwich at the co-op. A sign on the wall read WE GOT BOLOGNA, YELLOW CHEESE, AND BOLOGNA WITH YELLOW CHEESE.

The hardwood floor was worn smooth over the years, and the store smelled of dead fish and lubricant for rusted nuts and bolts. In front of the co-op, spades, rakes, hoes, red and green wheelbarrows, and Lilliputian tomato plants beckoned potential shoppers. Abigail bought her vegetable and flower seeds, bulbs, and cuttings from the co-op, but otherwise tried to stay out of a store mostly populated with men who ogled and leered at her when she wore thin sundresses. The unwanted salacious attention to a pregnant woman disgusted her.

During Abigail's first time in the dry goods store, she tried to place a wide-brimmed insipidly decorated straw hat, with a pink bow and dried flowers, onto Doretha's head. Doretha knew better—Negroes were forbidden from trying on any merchandise or fingering it unnecessarily—but did not have time to react. The size of the hat caused it to cover her forehead and eyes. In a flash, the sales clerk asked them to leave the store. Speaking loud enough for everyone to hear, the proprietor sent a comment in the direction of their departure, "Niggers need to be taught their place and manners." Abigail recoiled spontaneously when she heard it and turned around. Before she could get a word out in reply, Doretha grabbed her hand and hurried her out of the store. Repulsed by the incident, Abigail declined to discuss the occurrence when Doretha later brought it up. She never entered that store again.

Along the sidewalk, packs of people stood gossiping, with no intention of moving. This forced Negroes to the curb and street since they had to relinquish walkways to whites. Their ultimate destination was the Dixie—a nickel for the matinee, Coca-Cola for another nickel, and a bag of popcorn for three cents. They took their seat in the "colored" section balcony and were transported from the harshness of life on the farm to a fantasyland of romance and movie stars. There was Tyrone Power, his black eyebrows knitted in a troubled frown, and Joan Crawford, her huge dark lips bravely tremulous while her eyes filled with tears.

On Sunday, the fields were vacant. It was considered a sin to work on the Sabbath. Most things were sinful in rural Arkansas, especially if you were a Methodist. The church was located off the gravel road in a grove of oaks a few hundred yards from the edge of town. Small and white, it looked like something on a country calendar with its oak pews and frosted glass on the windows. The only spot of color was the burgundy carpet on the altar. The Reverend Lacey, a loud and angry man who spent too much time conjuring up new sins about which he preached, consumed a great part of the Sunday worship ritual. Accustomed to Papa's elegantly delivered sermons at the Tuskegee Chapel, Abigail didn't care for Reverend Lacey's ranting. But it was a festive gathering, with everyone in good spirits or at least pretending to be. It was a time for visiting or spreading news and gossip. Whatever the worries of the world—coming flood, Jim Crow laws, the war, the fluctuating price of cotton, making ends meet—they were all put aside during church.

Aside from family and farm, nothing was as important to the Negro Delta community as the church. With Doretha's coaching, Abigail soon knew every person in the congregation. It was a family—one that accepted her with some hesitation and tongue wagging—for better or worse. Mildred, Doretha, and the Duncan legacy had much to do with smoothing the reception Abigail received.

For anyone ill, all manner of prayer and Christian caring poured forth. A funeral was a week-long, almost holy, event. The fall and spring revivals were planned for months and greatly anticipated. At least once a month, there was some form of dinner-on-the-grounds, a potluck picnic under the trees behind the church. Weddings were important, but lacked the high drama of funerals.

The Meriweathers sat in their usual spot, same pew, halfway back up on the left side. The pews were not marked or reserved, but everyone knew where everybody else was supposed to sit. Even with the windows open, the ladies fanned themselves and the men just sat still and sweated. Abigail and Doretha sang in the choir and enjoyed showing off. Blending their voices above the others, they unleashed spirituals such as "Precious Lord" and "Blessed Assurance." *Amens, Yes Lords,* and *Sing it Sisters* exuded from an appreciative congregation. Occasionally, Abigail played the piano when Sister Gaines suffered from one of her influenza flare-ups.

The picnic grounds and baseball diamond near Briler's Creek, a mile south of the church, hosted the annual fall picnic for the combined Methodist and Baptist congregations. An impressive array of food accompanied the event. One table showcased nothing but raw vegetables—tomatoes of a dozen varieties, cucumbers, white and yellow onions in vinegar. Other tables hosted beans, black-eyed peas, crowder peas, green beans cooked with ham, and butter beans. At least a dozen bowls of potato salad, with no two looking alike, and plates of deviled eggs covered half of another table. Bowls of fried chicken, baskets of cornbread, rolls, and various kinds of bread covered yet another table. Waiting in the shade, homemade chocolate and peanut butter ice cream and fudge brownies were packed in coolers that were draped with towels and packed with ice.

The highlight of the affair for the men, at least, was the baseball game between the two faiths. Complete with umpires, coaches, and much haggling, this intense competition carried over from year to year. According to Doretha, the Methodists had not won since CJ left. By the third inning, the ladies of both denominations grouped into small clusters of conversation. For them, the game was of lesser importance. Abigail felt out of step with the flow of general conversation. She intuitively felt that conversation passing beyond certain limits might be a disruption, a form of showing off. Yet, trying to fit in, Abigail's perception of the limits was not reliable. She sometimes couldn't wait out the pauses or honor the common aversions to certain topics.

Women talked about who had a tumor, a septic throat, a bad mess of boils. They told how their own digestion, kidneys, nerves were functioning. Intimate bodily matters never seemed to be so out of place, or suspect, as the mention of a fact read in a book or magazine, or an item in the news, or anything, really, that was not materially close at hand. These women touched each other with their words not to do any harm, but to give themselves pleasure; little new was offered, mere pinches or slivers were added. Yet these almost meaningless remarks or glimpses did enhance the flavor of the conversation. The conversations, too, served a purpose of location, of placing the others on a continuum of happiness or its opposite. It served the purpose of satisfying whoever was speaking that others are within hailing distance in their dark passage through life, with its mating and birthing, its getting and spending, its gathering and scattering. Abigail did not understand about the connections and complications, obstacles and burdens of Delta women. Outside of church, they seemed to have a serious weariness. In contrast, Abigail's pregnancy seemed to agree with her. Her beauty remained undimmed, her looks as luminous as they had ever been. She enjoyed the attention, as did Doretha, from all the women at the afternoon gathering.

September and early October was a busy, anxious time around the farm. The months were filled with sleepless nights, doubts, and extraordinarily hard work. On a routine day, Abigail milked Isabel, gathered the eggs, and started the biscuits before Hatti Mae and Mildred arrived. The entire Meriweather family appeared at sunrise for breakfast, usually fresh eggs, milk, salt-cured ham, sorghum, biscuits, and coffee. Everyone ate quickly. Stuart and his boys wanted to get an early start before the sun got too high.

Stuart drove the boys to the field on a trailer that was coupled to the tractor. They worked the bottom fifty acres first in case of flooding.

Each took a twelve-foot sack—which held about sixty pounds of cotton—flung it across his back with the strap over the right shoulder, and attacked a separate row. By 8:00 AM, everyone was ready to weigh in their first load or should have been. Stuart did not tolerate laziness from his boys and everyone was expected to hit a "home run" by the end of the day, which meant picking at least one hundred pounds. Meeting that expectation involved twelve hours, unshielded in the sun and bent over, picking with both hands until their fingers bled.

Mildred was in charge of the scales, which hung from the end of the trailer. The straps of a sack were looped over the hooks at the bottom of the scales. The needle sprang around like the long hand of a large clock. Everyone saw how much each person picked. Mildred recorded the data in a small book near the scales. The cotton was piled into the trailer. The empty sacks were caught when they were tossed down. There was no time for rest. Another row was selected and the pickers disappeared into the fields for another hour and fifteen minutes or thereabouts.

Abigail and Doretha kept cold water coming to the fields by letting large chunks of ice melt on the porch. Relieving themselves and taking water breaks were barely tolerated by Stuart. To break the monotony, they kept up endless chatter and singing. They developed their own harmony and rendition to spirituals such as "Shall We Gather at the River," "What a Friend We Have in Jesus," "Rock of Ages," "Oh Master Let Me Walk With Thee," "Savior Like a Shepherd Lead Me," and "His Eye is On the Sparrow."

Sharply at noon, everyone came in from the fields, hot, thirsty, and with fingers swollen from tiny punctures inflicted by the burrs. Leftovers from breakfast along with fresh fruit and vegetables were offered for lunch. In most cases, all they wanted to do was find the shade and snooze for an hour. Later in the afternoon, Abigail and Doretha would take little pick-me-ups of crackers and sausage to the fields.

Doretha was entering her final trimester of pregnancy, and Hatti Mae kept a watch on both girls. She often had to restrain their enthusiasm. Hatti Mae directed the evening meal preparation, put together by Doretha and Abigail with Mildred's help when she came in from the fields. Coming in from the fields at six-thirty, shirt and coveralls soaked with sweat, everyone washed up at the pump, and dinner was served on wooden picnic tables in the backyard at seven. They sat around the tables, held hands, and gave thanks for the food and the blessings of a good day's harvest. A typical meal consisted of potatoes; vegetables, including corn-on-the-cob; poultry, pork, or fish; fresh fruit; biscuits or cornbread; and berry pies, cakes, or cookies for dessert. Through Saturday, for nearly two months, this was how the days unfolded. There were occasional casualties from the heat, but after a couple of hours, the person returned to the fields.

The Meriweathers tried to get the cotton harvested before the weather turned and brought the moisture. There were a lot of predictions about the sales price of cotton and what gin to use, but all the second-guessing was pointless because the regional market in the Carolinas set the prices. They were announced each day on the radio. However, Stuart Meriweather knew how well or badly they had done before all the cotton was sold, but he refused to accept the fact until the money was all in—a kind of gambler's logic. The cotton business was always risky. Machinery failure, rain, erratic market prices, and plain hard luck created bad years, in spite of how well Stuart managed the farm. Some years, the real question was not whether September and October would be good or bad, but just how bad it was going to be.

Aside from the fall picnic, the drudgery and monotony of farm life had other interruptions and distractions. Nothing excited Delta folks like the carnival. Abigail and Doretha could barely contain themselves and marked off the days on a makeshift calendar they crafted from one of the posters publicizing its arrival. Strict segregation prevailed in Walnut Grove. There was a clear social order with Negroes at the bottom. Everyone else was expected to know his or her place. Carnival weekend saw a few exceptions orchestrated by its owners who had no interest in race relations.

The carnival was run by a wandering band of gypsies with funny accents who lived in Florida during the winter. They hit the small farming towns in the fall when the harvest was in full swing and folks had money in their pockets. On Thursday, they set up in a large open field at the end of Main Street and stayed through the weekend. They had two moth-eaten circus lions that looked drugged, an elephant, and a giant loggerhead turtle. The troupe included odd humans such as tumbling midgets, the girl with six fingers, and the man with the extra leg. A Ferris wheel, merry-go-round, and three other rides squeaked and rattled and generally terrified all the mothers. The Slinger was one such ride. Comprised of a circle of swings on chains, it went increasingly faster until the riders were flying parallel to the ground, screaming and begging to stop. The prior year, a chain had snapped and a little girl had been flung across the midway and into the side of a trailer. It returned with new chains and was met by a long line waiting to ride.

Crowds lined up at booths and played with rings and darts, shot pellet pistols at little toy ducks that floated in a pool, watched a magician, or had a photo taken. Shrill music rattled from the loudspeakers. It was loud, colorful, filled with excitement and brought out the little girls in Doretha and Abigail. The smell of popcorn, corndogs, and something frying in grease filled the air. A cart with a glass box atop had a sugary concoction whirling into billows of pink, gooey clouds onto paper cones; the sign read: COTTON CANDY FOR A NICKEL. Candied apples were a dime. Abigail and Doretha had one apiece. For twenty-five cents, a lady with long, black hair; big hooped earrings; a scarf wrapped around the top of her head and tied in a knot above her ear; and dressed in a long skirt and a ruffled blouse worn off her shoulders told anyone's fortune. For the same price, a dark-eyed lady used tarot cards to the same end. A flamboyant man with a wig that kept slipping guessed a patron's age or weight for a dime. If he wasn't within three years or ten pounds, the patron won a prize. The midway had the usual collection of games—softballs thrown at milk jugs, basketballs aimed at rims that were too small, darts thrown at balloons, and hoops tossed over bottlenecks.

As Abigail, Doretha, and the Meriweather brothers strolled through the carnival enjoying the noise and excitement, a sense of danger nipped at their heels. Throughout the day, the Higley boys had been following them from one venue to the next with jeers and taunts. They were in their usual mode of hooting and hollering racial insults in an attempt to provoke the Meriweathers. Dirt-grinding poor, living on subsistence farming and occasional sharecropping, the Higleys lived in the back hills, but they hung around town on Saturdays. Negroes had no choice but to tolerate the ranting and raving directed at them. Any gestures or the slightest of glances in the direction of the Higleys was guaranteed to set them off. It was the town consensus that the Higleys had "crossed the line" in terms of civility, although it wasn't clear to anyone what the line was or exactly what it meant. Depending on whom you talked to, the Higleys had a reputation as strange, backward, illiterate, and feral hillbillies who hated everyone, especially Negroes. Since the Higley children didn't go to school or church, no one was sure how many kids were in the family. They were lean and hungry looking, disheveled, shaggy and dirty, wore ragged clothes, and most often were barefoot. Their father was a drunk—and their mother a burley, feisty, and surly woman. She once whipped a fully armed deputy who was trying to arrest one of her boys. She broke his arm and nose, and he left town in disgrace. The eldest Higley boy was in prison for killing someone.

The Meriweathers knew they could not risk a fight; the consequences would be far greater for them than the Higleys. Even people like the Higleys had dominion over Negroes in the eyes of the law and citizens in the Delta.

As the Meriweathers and Abigail were leaving the carnival, the Higley clan crowded them and tried to block their exit. Some jostling occurred as Jerome and Herbert, the two older Meriweather brothers, tried to clear a path for Abigail and Doretha who were panicked and unstrung. A crowd was beginning to develop just as Sheriff Barton arrived. He had been alerted that trouble was brewing once again with the Higleys.

Sheriff Barton was a man who was fond of the trappings of law enforcement. He had badges on his hat, shirt pocket, and in a wallet on his left hip. And he was dripping and festooned with bullets. Aside from being naturally effeminate, soft, and mealy, Sheriff Barton was a little too much encumbered with the implements of his office to have a chance of being nimble. He couldn't take half a step without leather creaking, metal jangling, and all of his free-swinging attachments threatening to beat him senseless if he tried to run. Sheriff Barton did not represent much of a discouragement to the Higleys and just about the whole town proclaimed him a mockery and laughingstock. On this day, the authority of his position must have prevailed. The Higleys stepped aside when Sheriff Barton yelled in a booming, slow-as-molasses voice, to break it up and let the niggers pass. The Higleys laughed and shouted more derisive comments, but they had turned their attention to Sheriff Barton and inquired in a slow impersonation of drawing a gun from its holster whether he had shot anything lately.

Thinking he was outside of earshot of the Higleys, Jerome, shook his head in frustration and allowed in a resigned tone, "White trash, hillbillies, dumb peckerwoods." Herbert winced at Jerome's disparagement and hurried everyone along, hoping no one had overheard.

Stuart was outraged when he heard about the debacle. Sensing the potential for circumstances to escalate and become harmful, he declared, "I'm suspending trips to town for a couple of weeks. Let things settle down and blow over."

It was well known that Little Rock, Walnut Grove, Pine Bluff, and the surrounding Delta area had its history of violence against Negroes. One of the more active chapters of the Ku Klux Klan operated in the area with members from the farmers and townspeople nearby. Jerome received an upbraiding for not exercising more restraint. Stuart was thankful that Jerome had not snapped and lost total control. As the problem child of the family, Jerome created too much commotion and could turn something small into an event. Everything was over the top. He never relaxed, pondered things over, or looked at things calmly. What began as an event would become a spectacle and finally an extravaganza and trouble. Even around the family farm, Jerome attracted noise and disorder.

A silence enveloped Abigail as though she had caught a glimpse of what lay ahead. Life in the Delta just seemed too out of kilter, tilted, and off balance to grasp. The extent of racism displayed by the Higleys and bystanders filled her with dread. She could not comprehend the enthusiasm with which they were ridiculed without provocation. Identified and in the company of the Meriweathers, she was a nigger or a Negro and nothing else.

Wanting to spare CJ her misgivings, she wrote to Papa about the terrible scene at the carnival and the fear and dread that was mounting up inside her, fueled by the feeling of imminent danger. Papa had expected a letter similar to this and wrote back with a promise of a trip home after the baby arrived. Papa's promise and the sentiments expressed in his letter provided brief solace from Abigail's empty feelings. She was desperate for something, anything that could make up for some of the lost objects, family, and ideals in her Delta life.

Abigail's spirits lifted a bit as the haze of late summer gave way to the diamond light of fall. Stuart was relieved that the year yielded a good harvest. Now it was time to haul logs in from the hills and top off the winter woodpiles. The smell of wood smoke laced the air like perfume. Temperatures got a little crazy; the midday sun struck like a hammer and felt hotter than it did in August, but stepping into the shade could cause a shiver. In the evenings, the shadows stretched longer and seemed darker and more mysterious. The days grew perceptibly shorter. When the sun dropped behind the western ridge, the night air had the ashy taste of winter.

Abigail remembered arguing with her mother about what brought on the best fall colors. Was it little rain and mild frost, no frost or rain at all, hot afternoons and cold nights, or how serious the end-of-summer drought had been? For certain, Abigail loved the fall in Tuskegee, but she had seen nothing like the pure light and blazing color on every ridge, river, creek, and wooded area in the Delta.

A black walnut tree stood in the near corner of the yard. Sitting on the front steps on restless October nights, Abigail heard the nuts hit the ground with a decided thump. In competition with the red squirrels, or "fairy" squirrels as Doretha called them, Abigail crossed the yard on the brisk mornings with the stew pot in hand and harvested the nuts. Doretha and Abigail spent many fall evenings cracking walnuts with a brick or hammer. Smashing off the husks, their fingers were stained a nicotine-yellow like chain smokers. They arranged the shucked nuts along a board against the east side of the house to "ripen up." Mildred taught the girls how to make an apple pound cake with black walnuts. Although many arrived in crumbs, their young husbands gratefully consumed the constant fall supply of cakes that came their way.

— Chapter Three —

The Meriweathers took the Delta winds for granted. The Duncan farm lay directly in line with a gap in the encircling hills to the northwest. It was through this notch that the prevailing wind tunneled, falling on the house with ferocity. The house shuddered as the wind punched it and slid along its sides like a released torrent from a broken dam. During the winter, week after week, it sank and rose, attacked and feinted.

In the early evening of January 4, 1941, there was something different about the wind and thunderstorm that was ripping, pounding, and volleying through the hills as though a war had broken out. Lightning crackled, trees split, limbs crashed, and hail rained down like shots. The Arkansas River was rising. The power had been out for more than an hour. Hatti Mae was bent over Abigail, with Doretha alongside, as James was delivered into the world by a lantern's light.

Herbert had helped his father batten down their property and herded everyone in before heading for the Duncan farm. He was strengthening the windowpanes with tape when Abigail went into labor. It did not take him long to fetch his grandmother.

Doretha had been visiting all day, afraid to leave Abigail because of the familiar labor symptoms Abigail was having. She had given birth a month earlier and had baby Will settled down in the cradle that had been given to Abigail by her family.

Hatti Mae held James up and pronounced him the first in a new generation of Duncans in the Arkansas Delta. "The farm be needin' another Duncan boy 'round here. You done good, Abigail." Hatti Mae cleaned him as best she could before attending to Abigail. "I know you be feelin' bad child. Just lay still while Hatti Mae takes care of things." It was a messy, difficult birth, and she feared there might be complications.

"Thank you for getting me through this," Abigail stated in a barely audible whisper.

"I likes being with my Delta daughters when their time comes, colored or white, it don't matter none to me. I gots me 'bout a thousand chillin walkin' 'round the Delta. I remember deliverin' that squallin' child CJ."

In the fields and woods outside the house, the wind bore down hard on the trees. The rains gouged the earth and swells of water from the river splashed over its banks into the creeks.

Herbert went into the bedroom and found Abigail exhausted and nearly asleep. His grandmother wiped Abigail's face with a cloth. Herbert said, "That be a fine night's work you done, Abigail."

"Thanks, Herbert. What about that storm out there? It sounds bad."

"Don't you be worrin' yourself none 'bout such things. I be takin' care of everythin'."

As Doretha fixed a pot of coffee, she felt the wind shuddering against the house and the low humming of the windows—the song of endangered glass. The water had risen to the level of the banks and would soon be flowing inland, virulent and urged by the wind.

Abigail asked for the white Bible her father had given her as a wedding gift. She opened it to the glossy pages between the Old and New Testament. She propped herself up a bit, and Doretha brought her a fountain pen. She steadied her hand enough to inscribe the baby's name: Christian James Duncan—after his father and grandfather. It had already been decided he would carry the nickname James.

Herbert put on his boots, rain slicker, and hat. Carrying one of the lanterns from the kitchen, he checked on the women and babies before going out into the storm. The door almost blew off its hinges when he opened it, and it took all his strength to close it. He leaned into the wind and staggered through the yard. A twig hit his forehead, cutting it like a blade. He shielded his eyes with his hand and listened to the sound of trees breaking in half along the river. He stepped into water midway up to his knees. Blinded by rain, he became alarmed and let the wind carry him back to the house.

When he reached the front door, he could not open it; the wind had sealed it shut. He ran toward the back door and was knocked to the ground by a limb torn from the oak by the bedroom window. Dizzy and bleeding from a wound on the back of his head, he got to his knees and crawled to the door. The storm felt like a mountain leaning against him. As he opened the door, rain poured into the kitchen. For a moment, he lay stunned on the kitchen floor. Regaining his senses, he pulled himself up, stumbled to the sink, and washed the blood from his head before moving toward Abigail's bedroom. In the light of the lantern, his shadow, huge and portentous, followed him. Hatti Mae was asleep in a chair as Doretha attended to Abigail. Herbert shook his grandmother gently, "Grandma, grandma, wake up. The river is rising."

Hatti Mae immediately thought of the storm in '23 and knew they had to get to the barn and higher ground. Herbert's attempt to get her out first was rejected.

She scolded, "I'm old, but not feeble."

Herbert took James from Abigail and placed him into Hatti Mae's arms. Herbert wrapped his grandmother's shawl around her shoulders while she held the baby tightly to her breasts. Herbert then placed little Will on top of a cotton blanket and covered him with his yellow slicker. Doretha stayed with Abigail.

Opening the back door, Hattie Mae and Herbert stepped into the howling bitter rain and headed for the barn. The winds gusted at what seemed to be one hundred miles per hour; it screamed around them, demonic and black. It yanked at Hattie Mae's clothing and shot up her sleeves. She was lifted by the wind and blown across the backyard, her shawl billowing out around her like a sail. She shielded James as she was thrown into the side of the outhouse.

Herbert struggled toward her, caught her with one arm around her waist and lifted her to her feet. Crying out in pain, Hatti Mae was hurt. He held her for a moment. Then mud-splattered and rain-soaked, they fought their way toward the barn. Once again, he struggled against the wind as it held the door fast. When he forced it open, the door splintered against the side of the barn. Once inside, he climbed the ladder that disappeared into the darkness above them. Herbert laid Will in a pile of fragrant hay. He left the hayloft and went back down for James and Hatti Mae. The restlessness and panic of the animals in the barn was palpable as they frantically paced, lurched, and pitched about. Injured and in pain, Hatti Mae could not climb. He lifted his frail grandmother up in his arms. Hatti Mae held him tightly around his neck as he climbed the ladder, leaving James behind on the floor of the barn. The wind tore through the open door. Herbert propped Hatti Mae up against a bale of hay. She reached for Will and tried to dry him off, but the blankets and her clothes were soaked through. So she unbuttoned her blouse and hugged him close to her bare breast and let her own warmth flow into him.

With James in his arms, Herbert climbed the ladder one more time and laid James beside little Will and Hatti Mae. Herbert hurried down the ladder and pressed into the heart of the storm again. He had no idea how he was going to get Abigail up to the loft. When he entered the house, he saw the water spilling through the front door. He looked out into the darkness; he would retell the vision he saw many times. The water from the river, wild and majestic flowed swiftly, powerfully, against the house. A rowboat, torn from its moorings, lifted in the wind. He watched it hurtling out of the blackness, illuminated by the strange light of hurricanes, and lifted his hand as if to stop it. He closed his eyes as it shattered the window and hammered the dining room table. A piece of splintered glass lodged in his arm. Disregarding the blood soaking his shirt, he ran to Abigail's room.

Herbert reached his hands under Abigail's back and lifted her off the bed. Then he turned to his sister, "Doretha, hook your hand under my belt and keep in step with me," he instructed. "If you jerk, you'll pull us off balance."

As they walked through the back door, they stepped into moving water. The wind and water attacked them. Herbert and Doretha walked slowly, deliberately, planting their feet solidly before each step. The rain was cruel and stinging. A moaning Abigail clung to Herbert like a child. Once inside the barn, Herbert had to adjust his grip on Abigail several times as he climbed the ladder. When they reached Hatti Mae and the babies, the blanket he had wrapped Abigail in was covered with blood. Badly torn during the delivery, she was bleeding profusely. Herbert gave Doretha a piece of his torn shirt, "Hold this tightly between Abigail's legs." With every beat of Abigail's heart, more blood pumped out.

Herbert helped his grandmother attend to the screaming infants. Abigail grew weaker before everyone's eyes; they all feared she might die. The rising, ungovernable waters moved through the barn. Below them, the sounds of frightened animals mixed with the ferocious, cataclysmic howl of the wind as it rushed through the barn. The tension in every nail in the barn could almost be felt. It was as if the wood, suddenly animate, had begun to swell with water running through long-dead roots and veins.

Doretha lessened the pressure on the shirt and almost wept when she saw the bleeding had stopped. Abigail, in shock, lay unconscious in her own blood. Herbert searched the loft and found an oil-stained tarpaulin, which he laid over Abigail. For added warmth, he blanketed it with straw. An exhausted Hatti Mae lay silent with the babies.

Well past midnight, the water still had not receded. Outside, the prodigious winds devastated the trees in their assault and rushed through the door of the barn like a train entering a small tunnel. Trees were lifted out of the ground as easily as a child pulls candles out of a birthday cake. Saplings hurtled through the air as though they were leaves.

Herbert climbed down the ladder to free the animals. In the pandemonium of the escaping livestock, he was almost trampled in their desperation to leave the barn.

When he returned, the babies were arranged like cordwood on Hatti Mae's breasts as she held them in her dark arms. Doretha was sleeping next to Abigail. Herbert fell down, spent and beaten. He listened to the voice of the storm; its whine became something almost human to him. Exhausted, he fought the urge to sleep, and so fighting, slept.

He awoke at daybreak to sunshine and birdsong; the shadow of the trees crept across the farm. He looked down and saw the muddy barn floor. The babies were crying. Abigail's eyes opened at the cry and her milk flowed in a reflexive, sympathetic reaction.

Hatti Mae continued to sleep soundly and Doretha had to pry Hatti Mae's arms loose from her child. James's first night on earth had ended. The storm that had killed some dozen people in its wake, was later called the Bathsheba storm by the Delta folks. James's birth must have been a sign, an omen ... but of what?

— Chapter Four —

In a world refreshed with the presence of a new baby, a slight shift in balance occurred within Abigail. Some of her fears receded, and she met her life with a new strength. CJ wrote of his melancholy over having missed the great event of James's birth: "After two months, I finally have a description of the birth as well as a picture of my son. He does bear my handsome likeness …. And how I wish I knew what that long night and its aftermath had really been like; you spare my feelings, I know. You say not a word about your pains and trials….So many weeks elapse between us speaking, the other hearing (through our letters), and so many more before a response arrives. Our emotions lag far behind the events. For me, it was as if James had been born today. Yet he is already two months old, and I have no idea what those months have brought." Absorbed in motherhood, Abigail shook off another one of CJ's self-pitying letters.

Abigail and Doretha came to rely on each other as the centers of emotional stability and vitality in their lives. They visited several times a day, gave each other treats they had cooked, and shared each other's troubles. The demands of newborns had them sometimes reeling from the lack of sleep. They stoked themselves up on strong tea and launched out on a rampage of talk—about their marriages, their personal deficiencies, their interesting and discreditable motives, and their foregone ambitions. They tried to keep track of each other's dreams. Doretha became "Doe" and Abigail became "Abby." A sisterhood sprang to life in full bloom.

Abigail experienced her first spring, an early one, in the Delta and stepped into its embrace. She began to notice the days were getting longer. At sunset, the treetops on the western ridge took on a reddish hue as the buds swelled. Days in early March broke warm. And then, often as not, snapped back frigidly for a few days, only to warm up again. This vacillating freeze and thaw made the sap run in maple trees. The Meriweathers had a dozen sugar maple trees on their farm and seized those few days—until the weather settled—to tap their sugar trees. When the sap was "runnin' good" they spent entire nights in the sugarhouse to keep the wood fire burning under the huge pan of boiling sap. Abigail loved to walk into the sugarhouse, an old log shack that had been put up for making syrup. Steam rose from the boiling sap and filled the sugarhouse with the fragrance of warm, maple syrup. Abigail took the small tin cup and dipped it into the syrup to sample it. The Meriweather syrup found its way around the Negro community and on the shelf at Pop and Pearl's where it had been bartered for several weeks of food supplies.

One of the first things Abigail noticed when she arrived in the Delta was the low, yellow flowers blooming along the road. Called coltsfoot, it was the last of the spring flowers. Abigail fell in love with the wildflowers that erupted every spring on the floor of the wooded areas—hepatica, spring beauty, bird-on-the-wing, wake robin, snow trillium, bishop's cap, showy orchid, bird-foot, violet, and scores of others. Abigail dragged Doretha into her wildflower binges. She pressed them, pasted them to brown paper from cut up grocery sacks, scribed a poem on the inside, and used them for all of her correspondence and to take note of special occasions for women from the church. Arnetta told Abigail that her letters smelled like a buried garden when she opened them.

The serviceberry was the first tree to blossom. It dotted the hillsides, ridges, and valleys with hazy white–like apparitions in early spring. Within weeks, the redbud trees bloomed and an astonishing variety of dogwoods blossomed—lime green, chalk white, ivory, pink, deep red.

En route to town, there was a patch of redbud about five acres wide, a band of pure lavender, that made Abigail dizzy with wonder.

As much a hallmark of springtime as bluebonnets and the flowering redbud trees was the dense thicket of bright dots of red berries that trailed along roadside ditches, hugged the base of fence posts strung with barbed wire, and lined the base of pastures. Called the southern dewberry, it was a wilder, more belligerent breed of blackberry. Doretha and Abigail donned their broad-brimmed straw hats and leather gloves, grabbed short sticks, and headed into the brambles for the tart-sweet morsels of fruit. They poked their sticks into the brambles to scare away any lingering deadly copperhead snakes, stepped gingerly around fire-ant mounts, steered away from poison ivy interwoven with the berries, and endured the itchy jiggers. Abigail waited for Doretha to tramp down the bristling vines before she dared place her gloved hand into a thicket of berries. After a morning of filling their baskets, the afternoon was dedicated to transforming the fragile fruit into succulent cobblers from recipes handed down through generations of Delta families.

Papa made brief visits as often as possible and brought Abigail rhododendron cuttings on several difference occasions. Each time, the cuttings died. Abigail concluded, with advice from the Meriweathers, that there was too much lime in the soil.

Robins, bluebirds, and other songbirds came back to the Delta. At daybreak, wild turkeys gobbled in the hills. The geese returned to the river. Flocks sometimes flew on moonlit nights. At dusk, Abigail stood on the porch and listened to them honk as they followed the course of the river.

By April, everything and everyone awakened. Out in the yard and around the barn, the Meriweathers mended the fences, rode the tractor to turn the soil, tried to time the seeding according to the spring rains, and cleared the winter debris. They burned the debris of crumpled stalks, perished grass, oak leaves shed in the dark privacy of winter, and twigs and vines that once pruned clung together in infuriating ankle-clawing clumps. These brush piles, ignited on many mornings, in the midst of the webs of dew, were still smoldering at the end of the day, making ghosts in the night behind them as they headed home. They could smell the warm ashes from their house. A couple of the boys were always handy to help Abigail turn the garden over. After a winter of pewter skies and gray afternoons inside, it was a wonderful time to be outside with James in the open air. She appreciated the feel of the dirt under her feet and the scent of the mushrooming soil.

Wild greens emerged in April. On cloudless days with skies of translucent blue, Doretha and Abigail took bread bags to gather greens. Walking along and stopping at various plants, Doretha told Abigail what to call each variety: turkey wing, turnip, mustard, bird tongue, thistle, narrow dock, and poke. "This here's poke. It's good eatin' if we can find enough," Doretha instructed. They found a few wild strawberries and ate them on the spot. Different locations had different kinds of berries. Doretha had her own special name for them such as *sheep tit* and *round eye*.

Doretha declared that the best green was poke—"picked me a mess of poke," "had me some poke last night." To Abigail, they had a pungent taste somewhere between leeks and strong garlic; her palate could not tolerate them. The Delta recipe for wild greens was, "ya'll wash 'em, parboil 'em, then fry 'em in butter." Abigail could always tell when Doretha or anybody for that matter had been eating poke. It did to the body what garlic did to the breath. After eating a healthy amount of poke, a funky smell emitted through every pore. Doretha was a persona non grata in Abigail's house if poke had been a recent part of her diet. It permeated her skin, her hair, and all of the rest of her.

Abigail could not quiet that pearly ache in her heart that was easily diagnosed as the cry for home. She kept that cry to herself. She had to concentrate on the task of raising a child in an almost foreign culture. Papa's visits to the farm contrasted her mother's contentment to write frequent letters. Guilt leaked off Abigail's fingers when she read most of her mother's letters. Elizabeth was never far away from Abigail. There were things she said or did that were her mother's teachings, her mother's actual words. As soon as the words left her mouth, she felt her mother walk up and stand behind her—listening—to hear if she'd gotten it right. And now and again, her mother came and stood so close that she imagined hearing her breath whistling down the long narrows of her imperial nose. Her mother had traveled this long way to find her and withhold her affection and tenderness again, just to remind her daughter, as a good mother should, that her forgiveness might still be won.

Abigail held her breath and then shook her head to clear it, turning to see if anyone noticed her looking like a fool with her eyes squeezed shut and her fists clinched at her sides, swept away in a fit of hope. And this image repeated itself again and again. It percolated up through the layers of the months she had been gone and bubbled out at Abigail's feet like a perverse spring. Abigail wondered, *if I give up hope of ever obtaining mother's absolution, will my time on Earth be free of the longing and tortured feelings I have?*

Abigail was relieved of the relentless yearning when her mother suffered a setback with her chronic health problems. Papa arranged a ticket for her to come home until her brother and sisters returned for the summer—Fletcher from Lincoln University, Margaret from Howard, and Ann who was in New York with Arnetta. Furloughs from military duty were hard to come by for Welcome.

Abigail had dispensed with her youth, walked out of her own life, and one year later returned home with a baby looking for traces of her former self. Papa was gone; he spent a lot of time in Washington, D.C. Her mother lay in her bedroom, taking her time about dying. There was absolute silence in the house; everyone, including visitors, spoke in whispers, laughed noiselessly, and wandered softly through the rooms that led to Elizabeth's door.

After getting James down for the night, Abigail drifted into her parents' room and took up Papa's spot on the large queen-size bed beside her mother. On the side of the bed near the window, she listened to her mother's breathing as the moonlight cast a shadow on her face. Out the window, the southern stars that were written in the sky like the alphabet above a blackboard confronted her. Their comradely light seemed familiar.

Somehow, Abigail's presence in Tuskegee made her ache for CJ. Her body reacted and she could still feel him, like the vibration of an old landmine being tripped and exploding miles away. The jolt registered in her body. The longing sharpened its knife against her heart. There was only anguish in its echo and encore. Within Abigail, CJ was the crashing sound of the sea and the wind's song. Staring at the stars, Abigail made a constellation out of CJ's handsome face. He visited her with light.

One night, as Abigail sought the cool side of the pillowcase trying vainly to find a comfort zone somewhere on that unfamiliar bed, she sat up in the old despair of insomnia and saw the moon crossing over her mother's exhausted face. Elizabeth's eyes were open; she too was looking at the night sky.

"Abigail, I'm not sure how much longer I'm going to be around."

"Mother, you're going to be just fine."

"I'm not. What's interesting is that I thought I'd be more afraid than I am. Oh, sometimes the fear nearly doubles me up. But mostly, I feel a great sense of relief and recognition. What I'm doing now is not living. I feel a part of something vast. I was just looking at the moon. Look at it, Abigail. It's almost full tonight and I've always known what the moon was doing and what phase it was in even if I wasn't paying attention. When I was a girl, I thought the moon was Virginia-born like me. I can barely remember what my mother's face looked like, Abigail. But she was a sweet woman who died so early in her life—like I'm doing.

"I'm glad I named you after her. You have that same twinkle, creativity, and mysteriousness. She once showed me the full moon and told me how everyone claimed they could see a man's face if they stared hard enough, but she had never seen him. Her mother told her there was a lady in the moon that very few people ever got to see. It took patience to see her because she was shy about her beauty. She had a shining crown of hair and a perfect profile. The lady in the moon was seen from the side and was as pretty as those women you see in cameos in jewelry shops in Montgomery. You can only see her when the moon's coming up to full. She doesn't show herself to everyone. But once you see her, you never even think about the man in the moon again."

"Why didn't you ever tell me that story?"

"I just remembered it. Memories of my past keep flooding in. I've no control over them. My poor brain seems to be in a hurry to think of everything it can before the end. My mind feels like a museum that takes in every painting it's offered. I can't control the flow."

"It sounds kind of nice."

"Help me with something, Abigail."

"Anything, if I can."

"I have a confession and apology to make to you, and I want to do it right. I'm no good at such things. You have asked repeatedly in your letters for my forgiveness. And I have never given you an answer. The truth is that I am the one who needs to be forgiven. I put you through so much unnecessary heartache and confusion because of jealousy. What kind of mother envies her daughter to the extent of withholding her approval and support?

"You had the potential to live the life I imagined, wanted, and prepared myself for as a young woman at Oberlin College. When I first arrived here with your father, I had the distinction of being George Washington Carver's first secretary. He was the director of agriculture. Starting out with a man who already had a distinguished career, there was no telling how far my ambition and education would have taken me. I gave that up to be a mother, make a nice home for you all, and support Papa's career.

"Oh, you were a handful, but it was my responsibility to shape and direct all of that creative energy and keep you safe. Instead, I pushed you away and forced you into perfect lockstep with my worst instincts. I know you will be angry with me for saying this, but you managed to marry the one person who thinks you are insignificant outside of the role as the caretaker of his son and the farm. You married a man who will ratify your most negative assumptions and sentiments about yourself rather than celebrate and give wing to your gifts and talents."

"Mother, please don't say that about CJ. He loves me. You don't know him," Abigail interrupted.

"Perhaps he does in his own way. But if he loved you in the right way, he would never have compromised your innocence and taken away a fifteen-year-old girl's future."

"Please don't blame him for the choices I made," Abigail defended.

"You're right, Abigail. I blame myself. Rather than worrying about this family's respectability and Papa's career, we should have kept you here to have your baby and let you finish school. Who knows what might have happened from there? Let's not talk anymore about this now. I'm a little tired."

Abigail nodded with tears in her eyes and propped her mother up on pillows so that they could watch the dawn break together.

"There it is again, talk about dependable," Abigail exhorted.

In the weeks that followed, Abigail displayed her newly acquired cooking skills for anyone who came to the house to visit her mother. Elizabeth's diet was greatly limited. Although she could eat very little of what Abigail prepared, her friends claimed they had never eaten so well. No one entered the house that Abigail did not feed. She was a consummate hostess—greeting people at the door and asking them to sign the guest book. Some evenings, Abigail helped her mother send thank-you notes to her visitors.

It seemed the entire town of Tuskegee came, and it moved Elizabeth greatly. More than enough eyebrows were raised by Abigail's sudden reappearance with a baby. Papa and Elizabeth had experienced some uncomfortable moments with friends and colleagues in explaining Abigail's whereabouts. For some, seeing Abigail provoked a new round of gossip, a search for improprieties to discredit and disgrace the family—particularly Papa who had become somewhat of an institution at Tuskegee.

Elizabeth seemed to rally one day. And for a week, the spirits of the entire house rode with her like a flood tide cleansing the marshes after a hard winter. During that week, Elizabeth passed on the mysterious rites of cosmetics to her daughter. Abigail had such natural beauty that she never had any interest or need for makeup.

"Apply the foundation moderately. When you put on rouge, begin at the bottom of the cheek and blend it up into the hairline near the corner of your eye. You want to accentuate your lovely high cheekbones. Remember not to put on too much color; you don't want to look like a clown. That's right. That's good. Now, let's go on to nails and perfume. Remember, less is more when it comes to perfume. The reason a skunk's a skunk is he doesn't understand moderation."

"Do I need to wear makeup mother?"

"Not now, but some day." Tears welled up in Elizabeth's eyes as she went on, "But I won't be here then. There are a lot of things I don't know, but I'm Leonardo da Vinci when it comes to applying makeup."

Elizabeth refused to let Abigail push her around in a wheelchair during their rare mornings in her garden. She came out of the house on Abigail's arm and walked deep into the rhododendron acreage. She carried a cane, but in forgetfulness, perhaps, hung it over her forearm and tottered along with it dangling loose like an outlandish bracelet. Abigail offered her arm. Elizabeth shakily brought her left forearm up and bore down heavily on her daughter's arm and wrist with her slender and freckled fingers. Her hold was like that of a vine to a wall; one good pull would destroy it, but otherwise it would survive all weathers. Abigail felt her mother's body jolt with every step, and every word twitched her head. Not that the effort to speak was so great, it was the need for emphasis that seized her. She wrinkled the arch of her nose fiercely, making her lips snarl above her near-perfect teeth with a comic expression that was self-conscious. It reminded Abigail of the funny faces Margaret made in constant confession of the fact that she did not consider herself beautiful. Elizabeth constantly tipped her head to look up at Abigail. In the tiny brown sockets affected by creases like so many drawstrings, her cracked brown eyes danced with captive life when she spoke.

Nearly every plant had a name and a story, "Oh, I don't like Mrs. Wolford; she always looks so washed-out to me. Papa loves these salmon colors; I say to him, 'If I want red, give me red, a fat red rose. And if I want white, give me white, a tall white lily, and don't bother me with all these in-betweens and would-be-pinks and almost-purples that don't know what their mind is. Rhody's a mealymouthed plant.' I've told some of my gardening friends, 'She does have a brain, so she gives you some of everything; just to tease you.' What are we standing here for? Sick old body like mine, stand still in one place it'll stick fast."

Elizabeth jabbed the cane into the grass, the signal for Abigail to extend her arm. They moved on down the alley of bloom. Her unsteady touch on Abigail's wrist bobbed like the swaying tops of the tall hemlocks. Abigail associated these trees with forbidden property; it always gave her great pleasure to be within their protection.

"Let's go see the plant I named after you. Ahhh! Now here's a plant." They stopped at a corner, and she lifted her dangling cane toward the small rhododendron clothed in a pink of penetrating purity. "I named this plant after you because it's the only rhody except some of the whites, I forget their names, silly names anyway, that say what it means. It's the only true pink there is. You know the story. When I first got it, I set it among the other so-called pinks and it showed them up as just so muddy. That's just like you. Even among your brothers and sisters, you stood out. You are something special. Remember, I tore those other plants beside the Abigail Louise right out and backed it with all crimsons." Abigail's eyes began to tear and she gripped her mother tightly.

Elizabeth clawed at Abigail's arm and moved on more heavily and rapidly. The sun was high; she probably felt a need for the house. Elizabeth bobbed past the overblown rhododendron blooms with Abigail. Back in her room, an exhausted Elizabeth slept for much of the afternoon.

Her mother had always been a mystery to her. In love with nature's bounty, she was a reservoir of tenderness for stray dogs and a shoebox full of baby squirrels rescued from a felled pine, tenderly wrapped in flannel and bottle-fed into independence. But that warmth had trouble flowing over the dam in her mother's heart to her.

During the bad days, Elizabeth rested with her head propped up on three soft pillows in the darkened room. Her face materialized out of the half-light, and the Venetian blinds, partially drawn, would divide the room in symmetrical chevrons of light. She just lay there and gave off an odor—maybe it was the medicine. Her flesh was jaundiced and sickly. Books and magazines were scattered on the night table beside her. Elizabeth insisted Abigail bring her grandson to her every night after his bath, no matter how she felt. Abigail placed James in Elizabeth's arms and watched in soft attendance at her mother holding him. Elizabeth sang to him until he fell asleep.

Those bedtime moments were filled with nostalgia as Abigail remembered her early childhood. All the Bryant children crowded together on their mother's bed, and she took them on miraculous, improbable voyages around Never-Never Land where they encountered perfidious and inimical characters. Each night, she devised ingenious ways to return them safely between the white sheets of her bed. Papa did not share in those journeys and was usually in his study reading. Elizabeth's imagination lit fires for her children in that room in a continuous shimmering ignition. These stories poured out of her in bright torrents, and there was always the promise of one more story.

Her mother led them out of her room, into the dimly lit hallway, past the door that led to Papa's study, up the winding stairs to the two large bedrooms on the second floor. Fletcher and Welcome shared a room, as did Margaret and Ann. Abigail then followed her mother back downstairs to her own bedroom, which sometimes sparked a bit of jealousy from Margaret. If a wind was blowing, the branches of the hovering oak tree scratched the windowpanes and she would notice the objects in her room cast enormous, ghostly shadows on the slanted enclosing walls. She would jump out of bed and scurry back up to her sisters' room and jump into bed with Margaret.

Abigail wanted to stay, but she needed to get back to the farm. Although the Meriweathers encouraged her to take as long as she needed, CJ had repeatedly expressed his concern about the farm being unattended. She had winced when she heard that Ann was living with Arnetta. Elizabeth had seen the tears welling up in Abigail's eyes and offered a utilitarian explanation about the arrangement, "… her illness, Papa's travels, her brothers and sisters away from home …." This did little to assuage a twinge of jealousy that she had been replaced, and her dream was now being lived by her sister. Abigail was also angry that she hadn't been told months earlier and had to hear it so abruptly.

Margaret unwittingly added insult with her vivid, almost histrionic description of her experience at Howard that included her adventures with boys and dating. In her highbrow inflected mode of speech—much the way she and Abigail used to be with each other—she launched into a testimonial about her dates, "They're mostly unmemorable. They prevaricate over insubstantial issues, small things with much indecision and intensity. They're far too disheveled and self-centered. They seem to dispense with the need to be thoughtful and interesting. I'm practicing moderation in my attachment to boys. The truth is they frighten me."

Margaret went on and on about sororities, classes, her girlfriends, pledge sisters and professors. There was no mention of Abigail's life in the Delta or motherhood. It was as though it needed to be kept bottled up. Otherwise, the tumult of it all could spill out and pollute and infect those around her.

Several days after Margaret's arrival from Washington, D.C., Abigail and James departed. Abigail had found peace with her mother, but left with torment about what she had lost and what lay ahead for her.

— Chapter Five —

Men swarmed around Abigail like flies, Negro and white alike. Since she arrived on the farm, even all the Meriweather boys had done something stupid to get her attention. One day, in the middle of August, a well-driller named Lucas arrived with an assortment of impressive equipment. Stuart warned Abigail that the water was starting to look a little brackish, and the well was drying up. Lucas was hired to extend the hole deeper into the earth. After several days of drilling, pure cold water could be pumped from the well. Lucas was a dashing, fervent, well-spoken, and flirtatious young man.

Doretha met Lucas when he first came to the farm and noticed the way he looked at Abigail. Not so innocently, Abigail gave him lunch and sat with him as he ate. In return, he charmed her with stories and opinions of public figures and politics, celebrities and movie stars. In a lowered voice broken by wildly disrespectful laughter, he told her rumors about private scandals and household triangles. These were all things Abigail felt giddy to hear; she realized she was blushing. Any misgivings Abigail had were easy to ignore. She was disarmed and distracted by Lucas who impressed her with the range of reading he enjoyed and caught her attention with his penchant for poetry, particularly work by southern poets. Several evenings, after Lucas finished drilling, he hung around and let Abigail entertain him with poetry from journals she brought with her from Tuskegee. It turned out that he had dropped out of law school. As punishment, he was relegated to the family well-drilling business until he decided to return to school.

It is not clear that Abigail saw it coming. She was absorbed, titillated, and radiant all at once. There was an instant mutual attraction. That he was white hardly mattered. They had become very playful and laughed a lot. The laughing seemed to make everything harmless and carefree. It took the danger out of it. Lucas found an old bike in the barn that Herbert had fixed for Abigail. He climbed onto the slightly rusted bike and wrestled it around for her to perch herself on the handlebars. Abigail felt self-conscious raising her rear end onto the crossbar; she was aware of him watching, but then they were off. Lucas pedaled firmly, and she could feel the bike vibrating with his effort. Pretty soon, they were flying around the farm, laughing in the darkness. The wind pressed her skirt to her legs and then caught it, flipping the hem up against her waist. Her slip billowed in the breeze, her knees and one thigh flashed in the moonlight. Abigail wanted to lean down, to fix it, but Lucas had her hands pressed under his on the handlebars. When she wriggled, he told her, "Hold still, love, I've got you." They came to a stop in the shadows behind the barn where Lucas propped the bike.

Abigail—every bit the sixteen-year-old—asked Lucas to push her on the swing that hung from the pin oak with CJ's initials carved into the wooden seat. He looked a little surprised—but the eagerness in her voice convinced him. Abigail settled herself in the swing. He put his hands in the small of her back and shoved firmly. Each time she swung back, he touched her lightly, his fingers spread across her hips. Lucas circled to the front of the swing as it finally came to a stop. The strands of hair that had flown loose fell back and covered her face. She tucked them away, all but one, which stuck to her cheek and throat, an inky curve.

Trying to gracefully get out of the swing, she took a step toward him, almost falling, stumbling into his arms. She kissed him—this well-driller she had known for less than a week. He kissed her back with force. She felt him turning her in his arms, as if dancing, and she tried to move her feet with him, but he held her too tightly, simply swinging her around. She felt dizzy. The pressure of his arms made it hard to breathe. She moaned softly, her mouth under his mouth.

When they finally stopped spinning, she found herself pressed against the cold, barnyard wall. Up close, it smelled sharply dank and rotten.

"I'm finished here," he whispered. "Will you miss me?"

She nodded in his arms, pressing her head against his chest, away from the wooden wall of the barn.

"I'll miss you," he told her, his lips to her ear.

She felt him picking at the button on her blouse. She felt a hand on her knee, fluttering with her hem and then under her skirt. "Beautiful Abigail," he crooned while sliding against the silk of her slip, against her thigh.

"Nice," he breathed. Her head was still bent toward him, but now she was straining her neck against his weight. She could feel the bony crook of his elbows between them, pressing against her side and across her belly. She could feel the tense muscle of his forearm twitching.

"Stop," she yelled at him. "Stop."

She felt pressure and then pain. Lucas was well-endowed and rough. He grunted into her hair, short, hot puffs of breath. If she dared scream, who would hear her? Who might come? She wondered if she was more afraid of being caught than of what he was doing to her.

She pushed her hands against the coarse wool on his chest, trying to somehow disengage him. Impervious, he grunted, "Almost, almost." He finished just as Abigail was able to pull away. She stumbled a bit as she ran toward the house tugging her skirt down and shoving her blouse back in. She expected him to come after her.

Before she reached the back door, she heard a shout, "Abby, Abby." It was Doretha. Frantically, she tried to button her blouse; her fingers fumbled. Abigail's stomach clenched. Her throat felt raw. She looked back at Lucas. He was scrambling to his truck and rig, and a second later, he was gone.

Abigail's body seemed heavy, waterlogged, her arms shaky. Doretha was already in the house. Weeping, Abigail fell into her arms.

Abigail suffered an agonizing guilt about her risky and provocative flirtation with Lucas and lamented her contribution to what happened. She pondered her weak resistance and whether he interpreted her spirited enthusiasm toward him all week as consent to his advances. She felt little anger toward Lucas; rather, she turned it full force on herself.

Doretha saw Abigail's anguish and didn't know how to respond. She hugged Abigail and kept repeating, "I'm so sorry. I'm so sorry. What can I do? I'm so sorry ...."

Days later, in an attempt to get Abigail to open up about what had occurred, Doretha made a promise to Abigail, "We'll keep this between us. And, we don't have to talk about it—unless you want to." She gave her word that what happened would never be spoken of, even between them. It was a secret she promised to take to her grave.

Abigail couldn't quite believe something so unthinkable could happen to her. She couldn't believe that she misjudged Lucas's intentions and been ambushed so completely. She had felt the jolt—the one that is supposed to alert her to danger—that registered in her body when she was around Lucas. As a married woman with a new baby, how could she have ignored such a strong voltage of adrenaline?

Abigail became preoccupied, always somewhere else, somewhere out of reach, rehashing in her mind a traumatic few minutes that were untouchable. She moped around, had little energy for the baby, and disappeared into someone blank and lifeless, joyless, almost mute. Elizabeth must have been prescient. A new dress accompanied a first-class sleeper car railway ticket to Arizona where CJ remained stationed at the army base at Fort Huachuca. A note was enclosed:

A mother can feel her child's unhappiness. The dress will stop him in his tracks. I love you Abigail. Mother

Hattie Mae and Doretha volunteered to care for the baby. A flurry of letters and arrangements had Abigail on her way just two weeks after her encounter with Lucas. Leaving Little Rock on a direct trip with no transfers, the rail headed toward Missouri. This Pacific route ascended hills and then gently rolled along the bottom of valleys and meandered as whimsically as the small rivers that it followed. At times, the terrain narrowed, weaved, and veered the tracks upward into shady forests and then glided down into the valleys. Again and again, Abigail lost herself to this dance as she stared out the window trying to purge herself of Lucas and generate an excitement to see a husband she barely knew and had not seen in over a year.

On some parts of the trip, the train went up one mountain and down another, like a roller coaster in and out of shadowy forests. It passed farms where cattle and sheep stood, sometimes on hillsides; it passed village-size towns with funny names that amused her. Between small towns, midsummer flowers crowded the shoulders of the track. Her mother loved the names of wildflowers, and on family drives, she often recited them. Abigail found herself saying out loud, "Queen Anne's lace, black-eyed Susan, ironweed, teasel, yarrow, Joe-Pye, vetch …."

It was her first trip of such distance. She had made numerous round-trips from Tuskegee to New York. The train ride provoked memories of those New York summers with her Aunt Arnetta. It was like looking out the train window into a kaleidoscope. Each look turned the cylinder and another memory, another pattern appeared. Since leaving Tuskegee, Abigail had not allowed herself to have those recollections. It hardly seemed possible that only a year ago her aunt was preparing her for her coming out as a debutante.

Abigail was beckoned back to reality when the train arrived in Texas, and all the Negro women were removed from the train. The porter told her that their seats had been reassigned to white soldiers; they would have to catch another train. A discouraged, bewildered Abigail began to collect her belongings to detrain until she was assured that white women were not being inconvenienced and she could keep her berth. It was not uncommon for Abigail to "pass" for white, but in this instance, she was offended by it. The indignity of those Negro women being removed from the train set her adrift. A feeling of displacement, profound and enervating, took over. It marked her sensibilities like indelible graffiti. But she remained silent about her race and felt ashamed. CJ was expecting her, and she was afraid of being placed in an unpredictable situation in the middle of Texas.

Abigail watched the Negro women descend from the train with an almost imperturbable dignity. As the train left the station, she wept softly. Trying to understand what just happened was like picking up a bead of mercury—something was clearly there in her heart, but she could not grasp it.

Abigail slept through the night. Sensing the loss of motion, she awakened. The train stopped at a railroad junction in the little town of Hereford, Arizona. *Why is the train stopping,* she wondered. Other than cactus and open space, there was nothing except a station with a ramp, a space to wait for the only activity in town—the arrival and departure of the train. The conductor came along and advised, "We've reached our destination."

A bit unsettled, Abigail apologized, "I didn't realize how close to the fort we were."

"We're not that close," the conductor responded, "but it's the end of the line for passenger trains. You've got another twenty-five miles to go."

Abigail got out with the rest of the passengers and retrieved her luggage. She was spared the long, bumpy ride in the old school bus that provided transportation to the fort. CJ had a car waiting to drive her. The dirt road was rutted out like a washboard. The driver, a Negro staff sergeant, made Abigail feel uncomfortable by staring at her through the rearview mirror during the entire trip. She fidgeted, pulled at her bodice to make sure she was not too revealing, and fumbled through her purse to avoid his glances. She later learned that CJ had secured the transportation by trading his special rations allotment.

Abigail was deposited at the outside gate of the fort, a treacherous spot that also served as the fort's red-light district. Perplexed that CJ was not there to escort her into the fort, she fended for herself among the prostitutes, customers, hustlers, and military police. She passed a Quonset hut that served as a beer tavern and a structure that housed the local whores. She stopped in front of a barracks providing temporary living quarters for visitors of the Negro men stationed at the fort. Abigail walked inside the guesthouse and was shocked to see rows of single beds and one latrine. She shuddered to think it might be her lodging during her visit. On her way back to the sitting area beside the gate, Abigail saw a woman being forced to her knees and punched in the face by a customer—or perhaps it was her pimp. As she plummeted to the ground, the man walked away from the woman with a studied nonchalance—unhurried and calm. Screaming engulfed the scene and MPs surrounded the man as he started to cross the street in Abigail's direction.

At just that moment, CJ arrived and Abigail tuned out the hideous situation. He met her gaze. Her beauty, opaque and carnal and disturbing, stirred him as it always had. "You look wonderful— wonderful!" was all he could say. No blushing schoolboy could have been more tongue-tied. They embraced clumsily, but passionately.

Their bodies felt like struck gongs, swollen by reverberations. CJ took Abigail's hand and realized how long it had been since he had touched her. Months of the deadening seriousness of military life had passed. All the illusions of being an army officer had withered and died under the intense Arizona sun. Aside from wondering how he was to survive their prolonged separation, CJ did not have the interior resources to dream and fantasize about Abigail. But it took only that moment of touching to restore the brassy luster and dazzling image of what he had missed.

Once inside the gate, a different facet of Fort Huachuca presented itself. It opened up like a city with an incredible pulse and flow of humanity. Purple mountains stood behind red-roofed buildings. Huachuca referred to the 7,600-foot high mountains that were known to local Indians as the "place of thunder." The fort had been in existence since the late 1800s and was described as an outpost with about 1,000 men and 1,000 mules. To accommodate the newly activated Negro divisions, the facility had been expanded.

CJ bartered for the use of a jeep and gave Abigail a tour of the base infrastructure that astonished her by its vastness—slightly more than one hundred square miles contained everything the men could need or want. They drove by theaters, bakeries, laundries, storage buildings, and artificial lakes used for pontoon and bridge training. There were firing ranges, tank facilities, classrooms, housing, hospitals, and entertainment areas. The fort was equipped with a modern power and sewage system to accommodate 25,000 people, including 1,100 employed civilians. CJ pointed out that to maintain segregation, there were two officers' clubs, two hospitals, separate recreational facilities, and dual living quarters for dependents. The only white men on the base were officers and most of the dependent housing went to them.

Abigail had enough of the sightseeing, and it didn't take much encouragement to get CJ heading to the Cooper Queen Hotel in Bisbee, an old mining town forty-five miles away. It was the best accommodation he could find and, at that, he needed the help of his superior officer to overcome reluctance of the proprietor to allow a Negro couple as guests. It was an efficiency room with a two-burner stove and an icebox that an ice merchant filled with provisions every day. The big, brass bed reminded them of a contemporary song whose lyrics fit the occasion, "Put me on your big brass bed until my face turns cherry red." According to Abigail's later telling of the story, they rarely left the room for three days.

They tended to each other with reverence. For Abigail, the more she lavished attention on him, the more of herself faded. That's what she wanted, selflessness. She wanted to forget that self, taken by Lucas, which lay awake at night full of dread, wondering, *how will I react to CJ after this?* CJ took her where she wanted to be: out of herself. She turned herself over to him, thinking of it as devotion. It even felt religious, she thought, although it wasn't really the devotional sort of selflessness they talked about in church. Her pliant nakedness unified to his senses of touch and smell, flickered in curved short circuits. Abigail's supine beauty was a continuous, calm, exultant entity, with rises and swells in dulcet shadowed corners. She was a giantess who met CJ's relentless thrusts with an embracing cavity. She did it all and could not suppress the loud moans she knew would disturb the guests in the next room.

There were fits of dozing amid a constant rejoining. Their closet of satisfied desire became nicely rank with a smell that was neither him nor her. "We're all mixed up together," she whispered. All territories lay open with them. "You're perfect," she sighed as morning was upon them.

He observed her in the hard morning light, "So are you."

On the second day, CJ took Abigail to the Mountainview Club for Negro officers. It was built on a hill overlooking a creek and surrounded by the mountains. Rock walls bordered the club and enclosed a garden containing red-flowered oleanders and green arbor vines. From nine different states, more than eighty paintings and other works by Negro artists provided the interior theme and ambiance. It was dinner, a little dancing, and back to that big brass bed at the Cooper Queen Hotel.

The surprise of the trip came the night before her departure. Lena Horne was scheduled to perform, and CJ arranged for seats near the front of the outdoor theater bearing her name. She had performed so many times for the men of the Ninety-second, they dubbed her the "Sweetheart of the Division" and the post commander named the theater in her honor. She had a nephew stationed at the base and admitted in the fort's newspaper, *Stars and Stripes,* of her special affinity and love affair with the 18,000 Negro soldiers at Fort Huachuca.

Abigail heard a special performance accompanied by other cast members of the popular musical *Cabin in the Sky*. Lena sang, "I've Got a Girl in Kalamazoo" and "You Are My Thrill." In addition, an ensemble of stars that called themselves the Hollywood Victory Committee headed by Clarence Muse gave a variety show that enthralled Abigail. Hattie Morrison's boogie-woogie piano got things going. Chinkie Grimes was called back for several encores of her red-hot dancing and singing. Sunshine Sammy, Mantan Moreland, and Montel Hawley each performed their one-man comedy acts. Clarence Muse closed the show with "Ol' Man River." Abigail was captivated by the performance. Once again, her Aunt Arnetta sprang to memory, particularly her heralded annual summer extravaganzas down in the New York Village for the performing acts that she hosted, showcasing Negro New York talent, including students from her own music studio. And, an ever-so-fleeting moment of regret for squandering her own musical talent slipped in and out of her mind.

In the few short days at Fort Huachuca, she managed to pick up some of the fort slang, like *solid sender that is a bender, that's no jive, five by five, hipsters, jitterbugs jitting, a jam that will end all jams, jump of the season,* and *root and toot.* The only detraction from their reunion was the discovery of the tattoo CJ never mentioned in his letters. Known as the Buffalo Division, CJ was assigned to the Ninety-second Infantry. Its slogan, "Deeds Not Words," was inscribed in blue pigment no more than a quarter-inch high and a couple inches long. A most unostentatious design as military tattoos go, and discretely positioned just below the joining of the right arm to the shoulder, the tattoo might easily enough be hidden. "Deeds Not Words" was a true expression of him. Those three words became an ineradicable biography of his time in the army. Contained in that insipid, but inspired tattoo, was so much of who he was. Abigail was angry that he had defiled his body, and she considered it unchristian. She easily forgave him, but warned, "You can never wear a sleeveless shirt in public in my company."

They spent their last night together, all night, making love, talking, and then making love again. Since the future was already scripted, there were no plans to make with only eight hours in the world left for them. They were no less ravenous, even though tender in their genitals, and slept for several stretches of an hour or more. Abigail sensed the night tilting and slowly swerving toward its end. In her sexual hysteria and exhaustion, she began to cry, smearing her tears, like a deer marking a tree, across his belly and chest, leaving kind of a glitter.

The next day, CJ got her to Hereford, onto the train, and settled into her compartment. Then he kissed her once and walked rapidly off the train without looking back, not wanting Abigail to witness his tears. But she called his name; he turned and heard her say, "CJ, remember our dreams, remember last night."

"I'll never forget it," he called back.

Seeing the flood of tears rolling down her cheeks, CJ rushed back to her. It broke his heart to see her crying. Their time together had been too short, and he didn't know when he would see her again. With their hands locked through the window opening, neither was able to let go. The train started moving, and their hands unclasped.

Abigail blew him kisses. Kindled in the papery light of the desert sun, he disappeared into the distance.

Abigail tossed a small prayer toward CJ. It was a prayer of gratitude for the extraordinary reunion with her husband. It was the honeymoon they had never had.

— Chapter Six —

In the blazing desert heat and the freezing cold of the surrounding mountains, CJ resumed the daily grind of training his company for combat. His men were often equipped with old World War I gear such as Bully Woolies, jodhpurs and wrap leggings, uniforms with high collars and the long, slit-type cap, pith helmets, and 1911 issue field rifles. As the company training officer, he pushed 250 men on twenty-five and sixty-five mile tactical hikes through the desert under the load of a sixty-pound full field pack.

A contentious vanity brought passion to his leadership and earned CJ an early placement on the first lieutenant promotion list. He trained his men with a vengeance and his company repeatedly received commendations during field inspections.

When they were not in the field, CJ challenged his men to attend literacy classes. He even set up his own unofficial educational groups to encourage his troops to assist one another. Although literacy had been eliminated as a requirement for induction, each man had to take a written examination to determine military specialty, occupation, and assignment. According to the white military brass it was not an intelligence test, only a quick and reasonably dependable measurement of working level and the ability to learn. But the test discriminated against men with minimal schooling and little or no exposure to world events. Despite its stated policy, the army interpreted the test as an indicator of racial differences and presented these as factors for keeping Negroes out of combat. CJ had a high percentage of illiterate and low-scoring individuals in his command, but as far as he was concerned, his men had all the requisite skills for the mission of his company as a combat infantry unit.

He bragged to his superiors, "Everyone in Foxtrot Company can strip down a weapon, set up a mortar emplacement, follow a compass heading on a night march, quickly find fields of fire for a machine gun, carry out a snappy rifle inspection, and even keep their appearance and gear 'spit and polish.' Those with low test scores are some of my best men."

Special services maintained a full calendar of USO entertainment functions, competitive sports, and special holiday celebrations. But there were too few opportunities for so many men, which presented CJ with constant problems. One was the cluster of Quonset huts just outside the gates of the fort that Abigail had encountered on her visit. The men drank and relieved their boredom at the Halfway House, a bar located in the middle of the cluster. CJ referred to it as the "Bloody Bucket" because at least once a month one of his men got into a fight at the bar. At night, CJ observed some of his men barely making bed check. By their own admission, they left the Halfway House at 10:15 PM and ran all the way back to the barracks, which was approximately five miles inside the fort. They were doing nine-minute miles to get back in time.

The huts where prostitutes plied their trade provided a serious recreational outlet for CJ's men. It was nicknamed "The Hook" because anybody who went there was going to get hooked by something—the clap, a knife blade, or if he was lucky, just a tough Negro fist. Fort Huachuca had an alarming rate of venereal disease. For every 1,000 soldiers, 368 cases were reported.

CJ had a rule for his company. If they visited one of the prostitutes they had to go through the prophylactic station located near "The Hook." If they didn't, and came up with a disease, they were subject to a summary court-martial. But the situation became so bad that CJ established "The Hook" as off-limits and applied disciplinary measures to individuals caught there.

The men joshed about the restriction. In their smothering proximity, they shared everything—snores, farts, bad breath, and odorous feet. Even the clumsy stealth of jerking off—the unsuppressed moan, the vibrating sheet glimpsed in the dawn light—was a matter for shared joking "Beatin' your meat again, Coon!" was not an uncommon ribbing dished out.

CJ worked hard to keep his men out of the way of themselves and out of the way of his promotion, including a restriction on gambling and drinking in the barracks. There were few slots open for promotion to first lieutenant from a Negro junior grade infantry officer. Military planners placed white, southern officers trained as staff and line officers at Virginia Military Academy (VMI), the Citadel, Clemson, and Presbyterian College in command of Negro troops at Fort Huachuca. These officers were presumed to have an understanding of Negroes by virtue of having lived and worked with them in the past. In a letter to Abigail, CJ wrote, "The so-called southern aristocracy runs the army. The white upper echelons in the military sit up nights thinking of ways to keep the Negro soldier, particularly officers like me in our place."

With the rules, regulations, restrictions, and built-in prejudice, CJ could not afford a major mistake within his ranks that had the potential to capture the attention of his superiors if he expected to remain on the promotion list. Relations between the white officers and Negro enlisted men had greatly deteriorated since CJ arrived at the fort. This big, sprawling camp contained somewhere between 17,000 to 20,000 Negro men in contrast to a small percentage of white officers who enforced the strictest segregation possible between themselves and the Negro officers. The only contact was strictly in relation to military activities. Social contact was out. How they would possibly function together in combat was a question that had passed many a Negro officer's mind, not to mention the minds of the enlisted men. Fights were regular occurrences on the post. Higher commanders made no effort to bring about a closer professional contact between Negro and white officers.

CJ faced many career-threatening situations resulting from the fragile state of relations between white and Negro officers. At a meeting of battalion officers from his division, he was instructed by a ranking white officer, "Boy, run up to the captain and tell him we're waiting on his officers." CJ was stunned to be addressed in that manner and became even more aggravated when the major said to him, "Boy, get going!"

CJ did not budge. Instead he replied, "Sir, are you addressing me? I was commissioned a second lieutenant in the United States Army, and as far as I know that hasn't changed."

The major responded with, "Oh, don't start that with me. I call all my junior officers 'boy.'"

That may have been the case, but not all of his junior officers got temporary weekend duty for a month to perform a low-level job. CJ was assigned to trash duty to investigate all of the garbage at the base to make sure no one was throwing out government-issue items. This type of treatment left CJ bitter. It also convinced him that he would be passed over for promotion.

* * * * * * * * *

Lucas came to the farm looking for Abigail. Stuart ordered him to stay off the property, and thus, rendered his motives—whatever they were—for the visit irrelevant. During Abigail's absence, Doretha had somehow alerted her father to the potential danger without revealing what had transpired between them. Nothing more was said between Abigail and Doretha about Lucas. Abigail wanted it to be a bad dream or make-believe. It was an exaggeration, she told herself. But the ghost of Lucas remained, and when she looked at the swing or the bike propped where he left it, she had trouble taking deep breaths.

Another shadow over Abigail's life in the Delta was the encounter with the Higleys. Nearly a year had passed, and the heightened vigilance on the part of the Meriweathers had all but disappeared. The Higleys were milling around the parking lot adjacent to Pop and Pearl Johnson's grocery store when they saw Jerome coming their way with an armload of groceries. As soon as Jerome noticed their presence, he considered a route for a hasty retreat. One of the Higley boys grabbed what looked like a two-by-four and sneaked up on Jerome from behind a parked car. As Jerome turned to run, he was surprised by a blow to his forehead and crumpled to the ground. The other four Higleys swarmed around him repeatedly kicking him in the face, groin, and back as he tried to curl up into a ball. He was kicked in the ribs so hard they made a cracking sound. The eldest Higley boy, the one everyone called Grunt who rarely spoke, made gesturing noises, and weighed every bit of three hundred pounds, picked Jerome up by the throat and threw him into the back of their truck. The onslaught had been so sudden and severe that Jerome had no idea what happened. He writhed and groaned and whimpered in a semiconscious state. A couple of miles south of town in a deserted backwoods area, they strung him up by his wrists to a tree limb, stripped him, and proceeded to whip him with a leather razor belt until he was unconscious and bleeding profusely from what seemed like every part of his body. They left him hanging there.

When Jerome did not return to their rendezvous location in front of the co-op, Stuart went looking for him. He found a bag of flour broken open dusting the gravel with flecks of blood splattered in the flour. Stuart quickly inspected the parking area for any signs of Jerome. He raced frantically back to Pop and Pearl's, distraught and angry with himself that he had let down his guard. Now Jerome's life was in jeopardy. From the looks of the parking area, his son had already been victimized. The rest of the family scoured Walnut Grove. No one came forth with any information; there was a sense that even if they knew anything they would refrain from offering it. As despicable as the Higley family was, the town had sympathy for them. When it involved white boys in some kind of trouble with Negroes, their meanness and other undesirable qualities were soon forgotten.

Word spread rapidly among the Delta Negroes about Jerome's disappearance and the likelihood that the Higleys had harmed him in some way. Baffled, but unsympathetic, Sheriff Barton looked like a big squirrel without a bushy tail, hunched over his notebook nearsightedly nibbling at every acorn of a clue. He and his deputies joined the search. Unsuccessful through the night, they continued to scour the area at daybreak. Sheriff Barton visited the Higley place up in the hills and found blood all over the back of the family truck. Threatening to have them all locked up, he coerced them to reveal the whereabouts of Jerome. Stuart was with the sheriff when they found Jerome's mangled body. He wept and hollered with pain as he cut his son down and laid him on the back seat of the police car. They rushed him to a hospital in Little Rock where he remained in critical condition for three weeks.

Whites, including Sheriff Barton, considered the brutal butchering of Jerome to be justice having been meted out—however extreme and vigilante in nature. The widespread Negro community condemned the brutality and the absence of any criminal actions against the Higleys. With the exception of a noticeable limp, Jerome recovered from his physical wounds. But the emotional scars remained evident. He refused to leave the farm and disappeared for hours at a time. When he reappeared, he would ask if the Higleys were gone or did he need to return to his hiding place. He suffered from the same recurring nightmares—violent, careening, and destructive—without plots or coherent scenarios. They were sudden drop-offs into deep sleep accompanied by images of dismembered parts of his body flying around, hurtling through trap doors, hanging from a tree, and dangling in an empty, screaming space. Jerome woke everyone with tortured crying. Everyone whispered that he was disturbed or had suffered brain damage and would never be the same.

Abigail's head was scrambled by more than the terrifying violence. During the usual morning chatter, Abigail was unusually quiet and staring into nowhere. She couldn't speak. Clutches of words, reasonable words, appropriate words, were all stuck in her throat. Abigail opened her mouth to see if that would free some of the words. None came out. After some prodding, she finally let go, "I'm pregnant again." Her statement was followed by a torrent of tears. She did not want another baby, not so soon. Some of her choices seemed to be taken away from her—like maybe returning to Tuskegee for good.

"I'm not ready for another pregnancy," Abigail admitted to Doretha.

Being the consummate friend, Doretha offered in earnest, "You be early 'nough to try and get rid of it."

Abigail's curiosity got the best of her, "And how do you suppose I do that?"

"Jumping up and down, sittin' in hot tubs, swallowin' castor oil sometimes works."

Abigail could not restrain her laughter and asked, "How do you come up with this stuff? Who gave you this information? Have you actually tried any of these remedies recently?"

"Everybody 'round these parts knows 'bout these things and have some other cures too," Doretha retorted, not appreciating Abigail's questioning condescension.

Abigail reminded Doretha that she was in her third month of pregnancy.

The news came from CJ that his company was being sent to Oklahoma for an indeterminate period of time for special training. Abigail wanted to let the pregnancy sink in before sharing the news with CJ and decided to hold off for awhile to let him acclimate to his new assignment and geography.

* * * * * * * * *

After a two-day train ride, CJ's company was taken in "six-bys" to a location an hour away from Fort Sill, the main base. The men were housed in rows of Quonset huts; each hut was equipped with bunks and a potbelly stove to hold back cold Oklahoma nights. The hushed and hurried manner in which the whole episode took place made him wonder what his company was in for.

Assembled in the area outside their quarters, a rather affable major welcomed them warmly as his newest protégés. Unsuccessful in his search for an opening line to preface his stunning news of what the future held in store for Foxtrot Company, candidly, he told them they were to be taught the fine art of the detection and removal of mines and booby traps. The suspense was over. *This is one of the army's integration plans for Negro soldiers*, CJ mused to himself.

Trying to make this new designation seem more exciting than foreboding, the major continued by explaining how they would be molded into demolition specialists, one of the most vital assignments in the combat army. He stressed the extreme danger of this delicate work and warned, "Here, you don't make mistakes. None! You will be an antimine infantry unit and carry out combat missions into enemy-held territory, far in front of our most forward lines. You will withstand the stealth, the gut-wrenching fear, and the hair-trigger pressure while trying not to blow yourselves up. Does anyone want out? Think about it." As expected, no one took the major up on his offer. The major further informed them about working in twelve-man special units doing the "dirty work" and "troubleshooting" for an entire regiment.

The training schedule was intense. Booby traps were planted under mattresses, behind the cast iron doors of barracks' potbellied stoves, under chairs or plates in the mess hall, beneath toilet seats and even in duffel bags. The engineer specialist from Fort Sill pounded the all-important message of constant awareness into them by planting insidious traps everywhere imaginable. The startling explosion of dynamite percussion caps whenever someone made a mistake served as a constant reminder that any shield of vigilance is not impenetrable. One night, a barracks door was blown off its hinges by a loud, but harmless, rigged booby trap when one of the squads returned to its quarters. The soldier, who had carelessly opened the door without checking it first, lost his composure for several days.

As the training continued, everyone became apprehensive, even paranoid. Many of the soldiers were almost afraid to move lest another planted "instructor's lesson" explode. CJ tried to emphasize to his men what the instructors were trying to drill into them, "Never accept anything at face value and never let your guard down. To do so could be deadly." In his bunk at night, CJ's stoic demeanor in front of his men gave way to lurid fears that Abigail was about to become a widow and his son fatherless.

The classroom was an acre of nearby land that was cleared and developed to simulate minefields. The first objective was to clear out all antipersonnel mines. Each deadly device, one after another, became part of their lives. The mines they were learning on were live, not dummies, which quickly brought the message home.

An equal amount of time was devoted to the anti-tank mines. When they reached the warfront, they would be called upon to remove hundreds of them buried under roads and snow to clear paths for the advancing tanks and infantrymen. CJ's company became adept at handling dynamite, nitrostarch, plastic explosives, primer cord, nitroglycerin, blasting caps, torpedoes to blast through barbed-wire defenses, and a host of other devices.

CJ and his men returned to Fort Huachuca in March. He could not get his troops to buy into the fact that they were specially trained, elite GI's with a skill not shared by others. On the basis of their twenty-one-dollar-a-month pay allotment, his men felt the government surely knew how to extract a bargain from its young Negro citizens who could possibly die for seventy cents a day.

* * * * * * * * *

Abigail could not overcome the feeling that her pregnancy somehow represented a failure and defeat. And she suffered all of its inward agonies. When she did inform CJ about expecting their second child, the news was couched in the struggle, the sorrow and despair, the sense that she was being pulled down by the dark undercurrent of Delta life.

She was not overwhelmed by CJ's enthusiasm about the pregnancy. His letters talked about trying to stay in touch without touch and how their bond to each other was changing as a result of the long periods of separation. He was trying to imagine her daily life, moving on without him, and he thanked her for the stories about James. He wrote about misgivings about their marriage and how he had changed. He even wrote about the young men who helped in the fields and around the house doing the tasks he ought to be doing and the parts of her life that were usurped by other men. A few of his letters frightened Abigail, as though he knew something.

— Chapter Seven —

Constant reminders were abundant about the harsh, unpredictable nature of the Delta. Two small Negro children from a neighboring farm were playing on a sandbar when the calm Arkansas River turned surly. A swift current surrounded the sandbar. With an angry and powerful suddenness, it collapsed and disintegrated like sugar, pulling the children into the current. Drowning was not uncommon in a river that had an average depth of fifty feet.

Recurrent and seasonal storms struck in an instant: the sky darkened, a slight breeze came from the west, as the sun disappeared behind the clouds, and the wind grew stronger. All storms in the Delta came from Little Rock through what was known as Tornado Alley. Hail hit first—hard, tiny specks the size of pea gravel. The sky to the southwest turned dark blue, almost black, and the low clouds bore down on everything. The wind howled through the trees along the river and pushed the dead cotton stalks to their sides. Lightning cracked. The rain hit with a fury—thick, cold, and sharp—falling sideways in the fierce wind. To the west, far beyond the river and high above the tree line, a slim funnel cloud dipped downward. It was light gray, almost white against the black sky, and grew larger and louder as it made its way very slowly toward the ground.

Tornadoes were common in the Arkansas Delta; in 1942, they seemed like a way of life. When it was nowhere near the farm and going away to the north and east, Abigail watched the funnel in muted fascination as it moved slowly, searching for the perfect place to touch down. Its tail, clearly visible above the horizon and way above the land, skipped along in midair, dancing at times while it decided where to strike. The bulk of the funnel spun lightly, a perfect upside-down cone whirling in a fierce spiral.

One Sunday, several tornadoes in close succession appeared to hit Walnut Grove. The funnels went slightly to the east of the farm and left only a sprinkling of brown rainwater and specks of mud. The storm raged for two hours and threw almost everything in nature's arsenal at the town and surrounding area.

Stuart made an inspection tour in the truck. The road was nothing but mud. In places, large sections had been washed away. A few flattened trees and debris were scattered for miles; a gaping hole or two was visible in the landscape. Aside from that, all the houses seemed to be in order, the stores along Main Street were intact, and God had protected the church. Much lying went on that afternoon in Walnut Grove, or perhaps a lot of exaggeration, according to Stuart. By the time he left town, he heard so many stories it was a miracle that hundreds had not been killed.

More routine occurrences on the farm included the hog killing in November. The cooler air this time of year lessened the possibility of bacteria. Every year, a hog was shot in the head, dipped in boiling water, and hung from a tree next to the tool shed before being butchered into a thousand pieces. Everything was used. From it came bacon, ham, loin, sausage, ribs, tongue, brains, and feet—everything but the squeal. Stuart did the gutting and performed the delicate removals, which proved too much for Abigail. She ran behind the house and puked.

Real winter did not begin until after Christmas. If there was going to be a blizzard or a heavy snowfall, it was usually in January or February. On most days, the sky was steel gray and the sun was a white blister above the river and ridges. At dusk, the breeze picked up and carried the taste and feel of moisture. The temperature hovered around the high thirties, and the dampness made it feel much colder. Abigail filled several bird feeders at dawn each day and scattered seeds, stale bread, and crushed apples on the ground. Back inside, she stood at the window to watch the birds swarm in—finches, sparrows, nuthatches, chickadees, downy woodpeckers, blue jays, and cardinals. Abigail ascribed something holy about seeing cardinals in the snow. This was the time of year for sewing quilts, reading and writing poems, and feeling safely tucked in with her son. A highlight for Abigail was receiving the summer catalogue from *Burpee's Seeds*. She loved seeing all the bright flowers in the middle of winter. It was her promise of good things to come—like a healthy new baby.

A couple of nights a week, Abigail wrote CJ a letter and more often than not prepared a special package for him. Doretha regularly showed up at this time for Abigail's help with her correspondence to Jimmy. He was with the Negro Twenty-fifth Infantry stationed somewhere in Georgia. She listened to the scratch and swirl of Abigail's black expensive fountain pen that her Aunt Arnetta gave her on her twelfth birthday. It sounded like the scrabbling of a creature in the underbrush. As Abigail wrote to CJ, there weren't any pauses or crossings out. In time, Doretha realized she could even identify the swoosh of a below-the-line "g" leaping diagonally upward into an "h," the crossing double zag of the ensuing "t," and, soon after, the blip of a period. When Abigail reached the bottom of the page, the sheet was turned over and smoothed down in a single, back-of-the-hand gesture.

The rush of writing and pages went on, while Doretha struggled to put a good sentence together and waited for the declarative final "A" or "Abigail"—the loudest sound of all. "Finished," Abigail announced. "Now, where are you? Let's put together a nice letter to Jimmy. You know, I don't think you ever told me how you and Jimmy met."

Doretha answered with a mischievous grin, "Would you believe at a Methodist revival in Pine Bluff?"

"Shame on you, Doe," Abigail playfully chided. "While the preacher was shouting his fire and brimstone message and the congregation was answering, 'Yes, Lord,' you and Jimmy had your own hallelujah going on."

"Somethin' like that," Doretha impishly acknowledged. "I guess the spirit came-a-calling."

"Well, it must be true what the Bible says, 'the soul is strong, but the flesh is weak.'"

"Preach Abigail, preach!" Doretha went on to share how much Jimmy missed his family. "Outta the blue they gave up farming and headed north to Ohio. I'm sure there's more to it than that, but Jimmy keeps stuff like that bottled up inside."

"That sounds familiar," Abigail mused. Off they would go for hours, like the two adolescent girls that they were.

Well into her second year in the Delta, Abigail remained prone to the mistakes and misadventures of her inexperience with the demands caused by nature and the hostilities of the geography. One that had the potential to be costly occurred when Abigail settled the fire in the stove for the night, which she had started from fresh-cut wood. She had been too lazy to fetch the seasoned logs located farther from the house. Aged wood burns hotter and faster. Fresh-cut wood still holds sap, which not only makes it burn less hot but also coats the stovepipe and chimney with creosote.

It was dawn when the flue fire started. As a result of the buildup from burning the wrong wood, black smoke billowed out of the chimney as sparks and flames shot up like fireworks. Stuart was already up and saw the black smoke and sparks coming from the farm. A small part of the roof had begun to burn. Just as he arrived, Abigail waddled out of the house, with James wrapped in a blanket, feeling more pregnant than usual. Stuart climbed up on the roof and swung a long, heavy chain around in the chimney to break up the burning creosote. Herbert had followed his father and was busy dousing the flames. Abigail received a lecture from Stuart that began, "The entire house could have burned down along with you and James in it. If the fire had started in the middle of the night, no one would have seen it until it was too late."

The incident on the bridge was even more unsettling. Leaving Herbert behind to care for James, Abigail crossed the bridge at least once a day en route to the Meriweathers. The deceitful bridge had cracks everywhere, some the width of a man, and was crumbling in spots. Long overdue as a major public works project, it was scheduled for summer renovation. On this hazy morning, fresh snow had fallen the night before and the glare was terrible.

As Abigail began her trek, she had been distracted by a swarm of sparrows flicking back and forth and did not follow her usual course, which included the careful testing and confident placement of one foot after another. A wedge-shaped crack gave way and she fell through the crevice and would have plunged ten feet below into the river had she not been so far along in her pregnancy. She felt a sudden loss of reality as her legs dangled into space. She was jammed into crunching, jagged, and sharp decaying wood planks and girders. There was a narrow slit where her body had broken through that called her back to life when she looked through at the river below. Her stomach felt like it was on fire, traumatized by breaking her fall and supporting her body weight. Time stopped, thinking stopped, everything stopped. Listening to the wood creaking and settling, Abigail was frightened that any movement might cause her precarious situation to worsen. With a cold wind swirling around, she dangled there for nearly an hour. Occasionally, she tried to relieve some of the pressure on her stomach by leveraging her hands at shoulder width and slowly pushing up. Exhausted, she began to cry out of futility, anger, and fear. At that moment, Stuart appeared. He had a knack for showing up when danger was knocking at Abigail's door or had already entered. The rescue took another half-hour. Abigail was bleeding and there was some fear that her pregnancy had been seriously compromised. Hatti Mae was called on to attend to Abigail and moved in for several days until Abigail was out of danger.

Hatti Mae administered to Abigail with herbal remedies and strange concoctions, especially her mixture of castor oil, lemon, and some of the black herb that she grew during the summer in a window box. It was her old standby and cure for most ailments. The dosage burned from the tongue to the toes.

In addition to being the midwife and country doctor, Hatti Mae was the Delta's oral historian and biographer. Abigail passed the time with her to fill in the gaps and vacancies in CJ's past. She needed to understand why life seemed so tilted, off balance, and surrounded in such secrecy. It shocked Abigail to learn that CJ and Hallie were battered and physically tormented and abused by Christian. "All that Bible-totin', preachin', and scripture quotin' and then harmin' his family like that don't make no sense," Hatti Mae scorned in an angry tone. More conciliatory, she admitted he tried to change near the end, but it was too late. The damage had been done. Hatti Mae talked about a stormy relationship between Stuart and Christian, CJ and Hallie's attempts to run away, and Christian's drunken rages.

Abigail did not know how to react to the revelations. Had she married someone with fatal, destructive flaws? What kind of father could CJ possibly be with such a tortured upbringing? What kind of love would ultimately come from those ruins?

The bleeding stopped and the last couple of months of pregnancy were assisted by a spring that seemed to be waiting for the homage Abigail ached to offer it. She had taken to walks along the river with Doretha. Here, the sheets of water from the flooded river flashed over the land and the banks of trillium under red-budded trees. Cowcatchers and pen cherries in the fencerows broke into bloom before there was a leaf on them.

* * * * * * * * *

I was almost delivered on one of those walks along the river. Abigail and Doretha had been ducking under branches of trees, stooping and stumbling, sometimes hit in the face by blossoms trying to get back to the farm. Mildred was caring for the babies, including Doretha's two-month-old boy. Abigail suddenly went into a labor that progressed rapidly. Unable to go any farther, she laid down with her head against the trunk of an apple tree. The root of the tree made a hard ridge under her, so she had to be shifted about. They fussed around weeding out last year's dark, dried apples, trying to get composed, when a labor pain hit. Abigail's screaming had Doretha on her way to get help. Five minutes after they got Abigail home in the truck, I made my inauspicious debut. Mildred was in attendance assisting Hatti Mae, who had been bedridden off and on for the past month. In her usual gracious reverence to childbirth, Hatti Mae announced the arrival of another healthy boy, Lander, as she handed me to my mother.

I was the last of the generation of children that Hatti Mae "midwifed" into the world—or perhaps the first of a new generation of war babies. Hatti Mae passed away in her sleep the day after my birth.

* * * * * * * * *

By her own definition, Abigail declared that she was one of those women who adored babies and took the business of raising her boys seriously. Abigail never left our side as we took our first steps and tongued those first ill-formed words. My brother and I played beneath the distracted majesty of our mother's hazel-eyed gaze. It seemed she always had her eyes on us and could not get enough of us; everything we did gave her pleasure. The sound of her laughter followed our crawling and barefooted gamboling around the farm.

Abigail's voice was clear and light, a voice without reason, like a snowfall on the roots of orchids. She pronounced each word carefully, as though she were tasting fruit. Her voice seeped into the gift she had inherited from Papa for storytelling, which made the complicated in the stories uncomplicated and the surprises not too surprising. We loved our mother's stories—some she read; some she made up. She brought others from her years of growing up with a fascination for make-believe that had been fed by both the promiscuous creativity of her Aunt Arnetta and her word-struck mother. Both women taught Abigail how to see parts of her world through a dazzling prism of imagination. Fairytales, mysteries, scary anecdotes and adventures, cosmic wars of good and evil, and her collection of childhood classics managed to find their way to the Delta from Tuskegee.

We crawled into her bed and took turns snuggling against her, our forms curving against her back. Her stories were filled with all our problems. *Why do we have bad dreams? Is there something weird that lives under the bed and makes noise at night? Why is our father gone all the time and for so long? Who is he fighting and why?*

The stories we heard from our mother were not prissy, however much they had to do with goodness. Abigail's wealth of imagination came out in its sheer, shining fullness. With her stories, she tried to get us to understand hard questions of our childhood. She did not shy away from the possibility that the answers could be sad, loss could be permanent, evil ever-present, and good exhaustible.

We had no comprehension for the letters our father wrote. My mother placed all of his letters since her arrival in Arkansas in a cigar box next to the radio. It was not uncommon for her to reread them numerous times. Sometimes, she read them to us along with the other bedtime stories.

Papa encouraged Abigail to flee the harsh Delta winters and spend them in Tuskegee. He assured her that the presence of babies and a daughter would bring back familiar sounds, commotion, and activity to a Bryant house that was much too still and serious with Elizabeth's illness. Abigail accepted the invitation—a muted cry for help from Papa—and I spent my first two winters with my grandparents. With CJ's blessing, Doretha willingly moved into the Duncan house and enjoyed the respite from a home that had grown more overcrowded with the new additions she brought into the family with her babies. Her overprotective brothers buzzed and hovered around her, as they had with Abigail, attending to many of the chores of maintaining the farm.

Elizabeth struggled heroically with congestive heart failure and pulmonary complications through the winter of 1944 with a tacit acceptance that the end was near. At Papa's urging, Abigail did not make her spring return to the Delta. She stayed on to allow Papa to keep his travel commitments and help with her mother who could no longer attend to her own basic needs. For Abigail, it was a temperamental turn of fate. Her relationship with her mother had come full circle.

— Chapter Eight —

World War II was in full swing and the United States was heavily engaged. Welcome's assignment to the Ninety-third Infantry Division and deployment to the rain forests of the Pacific Islands added to the grave concerns in the Bryant home. General Douglas MacArthur, commanding the army in the South Pacific, took an integrationist stand and assured the War Department he would not refuse the assignment of Negro troops to his theater of command. With this boldly stated stance, combined with the desire of both the secretary of war and chief of staff to assign Negro troops to different combat zones around the world, a change in military thinking had come about. Welcome, and thousands of other Negro troops, was placed directly in harm's way.

Welcome's letters arrived sporadically, sometimes in bunches. Unlike CJ, he wrote in a clipped, military prose that read like an order of the day. He described each mission as though he was speaking of an errand to buy bread or fill the car up with gas. Elizabeth did not open the letters, but waited for Papa to come home to read them. The contents of the letters painted a gruesome picture that held the Bryant household awash with fear.

After a fifteen-day trip to the South Pacific, the 2,500 Negro soldiers of the Ninety-third Infantry landed at Guadalcanal behind the first invasion force. Their mission was to protect the island from a

Japanese counteroffensive. A few days of acclimation to jungle warfare meant maneuvering through the humid, stinky terrain, half covered by mud and slime, and living with hordes of mosquitoes and green flies that were fat from the rotting corpses. From Guadalcanal, the Ninety-third Division was parceled out to numerous islands in the South Pacific. These volcanic mountains, island rain forests, coral atolls, and blue-green waters had been areas of serenity and beauty at one time. Welcome's unit moved through the Soloman Islands and the Slot fighting on the islands of New Guinea and New Georgia before heading toward the Philippine Islands. The island jungles defined the manner of war. Small patrols maneuvered through dense, wet, and nearly impenetrable forests. Welcome wrote that when large groups of troops landed on beaches, the Japanese fired with impunity from protective caves. In one letter, he complained:

The terrain is really tricky. A flat stretch of beach maybe one hundred to two hundred yards, then all of a sudden, I've got these sheer cliffs. The height! Up there the Japanese have caves and guns all along the coastline. We have been taking a lot of casualties ....

What was obvious from his correspondence was that at any time of the day or night, he and his men were subject to fire from antipersonnel artillery, phosphorous grenades, or jellied-gasoline bombs. Whenever he went out in small groups on patrol or reconnaissance, there was always the risk of a booby-trap ranging from trip-wire hand grenades to tree-stump "surprise" traps. The psychological impact of being in a war zone was difficult. He witnessed barbarities such as dead men hanging from trees with body parts strewn everywhere.

Everyone, except Papa, felt some relief when he reported that his unit was not being used in frontline operations but was involved in "mopping up" and perimeter maintenance. Papa knew it exposed Welcome to bombings, mortar and rifle fire, and bayonet attacks in their role as occupation troops. They stayed on an island for awhile before moving on to the Philippines.

Papa tried to edit the letters while reading them to Elizabeth to ease her worry. But it was difficult with the likes of some of them:

... Lord it's been a long haul. Our job is to hold the island of Halmahara, which is crawling with 37,000 Japanese soldiers ... sometimes their suicide units break through ....

... I am always on edge, anticipating the next attack, hoping to live through another day, another encounter ... I hate tricks, the booby-traps ....Every trail, every bush, every tree could prove to be disastrous ....

... the Japanese soldiers still follow the traditional code of warfare termed bushido—death before dishonor .... The Japanese are tough fighters, but their imagination is limited. They take orders and follow them, and that's it. No individual thinking ....

... this combat is taking a mental toll on my men. Many of the patrol missions I have to order them on are downright horrifying. Every day, I have to go out on one. Several of my men were killed and many others wounded in firefights with small bands of Japanese soldiers ....

... I sent out a recon patrol, lost communication with them, and had to go out and try to find them .... It was a day-and-a-half before my men and I reached them. We found their bodies, stripped of everything, bloated and covered with flies. Bringing back these putrefied bodies was difficult on my men ....

The letters became worse as did Elizabeth. Papa stopped reading the letters to her altogether unless she asked. And then he just skimmed them and tried to highlight any upbeat tone, which wasn't often. Elizabeth became drawn and wasted. Abigail witnessed her mother's daily diminishment, the evaporation of her fervent vitality. Elizabeth fell further and further away. Abigail thought that Elizabeth's eyes had already surrendered the light. The letters from Welcome depressed Abigail because she knew it was just a matter of time before CJ headed for Europe to fight.

Keeping two young boys entertained and out of trouble, doing the housework, cooking, greeting visitors, and keeping up with her correspondence with CJ were physically grueling for Abigail. But it satisfied her need to put some distance from herself as well as the Delta.

When Papa came home from campus, James, a precocious four-year old, was all over him, "Show me the nickel in your nose, Papa." With ostentatious sleight of hand and a few magic words, Papa extracted a nickel from his nose and handed it to James.

"Are there any more nickels up there, Papa?" he shouted, peering into his grandfather's dark, spacious nostrils.

"I don't know, James," Papa said playfully. "I blew my nose earlier today and nickels were shooting out all over my office. But look here, I feel something funny in my ears."

James searched Papa's great, hairy ears and found nothing. Papa repeated the magic phrases, waved his hands theatrically, cried "Presto," and pulled two nickels from behind his fleshy lobes and placed the coins into James's eager hands. Papa's supply of nickels and magic were endless.

* * * * * * * * *

CJ grew increasingly antsy that the Ninety-third Division was already in the Pacific and his division was still at Fort Huachuca. His men were over trained, tired of the routine, and getting nowhere. Then the news arrived.

"All colored officers report to Colonel Wood's tent!" echoed through CJ's company area. Quickly, a large number of officers from the Ninety-second assembled. Colonel Woods—Woody was his nickname—was seated on the ground with his legs folded under him like some kind of Indian chief. He had a carefully cultivated Irish brogue, a waxed handlebar mustache, and a rumored distinguished war record. Most of the old-timers knew Woody. He frequented the base several times a year and had a reputation as an intuitive leader that allowed him to wield strict authority without losing the common touch. The younger officers, like CJ, considered him flamboyant, slightly wacky, and challengingly insulting.

He spoke matter-of-factly, "My name is Colonel Sterling A. Woods, and I understand colored people. I had a plantation in the South. So I know your needs. Now, I know there has been much discussion in the colored newspapers as to whether this division will see combat. I was talking to the Chief of Staff, General Marshall, and he agreed with me that colored troops would likely see combat in Europe. Why is this? Because 10 percent of the population in this country is colored people, so it is only fair that in this war 10 percent of the casualties should be colored. Therefore, you will be trained, and you will be sent where the fighting is the thickest."

Many of CJ's fellow officers were pissed because Woody offered nothing concrete. CJ heard some muttering, "Why the fuck are we sitting here?"

"What a windbag. He's feeding us a bunch of garbage."

"Listen to this jerk. He's full of shit."

CJ had a different take on things. He sensed after Colonel Wood's little "pep" talk that heading for combat was imminent—because of some percentage nonsense.

CJ's company had been trained for anti-mine infantry combat duties and hoped they would be used in that role, not in the capacity commonly assigned to Negro soldiers in supply service and other noncombat jobs.

Abigail sent CJ articles from the newspaper about the "Double V Campaign" for victory at home and abroad. In the minds of many Americans, Negro and white, military service equaled full citizenship rights. Abigail also included a letter Papa gave her that had been sent to Roosevelt from the Fraternal Council of Negro Churches, an organization with more than six million members, appealing to his sense of justice. In part, it read:

Negro troops are begging for combat not just in the Pacific, but also in Europe. This war is producing a large number of mental casualties among Negro servicemen. Their dignity and humanity are outraged and insulted. These casualties are produced by our own military who insisted upon relegating the Negro troops to second-class service when they are prepared for first-class service. Our men are prepared for combat and want contact with the enemy. Will you give them that chance? Speak boldly to the military officials concerning the plight of Negro servicemen as you have so often done on behalf of the down-trodden nations of the world.

Another month passed before the Ninety-second was put on alert to ship out. Some of the Negro soldiers were skeptical; others were numb with silence. Because of their intense desert training, CJ thought they would be sent to Northern Africa where Rommel was kicking the hell out of the Americans. How wrong he was.

Called in by the battalion commander who had chewed him out and assigned him to weekend trash detail for a month, CJ was given orders that his company was shipping out immediately. They would join the Three hundred and thirty-third, a regiment of the Eighty-fourth Division at Camp Kilmer, New Jersey. The soldiers were heading for the European Theater of Operations. CJ was told he would be briefed when they arrived at Barton Stacy Camp, outside Andover in the British Isles. Recognized for his skill in training one of the most fit companies in all of the Ninety-second, CJ was promoted to company commander and promised his captain bars after getting a little combat under his belt.

Four years from the day he was commissioned, CJ's military odyssey began in earnest. CJ gathered his men together and proclaimed, "No more maneuvers; no more forced marches; no more racial clashes with white MP's, soldiers, and off-base police and civilians from small southern and western towns; no more menial or administrative assignments; no more ceremonial parades and army manuals."

"Hoorah," came back in unison from Foxtrot Company.

"No more life with the scorpions, snakes, Gila monsters, mountain lions, skunks, ring-tailed cats, kill bugs, horned toads, trader rats, and coatimundis; no more stumbling into clumps of barrel, prickly pear, buckhorn, or organ pipe cactus; no more desert and rattlesnakes."

Again, another shattering, "Hoorah" and utility hats were tossed in the air.

But there was another kind of hell waiting for them.

CJ routed his trip from Fort Huachuca to Camp Kilmer, New Jersey, through Montgomery, Alabama. He was cutting it close. Any delays or schedule changes could make him AWOL and miss shipping out with his company. He took this risk for a day with his family and a night with Abigail.

At a young age, CJ's likeness was pronounced in James—even the long arms and legs—and he took great pleasure in this. "Lander gets his looks from you and your mother's side of the family," was CJ's comment to Abigail when he saw me for the first time. As a two-year-old, I looked nothing like the three-month old in the sepia photographs he had. Abigail brushed aside this unexpected comment about my appearance as she prepared for her evening and night with him.

Papa had arranged accommodations for CJ at the guesthouse on the Tuskegee campus and even hired a babysitter to help him with his two young grandsons. A black dress from Margaret's closet hugged Abigail's curves with dangerous seduction. And it did not disappoint.

It was a night of lovemaking that had everything—robust sweetness, exhausting greediness, rhythmic motions, overwhelming finality, and fatigue.

As CJ departed, Abigail gave him a ribbon-bound box that held a gift for him: a series of letters. The first was dated two weeks after he was scheduled to ship out, the last more than a year hence; all were marked to be opened on certain dates or birthdays, holidays, and anniversaries. She wanted him to hold two strands of her life. One was the letters she would be writing to him; the other was the set of letters she worked on for weeks, trying to imagine what he might need to hear, what might comfort him. A rounded image of her could appear if he read them side-by-side. This was the only way she knew how to be with him, how to project herself into the future, sensing what CJ might feel like in a week, a month, a year from leaving her.

* * * * * * * * *

Papa summoned the other Bryant children home; Elizabeth was in her last days, perhaps her last hours. She had lasted far longer than anyone anticipated. Welcome remained in the Pacific fighting Japanese. There was no such thing as hardship leave, nor could he get across the ocean in time if there were. The house was filled with flowers, Elizabeth's closest Tuskegee friends, relatives from all over the country, clergy from the town and college, and enough food to feed a small platoon.

In the evening, a prayer service was conducted in Elizabeth's room. Through opened curtains, the moon entered the room like an extra communicant. Everyone bowed their heads and took turns praying for their mother with all the fierceness that had come to that moment. Tears got in the way of Abigail's prayers. Stained and waterlogged, her prayers did not float like wood smoke toward the heights of the world, but were set adrift.

Late that night, Elizabeth called for her children to come to her. She had already said her goodbye to Papa. They all went reluctantly; they were distraught and exhausted. Her stillness began its silent walk as they waited for her to speak. Her breathing had an agonized, desperate sound. Everyone grew still and leaned forward to hear her say, "After I'm gone, you will realize how much you were loved. You all have your own special gifts. Use them. Remember family and God. Take care of each other and Papa." There was silence; the ragged sound of her voice was gone. "Mother, Mother, Mother," Fletcher moaned, sinking to his knees beside her, sobbing. Elizabeth had just slipped away.

At the funeral, one was aware of an entire town in mourning. Elizabeth was buried at the Tuskegee Cemetery. After telling her mother goodbye, Abigail lost the word "mother" forever; she could not bear to use it.

Abigail gathered and arranged a large number of photographs that she had culled from various family albums stored in her mother's old brown trunk. Suddenly, they were of interest to her—these stern, suited figures that she had gazed past contemptuously in younger years. She hungrily studied all of the vague incidental backgrounds of street corners, parks, and seashores. Looking for premonitions of herself, she wondered how certain people had dared to look so pleased and self-possessed when their life's mission was still unfolding. Abigail stared at photographs of her mother and father in their younger years. She looked from face to face, from setting to setting, as if there were some code that could be cracked. She tried to arrange them in an alternating pattern that would suggest forward-moving events on one side of the family and then the other, the strands finally twining together when her mother and father stood side by side in the All Saints Chapel on Christmas Day 1915. Abigail tried different sequences, but could not achieve anything that approached the sense of staggered simultaneity or capture the thought, sensation, or dynamic narrative she sought.

Why had she waited? Her mother was the real archivist of the family and had a knack for conferring dramatic shape on past events, making them interesting. It was now too late. She came across a picture of her mother as a young woman that she wanted to keep. Elizabeth was anywhere between fourteen and eighteen years old. Photographed from the waist up, against fleur-de-lis wallpaper, her long braid was pulled down over her shoulder and across the front of her white blouse. Holding a sprig of wildflowers in her right hand, her left hand was reaching up to pinch a few stalks. It was the expression, however, that was arresting. Elizabeth's gaze was detached from any local object and directed wholly inward. The pretty mouth was set resolutely, as if to insist on a young woman's prerogative to look elsewhere.

The image was compelling to Abigail, not because it featured such innocence or because so much time had passed, but by what she knew outside the frame of the photo. Looking at her mother's face, imagining her in that room, in that moment, she couldn't purge herself of a simple reality. She knew some of what happened in that life. At the moment the photograph was taken, Elizabeth waited on the brink of it all and could not begin to guess how things would fall out for her. There was no innocent study of those photographs for Abigail. Everything that had happened—and continued to unfold in her life—was part of the peculiar figment that was the Bryant family narrative. The longer stories had grown up out of all the stories told. However, these photographs were the flimsiest, but most evocative tokens of a life.

— Chapter Nine —

I have no recollection of the next fifteen months of our lives. What I attempt to describe here are the coiling and overlays of memories of others, tightfisted with the limitlessly abundant and extravagant images of World War II. I am relying on mostly how my mother, Papa, Doretha, my older brother James, and a few others remembered those months. Herein is how my father, CJ, experienced the war through the letters he wrote home and his private journal. He wrote on any foolscap he could find in the most unusual places under the most trying of circumstances.

* * * * * * * * *

It was September 19, 1944, when the whistle blew. Instantly, pandemonium exploded. The men from Foxtrot Company grabbed cumbersome, bulging barracks bags, backpacks, rifles, gas masks, travel orders, and personal possessions as they stumbled out of the temporary barracks—covered with tar paper—and onto the "company streets." As he bounded out of the hut, CJ was ready. He was tired of being relegated to the sidelines and wanted part of the action in fighting the Germans. Many in his company, particularly those leaving wives and children behind as he was doing, failed to share his enthusiasm.

These were men who had no desire to die alone in some war-ravaged foreign country while protecting and defending a country in which they held tenuously to a precarious citizenship that segregated them, denied them rights, and subjected them to racial violence—even in uniform. Little could any of them know, as they stood shivering in the predawn darkness trying to wipe the sleep from their eyes, what lay ahead. For too many, death waited. For the survivors, a lifetime—however brief that might be—of tortured memories would be the only reward for patriotic service.

Each man in CJ's company carried a forty-pound pack, ten-pound rifle, gas mask, and helmet while dragging a forty-pound barracks bag along the ground, nearly a mile, to the transport trains at Camp Kilmer, New Jersey. CJ was ordered to board his company into the three rear cars. Sixty-seven men were crammed into each car that was originally built to accommodate forty-eight. Cinder particles from the coal-powered engine filtered through closed, loose-fitting train windows, adding to the cattle-car conditions and gritty discomfort of their sweat-soaked uniforms. About an hour into the move, the train slammed to a halt.

After a lengthy wait on the New Jersey side of New York harbor, they were loaded onto ferries that took them to a 786-foot troop transport, commissioned in 1928 and considered the largest of its class. The name in peeling paint on the prow proclaimed this was the USS *Edmund B. Alexander*. It had the appearance of an oversized tramp steamer straight out of a Humphrey Bogart movie. A volunteer group of Red Cross women went through the white ranks dispensing hot coffee and doughnuts in an attempt to bolster the sagging morale. The Negro soldiers were ignored.

The normal three-day voyage took thirteen days. The ship zigzagged across the ocean trying to avoid German "wolf pack" submarines that were patrolling the area. The ship had to make a last-minute change of course away from a major French seaport on the English Channel where heavy bombing and submarine activity had been reported. The *Alexander* dropped anchor beside a small Scottish village. The troops disembarked with the task of trying to maneuver half a ton of army gear up four decks on the ship's ladders.

Makeshift ferryboats took them to the Glasgow port harbor. A long march brought them to troop trains for a trip to south central England. CJ's company took their usual place at the rear in cars consisting of six to eight compartments that comfortably accommodated four passengers each. Eight to ten of his men were crammed into each car.

No more than an hour out of Glasgow, many of the buildings were in shambles. Malnourished, hollow-cheeked children ran along the tracks beside the train waving victory signs with their hands and yelling, "Any gum, chum?"

Sixteen bone-weary hours later, the train pulled into Newberry, and trucks took the troops the remaining fifteen miles to Barton Stacy Camp, an abandoned British facility outside Andover. CJ's troops were segregated in wooden barracks and not allowed to join other units already there.

For the next ten days, they were transported about an hour away for training on the infamous anti-tank Tellermine that the Germans had used so effectively against British and American tanks in North Africa and Italy. They also worked on clearing German anti-personnel mines.

Finally, the troops were told to prepare to ship out. They were herded to troop carrier trucks and then onto trains to Southampton, Britain's largest seaport in the English Channel. CJ's men endured the harshest of transport conditions, particularly the train ride to Southampton. With the blackout curtains tightly drawn, the car reeked of whiskey, cigarettes, sweat, and other overpowering bodily odors. Crammed into compartments while others sprawled in the aisles and hung from baggage racks, the trains looked worse than slave ships. Eventually, the men poured out of the train into another of England's pea-soup fog banks. After a shivering wait, they finally loaded onto a small space on the open deck of an LST (Landing Ship Tank). They fought off nausea as the LST pitched and rolled across the Channel.

They got to their feet for the first glimpse of war-torn France. They were greeted by the massive, ugly pillars lining Omaha Beach and overturned, burned-out half-tracks. Underwater German concrete anti-tank barriers snaked their way along the beach at water's edge. Twisted anti-tank cannons and rusted-out jeeps littered the beach. Gaping shell craters that had not been filled in by the tides littered the beach. Landing craft (LSIs) were everywhere, most of them with ragged holes torn in their sides from the artillery shells that had sunk them and their troops before they reached the beach. Amongst all of this were ammunition crates, sandbagged machine gun emplacements, and rolls of barbed wire.

As they scanned the beach and the hill beyond, everyone fell silent. The ghosts of the hundreds of men who had died there still lingered. Only the rumble of the LSI engine split the silence.

The LSIs took them to within fifty feet of the sandy high-watermark. Everyone jumped off the sloping ramp into chest-deep water. The troops paddled and waded, almost drowning. They spat out gagging mouthfuls of ice cold sea water. Stumbling, they bobbed up for air and eventually got a foothold on the beach. At last, they were on the European continent.

There was no turning back. Looking much like a rag-tag mob swerving across the debris-strewn landscape, they climbed over the gun emplacements and dragged their barracks bags along behind them under the hot French sun. CJ ordered his men into two columns as they wove across the desolate Normandy countryside on the most grueling, exhausting, spirit-shattering march. They now understood why CJ had pushed them so hard at Fort Huachuca.

Mile after mile, they stared at the muddy road in front of them and the obvious signs that the Germans had experienced a field day against the Americans. Devastation was everywhere. The road, the pastures, and orchards were pocked with artillery craters. Horse carcasses gave off the odor of rot and decay under the sun. Burned-out tanks, grotesquely positioned on their sides had been blasted into twisted junk by violent force. The men saw death and the elimination of village after village.

As they marched inland from Omaha Beach through the shattered French villages, grimy, gaunt children dressed in tattered clothing crawled out of the rubble and tugged furiously at the back of their uniforms looking for their tails and begging for food. They had been educated to believe that Negroes were monkeys or devils and possessed tails.

The march ended fifteen hours later and had covered an estimated fifty miles. Each man had lugged nearly one hundred pounds of gear. They had challenged another adversity and won.

When CJ ordered his men to fall out and dig in, most just flopped over backward in their tracks, packs still strapped to their back, and collapsed on earthen mounds. Most fell asleep instantly. CJ was irate when orders came to provide runners to carry messages from one unit to another. "Run? My men can barely limp," he sent word back to the battalion executive officer—but to no avail.

* * * * * * * * *

If it had not been for the exhausting pace of the late summer and early fall, Abigail would not have been able to cope with her worry. It had been five weeks without any communication from CJ. She gave him two weeks to reach Europe and another week for a letter to arrive. She pestered Papa to use his contacts in Washington to find out if the *Alexander* dropped anchor somewhere around the English Channel. The news was full of warnings about Allied ships being sunk by German submarines. It took Papa a week to track down CJ's whereabouts. He warned Abigail, "You've got to stop agonizing if you don't hear from CJ or you're not going to survive this war."

According to Stuart Meriweather, the postmen in the Delta had never worn neckties, never put on their gray, wool uniforms with stripes down the trouser legs, had never donned their postal-issue caps, and had never been so severe and proper until the war came along to make them extraordinarily significant. They knocked on doors and were greeted by mothers, wives, fathers, and sisters already on the edge of agony. The postman extended the official notice toward them. He didn't say, "I'm sorry," or "Forgive me," or "If there's anything I can do," but simply, "Ma'am" or "Sir." No one who received the official letter ever opened it immediately. They clutched it and bent it through their fingers; but they never neglected to say, "Thank you."

Newsreels at the Dixie showed airplanes turning cities into fields of fire and GIs storming sandy, island beaches strafed by fanatical Japanese. The great Eurasian continent seethed with moving masses and vast death. The oceans drank torpedoed ships. And in the United States, a land of women, children, and old men lived with price controls, rationing tokens, and war stamps. There was a speeding up of life, a sense that there were stakes higher than Delta life and cotton farming.

A distracted Abigail was reading the Sunday *Little Rock Gazette* when Doretha appeared unnoticed.

"What has you so preoccupied?"

Startled, Abigail reacted with hardly a greeting, "Doe, listen to this: 'Second Lieutenants Take a Pounding.'"

"Abigail, what does that mean?"

"I'll read it to you. 'No group among all the services has as high a casualty rate as second lieutenants.' It gets worse. There's an interview with a returning soldier from the Pacific: 'During the course of the long fighting on Okinawa ...we got numerous replacement lieutenants. They were wounded or killed with such regularity that we rarely knew anything about them ... and saw them on their feet only once or twice. Our officers got hit so often that it seemed to me the position of second lieutenant in an infantry company is a suicide mission.' CJ's not going to make it back home, Doe."

"That's no way to think. Where's your faith? God will take care of him," Doretha assured Abigail.

"Well, CJ is in Europe and not the Pacific," Abigail replied trying to calm herself down. She suddenly realized, "But my brother's still in the Pacific somewhere."

"Abigail, there's nothing we can do but pray. Come on, let's do some baking."

For most of the afternoon, Abigail was lost in her thoughts and did little talking. She wondered about all those second lieutenants that Tuskegee churned out. Were Papa's critics right? Abigail leafed through the dictionary for the word *martyr*.

"Doe," Abigail popped out, "the dictionary defines *martyr* as 'a person who makes a great sacrifice for the sake of a principle.'"

"What are you talking about?" Doretha quizzed.

"Our boys overseas, they're martyrs. My Papa defended the officer program at Tuskegee in the name of greater citizen rights for all of us. Do you think he made a mistake?"

"Abigail, you've got to give all this bad thinking up. It's making me nuts. I'm trying my best to hold on to the good news and keep us going. Now get over here and help with this last batch of cookies."

A couple of the Meriweather boys got jobs at a parachute factory in Little Rock. For the war effort, Abigail and Doretha took paper off of tin cans and flattened the cans by jumping on them on the cement floor of the chicken house while the chickens rustled and cackled on their rusty rungs or in their cubbyholes. The flattened tin cans piled up in a corner of the barn, making a shining mountain before being turned in. The eggs—brown, speckled, dabbed with dung—were sold to people around the Delta in reused paper egg cartons for a pittance.

Abigail received her first letter from CJ on November twentieth. As she did nearly every weekday, she waited at the mailbox and her heart nearly exploded when she saw the smile on the mailman's face as he approached. After kissing the letter numerous times, hugging us and twirling us around in the air, she cried and then became angry he had made her wait so long to hear from him. She was breathless and could not bring herself to read it until she had settled down with a cup of tea.

CJ's letter described a train-ride through Scotland, ... *its tranquil lakes and the brilliant reds and purples of the setting sun. One moment this beauty was at my fingertips and then it danced playfully away into my memory. I wish I had been clever enough to steal this enchanting example of nature's splendor and transpose it onto a canvas for you to enjoy. Each passing scene was truly a moment of exquisite beauty.*

He wrote of how unfair it was to be offered those tantalizing landscapes and then have them so abruptly replaced with the vision of war's atrocities, filth, deprivation, and destruction as he got farther into the European mainland. CJ's company was surprised to receive a twenty-four hour pass to London, and he shared impressions from his firsthand view of Hitler's "blitz" bombing that nearly flattened the fabled city. He described the mountains of burning rubble, the thousands of men, women, and babies who were now homeless refugees who filled the underground subway "tubes" and were forced to live like moles. He wrote of the thunderous roar from the rockets falling around London and the crying of frightened, bewildered children. A lighter, brief mention of the guards at Buckingham Palace and their crimson colonial splendor was followed by an abrupt warning that correspondence was going to be difficult.

They were preparing to make the twenty-six mile hop across the English Channel to Omaha Beach. He reminded Abigail to keep up with his whereabouts through newspaper and radio accounts about the progress of the war and the movement of the Eighty-fourth. He ended his letter with,

I will be thinking about you and the boys every moment. Take care of the homestead. I do love you Abigail. I will make you proud.

The letter ended, almost. A postscript was squeezed onto the bottom of the page that simply read, "Sorry about your mother." Abigail was put off that CJ relegated his rather trivial sentiment to an afterthought. It was true CJ held no affection for Elizabeth; he thought of her as an adversary and someone who had to be won over. Abigail realized she had to try to calm her expectations and adjust to CJ's rough edges.

Abigail was not caught off guard by her third pregnancy, but struggled with whether to tell CJ. It did not seem likely the war was going to end anytime soon, and CJ would miss the birth of yet another child. She ached for the birth of a daughter. Doretha convinced her that the news would be a source of joy for CJ and was too important for silence. This advice came from experience. When Doretha's husband, Jimmy, had come home on furlough, Doretha disappeared for several days. A couple of months later, she came to Abigail for help in writing a letter to Jimmy about another blessed event on the way. As it happened, Doretha was only a month ahead of Abigail. The boxes of maternity clothes that they had shared were brought out from storage.

* * * * * * * * *

As an anti-mine and anti-tank support company, CJ's troops traveled in vehicle convoys, rather than slogging their way to the next destination in ankle-deep mud. Passing through Versailles, on the outskirts of Paris, the convoy continued into Belgium and roared relentlessly toward the front. An air of urgency set in; the fatigue and danger of traveling in the daylight lost all significance. Leige was devastated—far worse than London and northern France. The convoy had traveled several hundred miles almost nonstop and still had not arrived at their destination. By midnight, the truck column pulled into a war-ravaged village and the men unloaded. A blackout was in effect, and the artillery-shattered town closed in around them. There was a shared sense of apprehension and dread. The war they sought was just around the corner. They could hear it in the distance; they could smell it. It wouldn't be long.

The German's scorched-earth policy hideously announced itself when they passed through Heerlen, Holland. The Germans had burned every building and barn they could, fired phosphoric shells and grenades into the orchards to burn the soil and make it useless for planting in the future, and slaughtered horses, cows, sheep, chickens, geese, anything that could be eaten. They crushed apple trees with tanks and ground apple crops to pulp with vehicles. Farmers were forced at gunpoint to shake apples from their trees so that the fruit could be sprayed with acids. Mattresses and blankets were slashed with knives and bayonets and the down contents cast to the winds. In a systematic plan to reduce an entire nation to starvation, the Germans contaminated wells and poisoned vegetable and fruit crops. They plundered everything they could find. As they marched or drove away, they taunted the Dutch people with, "Now you will have something to remember us by." These were the conditions in which CJ and his men found Holland.

CJ enjoyed walking along the miles and miles of earthen dikes that held back the North Sea. On top of some of those dikes, entire villages of single-story homes stretched almost endlessly. Apparently, in one last vicious act of vengeance against the Dutch, the Germans blew away an entire section of one dike, flooding miles of lowland countryside with seawater, rendering it useless for years to come.

A humorous moment revealed everyone's jumpiness. It was well after midnight when CJ and his men arrived in a bombed-out house in Marionberg, Holland. No one had eaten, so someone kindled the stove and placed a can of C-ration pork and beans on it. Exhausted, CJ stretched out on a couch and fell into a deep sleep. A horrible explosion awakened him. Instinctively, he hit the floor. CJ felt a sharp pain, a severe burning sensation on his arms and back, and thought he'd been hit. He put his hands to his face and came away with warm, wet flesh. "Medic, medic," someone cried out. CJ knew he'd been badly wounded from the amount of pain. Again, he put his hand to his face and came away with what appeared, in the flicker of candlelight, to be more blood. Reddish, brown stains covered the upper part of his uniform. The others in the room rushed to his assistance. Someone lit another candle to see how badly he'd been hit. They lifted him gently back onto the couch and by then, some flashlights had been found. Wryly, one of the men laughed, "It don't be lookin' like no blood to me." And, it wasn't. Only then did they recognize what covered his head and upper body was the can of pork and beans left unattended on the hot stove. The can had expanded and exploded, showering CJ with its contents. His men laughed for days about the incident.

As December pressed on, problems in the field were compounded by the heavy snowfall. If there was anything they didn't need, it was a ferocious Belgian winter. The German assault they had been waiting for still hadn't come; CJ resigned himself to spending more nights slouched and shivering in his foxhole. The temperature continued to plummet. There was no way to keep warm. As much as he wanted to stand up or stretch, making himself a better target for some Kraut's Mauser rifle was not appealing.

He tried to stamp his feet in the bottom of the hole, but the pain became too severe. The cold and heavy snowfall continued. When his feet finally went numb, he was relieved to feel the pain subsiding. Numbed by exhaustion, he didn't realize what was happening to him. Snow and sleet froze on his cheeks and filtered down his back. His feet became encased in snow and ice; he could no longer move them. And more disturbing, he just didn't care anymore.

The temperature had dropped well below zero. His whole body was numb, and he had given in to the sweet fatigue that had been building for days. He slept. He was awakened by Lieutenant "Showboat" Hayes, his second-in-command, who was punching him and telling him to move or he would freeze to death. He tried but couldn't and lapsed back to an unconscious sleep. The mind-numbing cold finally conquered his instinct for survival. He lay helplessly in the hole allowing the cold to take its toll.

It was almost daylight, and the snow hadn't slackened. His face was frozen stiff; his eyebrows, cheeks, and jaw were encrusted with ice. Because his eyes were glazed over, he could only see a few feet in front of his foxhole, and his feet were encased in a block of ice up to his ankles in the bottom of the hole. Two medical corpsmen found him in that condition and carried him to a meat wagon hidden in a clump of trees not far away. Given a mess kit of hot oatmeal and coffee, he was told to rest and thaw out. When the circulation returned to his legs, excruciating pain that had been dulled by the numbness gradually became unbearable. He was moved to a field hospital tent approximately a mile behind the lines. A team of doctors examined and probed at his legs, the sight of which was unnerving. Both feet looked like ugly, purplish-blue mutations with large, blistering pieces of torn skin peeling off them.

He was given painkillers. The doctors told him they would wait one day before making a decision whether or not to evacuate him to a rear area hospital where his badly frozen feet might be amputated. When CJ heard this dire prognosis, he hysterically pleaded with the doctors, "Don't do that to me. Don't take my feet. Please, please …" He was given an injection. The next thing he remembered was waking up as one of the doctors examined him and informed him there had been substantial improvement.

After a week of recuperation in the field hospital for frostbite and trench foot, CJ felt an overwhelming sense of relief and gratitude. He would rather have died than live the rest of his life without feet.

Several letters that week went out to Abigail. They all had a tone of gratitude:

This morning, I opened an envelope from the cache you sent with me. No one but you, love, would have thought to do this. During these times when I have no mail from you, I have words from your letters, which have been of great consolation. I wait like a child on Christmas Eve for the dates you have marked on each envelope to arrive. I obey you, you see; I have not cheated. Now that we are on the move, I treasure these even more. I wish I had thought to leave behind a similar gift for you.

* * * * * * * * *

Every evening at exactly six o'clock, Abigail tried to have the children settled, removed her apron, and sat at the kitchen table. The end of the table was flush against the wall and served as a large shelf that accumulated things. In the center was an RCA radio in a walnut case. She turned on the switch as the CBS news was delivered: "This is Edward R. Morrow, live from New York." There would be heavy fighting someplace or another in Europe and from the old map she kept tucked beside the radio, she knew whether CJ's unit was in the area. His letters arrived far too infrequently. Abigail tried to read everything she could into those few letters to get a sense of how he was doing. When Mr. Morrow got past his lead story about the politics, he started on the war. Abigail closed her eyes, folded her hands together, put both index fingers to her lips and waited. What was she was waiting for? Mr. Morrow was not going to announce to the nation that CJ Duncan was dead or alive.

Another letter surprised Abigail ten days later, but her elation was soon dissipated by its contents. The letter began with a touch of nostalgia and a funny vignette or two. The last paragraph sounded like a drowning man or someone marching toward an ominous unknown:

I have never been afraid of the dark before but I must tell you without shame, that on some nights I am. While my heart is pounding at times as we enter ink-like blackness and there is eerie silence, broken only by the occasional clanking of rifles shining against our steel helmets, and the uneven squishing patter of thousands of footsteps in this muddy hell, I force myself to think about you and home and my fear subsides. Pray for me. I love you Abigail.

Doretha learned that Jimmy had been reassigned to CJ's old Ninety-second Division, the Buffalo Soldiers. She proudly boasted to Abigail about their arrival in Italy where they joined the American Fifth Army. Jimmy, who was a field sergeant, sent Doretha a copy of an article from some Negro newspaper that his parents found. She could almost recite it:

Rumors of the arrival of the Buffalo Soldiers in Naples had preceded them .... As the thousands of Negro fighting men, in single file, debarked from the crowded troopship, they presented an impressive and awe-inspiring spectacle. Armed with basic weapons and full field battle dress, proudly wearing the circular patch with the black buffalo, they moved smartly and efficiently into their unit formations. As they marched away every man in step, every weapon in place, chins up and eyes forward, a low rumbling babble of sound came from the troops on the dock, then swelled to a crescendo of thunderous cheering that continued until the last Buffalo unit had disappeared from sight.

Abigail shared in Doretha's satisfaction. She knew how hard Papa had worked on behalf of the Negro troops to get them into combat in Europe.

But as time passed, Doretha began to sing a different tune. The Ninety-second was part of an Allied push from the coastal areas of the Ligurian Sea through the valleys and plains to the Apennines, and were engaged in pitched battles to clear out firmly entrenched Nazi strongholds. Jimmy was attached to the 370th Combat Team and was in the thick of the action.

At first, his letters read like a travel brochure trying to entice reluctant tourists to an exotic locale with descriptions of how the sun reflected on the snow-capped Italian mountains. By late October, Jimmy's letters suddenly changed. The letter Doretha read to Abigail dated November 10, 1944, revealed how far his communication had deteriorated:

Dear Doretha honey,

The German artillery and firing keeps me very jumpy. Five colored officers have been killed in action so far. Has the 92nd published any casualty lists in the colored papers? We are all getting a raw deal. We have been on the line 82 days, and we don't know when we are going to get relieved. We thought the election would change it, but it hasn't. The men are sick, frostbitten, shell-shocked and scared. It's good the Germans don't know the condition of some of us or we would be in a lot hotter water. I wish some of the papers would get a hold of this and ask the War Department when we are going to get relieved. It looks as if they want to wipe out the all-colored 92nd. The "all" means all colored on the line and a few on the staff. I don't know what the papers are saying, but it's really tough. A couple of the colored officers have been or are up for court-martial because they refuse to lead troops into death traps.

I just wish some of us here could get back and tell what we know. I'm really disgusted with the whole setup. It looks as if they don't even expect to give us a break. We can look right out of the hole and see Germans parading around on the skyline and it takes half of the day to get artillery on it, because we have to conserve ammunition and yet the Germans shell the hell out of us. It's no joke to see men you have known, lived with, eaten with, and slept with blown up or shot down before your eyes. The majority of the men are too tired to fight.

Well, sugar, I've blown off enough steam for now. The NAACP should know this situation. The Germans are beginning to shell us again, so I'll sign off. You know how much I love you and the kids, and I'm not going to let anything keep me from getting back home and holding you in my arms. Sorry to burden you with this letter. Pray for me.

Your lover,

Jimmy

Doretha was almost delirious with agonizing worry. Her spirit seemed to wither and shrivel. She just seemed to deflate.

Something broke through with CJ's last letter and Abigail wrote what she'd never permitted herself before:

Terrible scenes rise up before my eyes and they are as real as the rest of my life. I look out the window and I see the postman walk up to the door; he is bearing an envelope. I know what is in it. I know. I am already crying as I open the door. He looks down at his shoes. I take the letter from him. I open it; it is one from the government and I skip over the sentences, which attempt to prepare me for the news. I skip to the part in which it says you have died. It talks about an explosion. I read the sentences again and again. They confirm my worst fears, and I grow faint as hope expires in me and yet I will not believe. In the envelope, too, another sheet: the words of someone I have never met, who witnessed your last days:

"Though I am a stranger to you, it is my duty to inform you of a most terrible event."

And then a description of whatever befell you; and one more sheet, which is your last letter to me.

You see how I torment myself. Imagine all the things you might write. Imagine on some days that you tell me the truth, on other days that you lie to spare my feelings. I imagine you writing, "Do not grieve too long dearest Abigail. The cruelest thing, when we think of our loved ones dying in distant lands, is the thought of them dying alone and abandoned, uncared for ...." How can I imagine you alive and well when I have not heard from you for so long?

I am ashamed of myself for writing this. All over America other women wait patiently for soldiers and sailors— why can't I? I will try to be stronger. When you read this letter, know that it was written by Abigail who loves you, in a moment of weakness and despair.

Abigail received the Uncle Sam Christmas surprise that included a telegram and flowers. It was a package deal through the USO for men on the front lines. Some carved wooden Dutch pull toys, trucks, or a collection of model airplanes—P-51s, Zeros, Spitfires, and Messerschmitts—arrived for James and me weeks earlier. But the holidays came and went without a letter from CJ. Doretha suffered the same drought. They cried in each other's arms on Christmas Eve while listening to carols and holiday music on the radio.

The second week in January, Abigail received the letter she had been longing for. It had everything in it—love, devotion, a sense of humor, concern, news of his whereabouts, and the conditions around him. His letter provided emotional sustenance to help Abigail endure another indeterminate period of silence and worry.

The letter was lengthy and read like a novella. It began with how amazed he was that the stars over Holland were the same as the ones that shined in the Arkansas Delta sky. By looking straight up at night, he could be at home with her and the boys. He listed the new words he learned from a Dutch family. He described their demeanor and customs, and their struggle with food shortages. Members of CJ's company had started to meet each night, when possible, to read the Bible aloud. Abigail was happy to hear that he gained some inner strength and peace of mind from the scripture reading that pushed the war away for a few special minutes each evening. He commented in his letter about hoping for some divine protection. CJ described an incident in the little Belgium village of Heures. He had been without sleep for twenty-three hours and fell asleep in a hayloft. He was awakened by a strange weight on his chest—a chicken was roosting near his chin.

He and his men were constantly on the move or under attack. The letter described the likes of Marche, Belgium, and the artificial Christmas tree Abigail sent, which he stuck in the snow at the lip of his foxhole. A Christmas morale boost came with the lifting of the nine-day fog in England. Squadron after squadron of fighters and B-17 bombers streaked overhead on their way to German cities.

The subzero temperature and its consequences was a dominant theme: frostbite, trench foot problems, and foxholes as ice-encrusted chambers. His troops were experiencing temperatures thirty degrees below freezing. To stay warm, they wore long-john underwear, woolen uniform pants and shirt, a sweater, a field jacket, a full-length wool overcoat, two pair of gloves, a wool cap, a helmet, two pair of wool socks, combat boots wrapped in torn-up woolen strips, and oversized galoshes. They then wrapped themselves cocoon-style in as many blankets as could be found.

There were apologies about the absence of letters and his concerns about whether she was getting her military dependent allowance okay. He mentioned homesickness and even missed seeing old man Bailey dressed up like Santa Claus for the kids. Most importantly, he wrote of his utter love and devotion.

* * * * * * * * *

CJ returned to his unit in Grand Han, Belgium. He and his men were given a two-day temporary duty change from mine detection to grave registration. When they arrived at a building designated as a field mortuary, he was briefed that his company would be picking up American dead in the field. They rode around the area in three-quarter ton weapon carriers. Whenever they spotted a dead American, they jumped off, picked up the body, and slung it any way they could, usually by the arms and legs, onto the back of the truck.

As they hefted each twisted, frozen corpse, CJ invariably turned away. He averted his eyes from the glazed, blue, bloated faces of the dead, each grotesquely etched with the filth of war. The eyes of many of the dead were open—reflecting the terror and violence of their last moments on earth. It was almost as if CJ could reject death, push it away, and not let it intrude into his life, as fragile as it was hour by hour.

The bodies, frozen and stiff in every position imaginable, were stacked haphazardly higher and higher like cordwood until the men couldn't throw the bodies any higher. Then it was back to the field mortuary where they emptied their load and started the process again. They found bodies floating in the rivers, trampled on the roads, bloated in the ditches, rotting in the bunkers, twisted into foxholes, burned in the tanks, buried in the snow, sprawled in doorways, splattered in gutters, dismembered in mine fields, and literally blown up into trees.

They didn't try to identify them—that was someone else's responsibility at the mortuary. CJ had to turn off all mental sensibility and instructed his men to do the same, "Find them, load them, get rid of them." They didn't bother with German corpses.

CJ posed to Jiggs, his platoon sergeant, who usually relished personal commentary and philosophical discussions, "What's happened to me? I've become so indifferent and blasé to death. Look at that corpse; that boy was no more than nineteen or twenty years old. He has a family and friends who will miss him."

Jiggs was in no mood for such discourse and deadpanned back, "I'm numb from all this shit. Let's get those boys over there and get the hell outta here."

It was all the same, as were the towns of Haversin, Marche, Hootan, Geilenkirschen, and Prummern. The carnage of the struggle was everywhere: bullet-riddled overturned jeeps and wagons, horse and livestock carcasses, and bodies draped over smoldering tanks. Grotesque brown and green uniformed corpses covered the streets. Arms and legs were blown off, men were disemboweled, and mouths, noses, and jaws were blown away. Some men were still alive, foaming blood drooling from their mouths, gaping holes of bloody meat where chests had been, intestinal tracts lying stretched out on the ground like long twisted links of sausage. How would CJ ever get these images out of his head?

He and his company had to accept the middle-of-the-night, nomadic lifestyle which meant only more loss of sleep, more mud, less food, more cold, more work, and worse living conditions. They had been given an extra piece of equipment to carry around called a "vacuum cleaner" mine detector. Each man already carried a full field pack, field rations, gas mask, nine-pound M-2-rifle, three bandoleers of rifle ammunition, and other miscellaneous combat gear. They were always weighted down. CJ wanted desperately to complain to division-level command, but refrained. He feared a racist backlash that would propagate and serve to fulfill prophesies about the Negro soldiers' incompetence and unsuitability for combat.

There was a constant demand for mine detection, clearing, or planting squads from CJ's company. The entire 333rd Regiment depended upon them and for just cause. Mines had a terrible and deep psychological effect on soldiers. They would rather take their chances with small arms fire or even artillery than with those silent, deadly devices.

The losses CJ suffered after only six months were staggering: three full squads—thirty-six men—were dead and fourteen were injured. That was one-quarter of his company. They went out in advance of ground attacks to search buildings for booby traps, clear areas bordering roadway traffic, bury mines to slow down the approaching German infantry, plant daisy-chain anti-tank mines, and hide in ditches beside the road to pull the ropes in front of the lead enemy tanks. They also had to endure what infantry troops did—without their special training. CJ had to leave six men behind when a frontal assault by several squads of SS troops outflanked and overran their position. The snow was crimson with their blood.

As CJ was planning to draw attention in the national media through a war correspondent he had befriended to what he called "the slaughter of Foxtrot Company," the captain from the battalion paid his men a visit and praised them for their courage. Each of the men in CJ's company was awarded a Combat Infantry Badge for exemplary conduct in action against the enemy. Maybe the best thing that happened, in spite of its racist overtones, was the nickname bestowed on his company. They were now called "The Spooks" or "Spook Company." The moniker carried with it a badge of honor of sorts that truly inflated their exhausted egos. It was the closest thing to a small acknowledgement of acceptance of Negro soldiers. The captain explained to CJ and his men that the nickname came about because of their color and not being able to see their faces in the dark, their stealth in dealing with mines, and the way they sent so many Germans into the hereafter. They were getting used to it and chose not to be offended by it as a racial slur. "Go get the Spooks!" "Call the Spooks in for this!" CJ could imagine worse treatment and slander.

Racist propaganda preceded them. Written in their native language and posted on billboards throughout the region, the racist posters threatened the women with violent reprisals if they engaged in any type of association with Negro soldiers. CJ had one of the billboards translated:

Do you know that the Negro is a man
of the colored race;
that he must live in America only among his own;
that he is an inferior human being,
if not in name, at least in fact?
The machine gun will cut down the prostitute
who sells the honor of her race,
and the people will seek revenge upon her and her
black son when this crime has been
brought to light.

Even white soldiers were shocked by the tone of the placards.

Foxtrot Company also encountered a caricature by a German cartoonist that portrayed a Negro soldier as a dementedly grinning monkey. The caption, "Know Your Enemy," was written in several languages beneath the profoundly repulsive effigy that was complete with an unshaven face, disheveled uniform, grungy cap, exaggerated fleshy lips and broad nose, and watery bulging eyes. But it was the coiling, long tail that was drawn with such subtlety that one didn't immediately notice an elongated male organ gripped in the monkey's hairy paw. This last detail usually elicited a slow double take that got to everyone's funny bone. As was their norm to joke about such insults, wisecracking Dudley, known for his smart-ass bravado and cheap banter, slyly commented, "At least they got the size of my cock right."

CJ managed to get a long letter out to Abigail in early February 1945. He was still in Belgium in places with names like Odeigne and Webomont. He described the strangest face he'd ever seen: sunken eyes bloodshot and ringed with dark circles, cheeks and jaw with a six-week scraggly, black beard matted with encrusted mud, and a forehead with deep furrows crisscrossing it. It was his reflection in a mirror that he portrayed to Abigail and wondered whether he would ever again look like the person she remembered. CJ raved about the packages she sent filled with candy, Cracker Jacks, animal crackers, fruit, dried meat, popcorn, and gum. These not only kept him with a bottomless barracks bag of food, but also made him the envy of everyone. The envy, he wrote Abigail, was more about him having someone at home as beautiful as she. He added that the picture he was always waving around was getting a little frayed at the edges.

He wrote to her about a Belgium woman and her just-delivered, yowling, baby boy. He barely got them out of a burning house that had been hit by artillery. Carrying that little Belgium newborn made him realize that the birth of their third child was just around the corner and that he had not been there for the delivery of any of their children. CJ confirmed that he liked the names Daniel Turner and Nettie Olivia for the baby. He knew how much Arnetta meant to her, so thought Nettie was a good compromise. However, he expressed a little surprise that her father's name was not a candidate.

He did a little gloating about the combat infantry badges and the important contributions his company was making to the war. He knew Abigail would have a difficult time with the "spook" moniker. She would perceive it to be a disparagement and not a badge of honor. He ended his letter with:

Well, my beautiful Valentine, I love you with all my heart. Share some of my love with the boys and the one in the oven.

One by one, CJ's company was being reduced by the war. He could see it in his men's eyes. They wondered when their turn was coming. CJ had so many close calls with death. On the most recent occasion, he entered the front door during one of their house-to-house searches for booby traps. A violent blow punched him in the side, spinning him around and dumping him in a heap on a pile of shattered masonry. A sniper had been following him in his sights. As he lay in the rubble collecting his thoughts, another bullet slammed into the door jam over his head, throwing splinters of wood into his face. CJ rolled inside the building. Instinctively, he felt for the wound and couldn't understand why there was no pain, just a dull ache as if someone had walloped him hard in the side. There was no wound. The sniper's bullet had severed his cartridge belt and hit his M-1 ammo pouch. The cartridges had been flattened and twisted, but not one had exploded. CJ vowed to Showboat, "I'm going to carry this clip around with me until the war ends."

CJ survived the Ardennes and the Battle of the Bulge. In something called Operation Grenade, a push toward the Rhineland and Berlin, it was hell dealing with the assault across the Roer River. It was four in the morning, and they had exactly two minutes to sprint across a two-foot wide bouncing, swaying pontoon bridge that was heavily fortified by Germans on the other side. CJ's men were part of the first wave to go across. Occasionally, CJ had to hold rope handrails as the bucking bridge did its best to throw him into the Roer below. He felt as though he was running in slow motion. German Messerschmitts and Focke Wulfs strafed and bombed them. A body-battering concussion of shells and mortars and ear-shattering artillery made it seem as if they were trying to function in a black void of time where reality ceased. As American troops poured across the bridge, heavy casualties were taken. Hundreds of wounded soldiers fell into the water and tried to swim the last few yards ashore as the current or rifle fire claimed them. CJ lost another eight men.

The Germans were in full retreat with pockets of stubborn, sometimes fanatical resistance. CJ's unit moved eastward and had to endure the cold, penetrating March dampness, wet uniforms, and the lack of rest and food. The towns of Lindern, Doveren, Wegburg, Dulken, and Erkelenz had large concentrations of German soldiers who were in hiding. Truck-mounted public address systems rolled up to the edge of the city and blared in German that they had ten minutes to surrender themselves. They were told to take whatever possessions they could carry and were assured no harm would come to them. The warning that an artillery barrage would commence after ten minutes usually did the trick. Frightened civilians streamed out of town carrying battered suitcases, sheets, and blankets filled with meager belongings. Hundreds of soldiers surrendered. An intense howitzer barrage pounded the city for twenty minutes. Then, the dangerous house-to-house searches followed.

As they moved into the Rhineland, there was no resistance. White flags and bed sheets were draped everywhere, hanging from every house and building as signs of surrender. Civilians crowded sidewalks, some in business suits; women bicycled with shopping bags hanging from their arms; and even a few cars were being driven on the street like a normal German city. Cities such as Monchengladbach, Krefeld, and Moers were passed through without shelling.

Hitler's defenses were falling like dominoes. The resolve of his troops was weakening; each day, they pushed deeper into the German homeland. CJ and his men were now facing a different kind of war. His company was presented with another citation for "... facilitating the advance ... during Operation Grenade ...." Koko, the quipster and funnyman of Foxtrot lampooned the citation, "That commendation and ten cents would not allow us to sit at a lunch counter to have a cup of coffee back in the States."

The rest of the Ninety-second Division was elsewhere in Europe evidenced by the shower of German propaganda pamphlets:

To all members of the colored Division:

After they got you into the army they shipped you off to a foreign country to fight in a rich man's war. As for you fellows, you have nothing to gain but you may lose your lives or get your limbs blown off. Don't wait for that. Better say goodbye to war. Ship over to Jerry's some night, as many colored boys have done before you. They are now safe in a POW camp waiting for the end of the war. Stay alive for your folks and don't die for empty promises.

After two and a half months of waiting, Doretha received the belated news that Jimmy had been hospitalized for twenty-eight days with gunshot and shrapnel wounds and frostbite. His letter was cheerful:

... I've been wounded in the heel and arm. Don't get excited because you know that if it were bad I would tell you. I've been awarded the Purple Heart. It's a beautiful medal. I'm going to send it home as soon as I can. I walk fairly good, but not very fast. I'm getting good treatment. I should be rejoining my unit in a few weeks ...

Abigail was surprised that Doretha held up well with the news. The ambiguity and not knowing always got the best of both of them, they supposed.

CJ's company was about to join in the attempt at what Hitler said was impossible: to breach and penetrate the area east of Germany's largest natural obstacle—the Rhine River. If they could make it across the Rhine, the back of Germany's military might well be broken forever. There wasn't much conversation at the "last supper." A pall of uncertainty and apprehension hung over most of them as they counted the hours ticking by. Crossing the Roer had been a bitter, bloody fight orchestrated by the most intense artillery fire CJ had experienced. The Rhine was much wider, more strategically important, and better defended. It was the do-or-die campaign for the German army; it was the last defensible position before Berlin.

The Americans would move out north along the west bank of the river. Restriction to quarters gave CJ a little time for reflection. *How many times can one go back on the line and do what they do with the mines and still come out again in one piece? How long would it be before their* luck ran out? Was this going to be the end of the line for them? Is it that a man's destiny is determined strictly by how far fate is pushed? The fate of CJ's company had been pushed far, hard, and often.

Much to CJ's relief, the dirty work was already done for them. A crossing had already been made and a beachhead had been established. They crossed the river without a fight. When they hit the far bank of the Rhine, the German artillery waited and hell was unleashed.

The Americans drove toward a glowing red horizon. An entire city was burning, and they headed into the flames. There, in the city of Wesel, man had accomplished the ultimate obliteration. It was later called "the city of the burning dead," man's hell on earth. They advanced slowly through Wesel. Flames scorched the canvas sides of their trucks.

The 5th Armored Division cut a path into Germany's heartland, and the 102nd Division backed them up. The objectives of the 84th were the Weser River, the Elbe River, and the final destination—about four hundred miles away—Berlin. Sitting practically motionless in the rear of a bouncing truck with only a few ten-minute roadside stops during stints of twenty-four hours was brutal. About every seventy-two hours, they took a break in one of the many small cities in the heart of Germany's northern central plains and encountered little resistance. It was a command decision to shoot defenders of those cities on sight, regardless of sex or age, whether or not they were armed and threatening their progress. CJ countermanded those orders with his company. "Unless fired upon," he instructed, "keep your weapons in a locked, but ready, position. Too much unnecessary blood has already been shed." Bielefeld, Herford, and other cities came and went as hundreds of German soldiers surrendered along the way. Most of them were told to disband and find their way home. Homes and towns were reduced to smashed mortar and stone. Families had become refugees wandering hundreds of miles from city to city like nomads, seeking food and shelter.

As the convoy continued eastward from the Rhine, they approached an area where a nauseating smell permeated the air. A twelve-foot high fence strung with double rows of barbed wire enclosed wooden barracks known as concentration camp huts. A sign over a barbed wire gate read "Nord Stalag III." Everywhere CJ looked, he was aware of the genocide of Jews. It was difficult to differentiate between the living and dead skeletons on the wooden platforms that served as beds. Those that stared up at them with sunken eye sockets were too far gone to speak. Many had their teeth pounded out for their gold fillings.

CJ met his first German Jew, a man named Heinrich. CJ found him sitting in a desk chair in the administration building and was repulsed by his emaciated appearance. He spoke English quite well although his voice was but a hollow whisper. The German camp doctors had conducted experiments on his voice box. He had large scars on his arms and back where they had performed skin grafts for plastic surgery. He also had large, scarred areas on his legs and buttocks where skin had been removed for other experimentation. Facetiously, he told CJ this had all been done while he still had meat on his bones. The scars on his shoulders and back were from "the whip."

Heinrich took CJ to a concrete building with a tall chimney at the rear of the camp—*Das Krematorium*. He insisted CJ go inside to witness the skulls, bones, ashes, and experience the awful stench. A deep pit contained bones of what must have been hundreds of Jews. The walls were a gruesome mural of smeared blood. It looked as if they had bashed their heads against the walls to render themselves unconscious.

Heinrich took CJ to the ones he considered "the more fortunate." They had been frozen solid and then thrown into vats of hot water in a primitive cryogenic experimentation.

They proceeded to the nearby woods where cremation pyres of railroad ties and skeletal bodies were stacked in crisscross patterns. The concentration camp guards had not had time to light the last pyre before being overrun by American troops. Heinrich told CJ that this is how they disposed of the bodies. CJ threw up. Heinrich put his frail hand on the shoulder of an embarrassed, bent over CJ and in a crackly whisper entreated, *"Vergessen Sie nicht."* CJ knew he would never forget.

They stopped at the small village of Weinhausen. There, CJ found a large farmhouse to take a little private time to pull himself together. He thought he had seen everything in Belgium that war could spawn, but what he saw in Braunschweig was almost beyond human comprehension. It registered with him that there is absolutely no limit to man's destructive nature and inhumanity.

* * * * * * * * * *

With the demands of two active toddlers and in her sixth month of pregnancy, Abigail was less aware and less agitated that five weeks had eluded her without a letter from CJ. Her letter writing had all but ceased. The news was full of reports about the tide turning. Finally pulled off the front lines, Jimmy was reassigned to other duties in a quartermaster unit headed into France. His letters became more upbeat. Papa visited Abigail for a couple of days en route to Washington, D.C. He mentioned that he had accomplished his goals at Tuskegee. He was thinking about resigning to accept a high-level government position in Washington and continue his military career as a reservist with the rank of major.

It was the end of March when Abigail heard from CJ again. The letter came from the town of Krefeld near the banks of the Rhine. He complained bitterly about not having had a mail call in weeks and inquired about her pregnancy. CJ indulged himself by pouring out his sentiments about the hell of war and a winter that was almost beyond human endurance. He apologized for being physically and mentally unable to pen a letter to her that would not be filled with the atrocities and hardship of the past months and recent weeks. He described some of his experiences at the Bulge and Ardennes, the Roer River crossing, the furious push from town to town in Rhineland dealing with civilians, surrendering soldiers, and pockets of resistance here and there.

After all the complaining, the tone of the letter changed and flowed into the luxurious new accommodation he was enjoying for a few days. He explained that they moved into towns, evacuated the premises, and took temporary possession—an enactment of "to the victor go the spoils." The residents were allowed to return when the army moved on. He enjoyed the soft beds, sheets, radio, drapes, electricity, bathtub, paintings, ornate pastel tiling, and carpeting. But the best of the arrangement:

... is not the soft beds but rather a real toilet that works. After all these months of "slit trenches, four holers, and behind-the-bush relief," it was great to have a place to sit.

Slipping back into a more serious mode, he reminded Abigail of all that lay ahead, including crossing the Rhine. Abigail enjoyed the part of the letter about the difference in the German Rhinelanders from the Dutch and Belgium people, even the Bavarians—their carefree attitude, sense of humor (considering their predicament), and attitude toward Americans, even the Negroes. CJ explained that Negroes are a curiosity to them:

Many think we are monkeys or some sort of special breed of fighting animal developed by American ingenuity. Some of them wonder why we are not in cages or why we need to be segregated from the white soldiers. They thought we were well-trained and domesticated.

In closing, he asked Abigail to pray for him. She did not hear from CJ again until the middle of May.

The skirmishes with Germans were hit-and-run affairs, day in and day out. In Trebel, Hanover, and each village and town they passed through, they saw groups of unguarded German prisoners sitting propped against buildings, heads bowed, as though tasting the ignominy of total, unforgiving defeat. CJ wondered what was going through their minds as their almost endless columns of troops and armaments passed through.

Death was starting to hit hard. It was too close to the end. CJ just wanted all the killing to stop once and for all. A mind-shattering explosion knocked him senseless as the walls and ceilings caved in on him and some of his men. The house where they were billeted sustained a direct artillery hit. Two of his most dependable squad sergeants were killed. Their uniforms were covered from head to toe with their flesh and blood. CJ staggered outside and yelled in total frustration, "Enough, enough, enough now!" Later, he learned their own tank division had not been informed his company would be occupying that sector. Such accidents of war were referred to as "killed by friendly fire," a cruel misnomer. This accident unnerved CJ's men. Some even thought it was racially inspired.

Uninvited, CJ and a dozen of his men showed up at a quickly constructed portable outdoor venue, stage and all, for a Berlin visit by Bob Hope. A major ushered CJ and his men to the far side, out of sight of the hundreds of officers of every rank and senior enlisted staff who gathered for the highly anticipated event. Extravagantly, bigheartedly funny, Bob Hope brought along a troupe of showgirls. These beautiful, long-legged creatures in feathers and G-strings displayed a stupefying amount of bare flesh as they wiggled their butts toward the screaming mob.

CJ thought it added another surreal dimension to the ghoulish war experience: bimbos debarking from gargantuan transport planes, flashing their teeth, their groins gyrating. Then, almost instantly, they were airborne again. CJ expressed his sentiment to the group that dared accompany him to the show, "This is crazy. They're leaving behind hundreds of us doomed devils with aching gonads."

CJ marveled at the German autobahn. The multilane highway stretched through Herford, Hanover, Braunschweig, Magdeberg, and all highways seemed to lead to Berlin. At Trebel, a picturesque town only a couple of miles from the Elbe River, they reached the end of the line in their push to Berlin. They were halted at the Elbe and gave Berlin to the Russians who were coming from the west. At the rate they had been going, they could have beaten the Russians to the city. The decision to wait for the Russians did not sit well with most of them. They were told that at a certain time on May 2 their forces would fire a green flare out over the river. If the Russian troops had reached the other side, they would answer with a red flare. CJ let his men go to the river to watch. At 11:00 PM someone yelled, "There it is," and they stood silently watching the graceful arc of the Red Army signal. The war was over—although the official word came in a few days. Tears rolled down CJ's cheeks. He dropped to one knee and gave thanks for being spared.

CJ was going home to Abigail and his three boys. Daniel was delivered one month premature on May 15, 1945.

CJ's company had endured so much together through months of shared deprivation and hunger, survival-threatening cold and excruciating anguish, stark terror, shattering horror, crippling exhaustion, and personal triumph. A company notice was posted that Foxtrot Company (aka the Anti-Mine Company aka the Spook Company) had earned battle stars for the Rhineland, Ardennes, and Central Europe campaigns. Three miniature pieces of bronze on their ETO (European Theater of Operation) ribbon hardly exemplified or honored so much suffering and so much loss of life.

Of the two hundred men that left Camp Kilmer with CJ, only ninety-six were present to appreciate the symbolism of the battle stars.

Eighty were killed, twenty-two suffered service-ending wounds, and two mustered out because combat stress or fatigue had taken them over the psychological edge.

CJ's company had been on the combat line for an unheard of 171 continuous days in one of the riskiest assignments in the army. They were like a family. CJ knew each one of his men intimately and gave each, respectively, a nickname over the course of the war. These included Jiggs, Koko, J.B., Showboat, Long-Drink, Smitty, and Lil' Abner. Bonds were forged that were emotionally difficult to break. The courage of the Spook Company was legendary in the ranks of the Eighty-fourth. They were accorded considerable respect as the combat withdrawal commenced.

Six of his men were transferred to the division's Special Services unit as bandsmen. Officially, they were designated as part of the 333rd Regimental Band and were given deferential treatment as musicians. The other ninety Negro soldiers were moved to the village of Leutershausen where they began their duty in the occupation of southern Germany. Leutershausen was located midway between Weinheim bei Mannheim and the university city of Heidelberg, which had been declared an open city during the war to preserve its priceless history. Both armies honored the edict during the fighting and no bombs or shells had fallen on it.

During that occupation, CJ met Edith, a dark-haired, dark-eyed woman. At first, he spoke to her simply to be polite and to conceal his surprise that she'd addressed him in English and flirted with him—a Negro soldier—so openly. CJ encountered her while picking berries on a hillside. She wore no wedding ring; her dress was well cut although not elaborate; and her boots were sturdy and looked expensive. She followed CJ from bush to bush and spoke of plants, trees, and gardens in Leutershausen. It was a stream of conversation that felt intimate yet revealed nothing personal. In return, he told her a bit about himself. When they parted, she invited him to call on her a few days later. He accepted. Within the week, she let him know he would be welcome in her bed, and gently, that he would be a fool to refuse her. CJ didn't hide from her the fact he was married and would soon leave. But the relief he found with her—not just her body and the comfort of her bed, but her intelligence, her hands on his neck, the sympathy with which she listened to his hopes and longings—was so great at times that after she fell asleep, he nearly wept.

She told CJ how lonely she was and had been without company for awhile. She pressed her physical claims as if upon an invalid, with the soft, yet unyielding voice of a hospital visitor, coaxing him into vigor. As if he had been a teenager, she led him into certain byways of gratification that left her lipstick stains passed back and forth between their bodies like the ricochet marks in a squash court. The route to her orgasm could be torturous. She liked being bent backward over a silk cushioned stool so that her head rested on the floor a foot below her hips. Her green eyes groped for his face and the swirling pattern of the rug showed between the strands of her teased, expanded hair. She did not mind. She led him to slowly understand certain variations on the standard position. With wordless hints, she drew his masculine force out of its shell of shyness. His very reserve and hesitation seemed to enable her to break a seal on her own inhibitions. When they made love, CJ saw himself and her as two soldiers, survivors on a battlefield, sometimes too exhausted to moan, united by the fact they'd both gone through the barrage and both were miraculously still breathing.

CJ didn't insult her by paying her for their time together. She wasn't a prostitute, but simply a woman grown used, of necessity, to being kept by soldiers. Each time CJ arrived at her flat, he brought gifts from his stash that he liberated from dead Germans and abandoned homes and farms. Edith had a daughter who was about seven. Other than the gifts he brought her, such as carved toys and candy, he tried to ignore the little girl. Who was her father? What was her name? He couldn't think about that; he couldn't look at her. Edith somehow understood and sent her daughter off to play with the children in the village when he arrived. Through the open window over her bed, he sometimes heard them laughing.

Edith was wildly inventive in bed. After the frequent bouts with lust, she sat in bed naked and told CJ tales of her parents, now dead, her lovers, and friends—each with a story. During his weeks with Edith, Abigail receded to a voice in his ear or words on paper. CJ loved the carefully placed candles, the painted screen behind which she undid her ribbons and laces and emerged in a state of artful undress, and the daughter disposed of so that Edith could listen with utmost attention to him and concentrate on him completely. Once, they had a naked picnic in the deep-napped rug in the center of her living room. She sat cross-legged devouring the half-sandwich she had prepared beforehand. Her face beneath all that hair looked tiny. As she scrunched it into her sandwich, her face almost disappeared—the small straight nose, the myopic green eyes usually straining to see, but now vaguely swimming in her orgasm's aftermath. At each bite, her plump upper lip would leave a cerise blur of lipstick at the rim of the white bread.

The gossip flew swiftly among those remaining from his company. CJ was spotted several times with her—she was known to have a reputation. But to CJ's amazement and chagrin, the soldiers found this glamorous. They too had found solace in a brothel nearby.

He knew it was shameful. With some relief, his unit was given the job of supporting the provost marshal's office. It was time to leave. He held Edith's right hand in both of his and nodded numbly when she said she would write to him often, that he would write her, and hoped that they would see each other again. CJ said, "Don't write," aware the instant he did so of his cruelty by the look on her face. But she understood the tacit arrangement and didn't make a scene. Perhaps this was why he chose her. When they parted, he knew he would become simply a story she told to the next soldier she welcomed into her bed.

CJ was pleased that his assignment transported him to places such as Mosbach, Weinheim, Aberbach, Mannheim, Stuttgart, and every village and town in between. They searched the houses for illegally stashed weapons or Nazi propaganda materials. Townspeople were usually herded onto the streets while individual searches were conducted. Dozens of pistols, rifles, bayonets, knives, Nazi flags, propaganda books and pamphlets, swastika armbands, ammunition, and even potato masher grenades were seized.

He did not write to Abigail during this time. Other letters from her arrived, which he did not answer. What was he thinking? Not about Abigail, not about the life she was leading in his absence, not what she and the children were doing. Neither was he thinking about Edith. It wasn't as if his feelings for her had driven out those he had for Abigail. He just wasn't thinking at all. After all that had happened, maybe this was just his life trying to unfold.

— Chapter Ten —

The telling of the end of CJ's war odyssey became the Duncan's very own Christmas story. It was told on Christmas Eve. And each year, additional pieces were added like new tree ornaments and decorations in response to our growing awareness and James's temperament for detail.

Orders finally came through that most of CJ's company would begin processing and transporting to the States on November 20. It was a long journey home. First, they were transferred to Bremerhaven, a seaport on the North Sea, by freight cars and truck convoy. Bremerhaven was a former German post consisting of a parade ground and apartment-like brick barracks that had miraculously been untouched by bombings from the Allied forces. They were assigned almost lavish accommodations and could see an entire flotilla of liberty ships, victory ships, troop transports, and freighters from their windows. Fog, dampness, and the cold wind blowing in across the North Sea kept them mostly confined to their billets.

Once again, however, they were assigned segregated housing and separate chow times from the other troops processing back to the States. A notice was posted that henceforth boots would be shined, pants cleaned and pressed, close order drills would commence, hair would be cut, beards would be shaved, neckties would be worn, and the first bugle call would be at 0615, followed by reveille at 0625, and so on and so on. It seemed that everyone knew about CJ's company. When he marched around the camp, some of the white soldiers saluted. His company, "The Spooks," had surely distinguished themselves on the field of battle in other than just color.

The notice finally came that they would ship out on December 7. That's when CJ sent the telegram home: *Sailing Sunday 7th on Victory Frostburg from Bremerhaven. I'll be home for Christmas. Love.*

His company was part of the 911 men crammed onto the makeshift troop transport. As custom would have it, Negro soldiers were segregated deep in the bowels of the ship. The first sound heard was a loudspeaker blaring out Les Brown's "Sentimental Journey." There was no antisubmarine evasive routing this time, only flank speed, due west through the North Sea and the English Channel to New York City. Crewmembers, apparently aware of what many had gone through, couldn't do enough for the men. They even insisted they have seconds and thirds when it was their turn at the wardroom table.

One morning, lying on his bunk, CJ became aware of a strange shipboard sound that was louder than the pushing engines. Even from the bowels of the ship, they could hear the distant roar of soldiers cheering. They scrambled up to the deck and saw the distant New York skyline and the Statue of Liberty.

There was no hose-spraying harbor fireboat to greet them, no reception crowds, no hero's welcome, just the near-silent approach of the ship plowing through the outer harbor. Tugboats nudged the ship toward the slip. Dragging barracks bags topside and filing toward the gangplank, once on solid ground, many men knelt to kiss the American soil—or more accurately, the rotted New York harbor pier. Not one Negro soldier joined in this ritual. Absent were the same glad tidings and recognition of citizenship from a beloved country. When their boots touched the harbor planks, an odious feeling returned: the sense of having to walk the long arduous road in an America that bestows on its citizen of color a second-class status—even on those who fight on foreign soils for its liberty.

Herded passively onto trains, they were taken to Camp Kilmer, the same camp from which they had departed. CJ hiked to the PX and sent Abigail another telegram to let her know he was back on the continent. Another tedious extended twelve-hour train trip took them to Fort Gordon, Georgia, near Augusta. At 6:00 AM on December 20, the discharge processing began with a haircut, physical, dental and "short-arm" inspection, presentation of earned medals and ribbons, inoculations, travel pay disbursements, military record checks, and the mustering out of back pay and bonuses.

CJ received, among others, a Silver Star for Bravery, a Distinguished Service Cross, and a Legion of Merit Award. No fewer than four senior officers persistently hounded CJ to reenlist and continue his military career. He was promised a promotion in rank to captain and dependent housing for his family on his next base assignment. Having as much army life as he could stomach in one lifetime, he respectfully declined.

From the Augusta Greyhound Bus Terminal, he sent Abigail a telegram with his expected time of arrival in Little Rock. In his army dress uniform, with all the medals and ribbons pinned to his coat, CJ took his place in the back of the bus with all the other Negro passengers and slept nearly the entire trip.

As soon as the bus pulled into the Little Rock station, he could see Abigail. The picture he carried around Europe all those months had lied. She was more beautiful than even his wildest imaginings and memory. He was the last one off the bus, and Abigail grabbed him before his foot hit the platform. They hugged and kissed and cried for several minutes without a single word being spoken. Interrupted by a final announcement to claim baggage, Abigail proclaimed, "My honey's home." Papa had driven all the way from Tuskegee in his black 1941 Pontiac. He waited at the curb with James and me. Papa embraced CJ with tears in his eyes and whispered in his ear that he had prayed for him. CJ hugged us, got his first look at Daniel, and pronounced him another handsome Duncan.

It was Christmas Eve, December 24, 1945.

* * * * * * * * *

Judging from the difficulty Jimmy had with delays in deactivation and return to the States, CJ's Christmas Eve arrival was miraculous. In order to be discharged, a soldier had to acquire a certain number of points based on the length of time in service, length of time in combat, medals awarded, and rank. Because the Ninety-second was predominantly used in mop-up operations, most Negro soldiers had acquired fewer combat points. Though they had defended their nation by holding strategic locations, they were not awarded the higher points of "active combat" like CJ and his unit. Consequently, the Ninety-second was one of the last divisions to leave and came home in piecemeal fashion. As late as April, Jimmy was still in Europe relegated to rear echelon duty. Rumors circulated that many of the troops from the Ninety-second were being held back from discharge so that they could be used to rebuild bombed cities in war-torn areas of the world. The Office of War Information issued disclaimers that discrimination existed in their discharge policy after the usual hand-wringing and denials of inappropriateness. On May 8, 1946, Jimmy returned to the United States, but it still took another three weeks at Fort McClellan, Alabama, a post reputed to be hostile to returning Negro soldiers, before he finally made his way back to his family.

From the moment of reading about the GI Bill in the *Buffalo*, the Fort Huachuca newspaper, eighteen months earlier, CJ began to envision a future that did not include the Arkansas Delta or being a career soldier. Roosevelt had promised to finance—five hundred dollars per year for tuition, fees, and supplies and seventy-five dollars per month for subsistence—four years of his medical school ambitions.

CJ's hopes were written in his journal and carried in his heart. These elevated him above the mayhem in Europe when conditions were most desperate and finally came to rest on the strength of his will to go forward as the new year began. It was meticulously scripted. From Europe, he had corresponded with Meharry Medical College, the institution in Nashville, Tennessee, dedicated exclusively to educating Negro health care professionals. Meharry's reputation reached back as far as Reconstruction in 1876 under the auspices of the Freedmen's Aid Society and the Methodist Episcopal Church. Its goal was to educate freed slaves and provide health care services to the poor, rural, and underserved. CJ remembered the Negro doctors who had trained at Meharry and made their monthly rounds of the Delta. He never let go of those childhood images.

While CJ was in Europe, his transcripts were sent from Tuskegee to Meharry to be evaluated. In late 1944, he received news on his way to the Battle of the Bulge. If he fulfilled a semester's worth of missing biology and life science requirements and passed the medical entrance examination, they would grant him a provisional admittance. The end of the war and his timely rotation back to the States fell neatly into his most optimistic scenario: spring semester in a nearby Arkansas school to make up prerequisites for admission to Meharry, the two hundred-mile trip in June to Nashville to take the entrance exam, and a family move during the summer to get settled before fall classes.

But CJ's plans were illusory and as far away as those bitter and lonely nights in the foxholes in the Ardennes Forest where he dreamed of his future. His initial attempt to use the GI Bill and execute his plan hit an unyielding barrier. The dean at the Little Rock campus of the University of Arkansas repelled him, "I'm sorry, but we don't have colored boys studying here. Why don't you go to one of the Negro colleges? We can't have you taking the seat of a white student."

Disillusioned and disheartened, two days later he put on his uniform with all his battle ribbons and returned to the dean's office. Without an appointment, he barged in and said, "I risked my life on the soil of eastern Europe to make this country free. And you're telling me I can't attend this land grant college that gives preference to the citizens of Arkansas?" CJ refused to leave and was physically removed from the office and escorted off campus. Through Thurgood Marshall and the NAACP, an antidiscrimination lawsuit was filed against the public colleges and universities in Arkansas, all of which denied Negroes access and opportunity. CJ realized this to be a long process that had little chance to succeed within his timeframe, if ever.

Abigail called Papa and asked if he could help CJ gain a special, late admission to Tuskegee and allow the family to live with him for the remainder of the winter and spring during CJ's matriculation. Papa had already announced his resignation at Tuskegee and any remnants of political capital he possessed had greatly diminished. He was turned away by the dean and the new president of the college. He was told the days of favors and nepotism were over; CJ needed to apply for the fall term through standard admission procedures.

Crushed that his tenure at Tuskegee was incapable of affecting the grant of an exception that was well within the admission policy, Papa offered CJ an alternative. There was an empty house in the little town of Washington among the foothills of the Allegheny Mountains in southwestern Pennsylvania. The house had passed down to the Bryants from Elizabeth's side of the family. The most enticing part of Papa's solicitation was learning of the existence of a historic college—the oldest west of the Alleghenys and the eleventh oldest in America—spread out across forty-three acres of the southeast corner of the town.

Washington and Jefferson College or the more familiar name of W&J was notorious for its prehealth programs. Such was its reputation that nearly all graduates who applied to medical or health-related professional schools were accepted for admission. And, there was family legacy to ensure his admission to W&J. Abigail's grandfather, Dr. Jones after whom her brother Welcome had been named, obtained his bachelor's and master's degrees at W&J on his way to Western Reserve Medical School in Ohio. Awarded an MD in 1893, he went on to practice medicine in Norfolk and Newport News, Virginia, and gained a reputation as an expert in infectious diseases. His humanitarian efforts in treating dock workers earned Dr. Jones considerable national recognition.

Papa suggested that CJ follow Dr. Jones's footsteps as far as W&J and consider Western Reserve rather than returning to the South to attend Meharry.

CJ realized after the dean's office incident that he was still paying the price for those dark months in combat and needed to let the emotional scars from the war heal. War memories were easily triggered. Incoming fire was evoked by the snap of a tree branch; the low, throaty chugging sound of a V-2 "buzz bomb" came to mind when a diesel truck rumbled by; burning leaves and the smell of certain woods burning in the stove had the pungent, unforgettable smell of burning human flesh. The momentary flashbacks were always there.

CJ accepted Papa's proposition and agreed to get a job in Little Rock and save some money. He would get the affairs of the farm in order by arranging a transfer of title to the Meriweathers for a sum of money to be paid over time as the harvests allowed. He set his mind to moving to Washington in the late summer of 1947. Hope returned to the Duncan household. CJ did not feel defeated, only stalemated. But that state of mind was soon challenged.

It took weeks to complete the application process and test for civil service, state, and local municipal jobs. This resulted in no calls for interviews or being turned away by companies posting signs that read: NO NEGROES NEED APPLY. Sadly, it came down to toiling in laborer jobs, soliciting at sharecroppers shacks and poor farms to collect nickels and dimes from Negroes who bought insurance so that they could have a decent burial, or bowing and scraping for tips as a Red Cap and porter for the Missouri-Pacific Railroad.

When CJ made the choice to work for the railroad, he had no idea he would have to tolerate insults and humiliation in various forms, as well as flagrant indignities from passengers and his boss every day. He despised his supervisor's falsely grinning face and the fact that he had not spent a single day in military uniform or in a college classroom. CJ had to submit to scrutiny, to judgment, to prejudice, and to whim. He had to present an obsequiousness to the point of resembling "Step n' Fetchit." He was condemned to accept the dismissive, dominating treatment that attempted to shape him and turn him into whatever narrow idea or stereotype his boss had for the "colored boys" under his ruthless, almost sadistic control. CJ could do nothing but meekly say, "Yes, suh," if he wanted to keep his job. Every white person at the train station, no matter how well-intentioned that person was, dealt with Negroes with the presumption of intellectual inferiority. Somehow or another, if not directly by words then by facial expression, by tone of voice, or by impatience, they talked to Negroes as though they were dumb. If the Negro displayed even the slightest mentality, they were astonished, or angry, about their impudence.

Denied access to college and the lack of meaningful job prospects, CJ began to feel damaged, a failure, dispossessed, and lost. Acquiescence and defenselessness were not traits CJ wore very well. In the solitude of his private struggle, he came to realize that the failure of the country to acknowledge the sacrifice he made and his own contentious vanity made a defiant affair of honor. CJ spent nearly all of his spare time writing letters and preparing petitions, lobbying government departments, and provoking the filing of antidiscrimination lawsuits through the NAACP. A small corner of the front room of our house looked like a staging area from which he enacted the scene of indignant rage and strident propositions and arguments. His commentary and editorials on the mistreatment of Negro veterans returning from the war found a widespread and receptive audience through the national Negro media—*Crisis Magazine,* the *Pittsburgh Courier, Atlanta Daily, Baltimore Afro-American, Urban League Monthly,* and others.

This heavily decorated—Purple Heart, Bronze Star, four Oak Leaf Clusters—veteran's reputation grew. He became a spokesperson for the 650,000 Negro soldiers finding their way back to civilian life as second-class citizens—50,000 of these men had served some time in combat. His popularity as a fiery keynote speaker at Negro political, church, and activist gatherings brought a great deal of attention to the Duncan home, not all of which was desirable.

There is something intriguing about what moral suffering can do to someone who is in no obvious way a weak or feeble person. It is more insidious than what physical illnesses can do—there is no morphine drip or spinal block or radical surgery to alleviate it. Once CJ was in its grip, it was as though it would have to kill him in order to be free of it. A feeling of humiliating disgrace ate away at him. It was difficult to tear him free from his own bitterness. Even at home, CJ did not know how to disengage from the struggle.

Religion took on a renewed fervor when my father returned from the army. CJ looked upon his deliverance from the war as incontrovertible proof God was alive and still dabbling in the ordinary affairs of humankind. He brought a scrupulous obstinacy to his effort to become a better Methodist and to learn more about the theology and tenets of his religion.

My mother did not get carried away with religious zeal. The only change we noticed was the inclusion of the Bible with the other books she read to us most nights after dinner. She did try to teach James and me a bedtime prayer about guardian angels. Although she could never explain to our satisfaction just who these guardian angels were, she tried. She explained that these guardians sat nameless on our right shoulders and whispered to us whenever we stumbled blindly toward actions that offended God. Assigned to us at birth, they would never forsake their posts until we died. They monitored our sins like scrupulous accountants. On our left shoulders, an ambassador of Satan acted in malfeasant counterbalance to our guardian angel. This devil tried to lead us toward the succulents of evil and mischief. This duality led to much confusion. But we welcomed these two invisible companions into our life. We even gave them names that changed as the mood struck us. Sometimes we gave them funny names.

What started as our misunderstanding our mother's pronunciation of the word *guardian*, became our description of them as our "garden angels." These "garden angels" surrounded our house and were under a divine obligation to love and protect it. They watched over us, not because God required it, but because they cherished us and could not help it. We never believed the bad angel was an agent of Satan; we thought he was just a different religion from ours, like a Baptist.

My father taught James to fish the small streams. They'd slosh out into the center in old shoes and boots, flip a tiny minnow plug into deep pockets and likely ripples. I just stood in the water watching. The strike of a smallmouth bass by James or my father always made my heart jump. For CJ, it was the surest thing he knew. He already had a dinner menu in mind—bass fillets in cornbread batter, applesauce made from fruit picked from a neighboring farm, garlic potatoes with spuds from the garden, and Abigail's cornbread with honey. The Arkansas River and its streams are imprinted on my senses. The warm air with cool pockets, the river shining black and silver that rolled ahead and disappeared into a dark green tunnel of trees, the yellow light shining from the farmhouse kitchen across the pasture, and the fragrance from the barn in the air are part of who I am.

I can also remember how CJ smelled. After a day at the train station, CJ had a stale mustiness as though he had worked at a dump all day. And there was nothing that soap and water could do to change it. But on weekends, when he worked hard on the farm, his smell changed and became something different, something wonderful. Standing beside him as a small boy, I would press my nose against my father's shirt and take in the smell of some rich, warm acre.

We were treated to occasional Saturday afternoon drives. All five of us packed into the cab of the rickety, old 1932 Ford truck that he was afraid to drive more than forty miles per hour. After a half-hour ride engulfed in dust, he parked alongside the road. We proceeded to a footpath that took us a distance up the Petite Jean Mountains to a spot he had frequented as a youth. Standing on that mountain, it seemed as if the whole world had spread out beneath us. Not too far off, we could see the modest skyline of Little Rock framed in sunshine. My mother packed a picnic basket and laid out the red and white checkered tablecloth that she had found at the co-op. That square cloth with fringed edges always seemed to adhere to the rock and stubble on those windless and clear days. We playfully tussled with our father and our laughter pursued us across the mountains that were ours alone. CJ sometimes got a little rough with us despite Abigail's objections. He occasionally accused her of being too soft on us and wanting to put us in dresses. It bothered him when she used expressions such as, "her boys were going to be lovers, the sweetest boys who ever lived." He feared that while he had been away, Abigail defined us as such early on, turning us into the exact image of what she needed during his absence. Because Abigail was so young when we were born, there were times when she seemed more like an older sister than a parent.

The major connection with our father resided under the front porch in rows of dusty Mason jars. CJ had a collection of black widow spiders, a hobby that harkened back to his youth and an interest he inherited from his father. We were given the job of caring for those small malignant spiders, which floated like black cameos in their jars. We were never in real danger, our mother made sure of that. Most of the peril was in our imaginings. Twice a week, James and I descended into the moist gloom under the porch, carrying a naked exposed bulb attached to a long extension cord. We switched the bulb on and fed those mute arachnids through the screen holes in the lid—any one, of which, we were assured by our father, "could kill us deader than a stone." We had helped feed poultry since we could walk, but these trips under the porch required courage and an agitated sense of commitment that no chicken ever inspired. When the feeding hour approached, with careful instructions from our father, we crawled under the front porch to face the miniscule, satanic livestock that watched us in stillness like the approach of flies.

Every Saturday, we brought all the jars out from under the porch for our father's inspection. He eyed the spiders with discrimination. He counted the pear-shaped egg sacs and made notations in a small notebook whenever there was a crop of new spiders. Cautiously, he would remove a spider and let it walk back and forth across a dinner plate, turning it with a pair of tweezers when it neared the edge. He would point to the red hourglass delicately tattooed on the female spider's abdomen and say, "There. That's what you look for. That hourglass means 'I kill.'"

CJ's stock reply for why he collected black widows invariably acknowledged, "They are one of the many fears I had to overcome and master when I was around my father." Once he sarcastically teased, "Turning the black widows loose on some of those white folks down at the train station has crossed my mind. Something needs to scare them into a little decency and respect."

The care of black widows inspired a patience and concentration rare in young children. Out of fear of our father, we took our responsibilities seriously. Another motivation provoked our study of the lifecycle of the spiders with certain zeal: they were creatures that could kill us. My lifelong fear of spiders and insects began with my nose pressed close against Mason jars, observing the tedious and horrifying existence of black widows. They hung motionless in webs spun out of their viscera. They lived dangling and still, black in the high wires of their jar-shaped lives. When they moved quickly, it was to kill. Over the months, we watched the females kill and devour the males. We became attuned to the seasons of spiders; time poured out of the red hourglass in shimmering, ill-formed webs. We watched egg cases exploding into spiders newly minted that scattered like brown and orange seeds across a jar. We were fascinated. In some ways, we were young advocates for black widow spiders; however, our extreme fear could not be turned.

* * * * * * * * *

CJ was not the cadet Abigail fell in love with at Tuskegee. Military service and the war hardened him. They had been married for six years and were in their first year of living together. While there were many treaties and lulls, conferences and armistices, their life together was filled with conflict.

CJ always came home from work after dark. Usually, we were in bed when I heard his footsteps on the porch. I began to associate him with darkness. Abigail's voice changed and lost some of its music when he returned. As time passed, she became a different woman the moment he opened the door. The whole environment of the house changed. I heard their voices, speaking in crackling whispers over the late dinner, careful not to wake us, as CJ discussed the day of insults and degradation he endured at the train station.

There were nights when I heard my mother cry and only a bitter, harsh tone of my father's voice. But, the next morning I saw her kiss him on the lips as he went off to work. There were days when my mother did not speak to us at all. She sat on the front porch, staring out at the fields and the woods in the distance, her eyes hooded with a melancholy resignation and torpor that even our crying could not banish. Her stillness frightened us. Tears flowed out of her eyes, but her expression never changed. We learned to grieve in silence when these episodes came upon her. We could not break through to her; she would not share the hurt. What my mother presented to us and those around her was an impregnable essence, an elaborate façade that represented the smallest, least definitive part of her. She was always a little bit more than the sum of her parts because of the essential parts she withheld. I spent a childhood and part of my youth studying my mother with little success.

When my mother was sad or heart sore, I blamed myself or felt I had done something unforgivable. A portion of guilt was standard issue for all three of her children. Some part of our growing up consisted of convoluted, egregious apologies to our mother because of flawed people in her life who had hurt her, particularly our father.

Her face, ethereally lovely, was a window on the world—but a window in appearance only. She was masterful at drawing out the slim, wounded biographies of people around the Delta farms and equally adept at not revealing a single significant or traceable fact about herself, that is, except to Doretha.

My father had been home only a month, and my mother was pregnant. Born two months premature, Nettie Olivia was stillborn. Before he left for work, CJ carved her name in a tiny, crude, wooden cross and placed it atop the mound of dirt at her grave site. That was the extent of my father's participation in the small ceremony of grief. He never revealed any emotion over the loss of this child.

We buried Nettie Olivia late that day before CJ returned from work. Papa drove to Little Rock and picked Abigail up from the hospital and Nettie Olivia from the funeral parlor that had prepared her for burial.

Abigail stayed in her room until Papa went to get her for the ceremony. She leaned heavily on him and walked as though each step was hazardous and excruciatingly painful. She sat down on a kitchen chair Papa brought from the house to the cemetery beforehand. Her face was bereaved, anemic, and long suffering. Grief had changed her mouth into a thin, bitter horizon. When she was seated, she nodded for Papa to begin the ceremony. "Oh God, whose most dear Son did take little children into his arms and bless them. Give us grace, we beseech thee, to entrust the soul of this child to thy never-failing care and love." Papa then laid the open, small wooden casket on Abigail's lap.

The casket was not much longer than an oversized shoebox; the infant looked like a small plastic doll from the dime store. Abigail wept as she covered Nettie Olivia with kisses. She raised her eyes skyward and suddenly screamed out in helplessness and anger, "No, I don't forgive you, Lord. This is not allowed. It's simply not allowed. Do you hear me, Lord? I'm no longer interested in your holy will. How dare you take this little girl of mine! How dare you."

Papa took the casket, lowered it into the ground, and offered, "We have given the heavens an angel. Be gone to the arms of the Lord, Nettie Olivia. Watch over the family that would have loved and protected you and kept you safe from harm. You'll be one of God's small angels now. Keep watch over this farm and your brothers and parents."

Papa left before CJ arrived; he was in no mood for his bitter disposition. Doretha had taken Daniel from his usual perch in Abigail's arms and offered to keep him overnight. We were outside when our father's truck pulled up. He warned us to be especially sweet to our mother. "Pick her some flowers. Make her feel special."

By nightfall, Abigail still had not left her bedroom. CJ brought her a cup of tea and a bouquet of wildflowers before saying, "Abigail, it's probably for the best."

"Oh, CJ, how can you say that? I've lost my little girl. All I ever wanted was to have a little girl."

Abigail was inconsolable. CJ returned to the front room to read a magazine he had found abandoned on a seat of one of the Pullman cars. He was thumbing through it, looking back occasionally toward the room where his wife lay crying. His eyes glistened in the artificial light. The magazine was no remedy for such sounds of sorrow from

Abigail. CJ just let the magazine fall to the floor. He sat there in a daze, trying to shut out all thought of past and future—something he had learned to do during the war.

Catching James staring at him, CJ said, "James, you and Lander go in and make your mother feel better."

We went into our mother's bedroom. She was lying on her back, tears rolling down her cheeks, crying easily and softly. Afraid to approach her, we stood by the door, unsure of what to do next. She was staring at us with the most bereaved, desolate face I had ever seen. There was such defeat and hopelessness in her eyes.

"Dad told us to cheer you up," James mumbled.

"I heard what he said," she sobbed. "Come here, boys. Lie down beside me."

We climbed into bed next to her. She laid her head against James's shoulder and cried hard, digging her nails into my arm. The tears wet our faces with her kisses; we were paralyzed by such sudden intimacy.

Not having a daughter was a great disappointment in Abigail's life. She had produced a house full of boys. The noise level was always too high, and the small rooms were overheated with the sheer energy of roughhousing and life lived by the seat of the pants.

Abigail appeared too breakable to have produced such a tribe. We made her life boy-haunted and son-possessed. I am sure the birth of a daughter would have done much to alleviate that ache always inside her.

It rained when we went to bed that night. My father put out the lights and smoked a pipe on the screened-in porch before he retired. He seemed uncomfortable with us when my mother was not orchestrating the tenor of household life. Several times during the evening, he yelled at us when something minor and insignificant had irritated him. My father was an easy read. When there was real danger, we knew instinctively to avoid him. He had a genuine gift for tyranny but no coherent strategies. As a man who would always be a stranger in his own house, he was both emotionally brutal and ineffectual.

My father was the only person I ever knew who looked upon childhood as a dishonorable vocation that one grew out of as quickly as possible. I think my father loved us, but there has never been a more awkward love. It was a love that was not usable, that knew its place.

145

As a child, he had felt neglected and abandoned by his father. Most of the attention he received was rendered in the form of abuse. At night, surrounded by his family, my father looked trapped. He taught me a great deal about self-made loneliness.

— Chapter Eleven —

Beyond the perimeter of the fields on the east and west side of our farm were large deciduous woods. Our father told James and me that under no circumstances were we ever to cross through the fields to play in those woods. But we were children. Before long, we took a few forbidden steps and then raced back to the safety of the fields. The next time, we stepped off ten paces into the woods before we lost our nerve and returned to our own yard. Slowly, we began to demystify the outlawed woods—even the cemetery on the west side. Soon, we knew some of the acreage of the woods, particularly on the east side. We learned its secrets and boundaries; we hid in its groves and behind the gravestones.

On a warm August night, James and I slipped out of the house and walked through the fields to the edge of the woods. We heard a faint noise in the distance and summoned the nerve to follow it. As we came to a clearing, we saw an assembly of hooded and robed people gathered around a burning cross. They were chanting something we could not make out. We crawled toward the group for a better look. Mesmerized, we watched the restrained grandeur of the blaze and attended to every detail of the slowly evolving ceremony. It was like attending a church service, such was their seriousness and unruffled, ecclesiastical demeanor. They moved stiffly around the fire. We inhaled the aroma of burning logs made into a cross and watched the extraordinary rites and customs of those people.

As we got up to leave, a man relieving himself by a nearby tree saw us. With that robe on, he seemed like the largest, most powerful man I had ever seen. He grew out of the earth like a fantastic, grotesque tree. His body seemed colossal; his eyes were blue and vacant. A red beard covered his face, but there was something wrong about him. It was the way he looked at us—far different from the way adults normally studied children—that alerted us to danger. We felt the menace in his disengaged stare. His eyes did not seem connected to anything human. He zipped up his pants, let his robe fall back down around him, and turned toward us. We ran.

We made it to the side yard where our mother heard our screams and called to us from the back door. Surprised and angry that we had sneaked out, she launched into us, but ceased as we pointed toward the man coming through the fields. Several other men had joined him.

"What do you want, mister?" Abigail shouted to the red-bearded man.

"You and those pickaninies," he yelled in a strangely high-pitched voice for such a large man. He did not seem cruel or unbalanced; he simply seemed inhuman.

"What?" a frightened Abigail said.

"We want you niggers," he hollered, taking his first step to come out of the fields into the clearing.

We ran into the house and my mother locked the back door. I saw the men watching us through the kitchen window. I had never seen a man stare in such a primitive way. His hatred for Negroes was clear in his eyes. My mother walked over and pulled the shade. About a minute later, we heard the sound of our father's truck coming home from work.

"We'll be back," the man yelled, and we could hear the laughter. By the time my father entered the house, they were gone and my terrified mother collapsed into his arms. Distraught and furious, she fumed about the "Klucks" willfully trespassing into their backyard, terrorizing their children, and intimidating them with language of such racial hatred.

The next day, CJ got Sheriff Barton and his deputies to comb the woods. The only thing they found were the ashes from the burning cross. But that was enough to frighten everyone in the vicinity about the KKK operating nearby. We were severely disciplined and warned that the next time we disobeyed, the boogeyman was going to get us before we would make it home.

As youngsters, I think we truly believed we had summoned the visitation of the boogeyman. The boogeyman was the manifestation of our willful disobedience and had been called out of the netherworld to punish us for sneaking into those woods. We thought that we had profaned the land of the Klucks, the boogeymen who hated Negroes, and God had sent them to punish us.

We didn't enter those woods again, but those men had already exposed the gravity of our sin in being born a Negro. They required expiation. They brought the boogeymen into our home. They came to punish the sins of the Duncan children in a perverse and grotesque way. They knew how to do this most grievously.

During the next week, my brother and I were vigilant and cautious. However, my parents prepared in earnest and accelerated the plans to leave the Delta for Pennsylvania.

Abigail could not sleep at night after that. We found her hovering over us, obsessively checking and rechecking the locks on our bedroom windows. Once I awoke and saw her framed in moonlight, staring out toward the fields and scanning the moonlit yard for the approach of our enemy.

The word boogeyman changed meaning for us. It used to be just another scary character, a hobgoblin in one of our mother's frightening fairytales. We began to refer to the men who chased us through the woods as boogeymen. "Did the boogeymen come last night?" we would ask at breakfast. "Has the sheriff caught the boogeymen yet?" we asked as our mother read to us at bedtime. It became a catchall, a portmanteau word for everything evil or iniquitous in the world. When the Reverend Lacey described the terrors of hell in his fire and brimstone voice, he was explaining the boundaries and perimeters of the boogeyman to us. Boogeyman was a specific kind of person, a specific place, and a general condition of a world suddenly fearful and a fate uncontrollable.

CJ would not relinquish his activism.

Abigail pleaded with him, "You're being reckless and irresponsible and letting your rage and anger place us in danger. You're instigating something that's bound to come back on us."

CJ assured her, "The boys disturbed their meeting and provoked the KKK intrusion. They won't return to our house."

They reappeared two weeks later. We heard faint sounds of footsteps walking toward the back of the house. I saw my mother become flush and watched as she closed the door to the back bedrooms. With a drained, uninflected voice, she said, "They're on the roof."

We lifted our eyes slowly to the ceiling and listened intently for the direction of the footsteps. For ten minutes, we huddled together in the kitchen urging our father to get home. "Hurry, hurry," my mother repeated, knowing his arrival was imminent.

During the next five minutes we listened to them—probably no more than two or three men—moving unhurriedly about the roof. They made no attempt to enter one of the back windows or the door. The visit had no meaning except perhaps as a message to establish their credentials in our lives. Again. It inspired a renewed panic in our hearts. The sound of our father's truck in the distance came like the beating wings of a redemptive angel. We heard the footsteps run across the roof and were aware of them climbing onto the limbs of the huge oak that grew beside the house.

Abigail walked to the window in our bedroom and saw them as they reached the ground. They paused while looking back and then sneered and gave a salute common to the KKK. In an easy, unhurried gait they made their way toward the dark harboring fields.

CJ was enraged and contacted the Little Rock police the next day. They refused his request to patrol the area around the farm, citing the absence of manpower to respond to "perceived and not actual trouble" so far out of the metropolitan area. They advised him that the sheriff's office was his best bet. CJ grudgingly agreed with Abigail that his growing reputation as a troublemaker might well have contributed to the snub he received.

But for us kids, the boogeymen were there even when they were not. They inhabited each recessed corner of our house. We could not open any door without expecting them to be waiting behind it. We came to fear the approach of night. The nights they did not appear were as exhausting as the ones when they did. The trees outside the house lost their healthy, luxuriant beauty and became hideous in our eyes. Our fields and the woods became their domain, their safe hermitage, and a place of inexhaustible dread in our imagination. Their masked faces were portrayed subliminally in every window. If we closed our eyes, we saw their image imprinted on our consciousness like faces on a veil. They appeared in our dreams with their murderous eyes. Terror marked my mother's face; she slept during the day and roamed the house checking locks at night. Our father awakened several times during the night to check the perimeter of the house with his rifle in tow.

At night, with the lamps gleaming brightly, the interior of the house felt like an aquarium. We "floated" from room to room, feeling the eyes of KKK members studying us from beneath the gloom of oaks. We assumed they were watching and appraising us; we assumed they were omnipresent; we assumed they were biding their time, waiting the perfect moment to launch their attack against us. Swimming through the light of our besieged house, we waited in the charged, breathless atmosphere of our own obsessions. Our experience had a proximal effect on all the Negro families of the Delta. A heightened tension and vigilance was evident. Everyone knew CJ was an obvious target. The Meriweathers, as well as groups of Negroes, patrolled and made a point to swing by our house. They even entered the woods. But we knew that when they left, the night belonged to the KKK.

Our father worked on a passageway out of the house through a crawl space that led to the area under the porch where we kept the spiders. Up to this time, the only way to get under the porch was from the outside. All of us looked upon our father as the heroic figure, the redeemer, and the knight who would deliver us from harm's way and the fear of the boogeymen.

It was just another evening, two weeks from our scheduled departure. The bus tickets to Pittsburgh had been purchased. My mother was reading us a chapter from *The Yearling*. I was sitting on the floor between my mother's legs. James was lying on his stomach, playing with his green army figures, and Daniel was sitting in our mother's lap.

The room went dead with fear when Jimmy burst through the door. Out of breath, he surrendered the electrifying words, "The KKK is coming." While Abigail absorbed what she had just heard, he proceeded to explain in rapid fire, "A white woman stumbled while getting off the train. I'd just come over from another track to find CJ—we were riding home together tonight. The woman crashed to the cement platform. CJ smiled and offered his hand. He said, 'You took a good fall there. May I help you, Ma'am?' She seemed embarrassed by her clumsiness and hardly wasted a second to regain her composure."

Gulping for air, Jimmy continued, "She slapped CJ, spit in his direction, and screamed about being touched improperly by a nigger. I swear Abigail, he never laid a hand on her. A commotion started up and CJ was roughed up and restrained by a number of white passengers before he could get outta there. Word spread through the station that a colored man sexually assaulted a white woman. He never touched her and now it was a sexual assault. They've been out to get CJ for a long time. They dragged him to the station manager's office. There was cursing and punches were thrown. His face was all bloody.

"I tried to explain what had happened and was warned to stay out of it. A crowd formed in front of the station, but there were no police anywhere. A racial storm has been building up for a long time. I know vigilante justice when I see it taking shape. Other Negro workers, even those whose shift had just started, headed home. I got to see CJ for a brief moment. He told me to leave and warn you about the danger and he said that you'd know what to do. His boss told me as soon as they finished their investigation of the incident, they'd let CJ go. Abigail, I hated to leave him behind, but the longer I stayed, the more difficult it would be to find a safe passage home. I hitched a ride with Ben."

CJ and Jimmy Hayes had become good friends. He talked Jimmy into taking a job at the station while he was waiting for a position to come through in Akron, Ohio, at the rubber and tire factory. His father worked there on the assembly line and was pulling some strings.

This would be a night of horror that would change us forever. A part of me would always belong to that night. The KKK had stolen a portion of my boyhood, had stolen my pure sanction of a world administered by a God who loved me. In the trackless shadows of my subconscious, it became the night that changed my life and the fate of

Children of Secrets

the Duncans. We learned that fear is a dark art that requires a perfect teacher. We signed our names in the indifferent pages of the book of hours. Our perfect teachers had come in hoods and robes.

A sudden explosion of fire came through the window. The room rained glass and began to fill with a profusion of black smoke. The noise and smoke brought our mother screaming and running toward us. It was too late to get out of the house. Jimmy helped shuttle us through the emergency crawl space from inside the house. It took us under the porch and gave us temporary refuge.

We had another concern. The jars of spiders were near the heat, and one of the jars exploded. If any of the spiders survived, a small civilization of poisonous beasts was sure to head in our direction. Other jars exploded and fueled our trepidation. I screamed and beat at my legs convinced the spiders were on the loose and in the folds and creases of my trousers. This added to our panic and the urgency to get out from under the porch.

Burrowed in this cave-like sanctuary, we listened to the constant shouts of racial epitaphs —*coon, nigger, pickaninies.* We listened to the pounding footsteps of the KKK as the floor groaned and shuddered above us. The house was being ransacked and set on fire. The smell of smoke, the crackling of the fire, and a collapsing house turned our shelter into a torture chamber. We were suffocating from the intense heat as flames moved quickly through the house. We began a coughing, stumbling retreat from the crawl space.

Once we were outside, Jimmy picked up Daniel, my mother grabbed my hand, and James followed alongside as we ran across the short clearing. Jimmy wanted to get us to the protection of the cotton field where the stalks were higher than most adults' heads. We made our way past the clearing and ran straight ahead into the narrow path between the stalks. Abigail stopped, spit out soot-flecked phlegm, and let go of my hand. Ignoring Jimmy's vehement protests, she dashed back to the house and scooted under the porch. James hollered in the direction of the house for her to hurry up. Through the kitchen window, we saw the flames shrivel the lace curtains. Seconds later Abigail emerged from under the disintegrating porch, something clutched against her chest with one arm and holding two cloth bags that gave her considerable difficulty. One of the large pockets on the housedress she wore was smoking. The fire singed her eyebrows and gave her a sooty face. She dropped the bags, and Jimmy grabbed a handful of dirt to douse the smoke from her dress. When she reached out to pull us to her body, several loose photographs spilled to the ground. Her risky return to the house accomplished the rescue of her beloved album of photographs and poems. She also had grabbed the emergency supplies that had been put together a week earlier in the likelihood that something like this might occur.

As we proceeded down the narrow path, the leaves flapped in our faces and against our arms like streamers of oilcloth. Each stalk had its cotton bulbs, like babies in a shroud. There was a strong, almost sickening smell of vegetable growth, green starch, and hot sap.

The intent was to get a little way into the field and lie down under the cover of the large, coarse leaves. We would not come out until we could no longer hear anything coming from the burning house or the road—perhaps not even then. From our experience in the cotton field, we knew it was easy to get lost. It had happened to James and me several times while playing our hiding games.

We stepped over one row and then another, hoping we had not gotten turned around. In the dark, it was impossible for Jimmy to check the direction in which we were headed. At one point, we stood still and heard nothing but the cotton whispering and the faint, dampened sound of voices and crackling. As we continued on, the barking and yelling sounded louder. It turned out we had not gone far at all. We had stumbled around in one small corner of the field the entire time. We pushed our way through stalks and leaves, away from the direction of the noise. Getting across the bridge to the road was not possible.

Finally, we emerged from our serpentine path through the field. We followed the river and swampy marsh, wormed our way through the rank grass and sedge, and fell more than a few times into the brush and silt. Crouched in the shadows of the reeds, we slipped around like water rats just ahead of the gunshots, dogs, and bottles being broken by our drunken pursuers. We were frightened and panicky, but Jimmy refused to let hysteria and desperation overtake us. He knew if we got across the marshy shallow end of the river, the dogs would lose our scent. We could then make it to a shack the Meriweathers had shown him. Skinned knees and elbows, cuts from the cotton stalks, and exhausted, we stopped and huddled to take a breath. We had to be prodded and coaxed by Jimmy to continue. I refused to relinquish the space closest to Jimmy and my mother. Cold and wet in the gloomy, damp, and drizzling night air, our eyes burned and our throats were dry from the smoke. At last, we reached the shack. It was fully dark and shadows had settled under the skeletons of the trees. We entered the crumbling remains; the mildew and decay had an iodine smell like a bed of kelp. We huddled in the corner of the shack and waited for the sounds of dogs and voices to disappear. I did not move or speak. A paralysis of exquisite, impenetrable terror entered each cell of my body.

Jimmy had to leave to get back to his family in case the KKK came looking for CJ at the Meriweather farm. "I'll return at daybreak to get you out of here," he promised.

Abigail called after Jimmy, "Be careful and bring CJ back with you."

As the shock of the chase wore off, an overwhelming fatigue entered our bodies. We lay shivering, frail, and depleted before falling asleep.

As Abigail opened her eyes from what she thought had been a nightmare, she was startled by the morning brightness. She let us sleep and went outside to see if she could see or hear Jimmy coming. After an hour of pacing, she lost hope and thought something might have happened to him on the way back. *Get to a Greyhound bus station or bus stop and take anything heading north. I'll meet you in Pittsburgh at the main terminal.* Those were the words—the contingency plan—CJ had repeated often during the preceding few weeks. Abigail was upset because she had CJ's ticket. It would have burned in the fire if she had not taken it.

The distance from our farm to Little Rock was less than eight miles. Generally, it took my father about fifteen minutes at his usual forty-mile-per-hour clip. Highway 218 ran straight and flat through the farm country of the Delta. At this time of year, as far as one could see, the fields were white with cotton. With harvest in full swing, there was more traffic than usual.

Without Jimmy's help it was a struggle to get us moving, let alone reach the main highway. James and I maneuvered the bags up the side of the river gully. With a great deal of difficulty, Abigail got herself and Daniel to the top of the embankment. After another fifteen minutes of tramping through the brush, we made it to 218. We stood in the woods, a few yards off the shoulder, near the intersection of a gravel road. Abigail thought it was a good spot to hitch a ride to Little Rock. She was on the lookout for either hill people from the Ozarks or Mexicans from the Texas area who came to the region to work as field hands during harvest time. She reasoned they had no affiliation with the KKK and probably did not know what had happened.

After thirty minutes, a truck with a trailer behind it came from the west. From a quarter of a mile away, Abigail could tell they were Mexicans. We walked to the shoulder of the road and waited nervously as the driver downshifted; gears crunched and whined as he brought the truck to a stop. The truck was almost as old as ours, with slick tires, a cracked windshield, rusted fenders, and what looked like faded blue paint under a layer of dust. A tier had been constructed above the bed, and it was crammed with cardboard boxes and burlap bags filled with supplies. The driver and his wife sat in the cab with a small girl between them. The trailer was filled to the top with snowy mounds of freshly picked cotton; a tarp covered the front half, and two large shirtless boys stood at the rear, staring blankly at the asphalt beneath them. One had massive shoulders and a neck as thick as a stump. He spat tobacco juice out of the back of the trailer and seemed oblivious to us.

My mother managed to get through the language barrier that we needed a ride to Little Rock. They were headed to drop off their load at the nearby cotton gin. The driver sized us up and scrutinized our pitiful appearance. He glanced at his wife and then looked back at us. Waving two paper dollars, Abigail managed to get them to make a detour to our destination. We struggled onto the bed of the trailer and sat shoulder-to-shoulder with our feet and legs intertwined. As the Mexican pulled back on the road, the gears rattled, tires wobbled, crates and boxes and pots bounced around, as we did, and tufts of cotton escaped from under the tarp.

We arrived and carefully hopped down out of the trailer bed and onto the street in front of the station. We looked around bewildered and fearful. Our clothes were stiff with powdery traces of dried mud. With dirty faces and sooty hair, we had the appearance of neglected and abused ragamuffins under the charge of a down-and-out mother.

We found the "colored" facilities and drinking fountain and tried unsuccessfully to freshen up.

Walking into the bus terminal, I felt a thrill. I think we all did. I could feel the rush of adrenaline in travelers as they glanced at departure boards and studied the small numbers on their neatly inscribed tickets. The bus station was a place where you could actually see time move. People arrived and left through doors and gates like waves at the seashore. All around us, the world seemed impossibly ordinary: people chatting, people reading the paper, and people chewing gum. It was hard to know what we felt—relief partly, fear, longing, regret, but also sadness and guilt that we were about to leave our father behind. There were moments when each of us seemed to slip outside of ourselves and hover there, a spectator of an ordeal that seemed unimaginable.

Abigail found a phone and called Papa. Holding back tears, she explained that the fears she had shared with him a week earlier had been realized and asked him to get up to Little Rock to help CJ out of the trouble he was in. Papa told her to leave CJ's ticket at the will call window. He would depart within the hour for the Delta. Pulling out her tickets, she recited our itinerary: Nashville, Tennessee/Louisville, Kentucky/Cincinnati and then Columbus, Ohio, and finally Pittsburgh, Pennsylvania. Abigail gave him expected arrival times at each stop and noted that the nine hundred mile trip was going to take about twenty hours. Papa lectured Abigail about the seedy characters at bus stations, segregation policies, and the like. Then he tried to calm her with assurances that everything in his power would be done to help her through this. She was instructed to check in with Western Union and Traveler's Aid at the Louisville stop and there would be money and word about what was going on. And as was his nature, he reminded her, "God is on your side, Abigail. I know you feel overmatched. But you're going to have to show strength in this difficult situation. God has a way of leveling the playing field. Be strong for the kids."

As we waited for the Nashville bus, there was just enough time for James to probe with questions and worries he had about our father. "Where is he? Is he going to come and get on the bus with us? He'll be mad when he sees they burned down our house. If he thinks we burned up in the fire, he might not come looking for us." James relented when Abigail explained that CJ was hiding from the boogeymen who wanted to hurt him for something that happened at work; he would catch up to us as soon as he could.

Uncharacteristically, James cried. He was afraid our father was going to be mad because he had been left in charge as "the man of the house." Assurances that his father would be proud of him for helping to get us to the bus station safely did little to assuage his misgivings. I cried alongside James, caught in a contagion of fear and uncertainty that gripped us all.

Holding Daniel, Abigail took the long seat in the back of the bus. It actually held all four of us, with room to spare. It allowed us ample space in front of the seat to play without disturbing anyone. However, we were all nauseated from the cigarette smoke and diesel exhaust fumes that seemed to hover in the rear of the bus. We drew stares of bewilderment and pity. A stench of smoke, swamp, and manure accompanied us on our anxiety-filled bus transfers at the segregated Nashville and Louisville stations. Some people shook their heads in disgust and moved away from us as if we were capable of inflicting them with a disease.

The bus driver on the first leg of the trip had such pity for us; he handed my mother a bag of toys that had not yet found their way to Lost and Found. For intermittent periods, those blocks, plastic toy soldiers, a colorful top that made the whizzing sound as we pressed down hard on the wooden knob, Lincoln logs, and a Jack in the Box kept us occupied. But for most of the trip, we slept on the back seat on top of one another like a litter of kittens.

Louisville was the halfway point of the trip. And as Papa had promised, fifty dollars was waiting at Western Union. Traveler's Aid placed a call to Papa who had waited in Walnut Grove for our arrival in Louisville. We were only fifteen minutes behind schedule. Papa informed Abigail that no one had seen CJ. He had used his Washington, D.C. connections to get federal officials and the FBI on the scene in an attempt to prod the local and state police to help with the search. The KKK had a hold in the Arkansas political structure; their cooperation was abysmal. Papa could not get up the courage to tell her there was every indication that CJ had been lynched and his body disposed of. A grim-faced crew of volunteers was already searching for CJ's remains. The length and breadth of the Arkansas River was being dragged, enacting a disgusting form of Braille as boats felt their way along the mudflats, the pilings, and swamps.

"What about Jimmy? Why didn't he come back for us?" Abigail asked.

Papa had no choice but to tell her the truth, "The KKK dragged Jimmy out of the Meriweather house and beat him half to death with fists and the butts of their rifles in front of Doretha and their children. The Meriweather boys were held at bay with shotguns, unable to come to his assistance. They threw Jimmy in the back of their truck, drove him away, and continued to administer their vicious beating. Eventually, they dumped him on the side of the road bound up in an oyster sack and blinded in one eye." There was more he did not share with Abigail. The night brought bricks and a fusillade of rifle bursts through windows in Negro farms and homes all over the Delta.

After the news she had just received, Papa was not sure Abigail heard him when he told her Arnetta would be meeting them at the Pittsburgh bus station. For the remainder of the trip, Abigail sat silent, tearful, dejected, wrung her hands, and rubbed her forehead: a woman profoundly distraught at what she had heard.

Over blacktop and macadam, through towns and fields, past intersections and siren voices, the road evaded mountains and tunnels and rivers. The telephone wires continually whipped the stars. The road slid down through valleys like a chute dumping us in and out of farmland. As the bus moved through the thickening night, the road unraveled with infuriating slowness. Its black wall wearilessly rose in front of the headlights no matter how it twisted. The land sometimes refused to change—the same scruff on the embankments, the same weathered billboards for the same products—only the license plates on passing vehicles changed. The road was broad and confident for miles, but there were sudden patched stretches, that climbed and narrowed. This was not so much by plan as naturally, the edges crumbling in and the vegetation and terrain on either side crowding down. The road twisted more and more wildly in its struggle to gain height. without warning, it shed its skin of asphalt and occasionally wormed on to dirt. When the bus strayed from straddling the roadside weeds, brambles raked its painted sides. These roads did not last very long and eventually sloped back onto asphalt. There were times when the highway in front of us was empty.

It did not matter how many state borders we crossed on that bus trip. There was carry-on baggage from the Delta that we could not shed. We carried grievous wounds with us. When it was over, we would all think that we had survived the worst days of our lives and endured the most grisly scenario the world could have presented to us.

— Chapter Twelve —

We arrived in Pittsburgh and passed through the double doors into the cavernous, barn-like hall. My mother positioned us on a wooden bench in such a way as to see everyone entering and leaving. Four hours passed as we engaged in a shadow dance of time, recruited by our mother to participate in the intense nervous waiting and searching of every movement at the bus terminal doors. The sheer strain of anticipation, the fear of falling asleep and missing Arnetta's arrival—and maybe even our father—was unbearable.

Abigail was paged by Traveler's Aid and informed that Arnetta was detained. Her expected arrival time was an additional three hours away. Another call came from Papa to check in on us. After a long silence, Papa painfully admitted that CJ still had not been found. Information they had received from reliable informers within the KKK did not look good. "We are not giving up the search, but I believe it's in God's hands now."

Something in his words or tone betrayed hope for Abigail. She realized Papa couldn't bring himself to say that CJ had been killed and the whereabouts of the body was the focus of the attention and effort. Abigail dropped the phone and walked slowly and heavily, with head bowed and body stooped, back to the bench. We greeted her with an avalanche of questions.

"Was it dad?"

"What did he say?"

"When is he coming to get us? What's taking him so long?"

"Can we go somewhere else? I don't like it here."

Something snapped within her and she slipped away. Stunned, lost in thought, motionless, and unable to finish sentences, she spoke only when spoken to. Her responses were brief, perfunctory, and in a monotonous, sometimes inaudible voice. Her face became a mask with deeply troubled eyes. She began a retreat to some vacant, distant place of utter detachment.

"I don't understand what you're saying."

"Please mom, please mom, answer us."

"What's wrong, mom?"

"I'm hungry."

James kept scolding in my direction, "Look what we've done by disobeying our father. It's our fault. How many times did he tell us that 'no sin goes unpunished?' Why didn't we listen and stay out of those woods? We caused all these terrible things to happen to us."

"No, no, stop saying that. Mean, hateful people—that's what dad calls them," I protested, "they're the ones to blame, not us."

"We're going to really get it from dad when he shows up. I knew better than putting my nose where it didn't belong. I'm supposed to look out for everyone, help keep the family safe."

"Stop it James, please stop." I started to cry.

As children, we were reduced to the role of forgotten players in her private drama. She abandoned us. We didn't seem to matter. We slowly retreated into our own state of oblivion, waiting for someone, anyone, to come and rescue us. In forty-eight hours we had become serious casualties.

As best he could, James looked after Daniel. I had unraveled and spent considerable time huddled in a corner near the bench—acutely anxious and almost panicked. Arnetta arrived, surveyed our condition, and made several telephone calls. We sat petrified and bewildered as Arnetta explained that we were going to be given medical attention and food for a few days at a nice place. She gave her assurance that she would stay with us, "I'll be right by your side. Papa is making arrangements to join us and should be here soon." My mother hugged Arnetta without a word spoken and was helped into a vehicle resembling an ambulance. Abigail had given up and withdrawn into herself.

We were taken to the Mellon House, a children's residential treatment center, given a medical examination, cleaned up, and provided with fresh clothes and food. That night, I had a full-blown panic attack and was sedated. All I remember were the frightening sensations of ghostly outlines and washed out colors and an impossible urgency and discomfort—from which there was no relief. A violent alarm just seemed to go off in the form of rapid breathing, heart pounding irregularly, uncontrollable fear, threatening and taunting voices, and confusion about where I was.

Arnetta went to the psychiatric ward of Mount Eden Hospital where Abigail had been taken. Crouched in a corner with her arms wrapped around her knees, Abigail's head was turned away from the door and rested against the wall. She did not move or look up when Arnetta entered the room. Her spirit had been excised from her flesh. There was a natural stillness to her repose, an immaculate divinity to the black ensemble of her mental stupor. It was as though she had made a vow of silence and the renunciation of all movement. Arnetta, visibly shaken, hid her face in her hands.

Arnetta took Abigail by the shoulders, kissed her cheek, and sat down beside her. She held her tightly and snuggled her face against Abigail's hair. Arnetta pulled a brush from her purse and, as she stroked Abigail's tangled hair, she sang a song she knew Abigail loved. "Everything's going to be all right because your Auntie is here; I'm going to be right here until you get well."

Abigail's eyes registered nothing; they were two hazel gems lying inert in a field of off-white. The nurse helped move Abigail to the bed where she immediately curled up like an embryo. Arnetta stood over Abigail in silence for a moment, then comforted, "I'll be back in the morning and around here for as long as I'm needed."

Panic attacks, sleep disturbances, night terrors, and severe anxiety in some form or another started occurring every day. My world looked fuzzy and disorganized. After a week, my condition worsened. I was removed from the Mellon House and placed in a mental hospital for children, located twenty miles west of Pittsburgh. For several weeks, I fought severe panic reactions.

The KKK had perpetrated a crime against sleep and memory; its afterimage imprinted itself like an irreversible negative from the camera of dreams. The men who chased us taught us over and over of the abidingness, the terrible constancy that accompanies wounds of the spirit. Our souls had sustained damage beyond repair. Violence sends its deep roots into the heart. It has no seasons; it is always ripe, evergreen. A portion of our life had been mortgaged; our pure sanction of a world administered by a God who loved us had been stolen; our image of the universe had been defiled.

Two weeks passed and the search for CJ's body was abandoned. Papa attended a memorial service officiated by Reverend Lacey to an overflow crowd of Negroes from all over the Delta, including local NAACP officials and a Negro army color guard. Taps was played as Papa received a folded American flag on Abigail's behalf.

Reverend Lacey launched into an emotional testimonial ". . . telling the truth to ourselves about what happened to CJ cannot be redeemed, cannot be grasped, and is an unbearable weight to place on his wife, his children, his extended family, and all of his friends. The Duncan family has been a part of the Delta as slaves, as landowners and cotton farmers, and as Christians. There is no one up here to help us register and memorialize the snuffing of his life. He was erased from the living and leaves no grave, no sign, no physical trace of any kind. It was determined by a group of men in white sheets that he had no right to exist, not as an inferior breed, not even as a usable slave. He was obliterated like a contaminant in the way of a noxious and repellent insect. But brothers and sisters, his spirit lives and ...." The sermon provoked anger, grief, hatred toward whites, anguish, and most of all emptiness, meaninglessness, and an almost menacing sadness. The service concluded with the battle hymn, "We Shall Overcome." Papa left almost immediately for Pittsburgh.

Papa was shocked when he saw his daughter in the long-term psychiatric unit to which she had been moved. It was like a holding cell for drug addicts and other assorted miscreants, not a benevolent place in which to recuperate. The unit retained a sickeningly pungent smell with its mixture of urine, antiseptic, and cigarette-infused air. Stained and wrinkled clothes, disheveled and unkempt, Abigail had plunged beyond her catatonic-like state and somehow passed the reachable zones of the interior to some psychotic state in which she mumbled incoherently. When she saw Papa, Abigail babbled in a nonstop monologue that made no sense other than a few coherent questions: "Did they kill him Papa? Did they hang him, Papa? Where are my kids?"

Abigail had to be sedated. Visibly shaken from such a hideous experience, Papa had Abigail moved the next day to Washington Hospital, located in the town where we would be living. The combination of drugs and being in an environment in which she felt safe contributed to her improvement.

Two weeks had become six. I remained hospitalized, as did Abigail. James and Daniel continued their residency at the Mellon House. They were removed from private rooms and placed in a dormitory setting with as many as sixty other children.

Arnetta commuted back and forth from New York. All of her effort in Washington was directed toward the renovation of the house. When Arnetta first confronted the dwelling, she moaned in protest and stood there in silence. She was afraid to go in. It stood out like it had been placed there by accident. A somber, red brick color was still evident in a house that had not been painted for decades or occupied for years. At different times of the day, the light gave it a peeling, dried, blood-like, rusty, and sinister patina. Composed of sharp spires and an angled roof, this two-story house sat teetering on a crumbling foundation. Exposed two-by-fours propped up the sagging front porch. There wasn't a blade of grass in a yard littered with debris. A sidewalk and walkway were cracked in so many places that it resembled large gravel chunks interspersed with weeds. The windows were broken and the front door was caved in. The mailbox just laid on the ground in several pieces; the house number nowhere in sight. Inside, the house was claustrophobic and small. All the rooms had bizarre shapes, frightening corners, niches, indentations, and places to hide. Arnetta knew right away it was a house designed to nourish a child's nightmare. After all that we had been through, she feared for us boys. *How will they ever adjust to such a wicked looking place?* Everything was collapsing, broken, or had been destroyed by vagrants. The house was structurally unsound, had makeshift plumbing, no insulation, exposed wiring, roaches, spiders, and mice droppings everywhere.

Arnetta needed every minute of the two months it took to restore the house to the point of habitability. Still, it did not meet the minimum standards she had set. The trade-off was getting the family back together and beginning the process of facing a new reality. Abigail did not feel quite ready, but her doctor released her to outpatient care, Telling her, "It's time for you to go out and find a way to live with your demons, if not without them."

Papa, Arnetta, Abigail's brother, Fletcher, and sister, Margaret, who lived in Philadelphia, were there for the homecoming. Even Welcome had made the trip from Fort Dix, New Jersey, where he was an assistant to the chief-of-staff for training and operations. He had returned from the Pacific with combat ribbons, medals, the rank of captain, and the decision to remain in the army as a career. As the only Negro staff member, Welcome had Papa's influence in Washington to thank for his well-placed assignment that put him on a fast track to achieving significant status and power in the chain-of-command among Negro soldiers.

They all spent a couple of days helping to make the shadows lighter, the conflicts less intense, and bring Abigail back into contact with the reality of daily living. Several days later, James and Daniel arrived from the Mellon House. I rejoined my family the following week. My adjustment was difficult. About every other night, I had a panic episode. Night had an endlessness about it, an excessive number of unstructured and unknown hours that frightened me. Sleep seemed so deathlike and out of my control. I carried on a continuous dialogue with the hidden ones. Sitting up in bed, terrifying and surreal, I addressed something invisible against the opposite wall. Sweat poured off my face, my eyes looked disconsolate and pained. I usually collapsed and fell asleep after one of my fits—as everyone called them. It scared James when I was like that. James said I became someone else, someone he didn't know.

That first year was rough, but there was always family around for support. Doretha and Jimmy had moved to Akron, Ohio. Every opportunity brought Doretha and her children for extended visits. Although things were bad from time to time and the signs of Abigail's manic-depressive swings were there—no matter how hard she tried to conceal it—sometimes I like to think that she fought through it because of us. Our mother's "black seasons" hovered above our lives;

there would never be any brilliantly colored rainbows to remember from that time of our childhood. My hallucinations occasionally got out of control, but with less frequency. They seemed to exist outside of time or space or reason. I always felt different, unsafe, and alone. These disconnected fragments were firmly attached to a vague and debilitating sense of terror.

Papa visited as often as he could. Although he had resigned from Tuskegee as a faculty member, he retained his military designation as a major and the executive officer of the OTC Program there. Papa spent considerable chunks of time in Washington under the orders of Secretary of War Robert Patterson studying yet another proposal on the army's use of Negro soldiers. Even after all the studies, reports, investigations, inquiries, memoranda, and edicts regarding "the Negro soldier," the new secretary felt further analysis was needed. Better known as the Gillem Board, because it was headed by Lieutenant General A.C. Gillem, the active commander of the XIII Corps, Papa had an important role in the board's recommendation that "for the sake of national security every available and qualified man should be used in an assignment for which there is a need, for which he is best suited, and for which he has been trained." In a major shift of military policy, the board also held that it was "its duty to teach American ideals … realizing equality of opportunity and treatment irrespective of race was essential to military effectiveness … and that every member of the military establishment respects all other wearers of the uniform."

Papa had already been notified that if Harry Truman was elected president, he would have to leave Tuskegee and relocate permanently to Washington to answer an appointment to a civil rights post. Abigail prayed for Truman's election so that he would be closer to her.

Around the time of our reawakening as a family, my mother huddled us together in the living room. In a voice that was uncompromising, she compelled a promise from each of us, "You will never tell a living soul what happened to us in Little Rock."

James, predictably, responded with a rash of questions, "Why not mom? Did we do something that we should be ashamed of? Are we hiding from someone?"

"Stop it, James," Abigail impatiently scolded. "I don't care if you understand the reasons or not. When you get older, I'll explain."

"Papa said we were brave. People will like us for that, right, mom?"

"Lander, in a place like Washington, it's going to be hard enough to fit in. Negroes might pity us and whites despise us for bringing that kind of talk to their town."

"What kind of talk is that?" James chimed in.

"Just take my word for it; they won't want their faces rubbed in it."

"Rubbed in what?" I asked.

"Boys, I've had enough. I'll take a switch to you if you break that promise. I want to hear it. Do you promise?"

Almost in unison, we acquiesced.

We never broke that promise, any of us. We didn't even speak about it to one another until the summer James headed off for college. It was a private and binding covenant entered into by a ravaged broken family. In silence, we honored private shame and made it unspeakable.

The subject or mention of our father was taboo. The initials CJ became a landmine by themselves. We had been tacitly warned, and we honored the near sacredness of the silence. Only our mother could break this cardinal rule, which she did on rare occasions. One of those was Christmas Eve when she placed a gift under the tree for our father and recited CJ's special story of returning home on Christmas Eve 1945. She put on the scratchy 78 RPM recording, "I'll Be Home for Christmas" and played it over and over. She danced with each one of us boys—the shuffling, drifting, repetitious, inspired, mood-making two-step that she learned from Arnetta. Tears washed down her face. The story seemed to be a horrible treasure to us; it was something our family could claim that no other family could—a distinction, an event that could never be let go.

Nearly six months had passed; there were no friends or family around to lean on. Perhaps we turned the corner as a family without CJ when we awoke to eight inches of snow. The sky was bitter and gray, and the temperature hung around ten degrees during the day for an entire week. The pipes froze and then burst; the house was without water for two weeks. An icy limb dropped some of the power lines, which plunged us into darkness. We lived in the soft glow of kerosene lanterns. We built great fires and my mother melted snow from our shoes on the coal stove. There was a sense of gaiety and an atmosphere of some surprising and illicit festival in our house. We had our first snowball fight in the front yard, built our first snowman, and joined some of the children who said that we lived on the perfect street for sled riding. We discovered that we could cope and that the sky was not falling on our head. We slid down the packed snow, bouncing through the barricaded intersection, until the ride ended with a spurt of sparks on a bed of cinders the borough crew had shoveled from a truck. During a drab, damp winter, the packed snow, the sparks, and the glimpses of Christmas trees by living room windows along the walk to school lasted for only a few days, but these memories lasted all year and tugged time forward in a child's virtual eternity.

Part Two
Fall 1968

— Chapter Thirteen —

The winding DeNeve Circle chaparral-covered bluff overlooks the UCLA campus. Within the circle sits a quadrangle of L-shaped structures that house a small city of students. In my second year as a resident house advisor, I lived at the top of the circle in Hedrick Hall dormitory.

On a brilliant fall day in 1968, my return from classes took me along Bruin Walk and Sather Gate. They pulsed with an atmosphere that was as exciting as it was unsettling. It was like entering a kaleidoscope. Groups of students were engaged in a wide range of protests—the Vietnam War, ecological threats, apartheid in South Africa, the military-industrial complex, the arms race, and the exploitation of migrant farm workers. On this crowded promenade, other enclaves of students postured and proselytized about women's liberation and gay rights. Black and Chicano power contrasted sharply with the fraternity and sorority members. ROTC cadets diligently pursued recruits. Hare Krishnas, unaffiliated groupies, and self-styled "flower children" chanted and danced for attention.

Within this atmosphere, I tried to navigate through such a weary, almost hallucinatory maze with no signposts or catechisms or rules of the road. All the old certainties I had come to expect of campus life seemed marginal and hollow. The tangy confidence and strut I possessed when I had first arrived on campus turned hesitant in the face of a slippery, rampaging past couple of years. In some ways, I was traveling incognito, even to myself.

Feeling curiously invigorated, I looked forward to getting back to the dorm and taking a jog. However, the awaiting telegram deflated me. Maybe it was the premonition I had as I studied the yellow envelope.

Almost a decade had passed since I had made any contact with my family. Whenever questions came up about my family history, I reached for my well-rehearsed fiction about being orphaned. I rationalized that I never really knew my father, and my mother scarcely belonged to me. She was always so far out of touch. I had managed to subdue any longings I had for family. Hesitantly, I opened the telegram: MOM'S DYING OF CANCER. CALL WASHINGTON HOSPITAL. HAVE THEM PAGE ME. JAMES.

I went out to the back patio of the dormitory and sat on one of the benches facing the campus. Laughter erupted that I could not suppress. It broke loose all the inhibitions that clustered about those words, arranged like forbidden fruit in the telegram. It was both helpless and pain filled. I thought to myself: *My mother's not even sick. She's just after something. Something big. Abigail's a great strategist. She's used the imminence of her own demise before to get attention. She's not dying. She's acting out. She's got something spectacular up her sleeve. She thinks that cancer will elicit sympathy from her callous and ungrateful child and bring him home.*

I convinced myself that my reaction was perfectly reasonable, even justifiable. The idea of James tracking me down was incongruous with these musings. I could not have been that easy to find. I did not think this moment would ever happen. My mother would die and be buried and none of my family would bother me about it. That was the way it was suppose to be.

I had no choice but to call and headed nervously to my room—rehearsing and discarding something so simple as a common greeting. The time difference placed my call during normal hospital visitation hours. Several minutes of waiting and passing the call to various extensions produced my brother. James said, "Hello?" in an intonation that I could have recognized had I been gone for a hundred years.

"Hello?" James said again.

"James, it's me, Lander."

There was a long silence.

"The name's vaguely familiar, and I've heard legends about the boy's existence, but ...."

"Very funny, James. I'll accept some good-natured ribbing, but not much."

"Oh, did it appear I was being good-natured? Excuse me, you rotten SOB. I'm mad as hell and I plan to beat the crap out of you as soon as I see your sorry ass ...."

"The telegram?"

"You're calling to see if it's bullshit, right? It's true. Mom's got leukemia."

He started to say more and then stopped. I could hear his tone change. "She's in a coma and may not come out of it. 'Find Lander and bring him home.' I've heard that tearful refrain incessantly in recent weeks. She lost consciousness before I could find you."

I thought about plane schedules, reservations, canceling my date for the USC game, midterms. "I'll be in Pittsburgh sometime tomorrow. I'll call you later with the particulars."

I had so many reasons to distrust this news even after James's confirmation. A recollection took me back to when I was eleven or twelve and just on the brink of ceasing to be a little boy. One Sunday afternoon, my mother and I hiked up to the top of Prospect Hill, which was a mountain to a child. It had formed on one side of the valley that held our town. The town lay before us, exposed beneath a thin slice of haze. I did not feel uneasy standing alone with her next to a wind-stunted spruce tree on a long spine of shale. Suddenly, she dug her fingers into the hair on my head and announced, "There we all are, and there we'll all be forever." She hesitated before the word "forever." She hesitated again before adding, "Except you, Lander. You're going to fly."

A few birds were gliding far out over the valley at the level of our eyes. And in her impulsive way, she had just plucked that image from them, but it felt like a clue I had been waiting for all my childhood. She gave me a consciousness of a special destiny. I came to believe my mother's definition of me. She had defined me early on and succeeded in turning me into the exact image of what she needed at the time.

Because there was something essentially complacent and orthodox in my nature, I allowed her to knead and shape me into the smooth lineaments of a *mama's boy*. I adhered to the measurements of her vision. She succeeded in making me a dull, plain, and courteous child. I carried sensibilities primed and calibrated to register her slightest unhappiness. I longed for her approval, her applause, her pure uncomplicated love for me. Abigail was impulsive and romantic and inconsistent. No boy can endure for long the weight and magnitude of his mother's displaced passion. Yet few boys can resist their mother's innocent seductions to get her way. There was such forbidden sweetness in becoming the *mama's boy*. While there is nothing more natural, exquisite, and carnal on earth than a boy in love with the shape and touch of his mother, there is also nothing more damaging.

I was never able to develop this spirit of reassurance into a steady theme between us. That she continued to treat me like an ordinary child seemed a betrayal of the vision she had made me share. For years, I was captive to a hope she had tossed off and forgotten. I made attempts to remind her by appealing to the image of flight when I excelled at something. These efforts were received with a startled blank look as if I was talking nonsense. It seemed outrageously unjust. I'm not the first son to be completely fooled and wrong about his mother.

I hung up the phone and began the logistics of leaving school. I was breaking my solemn vow that I would never return to Washington or any place my family might call home.

I convinced myself that leaving someone isn't the worst thing you can do. It didn't have to be a tragedy. If you never left anything or anyone, there would be no room for the new. Naturally, to move on is an act of infidelity to others, to the past, to old notions of oneself. Perhaps every day should contain at least one essential infidelity. It would be an optimistic, hopeful act, guaranteeing belief in the future—a declaration that things could be not only different but also better. This was not the case when my mother committed her act of desertion.

On the flight, I had time to compose myself before I had to face the abundant, guilty love of brothers who would not know how to welcome me home. I wanted to find the right words, the safe words, and painfully avoid the wrong subjects. I was lost in thought when I heard the flight attendant's voice.

"We are beginning our descent ...."

My stomach began to hurt as the engines changed pitch to descend into the city. I blamed my pain on the freeze-dried salted nuts that had come in the little, silver-foil packet with the orange juice. The tempting young stewardess, with a delineated boundary on her throat where the pancake makeup stopped, had given me not one but two, and I ate both even though the nuts had a bitter aftertaste. The near engine of the 707 was haloed by a rainbow of furious vapor in a backwash of sunlight from the west as the plane droned eastward. This drone, too, had eaten into my stomach. Then there was the time crunch of my departure and the pressure of elbows on the armrests on both sides of me. I had arrived at the airport too late to get an aisle or a window seat.

I leaned my face toward the window, imbibing the Pittsburgh skyline. My stomach pain was replaced by a pang of anxiety, a kind of visceral reaction, the familiar symptom of which is fear. In all these years, I have never been able to purge myself of this loathing for Pittsburgh. Just hearing the name was enough. Every effort I made to sanitize the memory of what happened there—as a part of the saga of our exodus from Arkansas—turned into cheap sentimentality.

James waited for me at the gate. I saw him moments before he saw me. As we walked toward each other, I felt something I cannot explain. I felt it in the deepest part of me, an untouchable place that trembled with something instinctual and was rooted in the provenance of the species. It wasn't the unexpected tears that swelled up in my eyes that caused this resonance of fierce interior music of blood and identity. It was the beauty and fear of kinship, the ineffable ties of family, which sounded a blazing terror and an awestruck love inside me.

"Welcome home, Lander."

"It's good to see you, James," I said, shaking his hand.

As we walked to the baggage claim, he launched his reprimand, "You never stayed in contact with any of us."

"You don't waste any time."

"You've got a lot of answering to do."

"I've got nothing to answer for, James."

"You can't just walk back into a family after ten years like nothing's happened."

"Yes, I can. No one gave a damn about me in that rooming house."
It all came rushing back.

* * * * * * * * *

My mother had trembled as she tried to explain her acceptance of
a marriage proposal from Bryce McNair, which carried with it the
condition that she could not bring me with them to Buffalo. I recollect
that morning when she dropped me, along with my few possessions,
at the boarding house run by a woman she knew from a previous
employment. Her parting words carried a tone of finality. "Your mother
will always love you."

A better son would have embraced his mother, comforted her, and
made her feel less guilty. I can remember every agonizing detail. I put
my hand out toward her shoulder and then withdrew it as soon as
I came in range of her body. Her extreme sadness seemed to make
her dangerous, electric at that moment. Again, I reached out toward
her, but my hand did not travel the distance that had suddenly grown
between us. In the heat of the unseasonably warm morning, I felt a
film of ice form over my heart. Wordless, I tried to find the words
that would bring peace to my mother and her decision. Knowing I
should take her in my arms, I was paralyzed—thinking far too much
about myself and how I was going to make it alone. Thus, I lost a most
precious and life-defining moment forever.

The terror in discovering I did not know how to live without my
family gathered around me surfaced a semblance of the anxiety and
panic I had suffered as a young boy. Only a few times in my life had
I slept away from the sounds of my mother and brothers sleeping. I
was not quite ready to be abandoned from the life I had known. A
seventeen-year banquet of hope, an abiding place, and even grief was
coming to an end. I couldn't bear it. Why could I not tell my mother
what I felt? Is family one of nature's soluble gifts? Does it dissolve in
time like salt in rainwater?

There was the denial: It's all a mistake! She'll be back! She would
never leave me! There was anger, grief, and despair that chased each
other in an abject downward spiral. What tormented me most was an
overwhelming jealousy. I was the *mama's boy* and had paid the heavy
price for this advantage over my brothers. I was the one who gave up

so much of his childhood trying to make her happy. How could she choose a drunk with a gambling addiction over me? I felt betrayed by the person to whom my heart had been committed since birth, a woman who knew almost everything about me and wanted to know no more.

It was a year of deadening seriousness; all the illusions and bright dreams of my adolescence and final year of high school wanted to wither and die. I did not have the interior resources to dream new dreams; I was far too busy mourning the death of old ones and wondering how I was going to survive without my family.

Bryce McNair saw to the cessation of payments for room and board. He managed to cut my mother off from me completely or so I told myself. She wrote to me for the first few months and then nothing. They moved. I never heard from her again, not that I made any concerted effort. The woman running the boarding house contacted social services and the end result of their intervention was to enroll me as yet another abandoned youth under the care of the welfare system.

* * * * * * * * *

"Lander, I know this sounds harsh, but you need to get over yourself. You missed it. We missed it."

"Missed what?" I asked in frustration.

"We were no longer her little boys. I was heading for Penn State. Our mother finally turned her energies to finding a replacement for our father. She waited ten years for an intimate relationship with a man. Her time had arrived. She just made a bad choice."

"She did more than that! She deserted me. I was still a minor. I didn't begrudge her happiness. Couldn't she have waited another year until I graduated? I can't talk about this anymore. It's just too difficult. Let's change the subject to the reason I'm here. How is she doing?"

"She's worse today."

"Who put her in Washington Hospital? I remember people going there for hemorrhoids, blood blisters, and cold sores, not for something serious. Hey, there's my baggage."

"Washington Hospital has improved over the past few years," James said almost defensively, "but I'm not going to take any grief from you about the kind of medical care mom's receiving. Lander, I want you to know, the decision to call you was not unanimous."

James's anger was not subtle. I knew our conversation about my disappearance was not over. No one walks out on their family without reprisals. James, particularly, was far too disciplined to offer compassion to a deserter. No matter how much sympathy there might be for my motives, my brothers would still read a clear text of treason for my actions.

"I wish you hadn't," I snapped as I removed my bag from the conveyor belt and started following the crowd out toward the parking lot.

Taking my bulging briefcase filled with course texts and lecture notes, he said, "It was a request from mom that I couldn't ignore."

"You should've done it after she was dead." I regretted uttering those spiteful words the minute they slipped out of my mouth. But they served to neutralize the growing acrimony.

"Mom has changed a lot, particularly this past year. Too bad you didn't get to see any of those changes. Look, forgive my rancor. I got my MD from Case Tech Western Reserve University in Cleveland. I'm now doing a joint cardiovascular surgical residency at Cleveland Clinic and the University Hospital and Medical Center. Cleveland Clinic is one of the premier hospitals in the country for the treatment of cancer, particularly leukemia. I could have gotten her into the Cleveland Clinic, but mom insisted on staying in Washington."

"What is she doing in Washington anyway?"

"It's a long story. We'll get to it later."

"Congratulations James. or should I say Dr. Duncan"

"What about you?" Did you play ball anywhere? When I left, you were already getting recruiting letters from Nebraska, Pitt, even my alma mater."

I told him the nickel version that I had rattled off so many times before. It sounded more like a graduate school placement interview than the life I remembered having lived. "I played for a year at a division II school, dropped out and volunteered for the draft. There was a tour of duty in Vietnam, junior college, state colleges, and on to UCLA. I finish next year and will be applying to doctoral programs. My senior thesis is pointing me toward Princeton's interdisciplinary program in cognitive and behavioral sciences. I'm enjoying the lab, seminars, and academic fellowship. I'd like to hide out in an ivory tower some day as a research scientist and professor."

"Uncle Sam wasn't interested in me with my heart problems. You did a tour in Vietnam?" James asked rhetorically. "What was that like? Was it as bad as I've been hearing? You, in uniform and combat ..."

"In order to benefit from the GI Bill and keep my active duty stint at two years, I volunteered for the draft," I quickly offered, afraid James might attach some stigma to a regular enlistment.

I sensed James's interest in Vietnam and my military experience was his way of calling a temporary truce or moratorium between us. I indulged him. "Let's see. My basic and advanced infantry training was at Fort Gordon, Georgia, and airborne school was also in Georgia at Fort Benning. I spent six months at Fort Sam Houston in Texas with a bunch of conscientious objectors who were being transformed into combat medics.

"At the outset, I was on a trajectory for Vietnam and landed with a Special Forces team at Khe Sanh as their medic. Khe Sanh was the northernmost Special Forces outpost in the rugged highlands of South Vietnam about six miles from the Laotian border. Our assignment was to help intercept the flow of material and block guerilla activity along the Vietcong supply routes that ran from Laos to the coast. We were also there to win the allegiance of the local tribe's people, the Montagnards, who lived in key mountain and jungle areas where the Vietcong were establishing bases.

"The countryside was as beautiful as it was deadly. Just down the road was a coffee plantation owned by a wealthy Frenchman. Banana trees grew in our compound. Oranges, lemons, and grapefruits were in abundance and at our fingertips in the nearby jungles. After six months in Khe Sanh, I was transferred to an evacuation hospital unit following behind an infantry battalion."

"How much medical care were you able to provide with just six months training?" James queried with somewhat of a disdainful tone.

"By your standards, probably not much. In combat environments, the ability to triage and evacuate the wounded; tag and bag the KIA soldiers; handle field hospital sick calls dealing with trench foot, dysentery, malaria, lice, leeches, paddy algae, various rots and molds;

and day-to-day medical problems make a medic's role in the scheme of things fairly significant.

"Anyway, enough of this. I've spent the last two and a half years trying to distance myself from that nightmare. Speaking of nightmares, do I have to see mom's husband?" The thought of adding any more emotional weight to my homecoming seemed unbearable. I had not thought about the possibility of encountering my stepfather. "I'd rather not see him. I consider the man contemptible."

James followed up by surprising me with a little sentimentality, "I've missed you Lander. We were close. There was nothing we didn't share. Then we *all* went in different directions. But the rest of us stayed in touch, visited, wrote—all but you."

"I received a few letters from you during your first semester at Penn State. You had everything I didn't have. Our lives were going in different directions. I couldn't bring myself to respond to news about the exciting campus pursuits and academic life you richly earned and deserved. Call it sour grapes, feeling sorry for myself, a bit of jealousy."

"Lander, I never stopped to consider your circumstances and appreciate what you were going through. In retrospect, I can understand how you might think I was rubbing your face in my happiness. I just stopped writing when I didn't hear back from you. Then it seems I got caught up in my own life and the months seemed to fly by. When I finally started writing again, the mail came back with a "no longer at this address" stamped across the envelope. I contacted the woman at the boarding house, even Reverend Butler, but no one had a forwarding address. I guess I didn't try hard enough. We all kept waiting to hear from you. You just disappeared—and I guess no one came to find you, until now."

Trying to steer the conversation away from a blame game in which I had no chance of prevailing, I agreed with James that we should have been more diligent—and without hesitation, inquired, "James, are you married?"

"No, but I have someone pretty important down in Charlotte, North Carolina. We appear to be heading that way. How about you?"

"Not even close."

"Great to have you back," James said. He started the car and eased out of his parking space. "I'm glad you came."

"Where am I staying?"

"Aunt Ann insisted you stay with her and the girls. Daniel and I are at the Washington Plaza."

"I haven't even thought about facing Daniel's wrath and acrimony. I wouldn't be surprised if he took a swing at me."

Daniel had a fatal attraction for the extraordinary gesture. There was always flamboyance, exaggeration, and outrageousness to his response to even minor events. He was instinctive, not thoughtful. My younger brother functioned best as a connoisseur of hazard and endangerment. He was not truly happy unless he was engaged in his own private war with the rest of the world. I could always feel the tension of approaching risk with him. Thin ice and falling rocks composed the milieu he seemed to enjoy.

"You'll be surprised. He's done a turnaround with his life. The air force has been good for him. He finishes his reenlistment commitment in a few months and has been accepted at Tuskegee. The ghost of our father is calling him."

"That's great news."

"He worked in the judge advocate's office as a legal aide for most of his stateside military career. He was in Germany for awhile. Can you imagine Daniel as an attorney? He's someone who considered screaming as a higher form of discourse and a shouting match the upside of dialogue."

"He's bright, James, and law has some built-in safety features that will keep him on a more conventional path while allowing for his passion. Watch the road, doctor."

As we crossed over the long, graceful bridge that spanned the mile-long junction of the Allegheny and Monongahela rivers, I breathed in the noxious air from the industrial effluence that distilled in the bright sunshine of Pittsburgh. I could smell my boyhood sneaking up in a slow, purloined dream as I closed my eyes. The chemistry of time allowed me to repossess those chased-off, ghostly scents of my lost youth. Despite my ambivalence, I found my entire body leaning forward in anticipation of seeing the rest of my family again.

On its own, my spirit seemed to relax. While I had become a prisoner to the voluptuous latitude of southern California and its coastline, southwestern Pennsylvania had laid its imprint on me like an image on a coin.

Washington Hospital had received a facelift and expansion, but once inside, it gave off that recognizable, institutional antiseptic smell. The hallways were lined with drawings of schoolchildren and octogenarians who had excelled with crayons and finger paint during occupational therapy. For the last twenty-four hours, I had made a grand effort to think of everything except my mother's condition.

The past was one destination where I tried to limit my mental visits. When we approached the waiting room where the family had gathered in a mute, rough-hewn vigil, I felt as if I was walking into a minefield. "Hello, everybody," I said, trying not to make eye contact with anyone.

"Hello, Lander," an unfamiliar man's voice said. It was my mother's husband. "It's a pleasure to see you again."

"What pleasure?" I ignored the hand he extended. This was the man who had caused me such heartache.

"Your mother will be grateful that you came," McNair replied, seemingly undaunted by my snub as though he was expecting it.

James jumped in with a biting tone, "How would you know?"

"How is she?" I asked politely, feeling a bit guilty about not extending him the common courtesy of a handshake.

McNair looked perplexed and then frightened. I saw that this tall, gray-haired stranger was close to tears. When he tried to speak and no words followed, he could not have given me a more accurate or devastating portrait of my mother's condition.

"The name is familiar," my brother Daniel uttered sarcastically to the room, "but I can't place the face. You from these parts, stranger?" Daniel said, winking at James.

Daniel rose out of his chair and gave me a hug. He was the only person I knew who could embrace you and keep his distance at the same time. As the youngest, he had that natural gift for being outspoken and the ability to send us into scattered disarray.

I returned his embrace with a full-fledged bear hug. His emotions were always out front, running over the banks. I could feel his edge, the chronic anger he carried. He held the biggest grudge against our mother—the only one among us who would say, out loud, that she had crimes of incompetence and inattention to answer for. According to James, it was because of this that her coma had hit Daniel particularly hard.

I inquired from James why McNair seemed so uncomfortable and removed. Avoiding a direct answer, he smirked and offered sarcastically, "McNair has every reason to keep his distance."

As I walked down the corridor toward the intensive care unit with my brothers, James warned, "Brace yourself. She looks terrible, worse than I'm sure you have imagined."

Once the door shut behind us, I closed my eyes, took a deep breath, and leaned against a wall to regain whatever equilibrium I could before looking at the mother, my mother, who I had not seen in years. I approached the bed where an unrecognizable woman lay. For a moment, my heart swelled thinking that a terrible mistake had been made, and this broken woman was masquerading as my beautiful mother.

Whatever else people thought of Abigail, we were often told, by blacks and whites alike, that she was the prettiest woman in Washington. When we would tell her about the compliments, she would just blush and say, "I'm just a woman who does the best she can with what God gave her."

On one of her rare dates, she had emerged from her bedroom in a navy blue dress her current suitor had given her for Christmas. It was not her style to accept such personal tokens of affection. We took this to mean that maybe this one might be different from the others. We were walking proof that being fatherless can cause one the greatest thirsts of the human condition. My brothers and I were always on the lookout, always sizing up men that crossed our path as a potential husband for our mother and a father for us. We clung to the hope that one day she would bring home that special man—a man who would give a sense of harmony to our unbalanced lives and take away the sting of staying just a footstep ahead of poverty.

On this occasion, she could not quite hide her pleasure. She created a field of vibrancy with her beauty; her prettiness impinged softly as we turned to watch her entry. Our applause rested in the margins of our silence, the delicacy of our awe. She stood in the living room awaiting our approval. She spun in a slow circle, lovely in the places where a woman is lovely. Adhering to the tenets of her Adventist faith, she wore no makeup, but her complexion was flawless, her hair brushed and shining. James rose from the couch and began clapping his hands and Daniel and I joined him. Together, we began to cheer. She lifted her arms in a gesture of choking us as she approached, thinking we were making fun of her, but stopped when she realized we were praising her. Her eyes filled up with tears. She was the woman of dreams—but she had stopped dreaming that she could ever feel beautiful again. This was a rare moment, a perfect tone of feeling between us.

Our mother's body was now frail and covered with bruises. I touched her face; it was hot and her hair was wet and unkempt. I leaned down to kiss her and saw my own tear fall on her face.

"Jesus," I said, "She's not faking."

"Be careful. The doctor tells us she might be able to hear us, even in the coma," Daniel cautioned.

"Really," I wiped my tears away. Then I leaned over again and said, "It's your son Lander who's always loved you. I've never stopped being your biggest fan, your number one cheerleader. When you wake up from all this, we're going to listen to those Jackie Wilson and Sam Cooke records and dance the way we used to."

I took my mother's hand, pressing it softly against my cheek, and said, "I keep expecting her to open her eyes and scream, Surprise!"

"Not this time." After a lengthy pause, James motioned us away from the bed and whispered, "Lander, mother thinks you hate her."

"I've had my days. Okay, Daniel," hoping to get an answer from him, "what's going on? What's she doing in Washington?"

"McNair is a drunk and was physically abusive with mom, particularly after I left to join the air force. Apparently, one night a couple years ago, he was all boozed up and came after her with a gun. You know how mom can turn a man's head. Well, McNair was the jealous type. From what I gathered, he planned to shoot her and then turn the gun on himself. Fortunately, he was so drunk he couldn't even hold the gun still—let alone pull the trigger. Mom ran out of the house in fear for her life. She left him after the incident and returned here to live in our old house with Aunt Ann and her two daughters."

"Did she press charges?"

"Yes, but after a month, she dropped them. This is the first time he has seen her since that night. He just sends money and apologies. He's been by her bedside whenever possible and refuses to leave the hospital. He's taken the news hard; he says he still loves her and is lost without her."

"Why didn't you find me and let me know?"

"Mom asked us not to. She didn't want you to know. Besides, you don't get to play it both ways. When you leave the family, the family isn't accountable to you."

It was true I never wanted to hear from any member of my family ever again; I didn't wish to communicate with anyone who knew me. I wanted to start life anew, afresh, reinvent myself. Barely seventeen, I had felt abandoned, deserted, and on my own.

I returned to my mother's bedside and knelt down beside her. I tried to pray, but none of the old words she had taught me seemed adequate. I listened to her hard, rasping breathing and laid my head against her chest. Her valiant heart sounded strong and certain; that heartbeat alone gave me reason to hope. There was suddenly a slight change in her breathing and something must have registered on a machine at the nurse's station. A nurse came and took her pulse, adjusted the flow of the intravenous fluid into her veins, and hustled us out of the intensive care unit. Outside in the hallway, I felt hammered, flattened.

"She's really gonna die?" I whispered to James.

"They tell us the next seventy-two hours are critical."

James sensed my fatigue and suggested that he take me to the house to get settled. Daniel did not want to leave the hospital and declined an invitation to come along for the ride.

The passage of time had done little to change Washington. As the car eased along Spruce Street, which cut through the two blocks of downtown, the facade of the stores had retained the characteristic 1930s small, eastern, industrial town appearance. Each store was different. But seen together, they gave Main Street an undisclosed unity. I always wondered how a town so unassuming and modest could produce people so mean.

When we arrived nearly two decades before, the borough of East Washington had a totally white population of just over twelve hundred residents, its own law enforcement, and its own school systems. Outside of the gates of this wealthy borough, the population of the town was approximately twenty-six thousand residents within an area of three and one-third square miles. There were fewer than two thousand black citizens living in Washington. They were also enclosed behind gates, but not voluntarily. A circumscribed area of about three-quarters of a mile, called "The Hill," was dominated by row after row of government subsidized projects.

We crossed Lincoln Street on to Forrest Avenue, which was considered the color line. One side of the street was in Washington and contiguous with "The Hill" that collided with East Washington so sharply it was very nearly possible to stand with one foot in each. This abrupt juncture was dramatic, but so familiar I barely noticed. For most, the divide reflected a racial split familiar in many Pennsylvania towns; blurred by geographic distance, it managed to be abrupt and plainly evident. The disjunction I felt while living on the white borough side of Forrest Avenue is difficult to describe.

And there sat 142, lit by the last light of day. James pulled the car along the curb, and we sat for several minutes. He reached across the seat and squeezed my shoulder. Coming from him, that gesture was more than a welcome home. He was assuring me I could always find rescue in the country of my brothers. Their friendship burned as a soft fire; my absence did not appear to have extinguished the flame.

James walked me to the front door. Ann had heard the car pull up and was at the porch waiting. It had been ten years. Her face had turned harder and more chiseled, her unpainted lips thinner, those Bryant hazel eyes more opaque, and her body had grown wider—which she carried well. She gave each of us a hug as her daughters retreated behind her and peeked at me with suspicion. I watched as they reemerged and gave James affectionate pokes to get his attention. My facial expression gave away the hint of envy I felt at the playful closeness in evidence. "Serves you right for being a stranger for so long," Ann teased.

Iris and Melvena, my cousins, had little interest in their mother's introduction and continued their antics with James. Refusing a cup of coffee and making his exit to return to the hospital, I walked him back to the car and thanked him for not making my return more difficult than it already was.

I turned and walked to the end of the sidewalk. I looked up and down the street where I spent a part of my childhood. You could call this *my* homecoming. While it did not contain the same exigencies or pathos of my first arrival, I had the same sense of denial and disillusionment, looking for something I had lost. By the time I returned to the house, Iris and Melvena had retired to their bedroom, and Aunt Ann was waiting with coffee. There was something about the odor of the house. Maybe it was the smell of bread pudding, the familiar incense of the past coming to me in the envelope of that aroma. Aunt Ann confirmed it was my mother's recipe with the raisins. She had obviously been tipped off about how much I loved it.

I didn't know Ann very well, but my recollections were of a conflict she perpetuated with my mother. Their relationship held distances, jealousies, evasions, and unspoken recriminations. What I remember most was her complaining, wheedling attention, and looking to promote discord within the family. Nothing was ever right or enough. She plagued Abigail with telephone calls about her husband, her siblings, or other family members—what they had done or failed to do, what they had said or omitted to say. Conversations became heated and words were released with a ferocity that forced the slam of the receiver. Whereupon, Abigail generally collected herself, sighed, and picked up the phone again. The slow retracting whir of the rotary dial signaled the start of the next round.

It was apparent that Ann wanted to talk about her sister. She acknowledged that Abigail had a premonition of bad news when she arrived in Washington. She felt a slight, almost imperceptible change in her body, like the tiny rustle of cylinders shifting in a combination lock. She had always been able to read the signals her body gave off. The doctors confirmed her intuition and gave her the verdict of an advanced stage of leukemia. A death sentence had been passed on her.

Ann described how Abigail was spending the last months of her life. She did a lot of crying. Ann did not think her tears were out of self-pity, but a way of helping to water the path toward acceptance of dying. "She started the chemotherapy treatment right away, but it put a lot bigger hurt on her than the leukemia did," Ann said. "Abigail looked up her type of leukemia in medical textbooks and learned her cancer was particularly ornery. She didn't have a chance in hell of surviving, whether she got the chemo or not. But her doctor told her there was always a chance.

"She spoke often about living out the last months of her life and how important it was for her to get her affairs straight. She wanted to 'tell the truths that needed to be told.' I don't know what that meant, but she spent a lot of time at the Adventist church with Reverend Butler.

"Abigail summoned the courage to kick Bryce out of her life. He wanted her back, but there were too many broken promises, and she simply didn't want him to be a part of her last days. She wanted closure on the havoc Bryce left on the trails of his binges and blackouts. It's not fair, her life is ending just when she seems to have it all figured out."

I waited for Ann to tell me how my mother had poured her heart out over me. That satisfaction was not forthcoming. In its place were secondhand regrets, apologies, and excuses. But maybe there was no explanation that could redeem the pain and disappointment I carried around all these years.

However, I was not ready to let go of my suffering. Ann did her best to convey my mother's sentiments. "In her heart, she had not abandoned you. Abigail felt constant torment about the decision she made to leave you behind and desperately wanted a chance for atonement and forgiveness. Don't judge her too harshly. She had her hands full with Bryce and felt imprisoned in Buffalo. Abigail came back to Washington to get you, to reach out from here where she left you, and bring you home. James has been trying to find you to give her the opportunity for this peace. In families, there are no sins beyond forgiveness. Let her have this from you."

I sublimated my answer into interest in Ann's life, "What about you?"

"David died five years ago from a stroke, a cerebral hemorrhage. He was only thirty-five and left us a small life insurance policy and death benefits from the railroad. David worked the dining car on the Silver Bullet on the Philadelphia to Miami trip. This house was empty, so I came here from Philadelphia. I'm studying nursing and work part-time as an orderly at the hospital. We manage."

"Ann, I'm so sorry."

"Abigail's coming to live with us was a godsend. We had wounds we had inflicted on each other to mend. She encouraged me to go to school and helped with the girls. We have leaned on each other. That's the way God works."

We talked a little longer. I rose heavily, more fatigued than I knew I could be and still be awake. Ann was also exhausted. She showed me to the room my mother had occupied.

It did not take me long to fall asleep. But from the smoke of a dream too dark to remember, I woke in this bedroom, which was adjacent to the one where my boyhood was locked in a fixed position. A car horn was blaring on the street somewhere. I had grown up flanked by noisy streets that carried traffic in and out of East Washington and the black section of town.

Hours later, I heard the sounds of my aunt and her girls begin to stir in the same bedroom my brothers and I marched out of to encounter our lives. The movement of these relatives made a delicate, sustaining noise in this resurrected, reorganized household. I smelled the coffee brewing as I shaved and dressed to join them for breakfast.

As Ann scolded my little cousins, I could almost hear my mother's voice yelling, "Lander, don't you be eating from one end of this house to the other. You constantly have your mouth full. If you must eat all the time, eat over the sink." As a child, I had been afraid the food would run out and would march through the house always nibbling on something. And, I hated eating over the sink; it made me feel like a dog at his bowl. "That's why we have problems with roaches. There are crumbs on the floor—everywhere." It was incessant. "Don't slurp. Where are your table manners? Manners are a form of courtesy and courtesy is a form of goodness. Look at me when I'm talking to you. Take off that absurd hat in the house …"

Walking through the living room, I remembered the ritual we developed that started during our first few days in Washington. Each morning, before leaving the house, the four of us held hands and formed a circle together. In the living room, beside the potbellied coal stove that warmed us during cold winter mornings, we clasped our hands in a perfect unbreakable circle. I held Daniel's hand, Daniel held James's hand, James held my mother's hand, and she held mine. All of us touched, bound in a ring of flesh and blood. We would recite the watchword: "May the Lord Watch between Me and Thee [breathe] While We Are Absent [breathe] One From Another [breathe] Amen."

We recited this prayer so many times, the punctuation marks and capital letters had all worn away and the words had rearranged themselves to best match our breathing pattern. My mother would give the signal by bowing her head and we would begin. After saying the watchword, each of us, silently, was expected to say a small prayer or Bible verse. We remained silent with head bowed until we felt the squeeze of our hand, which we passed along. Occasionally, I would open my eyes and lift my head and not only feel, but see, the dazzling connection between us. With our pulses touching, it was a circle of uplifted love as we prepared to leave the house to face the difficulties of our life. This little ritual was like a momentary sanctuary. Knowing the teasing insults we would receive at school, my mother would always say before we left the house, "Be strong in God."

* * * * * * * * *

The next morning, the family gathered slowly again as the ruined cells skirmished in the silent lanes of Abigail's bloodstream. This gathering was irregular and off center. None of us wanted to be there. In her coma and attached to all the machines of measurement and warning, my mom could not hear the house of Duncan rallying to her side. No one loved theater and spectacle more than my mom, but this coming together contained no aspect of whim and it was not something to be taken lightly. She had taught her sons to laugh, but not to grieve. And so, with nothing to do, we sat around and waited, trying to learn the laws and courtesies of dying.

Under such extreme pressure, we got to know each other again. We had come to a meeting place in our lives that would be part telling of our hopes and dreams for the future that was upon us and part winking at the gods of darkness. The waiting room filled up with strange openings, disorders, and slanted windows facing out to the past. But all exits were barred; there seemed to be no way out as we groped for common ground and looked for a straight line to share.

Though we thought we were learning the protocols of dying, we did not know which ones applied to our mother. I had arrived at the hospital at seven that morning by cab and had visited her amid the humming machines that were monitoring her vital signs. The nurses told me there was no change, and I soon retreated to the waiting room where I shuffled through the books I was required to digest for several of my classes. Concentration was difficult in a room whose décor offended sensibilities at the lowest levels and could only be described as jarring.

Daniel and James made their way down the long hospital corridor toward me. I brought them up to date on mom's "no change" status. McNair approached us from the other corridor, his step military and even sprightly. He lifted his hand to stop James from going to check on Abigail, indicating he would like to talk to all of us. There were so many reasons why I resented this man—his transgressions against me by marrying my mother and mistreating her were at the top of the list. My mother's condition had forced us into an alliance none of us wanted. He was a measured, soft-spoken man whose sentences took time in the saying. When he was nervous, a slight stammer caused an even greater logjam of words. He apologized for his failures with Abigail. "I am here to give your mother all the support within my reach. I pray that I get the opportunity to ask her forgiveness. If I make you uncomfortable, or if you …." He broke down before he could finish his sentence.

James hadn't changed. He was quick to respond, "You are still her husband and have a right to be here."

Blowing his nose and wiping his eyes, McNair said, "That's very kind of you."

Daniel fidgeted and finally blurted out, "I don't like you, and you're nothing but a drunk. You're disgusting. Just stay out of my way." With that said, Daniel stalked off.

I almost felt sorry for this man, who apparently still loved my mother very much.

We took one-hour turns at her bedside. I spent my time holding her hand and kissing her cheek. I softly told her everything I could about my life. I also assured her that her face was still pretty by any measure or at any age. My mother used her beauty in Washington as she had during her youth. It was the most important weapon she had brought to a luckless life. It was not just her beauty that made her stand out in Washington. Her beauty was more sensual, or indeed, more overtly sexual. When Abigail left for Buffalo, her figure was full, yet slim. She was the envy of most women and the wonder of her sons. How often my brothers and I embarrassingly heard the veneration, "Your mother's a package; she's a real package."

Although we knew about mortality and accepted it on both an intellectual and primitive level, we now had to focus on the fact our mother was dying and perhaps within hours would leave us.

Her complexity had continued to surprise us right up until the time she left for Buffalo. It would have been impossible for any of us to describe her in a couple of glib, tossed-off sentences. If each of us had been compelled to do so, there is no doubt descriptions of three different women of various latitudes would have been the result.

Abigail never quite finished the task of creating herself; she was always a work in progress. In a thousand days of my childhood, at the point when I began to pay attention, she offered a thousand different mothers for my inspection. Growing up, I never had a clear sighting of her. The geography of my mother's character had boundaries I could never approach. She could smile one moment and make me think of the shy commune of angels; the next moment, the same smile could suggest an asylum for terrorists. With all of her psychological infirmities, she was always too complex for her sons.

Within her secret self, she constructed a unique masonry. She was easy to underestimate.

She looked upon her children as something to be cherished. It was extraordinarily rare for her to complain about her fate. She could not bring herself to admit, except during rare outbursts of candor, that anything was that unpleasant. There were times she was tired of feeling ill-made and transitory and just wanted to set the flags of her tomorrow at half-mast. Abigail could feel those periods of great sadness coming and warn us she was going away for awhile, but she'd be back. She was such a contradiction—suicidal and chronically depressed, yet she possessed a heroic glossary of optimistic phrases.

In public, she overdid happiness. She was militantly cheerful. Though we could be classified as indigent, she volunteered for every charitable function in Washington—both black and white—that would have her and didn't cost more than her time. In the town, she slowly became known as someone you could depend on in a pinch *when her mind was right.* It was not a very well-kept secret that she suffered from what people whispered were emotional problems, but she was harmless. Everyone considered her sweet, Christian, beautiful, industrious, and much too good for the circumstances she was in with three boys and no husband. She was all these things and an enigma to boot.

We received so many valuable gifts from our mother. She gave us a love of language and natural beauty, the ability to camouflage and delude without remorse, a survival instinct, fanatic obsessions, and a color blindness with the refusal to be stereotyped in a racial sense. There was also an unwitting attraction to danger, arrogance, honor, selfishness, self-righteousness, and belligerence to account for. Did we inherit those attributes from our father? James, Daniel, and I acquired all these tendencies in a deadly and varied mosaic of genes. In an outcry of pure bitterness, my mother would later sum it up by saying, "Lander, the lunatic; James, the fanatic; Daniel, the terror."

Abigail wanted us to be a family to be reckoned with. I was eight when our mother first got the job as a full-time downstairs day maid for the Fitch family. She informed us that she worked for very, very rich people. Mr. Fitch was the mayor of the town and the CEO of Washington Steel Company. Whenever she spoke of them, it was as though she was describing a family of some scrupulous peerage. The Fitch's were the nearest thing Washington had to a royal family, and she was proud to be part of their walled baronage.

In Washington, our status in town was set, but she refused to accept this painful social reality. As evidence of that, somehow, she managed to get herself nominated to the Washington League. Mrs. Parkinson's great-grandmother had founded the Washington League. In its charter, the stated purpose of the league was to initiate good works and worthwhile projects among all citizens of Washington. The women of the league were usually drawn from "remarkable women living within the borders of Washington." It was this final proviso that endowed my mother with the cheerful expectation that one day she would find herself inducted into full membership. What began as an aspiration soon turned to heartache. The membership committee unanimously rejected her nomination. In a withering summation that eventually reached my mother's ears, Mrs. Parkinson had said, "Abigail Duncan is definitely not league material." Not league material. How this delicate, summary phrasing must have devastated my mother when she heard it. She was not white or wealthy; those were shortcomings in herself that she refused to accept as thresholds for being a league woman.

Life in Washington was difficult no matter how resourceful my mother tried to be. Aside from her job with the Fitch family, which paid meager wages, her once-a-week housekeeping for Blaine Buckley, and the laundry she took in, there was not enough money to pay the bills and maintain our day-to-day welfare. From time-to-time, the electricity was turned off and the phone was disconnected. My mother's face looked vulnerable and worried beneath the soft light of kerosene. We were always out of coal during the winter, and food would often spoil because there was no money for blocks of ice for the icebox. When mice got into the plumbing, little hairs appeared in the kitchen tap. We never knew what was next. The teasing we got for the appearance of our clothes was well deserved. My mother tried to get a job in every store in Washington, but there were no openings or she was found unsuitable because of her history of mental illness, an insufficient formal education, or the lack of experience.

When James turned ten, we began our careers as gardeners, errand boys, or "handy" boys to earn a nickel any way we could. We scavenged and scoured for jobs. During the week of the Washington County Fair, all three of us worked cleaning up dung from the animals, picking up litter around the grounds, and other odd jobs that came our way. We grew into the rhythm of work, and became quite good at what we did. We learned industriousness and economy, but mostly humility.

From the time we were in control of the arithmetical principles of adding, subtracting, and making change, we each had paper routes and Saturday corners from which we sold the early edition of the Sunday *Pittsburgh Press* and *Sun-Telegraph*. James objected to any reference to it being *our* paper route—he was ten and it took considerable convincing and a little deceit to get the job. Our paper route ritual began at 5:00 AM on school days; our territory ranged far and wide, but mostly in East Washington. We were the objects of derision and jokes with the large canvas bags strapped to our backs and the overflow of papers stacked in the wagon we pulled behind us. The jangling and weight of the pennies, nickels, dimes, and quarters kept our mother repairing the holes in our pockets—until each of us got a change maker that we wore strapped to our waist.

We had almost a scholarly appreciation of coins. One of the advantages of being poor is that it takes very little money to gladden the heart. The Lincoln pennies that we collected in milk bottles, piggybanks, and socks were not negligible. One penny would buy a scoop of jelly beans or a licorice stick, five would buy a Hershey bar or Popsicle, six a Tastykake, and ten a ticket to the carnival. We attended knowing full well that we were upsetting our Adventist teachings about things that excite the imagination. Two hundred pennies, dutifully accumulated over weeks and packaged in four paper wrappers holding fifty each, could be exchanged at the Woolworth's five-and-dime book counter for a boy's lightweight adventure novel.

The coin wrappers were solemnly broken open, and each penny was respectfully counted by the saleswoman. Guilt accompanied our purchases since "books of romance, frivolous and exciting tales, sensational stories and myths and fiction of any genre" were off-limits. Again and again, we were confronted with salvation-inspired preaching against books filled with perversions of truth, misleading ideas, and false views of life or which fostered a desire for the unreal. It was yet another attempt to save us from our imagination.

To be denied the magic and wonder of the great childhood classics was an attempt to imprison our minds. James and I refused to abide by this hoax and read this forbidden literature in school and stealthily brought them into our house. When our mother discovered the books we had hidden, she admonished us with warnings that such books were a cunning device of Satan, who sought to divert our minds with soul-destroying deceptions. The Adventist church had a tight lock on our mother. "You don't have to go to a polluted fountain to satisfy your thirst for knowledge," she warned.

At the age of nine I realized that reading was a form of getting away that drove me, paradoxically, deeper into myself and my sense of possibility. Reading became my other place, something I had to hold like a secret. I remember the covetous excitement with which I stood in front of the section of biographies in the little school library that my third-grade class filed down to twice a week. I sought out books about inventors and pioneer heroes: Thomas Edison, Lewis and Clark, Jim

Bowie, and Sam Houston. Then I devoured all the books about Indian chiefs and warriors: Sitting Bull, Osceola, and Geronimo. Animals and dogs became a favorite: Rascal and Old Yeller.

One afternoon, kneeling down in a new section, I pulled out a book called *The Tower Treasure*, one of the first of the Hardy Boys series. And with that began a reading obsession that continued into the fifth grade. I read and reread the books—there were forty-some, I think. I borrowed them from the library, used money I earned to buy them, and sometimes stood in the Ward's Book Store and read, knocking off forty or fifty pages at a stretch, dreading the shoulder tap that would mean I had overstayed my patronage. The Hardy Boys series provided a complete and ongoing world of danger and intrigue offset by the clichés of the ideal home life that was distinctly absent at 142 Forrest Avenue.

Their town, Bayport, managed to condense the whole voluptuous larger universe, complete with gangsters, police, shady establishments, boathouses, deserted farmsteads, warehouses, train stations, worlds of all descriptions—everything required for every imaginable adventure. I entered a state of joyous trepidation. To have one of the books underway, safely secreted under my mattress, was to have a validation to immunity. Nothing seemed to matter—not even all the hardships. I had only to think of my book, the marker like a signpost showing me that road back in, and I would feel safe.

Dickens, Scott, and Kipling offered loftier excitements about growing up; I could not hurl myself into those other imagined worlds in the same way. Part of my Hardy Boys obsession had to do with my susceptibility to renderings of the boyhoods I saw around me. I was drawn by the mysteries, of course. But I was no less deeply compelled by the settings, images I derived of an ideal world for a boy. I loved the idea of those brothers with their lightly nubby loyalty, their constant interactions with their buddies, and the extraordinary freedom with which they went about their complicated and endlessly exciting business. Nothing could have been more different from the way I lived. When my brothers and I went out on our extended explorations and tiptoed along the dark paths in the woody section of Washington Park, I was also, in some elusive way, moving along in my life. I was stalking clues, developing possibilities, and James, while not much of a Hardy

Boys reader, was responsive. He accepted and amplified my suspicions; he embellished my notions of conspiracy. That he knew how to be a believer made our bond, in those early years, endlessly renewable.

But it wasn't just about the censorship of books. The net effect for us being raised in the Adventist faith was the sense of being chained to a strict dogma and its related practices that made us feel like prisoners. Our mother was the self-designated warden of our incarceration and relaxed the rules of our confinement only when it was convenient for her.

We were forbidden from going to dances, movies, the roller rink, carnivals, amusement parks, and other places that Adventists called "places of the devil's worship." The human body was believed to be the temple of the Holy Spirit and there was an impressive list of things considered as unclean, unnatural, unwholesome, unsuitable, un-this, and un-that. When we weren't in a fasting mode, the restrictions on diet exceeded any sense of temperance and moderation. The seemingly endless list of prohibitions included meat, pepper, salt, spices, pickles, tea, peanuts, cider, alcohol, coffee, butter, milk, eggs, sugar, and certain kinds of flour. We considered some parts of our persecution just plain stupid, such as the obsession with water that Adventists called *one of heaven's choicest blessings*. It was felt to be God's beverage of choice. We couldn't even have Kool-Aid.

Indian head pennies, Mercury dimes, and Buffalo nickels were all prized possessions. The Ben Franklin half-dollar and the Liberty fifty-cent pieces and quarters projected a potent magic to us. James and I treasured the Miss Liberty quarter—shameful to say—because of the erotic insight the reverse side provided. If it was turned upside down and partly covered with a knowing thumb, the wings and head of the flying eagle on the reverse side became striding legs and a penis.

We each had our own repository for our coins. James had a little tin box for his money that he showed off with an avid, ceremonial secrecy. My own, more meager hordes resided in a relatively frivolous piggy bank and a grinning red-tongued Mickey Mouse guarding a slotted treasure chest with a bottom that could be opened with a key. I had won the bank in a third grade spelling bee—the clinching word, I think, was "lonely." The disappearance of this quaint little bank, when I was in the sixth grade, constituted yet another of the inconsolable losses of my life. I resorted to an opaque glass milk bottle with a slot cut into the round tin lid as a replacement. I remember the satisfying noise the bottle made when it was weighty with change. Daniel had an identical bank, and I was convinced that he swapped banks occasionally.

My brothers and I understood money. More than that, we were trained in the hazardous complexities of understanding money at an early age. For instance, we learned money was better than poverty; we all need money, but there are degrees of desperation; money can either be abundant and very unreliable or reliable and very scarce; and money can be "the root of all evil" and easily wasted. While the rudiments of saving for a rainy day were imparted to us, the fact that most days were raining in our life made that fact a pecuniary blur.

Why we had to put 10 percent of our meager earnings into the collection plate never made much sense to us. We worked around that by sitting in the back pew so that we could easily excuse ourselves for that portion of the service. On one occasion, when we weren't paying attention and the plate was coming our way, we tried to fake our contribution and were lectured soundly after church by one of the deacons. He warned us we were putting God's blessings at risk.

Money worked in our house by way of a cash economy. Our mother's income went into a red-and-white recipe box that sat on top of the icebox. In addition, James and I were required to contribute five dollars each week from our paper routes and odd jobs to the family kitty. To dip into it, we had to stand on a kitchen chair. Our withdrawals were supervised. Even our mother's withdrawals from it were announced. When the box was empty, we were out of money— which was a common condition.

At one point, all three of us boys manned different Saturday corners. I had the A&P corner, James got Main Street, and Daniel took the Greyhound Bus Station. It was a ritual for us to pool our coins and count them. The various denominations were mounted in slick stacks. When they reached a certain height, James deftly slipped them into paper cylinders and smartly tamped them at both ends. When Daniel and I tried it, the coins rolled over the edge of the table onto the linoleum. A coin often ended upright on its edge. We all marveled at the willful, kinetic quality of the quarters that fell on the floor and unaccountably wobbled to their feet, as it were, before traveling across the floor as if seeking some other destination. A final tally was made and James distributed our proceeds in equal thirds. It was his idea that all of us had good nights and bad nights on our corners; this was a way to help each other. He said we were the Three Musketeers, "All for one, and one for all."

We considered Pennsylvania millionaires, Andrew Carnegie and Andrew Mellon, as folk heroes. But we did not have to go very far to see wealth. We lived amongst it in East Washington. We did not begrudge the tuxedoed personas their pillared estates, their lawns and swimming pools, their buffed and sometimes chauffeured luxury cars, and their giddy daughters in chiffon and pearls. To be among such well-endowed lives was pleasurable. It was similar to feeling coins swim through your fingers or imagining, as in some of those crime books we read, a suitcase full of bundled bills. Even with the bigotry, we maintained this ability to identify with the riches of our classmates and their families, which alleviated our own poverty by the vicarious enjoyment of their substantial assets.

I have often wondered if this had an effect on our strivings and lifted the ceiling for us as to what was possible. We refused to crack beneath the dire load of our poverty—although, at times, we were dangerously close. We found some solace in things we would hear that found their way to school or something we read in the *Washington Reporter*. It showed us that our wealthy neighbors were often foolish and not infrequently miserable. They suffered from ulcers, financial reversals, and discontents of excessive propriety; they were hostages to their fortunes, and prey to complications from which we were exempt.

My brothers and I learned other things about money. Similar to words and feelings, money's value is intangible. Yet, it can last; it doesn't have to flit away. Nor does it ask anything of its possessor. It melts away in the steady rise of our wants and needs. We have some control over that. It has warmth and extension. Rich or poor, a penny is a penny.

In some ways, the larger meaning of money—its social potency—was deliberately kept veiled by our circumstances. Like a secret weapon, it was a force that could send things spiraling fatally out of control. I was about ten years old before I heard us referred to as poor. Nigger, yes, but not poor. Poor? Until I was older, I didn't feel remotely poor. There were just lots of things we didn't have.

James's relentless industriousness attracted a wide audience of advocates and mentors willing to lend a hand of opportunity or offer advice. No one made a more significant impact on James's adolescent life than Dr. Wade. They met during the first week of summer vacation in 1951. James's plan to increase his paper route in East Washington had fallen flat. I tagged along and listened to him offer a noticeably rehearsed, but polite, greeting to begin his solicitation, "Would you like a subscription to the *Pittsburgh Press* daily newspaper delivered to your door?" Sometimes in mid sentence, before he could offer the week of free delivery, extol the virtues of the paper, or promise personal dependability—all of which he was prepared to do—the rejection was rendered. Door after door was closed. I admired his ability to take rejection. Maybe he didn't understand the satire in the previous week's sermon: *Blessed is the man who expects nothing, for he shall never be disappointed.*

James's resolve was strengthened by the promotion being offered to paperboys. Five new subscriptions would earn a bus ride, box lunch, and bleacher ticket to Forbes Field and the doubleheader between the Pirates and the Dodgers. He told me, "It's going to take some doing for both of us to get to go. That's ten new customers and so far we're batting zero."

We spent many hours listening to the radio broadcasts of the Pirates's games. We further entertained ourselves by pretending to be official scorekeepers and carefully documenting the box scores for each inning. James was a prisoner of the morning sports section and memorized its long, clean columns of statistics. Because of its heretic obsession with numbers, baseball was James's favorite season; each day was framed by the lucid numerology of box scores. He could recite daily statistics for the player and important facts about their careers. He was a walking baseball card.

Consistent with the circulation principle of neighborhood paper boy, our proximity to East Washington earned us route locations in its reclusive affluent borough. It did not matter that our home barely qualified—situated quite by accident on the East Washington side of the color line. As James saw it, he had the job by a precarious grace.

The streets were lined by chestnut and elm trees; branches from both sides of the street overlapped to form promenades. Stately homes in forms borrowed from the Victorian and revivalist styles were set far back from the street by expansive lawns and brick and rock walkways and driveways. Carefully coifed hedges separated each estate into its own private enclave. Doctors, lawyers, bankers, and executives of the steel, oil, glass, and gas companies resided in East Washington.

"Go out there and make opportunities out of obstacles," was our mother's standard and often repeated pep talk. But even at twelve, James needed no encouragement. He was tough and could seem to live without illusions and hold back disappointments. James was already engaged in the task of figuring out how to get beyond the first sentence. "Maybe I should change the order of my sales pitch and offer the free trial subscription first."

James knocked on a door with a small brass plaque that read *Dr. Nicholas Wade*. We were ushered to the back entrance by a woman dressed in a maid's uniform.

"What do you colored boys want?" asked the approaching voice.

I begged James to leave when I heard its vitriolic tone. He didn't budge, and I pushed myself as close behind him as possible. An old man appeared and sharply ordered us to state our business. James was interrupted in the middle of his revised pitch.

"What's in the news today?"

I relaxed knowing James always took a few minutes to read the first couple of paragraphs of the first four columns of the newspaper before beginning the deliveries. Unflappable, out came, in headline form, something about the coal miner's strike, the hydrogen bomb, France's objection to the Soviet recognition of Ho Chi Minh rule, and Winston Churchill's expected book on World War II. In closing, he added that the Pirates routed the Phillies, 11–2, and Dale Long had extended his home run streak to eight games. Sensing Dr. Wade's interest and having listened to the game the night before, James gave all the highlights. With his recitation on that ball game, he had earned his first new customer. Dr. Wade was an avid fan of the Pittsburgh Pirates and an instant fondness developed between them. Although it had its stormy moments, they always had their baseball to fall back on.

The doctor happened to be among the group of wealthy residents who had petitioned the Washington County Court to incorporate the town of East Washington into a separate borough. Formidable and respected around town for having led the drive to establish a hospital in Washington, he practiced and headed the board of directors for three decades.

Dr. Wade provided us with odd jobs around his estate. "His boys," he liked to call us, and sometimes he surprised us with his company. I could not find the same confidence and comfort level that James enjoyed with him. They engaged in repartee about the Pirates, the pennant race, and players around the league. He constantly quizzed James about baseball statistics and facts. On those rare occasions when he would catch James wanting for some piece of baseball trivia, he celebrated by saying, "Humble yourself, young man, at the feet of the all-time great fan." His stern countenance over the summer softened. He smiled more than he scowled and the foreboding wire-rimmed glasses that he wore made him look like someone's genteel grandfather. But he had no children or grandchildren, and his wife was dead. His voice was tremulous and hoarse; his carefully parted and combed hair and trimmed mustache were white. He had a potbelly, wore a hearing aid, and shuffled uncertainly. Some things did not change. His expression remained inscrutable. His pale blue eyes were small and set in a wide, bullish face; his stare was coldly foxy. The many lines around his eyes came from his smile, which appeared suddenly and evaporated just as quickly.

He was almost eighty-three, yet every word seemed well chosen and mordant. His commentaries were bright and swift summations of major themes. There was an insatiable quality to Dr. Wade's maneuvering of the conversation.

Working at his house during the week and sometimes on Sundays—Saturday was our Sabbath—he would invite us to join him on his veranda to listen to the game and have cookies and lemonade. Invariably, a heated discussion would break out. He leaned forward, positioning himself like a praying mantis. His eyes had the shining concentration of a predator. James became irate when Dr. Wade talked about "his rules" and what whites were supposed to be good at and what coloreds were supposed to be good at. "In football, whites play quarterback and coloreds play running back; in baseball, whites pitch and coloreds play the outfield; in track and field, anything under the quarter mile belongs to the coloreds."

James irreverently objected and called his views bigoted, racist, and prejudiced. The doctor enjoyed James's fierce defense and baited him. I'm not sure he even meant some of the things he said. "Why can't I talk about whites and coloreds as being different? Under the skin, we are not all the same." As a retired physician, he enjoyed playing devil's advocate with medical facts, thereby keeping James ruffled and defensive.

When Dr. Wade commented that any colored man a white passes on the street is just plain dumber, James got up and left. This started to happen with greater frequency. I would be left standing there, and he would devilishly chortle, "Tell your brother to come back and put up a fight." James always returned; the baseball brought him back. His greatest defense was himself. James had this self-reinforcing belief in his ability, a rare form of tunnel vision. "What about desire? You can't measure that and you can't trace it to differences between races." There were times when he was reduced to yelling, "I'm smarter than anyone in my class. I'm going somewhere with my mind. I just hope you're around and have to eat your words!"

James could fix lamps. He knew how to insert and screw down hook-shapes of copper wire into the terminals of a switch. He knew how to splice the wires of our Christmas lights when a bad socket made the whole string go dark. He somehow managed to get his hands on *Popular Mechanics* each month and had sent away for a make-it-yourself radio kit that he assembled to the point where we could hear static and a faint voice pulsing in and out.

We "inherited" Dr. Wade's defunct plug-in washing machine. He finally gave up on it and offered it to us. We pushed it home, nearly two miles, on a borrowed dolly. James went to work on it. After a few blown fuses, much to our mother's delight, he had that old, tub-shaped machine with a wringer of rubber running flawlessly. The wet clothes would emerge from between the two cylinders of white rubber like giant wrinkled tongues and slowly spill into the wicker clothes basket. I was enchanted by the powerful, rhythmic back-and-forth beating action, stirring up a mass of bubbles; by the smell of soap flakes, so strong it seemed to scour clean my sinuses; and by the woody, springy scent of the large wicker basket.

It was inevitable that some day I would stick my fingers in the wringer. In a quick rush, I felt the relentless pressure climbing toward my wrist and screamed in terror. A safety device popped the wringers apart even before my mother could dart around me and reach the release lever. In the way of childhood confusions, the look of horror that distended her face and the scolding she gave me afterward was lumped together with my moment of pain—as if she had caused it. Still, I remained an admirer of the process: the wash made its way through the wringer into the basket and up the cellar stairs through the bulkhead door into the backyard. There, the white bed sheets hung about me like the billowing walls of a fragile castle, a jungle palace I was exploring all by myself. A shift of breeze would cause the clothesline to lean in a different direction, so that my face was brought into abrupt contact with the towering, damp, light-flooded cotton. Handing up clothespins to my mother was one of my first ways of feeling useful and bonding with her. However, it did not register in the same way for her. The little clothespin basket had no fresh wicker smell; it had a musky darkness from being handled by so many hands, year after year. It was a little heavier than expected when you touched it, whereas the clothespins were lighter. With their two legs and flat knobs at the other end, the clothespins were smooth in my hands. With the aid of colored pencils, the clothespins could become staring, smiling, little men, wearing sailor hats and blue coats. They could be made to do tricks, stuck together like acrobats.

But no matter how we labored around town, we could not bring in enough money. Each year, things became worse: from the serious disrepair of the house to having acceptable school clothes to wear. We were made desperate by our mother's silent but explicit terror. It was understandable why she fell into her depressions and had to be hospitalized.

She would not let us tell anyone, not even Papa, of the seriousness of our dilemma and refused to take money from him. He would slip money to James to put in the "kitty." The amount of the subsidy we enjoyed from Papa was not inconsequential. It became painfully clear when he suffered a series of debilitating strokes and his miraculous intervention ceased. The loss of forever-present Papa—our underpinning, our foundation, our anchor and safety net—left us feeling vulnerable and defenseless to life's capriciousness.

Papa was passed among his eldest children for care. Our home was the exception; we couldn't even take care of ourselves. Papa required almost round-the-clock attention. Eventually, resources were pooled, and he was moved to a nursing home in Washington. Now we had our turn to help Papa. Abigail's contribution, which she willingly took on, was to oversee his care. Three weeks after his arrival, a succession of little strokes brought him to the point where he could not swallow. The doctor broached Abigail, "The decision is yours." His face was heavy, kindly, self-protective, and formal.

The decision was whether or not to move her father to Washington Hospital where he could be fed intravenously and his life could be prolonged. Seeking escape from this responsibility, Abigail called her sisters and brothers; they all agreed that not compromising their father's dignity was uppermost. The doctor seized Abigail's hand and pronounced with a solemn artificial clarity, "You have made a wise decision."

Abigail hated the nursing home with its cloaked odors, its incessant television, its expensive false order and hypocrisy of false cheer, its stifling vulgarity. "Well, aren't you the handsome boy!" the supervisor had exclaimed to Papa upon admittance and tapped him on the arm like a brash girlfriend. We spent many hours with our mother at the nursing home and occasionally held Papa's hand. It felt warm and strong, though he lay unconscious, dying. He was starving and dying of thirst. His breath stank. Yet the presence was still his. In his unconscious struggle for breath, his sallow face flitted, soundlessly muttering, into expressions we knew—the helpless raised eyebrows that preceded an attempt to be droll or a sudden stiffening of the upper lip that warned of one of his rare, pained, carefully phrased reprimands. His face was sinking in upon itself with the startled expression that mummies have; the distance between his raised eyebrows and lowered eyelids seemed enormous.

His hand would twitch, or my hand would come upon his pulse. Oddly, the sign of life horrified me. It was like the sight of roaches scuttling in the sink when, in the middle of the night, the kitchen light is suddenly turned on. Ten years old, Daniel was frightened by the nursing home. The heads of the dying bobbing amid white sheets as he strode down the hall was too much for him. On one visit, a little gauzy-haired, red-faced lady was strapped into a geriatric chair. She kept crying "help" and clapped her hands. She paused when we passed and then resumed, "help" clap, clap "help." Daniel ran out of the nursing home. He refused to go again.

Papa had never begrudged Abigail his time, ever, and she wanted not to begrudge him her company now. After announcing her presence in his deaf ear, she would settle herself by his side and hold his hand for hours. Dry and uncallused, his hand rested warm in his daughter's. sometimes his hand returned her squeeze or perhaps the agitation that passed across his face caused his shallow pulse to race. "Just relax," she would chant to him. "Relax. It's all right. I'm right here Papa. I won't go away."

Abigail came and went, marveling at the fury of her father's will to live. Abigail saw the force that had carved a shelter for his three daughters and two sons and had urged respectability upon them. His face, parched and unfed, grew rigid. His mouth made an O like a baby's at the breast. His breathing poured forth a stench like a stream of inexpressible scorn. His hand lived in hers. There were times when she could not make herself stay for very long. "Papa, I must leave for a minute," she would say and then flee. He could not die; she could not stay. As with the participants of a great and wicked love, there was none to forgive them save each other. Abigail had been raking leaves from our frostbitten lawn—thinking she should be with Papa—when a nurse called to notify us. Papa had died unobserved.

The world, which had made a space of privacy and isolation around us, gathered and descended in a fluttering of letters and visits, of regards and reminiscences. From the White House to the head of the NAACP, from presidents of Negro colleges to the U.S. Defense Department, from the national media to parishioners whose lives he touched, Papa's long, successful life was rebuilt in words before us.

The funeral was a rally of the surviving, a salute to a remarkable man who had passed away some time ago while his body was still alive. Family and friends honored him and cried. Elderly faces that had floated above Abigail's childhood, her father's old friends, materialized.

Abigail was kissed, hugged, caressed, and complimented. Yet she felt like Papa's executioner by not fighting to provide life support. There was no paradox, she saw. Everyone was grateful to Abigail. The world needed death. It needed death exactly as much as it needed life.

The fission of Abigail's unaltered pride made her incapable of asking anyone for help. She refused state aid programs to families with dependent children. However, she could not pay her bills at several of the stores that granted her a limited amount of credit to buy groceries. During those times, she simply refrained from going to town. She turned inward. Her silences became prolonged and troublesome, barely short of being debilitating enough to be hospitalized. She worked her garden in the backyard with a compulsive rage. Tentativeness settled over our house.

On the day before Thanksgiving 1953, a car pulled up to our yard and four immaculately dressed women approached the house. I opened the door to Mesdames Potter, Randall, Wright, and Parkinson, the four officers of the Washington League. Mrs. Parkinson asked if she could speak to Abigail.

My mother came to the door and something died in her eyes the moment she saw them. She dried her hands on her apron and asked them to come inside. "We can't stay long, Abigail. We have three other turkeys and bags of groceries to deliver by dark," Mrs. Parkinson said sweetly.

"I don't understand," my mother said as the four ladies seated themselves uncomfortably on the edge of the couch, their eyes darting about the living room. I watched as Mrs. Randall carefully adjusted her dress to ensure her skin not touch the fabric of the couch. I remember thinking, *I bet she's afraid of getting cooties.*

"Abigail, you must have heard that one of the functions of the league is to distribute turkeys at Thanksgiving to less fortunate families around Washington. We wanted to make sure you and your boys didn't go without," Mrs. Potter explained.

"There must be some mistake. My family is doing just fine. I thank you ladies for thinking of us." My mother controlled her anger with considerable difficulty. "There are many families in Washington who are in need of your charity far more than this one."

"Please don't think of this as charity, Abigail," Mrs. Wright implored. "Think of it as a gesture of goodwill among friends who are worried about you."

"Please, don't do this to me," my mother pleaded. "Please, I beg of you."

"Think of your children and their Thanksgiving. Don't just think of yourself."

James spoke and his voice quivered with rage, "Get out of our house."

"What a rude young man," Mrs. Randall said.

"My son asked you to leave."

"We are Seventh-day Adventists and vegetarians. It's against our religion to eat your old turkey," James yelled.

"Well, there are plenty of groceries here. Maybe one of your poor friends living up the street in those projects would take the turkey off your hands. We'll leave it up to you."

Regaining her composure with some difficulty, my mother said, "Leave the stuff out in the yard when you go."

"You made this very difficult for us, Abigail," Mrs. Parkinson said.

"Not as hard as you made it for me," my mother responded as the women got up to leave.

We listened as their car pulled away and then followed our mother out into the yard. We saw the tears of rage in her eyes as she stood staring at the turkey and groceries she had been granted as an act of charity and debasement by the Washington League. "They were waiting for this opportunity. They've been biding their time and waiting," she said. "I want you boys to remember this. They tried to take away our dignity. Never let something like this happen to your family when you grow up."

Strangely, I do not remember any Thanksgiving dinner that year. But I do recall what happened in late December. We found a dead raccoon in our backyard. My mother ordered James and me to remove it before it began to decompose and stink. At breakfast that morning, James just happened to read in one of our leftover papers, in the social column, that the Parkinson family was in Barbados for their annual winter vacation. It was Daniel who made the connection between the raccoon, the Parkinsons, and Barbados. But it was James who hatched the plan. Daniel and I were terrified and exhilarated by the boldness of his proposal, but neither of us wanted any part of it. James continued to urge us quietly about getting revenge on Mrs. Parkinson. We became mesmerized by his magnetic, but gentle eloquence. His decision was already made. He spent half the night enlisting us as recruits in our first real dance on the wild side.

We awoke an hour earlier than usual and slipped out of the house. Soundlessly, we folded the papers and proceeded to make our deliveries. We were carrying extra cargo in our wagon—the dead raccoon. We moved through the dark abandoned streets of East Washington toward the Parkinson house. We passed beneath the oaks that formed the leafless canopy along this distinguished neighborhood. The air was cold, and Christmas tree lights winked in some of the windows.

When we reached the Parkinson house, we set the raccoon down in the backyard, and James went around checking the windows. He shimmied up one of the columns and found a bathroom window unlocked on the second floor. Daniel and I heard the door open and saw James motion to us. We lifted the raccoon again and moved as quickly as we could up the back stairs. We went directly to the master bedroom, where James had thoughtfully pulled back the covers on Mr. and Mrs. Parkinson's immense four-poster bed. We laid the raccoon between the sheets and propped its head on a pillow and then covered it with the blankets. I turned the valve on the radiator full blast. Daniel found one of Mrs. Parkinson's sleeping bonnets and placed it rakishly on the raccoon's head. The room permeated with the foul stench. We completed the paper route and were home when our mother called us to breakfast.

After they returned from Barbados, the Parkinsons could not live in their home for weeks. The raccoon's decomposition had been ghastly and hideous in the extreme heat of the bedroom. The four-poster bed and the mattress were burned. My mother heard that no maid could enter the room for several weeks without vomiting. Mr. Parkinson promised a thousand dollars to anyone who could provide information leading to the conviction of the person or persons who had committed the heinous crime. An editorial appeared in the *Washington Reporter* regarding the incident. I have never seen my mother happier than when we drew her attention to that editorial.

Months earlier, the league had announced in a full-page newspaper ad that it was inviting all the women of Washington to make their submissions for the league's cookbook, which would contain the best recipes in the entire town. My mother viewed it as a splendid opportunity to impress the members of the league with her culinary skills and wasted no time submitting her recipes for approval. When compiling the cookbook, the league had refused to consider inclusion of the recipes she submitted. Shortly after the raccoon incident, we bought my mother a copy of the Washington League cookbook for her birthday.

The cookbook was a gift from the three of us. We could see the old look of hurt and disappointment in my mother's eyes as she held the book in her hands. The gift troubled her and we could tell she was wondering if we were making fun of her.

"Open it to the back page," James said. "We wrote you a recipe."

Raccoon chez Parkinson

One raccoon, preferably ripe
Choose an early morning when it's still dark
Make sure mother is sleeping
Head for East Washington
Be careful that no one sees you
Find an open window
Unlock the back door
Place the raccoon in the four-poster bed
Turn the heat on high
Simmer raccoon until done, usually two weeks
Remove done raccoon and evacuate
Putrid and repugnant odor guaranteed

Happy Birthday, Mom

With Love,
James, Lander, and Daniel

At first, my mother scolded us—screaming that she was raising us to be decent, law-abiding citizens and not hoodlums. She threatened to talk to Mr. Parkinson and collect the thousand dollar reward. She told us we had to turn ourselves in to the sheriff and that we had disgraced the family. This would make us the laughing stock of Washington. Then she giggled like a schoolgirl and could not help herself. She grabbed the three of us together and hugged us in a rare, physical embrace. Then she whispered, and there was both fury and exaltation in that whisper, "My kids are something. Abigail Duncan may be nothing, but by God, her kids are something."

— Chapter Fourteen —

Daniel relieved me and I noticed we were instinctively obeying an innate chronology, taking turns from oldest to youngest. Other family members who spelled us occasionally interrupted our rotation.

As we sat in the waiting room, the weight of my brothers' gazes was almost too much for me. My exile had changed their understanding of me, and I could feel their morbid curiosity. They no longer felt easy in my presence, nor I in theirs. In some way we all felt measured, discarded, and dismissed.

At 8:00 PM, the doctor gathered us together for a final grim prognosis. The critical seventy-two hours had become twenty-four. We stood uncomfortably before him like prisoners before a judge famous for his harshness. His words frightened us.

We did not leave the hospital until two in the morning. Ann had left the front door unlocked for me. Unable to sleep, I showered, shaved, put on fresh clothes, and returned to the hospital by cab. James and Daniel were already there and it was only 5:00 AM. Emotional and physical exhaustion, tension, and stress had frayed our nerves.

There were some exchanges between James and Daniel. At times, James seemed wound as tightly as a watch. Daniel, however, had some inner coolant that kept his psyche from overheating. The tension between them hung like a power line. At one point I heard Daniel say, "You talk to me like I'm still a little boy."

"You'll always be my baby brother," James said into the newspaper he was reading.

After that exchange, Daniel separated himself from the rest of us and moved to the window watching the sparse traffic pass by the hospital. He gave off an impenetrable aura of solitude and danger. The room was emotionally charged. Daniel just stared without malice and with perfect equanimity. I approached him cautiously with an invitation to join me for a cup of coffee at the kiosk in the hospital lobby.

As we walked, he described in vivid detail a visit to mom during her hospitalization a few weeks earlier. "I was asleep on a chair in the corner and woke up when I heard her cry out. A nurse was standing by her bed fiddling with the IV when mom started to vomit uncontrollably. As the nurse wiped the vomit from her gown and cleaned it off her face and arms, she squeezed the nurse's wrist. Mom continued to vomit again and again. Mom whispered that everything was breaking up and coming apart. Her breath was ragged and coarse.

"She said she needed a shower—she was a mess and had a bad smell. The nurse helped her frail body off the bed. Mom's legs collapsed when her feet touched the cold linoleum floor. The nurse, a large woman, lifted her from beneath her armpits and carried her like a rag doll to the bathroom. The tears flooded down her cheeks and she whimpered in humiliation and pain. There was a terrible stench in the room; I saw a trail of diarrhea across the hospital room floor. I heard the spray coming from the showerhead and thought how courageous she was. When she returned to the room, a towel was wrapped around her head like a turban and she had on a fresh hospital gown. The nurse helped her to a chair, stripped the bed and proceeded to quickly change the sheets, pillowcases, and blankets. She then helped mother back into bed. That's when the nurse realized that I was awake. She gave me a quick glance, smiled, and went about reinserting the IV and chemo. She cleaned the trail of excrement from the floor with some disinfectant. I could never do her job.

"When she left the room, I went into the bathroom and puked. That's when I saw the tufts of mom's hair lying on the floor in the shower stall. I went down to the gift shop and bought bunches of flowers so that she'd awaken to the smell of roses and lilacs. I wish I could have disposed of that last clear bag of chemotherapy that hung above her bed." With horror in his voice, he said, "You ought to know what that chemotherapy did to our mother. She couldn't keep food down. She wouldn't eat anything because she threw it right up. It took everything out of her and was killing her from the inside out. I pleaded with James and the doctor to discontinue the chemo. They kept repeating that it was her only chance."

Daniel shared the conversation he had with her when she awakened in the morning. "Her lips were chapped and feverish, and she acknowledged having thought it was all over. When I told her she was going to be just fine, she told me she wasn't going to walk away from this and everyone should stop pretending. She thought she would be more afraid than she was, although at times her fear nearly doubled her up. Mostly, she said she felt a great sense of relief, of resignation.

"She admitted to making our lives hard and raising three boys who all seemed unhappy because there was something cracked or missing in our family. Lander, she singled you out as being the most angry. Every time she tried something, it was the first time she ever did it—a girl who had to learn everything on the run. Trial and error was the only school she attended.

"Lander, can you imagine that clear, foul-smelling chemotherapy dripping into her vein? It burned as it entered her body and killed every blood cell it touched, good and bad. Her body turned inward on itself and her vital signs wavered. The doctor monitored each step of the descent. He took mom all the way down to the point of death and then stopped the chemotherapy treatment and left a withered tormented body. At least, she was free of all that poison and its side effects."

I was beginning to piece the chronology of events surrounding my mother's illness and the undertone of conflict between James and Daniel. After her prior hospitalization, she had returned to the house on Forrest Avenue to live out the time that was allotted her. According to Daniel and James, she gave them lessons in the art of dying well. Although everyone knew Abigail was complicated, unknowable, and difficult, none of them knew exactly how courageous a woman she was until she began the business of dying.

Ann had given Abigail her old bedroom and made her feel like the head of the household and not an escapee from Buffalo and her marriage. She made the house comfortable as friends and acquaintances dropped by to say their farewells when they heard the news of Abigail's health. To their surprise, they came to a house that was not filled with sorrow. As was her secret to survival, she charmed her visitors with her vivaciousness.

The conflict between James and Daniel centered on the continuation of the chemotherapy. Daniel bitterly complained it should have been discontinued much earlier. He argued that our mother was in more danger of being killed by the chemotherapy than by the leukemia. James would not relent. Because her white blood cell count was off the charts, he supported her being put on the most powerful chemo available.

The waiting room began to fill—Ann, Fletcher, and Margaret, neighbors, people from the church, Mrs. Fitch, and others I did not recognize. Although they were not permitted in her room, many came to the waiting room to pay their respects and hold a vigil.

Doretha had her hands full in Ohio. Jimmy struggled with the disabilities he suffered from the Klan beating he took in Arkansas. He missed a lot of work; Doretha had to maintain full-time employment to keep things afloat. I must have been nine or ten the last time I had seen her. I ran into her when she first arrived at the hospital. I knew it took moving heaven and earth for her to be there. She gave me a proud unabashed smile—her cleft palette had been surgically repaired. For an uncomfortable few seconds, we just stared at each other. She seemed as startled by my appearance as I was with hers. "Lander?" She quizzically intoned. We hugged as I thanked her for her presence and support. *What had caught her attention that made her stare at me like that?*

The number of flowers, potted plants, gifts, and cards surprised me. Most were forbidden in the intensive care unit, so my brothers and I fanned out through the hospital dropping off bouquets and arrangements to cheer the dreary rooms of other patients. It moved us greatly that Abigail's life had not gone unnoticed by her townspeople, even after her seven-year absence. As her children, we knew all about Abigail's strangeness and insecurity, but we also knew about the unstinting nature of her sweetness. She had camouflaged the vinegar factory in her character with a great honeycomb along the sills and porches of her public self. Abigail possessed a small genius for the right gesture. She had done thousands of things she did not have to do only because they felt comfortable to her. She had been prodigal with unnoticed, artless moments of making people happy to be alive.

At our command post in the waiting room, my brothers and I received people—some we had never met before. Others, such as Mr. Bingham, our mailman, was one of the suitors Abigail had rejected. With the heroism of the well-publicized postal service slogan, he heroically plodded his way up and down Forrest Avenue twice a day, leaning at an angle from the weight of his leather pouch. On our lucky days, he delivered books and secret decoder rings and signed photographs of sports' stars.

If my diffuse childhood happiness could be distilled into one moment, it would be the day of a snowstorm around Christmas. On that mid-afternoon day, the outdoors had already darkened under the cloud cover, tinsel and dried needles fell off the holiday evergreen in the living room onto the miniature landscape below. My mother had concocted snow out of cotton and flakes of Lux soap. Toothpicks stuck into bits of green-painted sponge became trees and habitation. Fragile store-bought papier-mâché houses gathered around the speckled mirror of a pond. Around the three-rail track, my blue Lionel train ran with its obedient speed shifts and translucent smell of lubricating oil. Suddenly, a noise jolted me—it was the clacking of the letter slot that announced Mr. Bingham had dredged through the blizzard for the second time that day to deliver the mail. It seemed to confirm a version of the reality I precariously clung to; we were safe and lovingly regarded from on high as the ageless figures in a shaken snow globe.

Mrs. Fitch was uncommonly gracious. She liked Abigail, and, early in their relationship, she abandoned the protocol she maintained with the other maids. She enjoyed telling Abigail some of the secrets and scandals that had disfigured the histories of the old families of East Washington. Some of those secrets floated about like sawdust from a termite-ridden beam. There was nothing like a scandal to dull the sheen and vigor of some of those grand old East Washington names.

It did not surprise me to see Mrs. Liggons around the hospital. She had lived across the street from us on Forrest Avenue. The day we arrived in Washington, she became our nosy, irascible fairy godmother. Like Papa, when life seemed to be getting the best of us, she was most present. As children, her elevated status was directly related to her television. She was the first neighbor on our street to have one. After getting beyond the hard, flat tone of antagonism and distrust in her voice that sounded angry, we realized she was a lovely and kind old woman who considered it her calling in life to monitor the movements of everyone in the neighborhood. So any question was usually answered with another. I would find ways to watch her television, even if it cost me an errand or two—like going to the neighborhood grocery store to get her snuff which she dipped with regularity. Three Thistle was her brand.

Queen for a Day was one of her favorite programs. I would sit with her on the sofa and listen to the women whose children were crippled by polio, whose houses had been struck by lightening, or who had suffered the death of a loved one or a divorce. The one with the saddest life and loudest applause from the audience traded her troubles for a velvet cape, roses, and modern appliances. I clapped along with Mrs. Liggons and the studio audience—longest and hardest for the women who broke down and cried in the middle of their stories. I made my hands sting for these women. I always thought my mother was a perfect candidate for that television show except she would never admit—at least in public—that her life was sad or we had troubles.

Mrs. Liggons was the only adult I knew who insisted I call her by her first name, Alta. However, I was only to use it in her house when no one was listening. When my mother was not at home, Alta could always be counted on for mercurochrome and Band-Aids for my skinned knees and a Tootsie Roll from her hidden jar. Early on, she had taken an interest in my penmanship and cursive writing. "Not bad for an eight-year old," she would tell me after her inspections. This was a woman who had to sign her name with an "X." She never learned to read or write.

We had no illusions about ever having the luxury of a television in our home. But a radio was a different matter. I wonder if we could have survived our childhood without the radio. Those radio programs allowed us to fly, let bullets bounce harmlessly off our chest, beat up whoever picked on us, and enabled us to become invisible. James was my accomplice; we each found our own escape, our own reassurances in listening to the radio.

The world we found was not identical, but many compass points were the same. James liked the comedy of stingy Jack Benny or the pompous Gildersleeve. I delighted in the late afternoon serial heroes and heroines. We shared a fondness for the nighttime killers, crooks, and detectives. At times, various shows rivaled in the same time slot. But it was James who decided if we would ship out with Terry and the Pirates or leap tall buildings with Superman, be copilot to Sky King rather than Captain Midnight, occupy the territory around Gene Autry's Melody Ranch or take up residence in London with Sherlock Holmes. I did not protest his choices. He could tune the radio better than anyone. His kick or smash with his fist cleared the air of all the crackle and hiss.

Once tuned, we lay on the cold linoleum floor in the living room in front of the hulking four-foot high console with its silky walnut finish and intricately carved wooden frame over the cloth-covered speaker. It was the best piece of furniture in our home and took up what seemed to be a third of the living room space.

Blaine Buckley, the chain-smoking, heavy drinking washed-out blond owner and operator of the only cab company in town, had given the console to my mother in exchange for her housecleaning and laundry services. It turned out to be a bargain since Mrs. Buckley withheld only one day's wages of eight dollars. Although the phonograph worked, Mrs. Buckley had expressed her irritation with the constant static and repeated often that she was going to dump it. My mother was quick to offer the solution that she would take it off her hands.

Sometimes I think my mother endured this extra job, fitting it in on Sunday afternoons, just for the day when Mrs. Buckley would follow through on her threat. She despised working in a home she referred to as a "den of iniquity" and vilified this woman as a foul-mouthed, loose, filthy drunk. By her own admission, she drove away three husbands and a number of housekeepers. On Sundays, my mother would find Mrs. Buckley blacked out on her bed soaking in her own urine.

James and I earned a few extra dollars at the cab company by cleaning up the garage once a week. The two of us shared another viewpoint on Mrs. Buckley. We were in awe as we watched and listened to her dispatch cabs nonstop—a cigarette always hanging out of her mouth—all over town. It took awhile, but one evening, two of Mrs. Buckley's drivers showed up in a cab with that RCA console hanging out of the trunk. They wore their gold and navy-blue cab uniforms, making them look like refugees from a military junta. They ascended the rickety stairs sideways. Although my mother was not the type to tell other people their business, men particularly, she warned them to be careful. They plugged it in and began to do things to it as though they were uncertain it had survived the bumpy transport. Condescendingly, one of the men in a salacious disrespectful tone said to my mother, "Okay, girlie, twist this button here to get the record player to work. Like this." He put his callused hand on my mother's hand, between her fingers, and then turned a plastic knob. My mother was too excited to take offense. She pulled away and came back with a record. I was disgusted and glared at the man; he returned my look with a sinister grin. He clicked the speed on the turntable to 78, plunked the record through the spindle, and after a little static, out came a velvety voice "… *heavenly shades of night are falling, it's twilight time* …."

I cannot recall ever seeing my mother so vibrantly alive and ecstatic. "Thank you, Lord! Thank you, Lord! Hallelujah!" she kept saying as she lifted her apron to wipe the tears. Finally, she could listen to those 78s—The Ink Spots, Nat King Cole, The Mighty Clouds of Joy, Sarah Vaughan, Etta James, Ella Fitzgerald, Della Reese—that she had rescued from rummage sales.

For James and me, the console was an alternative to the small plastic set in our room with the big yellow dial that we would listen to at night with our heads under the covers. It remained another one of the mysteries of the Duncan house why our mother scrutinized and policed the books we read but gave us unfettered access to radio programs. The only restriction: the radio had to be off from sundown on Friday to sundown on Saturday—our Sabbath.

While in the waiting room and greeting visitors, Daniel told James and me about McNair. He called it five years of a living hell in Buffalo, which was why he joined the air force right after graduation. McNair refused to help him with college and would not let him live at home to attend the University of Buffalo or Buffalo State College.

McNair appeared at the waiting room door clean-shaven and impeccably dressed. He stood erect, his eyes swept the room like a raptor surveying an acre of hunting ground for prey.

Daniel sat down next to me and instructed, "Count to four and then inhale." The smell of English Leather cologne stormed my nostrils. Daniel continued, "That smell brings back everything that was wrong about our life in Buffalo. English Leather was a sign McNair was going to try to clean up his act and not drink for the next several days. He had some kind of internal barometer that registered when he had crossed some line of conduct that required fine-tuning. He wasn't just an alcoholic; he was a complicated alcoholic. He used sobriety as a weapon of surprise. McNair would suddenly stop drinking, splash himself with cologne, and give mom reason to hope that life would be better with him. Eventually, she learned never to trust a sober McNair."

"Living in the same house with that man must have been hell," I sympathized. "And to think, I was jealous that you were living with him and mom."

James began to move about the waiting room, jangling his keys in his pocket so loudly that all eyes turned on him. Even during our Washington years, he thought by conducting himself with restraint and dignity, he would be spared the more baroque and unbridled excesses of our family's behavior. We always embarrassed him. He sought immunity from our extravagances and lack of caution or reserve. James longed for dignity and thought that was precious little to ask. He knew our family was capable of anything, particularly mother and Daniel.

Daniel walked me a few feet away from James and continued to hold court. "I get physically sick when I smell that stuff. I swear I do. Mother bought him a new kind of aftershave lotion. Think he ever wore it? Hell, no!"

He then lowered his voice and directed his assault on James. "He baits me. You've witnessed a couple of times today how he drives me crazy. It's subtle, but there's an undertone that's barely perceptible. He's always construing what I say as something negative. It's always disapproval—an editorial, a commentary that's disparaging. What you see is what you get. You know that about me. I've always been that way."

The door opened at the end of the room and Dr. Leyton walked in. Abigail had checked into the hospital as Mrs. Duncan. It was evident that McNair was more than a little upset when Dr. Leyton announced to the silenced room, "Mrs. Duncan is losing ground. You may want to call your minister."

James understood the gravity of the situation. I looked in his direction and was stunned to see tears in his eyes. Tears were rare in that severe treasury where he stored his grief.

I began to feel the roots of exhaustion curling into the deepest tissues of my body. I stood up, restless, eager to move around. As I walked down the corridor, James followed me and we continued walking until we were standing outside the main entrance. Concern was written all over his face as he stated flatly, "We should call the church and get Reverend Butler out here to administer last rites."

Although I had issues with Reverend Butler and the church, I agreed with James and walked to a bank of telephones in the lobby. The rectory secretary informed me that Reverend Butler was in a counseling session. I gave her the abridged version of what was going on. She assured me the reverend would return my call as soon as he was free. I gave her the number and told her I would be waiting by the phone. Ten minutes later, the telephone rang. Before I could get a word out, Reverend Butler registered his infuriation, "Why wasn't I notified earlier? Would you mind coming and getting me? All the church vehicles are in use. I need to be there for Abigail."

* * * * * * * * *

A year after we arrived in Washington, my mother went through some kind of conversion. For her, it was a perilous and invigorating voyage on weedy, doctrinal seas. People calling themselves missionaries came to our home and spent several hours proselytizing about what they called "embarking on a well-worn road of personal and family well-being." Maybe she was seduced by their doctrine of a "carefully guarded Christian home as the surest safeguards against the corruption of the outside world … and the family as a place of refuge for the tempted youth." Perhaps she felt she would get help from the Adventists in raising three boys alone. She thought our conversion from Methodist to Adventist would mean some automatic improvement in our circumstances. She would learn slowly, and painfully, there was nothing stranger or more alien around Washington than Seventh-day Adventists.

My mother came to her roaring faith with her ignorance shining and intact. She knew nothing of that immense, intricate architecture that supported Adventism. She learned about it piecemeal, a tenet at a time. Her deeply religious faith stalked her through days and nights of despair. When it finally chose to pounce, she was ready for it and let herself, and us, be devoured like lambs. Readiness is the opening God needs. And she moved quickly with us in tow into the netherworld of prayer and Seventh-day Adventism.

How often we repeated the ritual. When the hymn was done, the preacher told some version of the story of the narrow gate; the strict accounting; the raked, leveled, and weeded ground of the Promised Land toward which we all traveled in a sure and certain hope of the resurrection. The worst part was staying for the baptisms and the feet-washing ordeals.

When it was our time to be baptized, there was considerable anguish around our house. Not one of us could swim. The thought of being submerged as part of the ceremony had us trembling. We were sure God was going to finally get us for all the many things we thought we had gotten away with. God certainly was going to take issue with our stealing his money.

One evening a week, we were required to solicit for the extensive missionary programs. We carried a container into which money was to be dropped. A short speech was offered to whoever answered the door: "Good deeds are twice a blessing, benefiting both the giver and the receiver of the kindness. Would you like to give to our good works?" Occasionally, we acted on the temptation to keep some of the collection for ourselves to buy candy.

So sure that we were in for it, we hid when the ceremony commenced. We made quite a commotion when we were found by several of the elders and wrestled to the baptismal.

James reasoned God did not visit his vengeance upon us because he had a sense of fair play, he had done plenty of bad stuff to us ... and the score was now even. More than anything else, the Seventh-day Adventists laid a foundation of pure guilt inside us and raised a temple in our soft center. Floors were paved with guilt. Statues and replicas of Jesus were carved out of great blocks of guilt. We always acted as though guilt was something tangible, something we carried around in our pockets. And our pockets were always full.

The Seventh-day Adventist Church of Washington was located in an isolated area on the edge of town. The campus was comprised of the main chapel, administrative offices, classrooms, a large activity center, and several guest cottages. It had been a refuge for us when my mother was either hospitalized or incapacitated at home with her depression. There were periods when life was suffocating us; we could find a safe haven and escape on the Adventist campus. We would stay in one of the guest cottages and heal our broken spirits by going to church each day for Bible study and playing around the vast wooded grounds. My mother would walk in those woods with Reverend Butler for hours. I grew up believing my mother was in love with this baffling and quiescent man.

I volunteered to get Reverend Butler, relishing a respite from the hospital drama. The car moved through pools of undisturbed shade, giving me a lost feeling. As I turned into the long driveway leading to the rectory, I spotted Reverend Butler waiting beside the bell tower that rendered hourly chimes. We exchanged handshakes. I opened the passenger door for him, and he slid into the seat with a polite, but chilly, "Thank you."

He was a tall man, built like a heron. His face had a lived-in and tortured look with flesh like white asparagus. He seemed vaguely off balance. He always seemed maladroit and overcautious with his parishioners. To my mother, Reverend Butler was an indisputably holy man. But to my brothers and me, he made faith seem melancholic. As the only black members of the church, we thought he was afraid of us, as though we were those heathens he talked about in his sermons that needed to be saved. He avoided all eye contact with us as we got older. I headed the rental car I borrowed from James toward the same roads that had brought me to him. He was so jumpy you would have thought I was driving him to a whorehouse.

During the drive, he spoke very little and acted oblivious to my presence. As we got closer to the hospital, he found his voice. "Do you miss God?" he asked.

The pure presumption and simplicity of the question startled and angered me. How did he know I had lost my faith? Or perhaps he expected a rebuttal and confirmation that God was very much in my life. I resented the misdirection and obtuse approach he took with me. "Why do you ask?"

"You were a very religious boy once."

"I believed in the tooth fairy then, too," I said with uncharacteristic derision. "But, of course, I had solid proof from that nickel underneath my pillow."

"Before your mother left for Buffalo, she came to see me with a very heavy heart. She didn't want to leave you behind and was going to call off the marriage. I encouraged her to go. It was a difficult recommendation. She needed the love of a man in her life more than you needed the physical presence of a mother. I promised her I would look after you. You refused to take my calls and would not even come down from your room at the boarding house when I came to visit. You never came to church. And then, you were gone."

"That was some decision you helped her make. Who were you to say what I needed? Who tells someone to leave a child behind?" I ruefully questioned.

"You're angry with me, I understand. But God, what of him?"

"We're not on speaking terms."

"Why?"

"I needed my mother. I wasn't ready for her to let go of me. It's easier to blame him."

"That's an odd take, Lander."

I looked over at the thin-faced man with his profile of a minor saint. His gauntness gave him a fierceness his soft voice lacked. "We thought our mother was having an affair with you when we were younger. We were all sure of it."

Reverend Butler smiled but did not look shaken by the revelation. "You were too close," I continued. "There was always something strange and unspoken when you two got together—whispers and touching of hands, going off together in the woods. You would not be the first man to fall to my mother's beauty. We thought you were the reason she didn't take interest in other men. James thought you were taking advantage of your privilege and our mother's substantial vulnerabilities. He always distrusted you. But he's the one who advised I call."

"Your brother has always been insolent and disrespectful," a slightly perturbed Reverend Butler fired back. "He confronted me on one occasion with unfounded accusations and what he described as proof that Abigail and I were lovers. How naïve and impertinent you both were in these unchristian assertions. Neither of you knows the damage your petulance caused your mother as well as myself."

"What are you talking about?" I asked.

"You figure it out. I'm through with this conversation."

* * * * * * * * *

I was aware of the evidence for his assertion. It first presented itself on a Columbus Day weekend. I was eleven years old. The church owned a big wheat-yellow farmhouse with a barn and twenty acres for family and congregation retreats, conferences, and workshops. It was located about 120 miles north toward West Virginia. We were one of the six families invited by Reverend Butler for a getaway of "autumn reflections and renewal of the spirit."

The church van had picked us up and threaded its way out of the crowded highways and then smoothly northeast, across the Ohio and Allegheny rivers onto the winding state roads. We passed towns much smaller than Washington. We noted their irregular, casually mowed lawns and red-painted country stores advertising the Fudge Factory or the Pumpkin Patch, which showed a sharp-edged charm, a stagy, calendar-art appearance. The leaves were glorious. There were entire valleys and mountains of them. Showy maples in strident pinks and scarlets, the clangorous gold of the hickories, and the accompanying brasses of birch and beech could be seen on both sides of the road. Rise after rise, this heavenly tumult was tied to the earth only by broad bands of evergreen and outcroppings of granite.

We were excited about the weekend excursion, none more so than our mother. We arrived and felt graced by the natural splendor. The dirt driveway—ruts worn into the lawn and given a dusting of gravel—came in at right angles off an unmarked macadam road. Several of the families had already arrived and were standing on the side porch when we pulled up. My brothers and I uncoiled from the confinement of the car and were met with a pleasant reign of confusion. Piecemeal unloading and a swirling of people back and forth finally culminated in some instructions from a paternal sounding Reverend Butler, "It's girls' and boys' dormitories. At the head of the stairs, men turn right, women left, boys twelve and older out in the barn. Each man will split his weight in wood. Each woman is responsible for one lunch or dinner. Breakfast is a free-for-all."

I remember this trip vividly. The air was deliciously crisp and dry. The sounds were fewer and different. They were individual noises: a single car passing on the road, a lone crow scolding above the stubbly side field, a single window sash clicking back and forth in the gentle wind. Even the smells of the house were different: linoleum, ashes, split wood, plaster, and a damp cellar with its own characteristic scent. The scent rose through the floorboards and followed the steep, wear-rounded stairs to the second floor where the younger children and their sleeping bags settled in the tangle of middle rooms. For the adults, two large bedrooms were set up as same-sex dormitories. Suitcases became claim markers.

Abigail did not bring a sleeping bag, and her suitcase followed Reverend Butler into his private bedroom downstairs. It was not clear that anyone noticed but James. He brought it to my attention. Abigail seemed to be familiar with the farmhouse and its surroundings. But when had she been there and how could we have not known?

In addition to the adults, there were sixteen children; three dogs, Fritz, Toby, and Wolf; and two cats. A long-haired gray feline with extra toes appeared throughout the house in the strangest places, in locked rooms and dresser drawers, like an apparition. Several teenagers, including James, were embarrassed to be in attendance.

Reverend Butler and my mother collected all the children and took us on what they called a leaf walk. We filed diagonally through a field into the long strip of woods along the creek, leaving the barn behind us on the right. The sound of the cars on the road could barely be heard. Abigail was in her glory. Reverend Butler gazed at her adoringly and let her do the talking. She had learned so much about nature from her mother and Arnetta.

Abigail gestured up and around her before saying, "We've come all the way up here to admire the bright colors; above all, the turning leaves of the maple tree, particularly the sugar maple, from which we get maple syrup. But all the trees contribute. The stately beech can be recognized by its smooth gray bark. The birch family, which is especially known for its white, or paper birch, from which the Indians used to make …"

"Canoes," several of the kids said almost in unison.

"The last trees to let go of their leaves are the oaks," Abigail continued. She picked up an oak leaf and held it out to impress upon us its lobed, deeply indented shape. "Even in the winter snows, the oak will cling to its old brown leaves. The first tree to let go of its leaves tends to be another giant of the forest—the ash. Its leaves turn an unusual purplish-blue color, unlike anything else; then suddenly, one day, the leaves are gone."

Reverend Butler chimed in, "Standing here, who can see a leaf fall?"

No one spoke. A minute passed. No leaf fell.

"If we stand here long enough," Reverend Butler conceded, "or if there was a wind or a hard rain, we might see the moment that the leaf begins to fall. But normally, that moment happens unobserved, that moment when the root of the stem, where the bud once was, decides the time has come to let go. But it happens." Reverend Butler looked upward and lifted his arms as if he were delivering a sermon. We all grew still, expecting him to pull something out of the air from the reds and golds trembling around us. "Nobody sees it happen, but it does. For suddenly, it seems, the woods are bare."

We returned from the leaf walk, feeling proud of our mother. At the sounds of food being prepared in the kitchen, we gathered like birds at a tray of seeds and ate our share of peanut butter and jelly sandwiches. It did not escape James's notice that Reverend Butler and our mother had withdrawn to his downstairs bedroom and shut the door. James was agitated by Abigail's disappearance and kept looking around for her return. I was inhaling my second sandwich—my eternal fear of running out of food—when one of the mothers warned me to leave room for the traditional big vegetarian hot dog and chili dinner.

Abigail and the reverend emerged in time for the softball game that was organized on the side field. Everyone played. As the sun began its descent, people drifted toward the house.

Standing in the long, narrow living room, one of the parishioners remarked about the need to repair the ceiling, which drooped in the center like the underside of an old bed, before the whole darn thing collapsed. A fresh fire was built of dry and seasoned logs from the wood box beneath the stairs.

Toward 7:00 PM, the children were fed and then scattered to the rooms upstairs or out to the barn. The adults retired to the living room after dinner for Bible study and a discussion on family values. Above their heads, on the swaybacked ceiling, footsteps scurried and rustled like those of giant rats. This weekend invited us to make our own societies and exist like a pack of shadows in the corners of the "grown-up fun" that had James in a torment.

I could not fall asleep; the noise from below was too great. Spread out on the floor in sleeping bags, all the other kids fell asleep swiftly; many snored or made strange noises. The most spectacular was a nasal arpeggio that encompassed octaves that ran up and down the scale. A boy about my age plugged steadily away, his rhythmic wheeze like a rusty engine that would not die. A few feet away from my face, Daniel demonstrated his odd talent of coughing incessantly in his sleep without waking himself. And, when at last, things concluded and the adults began to clatter up the flight of stairs, I still could not sleep. I heard some faint, halting footsteps. One of the cats had pushed open the door and was nosing about. I strained my eyes and saw it was the gray one with extra toes. I reached out with my foot and nudged the door shut again. The various sounds of people in the house ebbed in little stages into quiet, into sleep: twenty-seven other human beings— including the boys in the barn.

The next morning, smells from the kitchen penetrated the room, my nostrils, my brain. Most of the kids were already up, the day was well advanced. I must have fallen asleep after all. The house moved with activity. One of the mothers bossily prepared breakfast. She flipped wave after wave of pancakes two at a time with an extra large and long aluminum spatula. I was grateful she volunteered to do this. "Three pancakes per person and that includes you, Lander." I smiled embarrassingly at the attention directed my way. It was the same woman who caught me choking down my second sandwich.

"Those who like their scrambled eggs runny, come serve yourselves right now. Those who don't, get at the end of the line."

I thanked her profusely and indicated I was not looking forward to a bowl of cold cereal which, had I been on my own as Reverend Butler indicated, would have been the case. She replied, "We don't believe in Sugar Pops around here."

Abigail came sleepily into the kitchen. She wore tight shiny red pants that made her legs look even longer and thinner—and sexier if I can say this. She was barefoot and came from the direction of Reverend Butler's room. The knowledge ran silently through the mingled families, chastening them. *It was unthinkable Reverend Butler could be cavorting with a colored woman under the roof of his parishioners and their children.* James and I overhead the whispering.

Someone went to the nearest town and bought several Sunday papers. The children, including me, fought over the funnies; the men reached for the sports and financial pages. The day proceeded with that unreality peculiar to Sunday; one hour seemed as long as two and the next went by in ten minutes. A great deal of the conversation concerned where everyone was—particularly Abigail and Reverend Butler.

Abigail joined James and me in the garden salvaging tomatoes and zucchini from the previous night's frost. James quizzed mom, "Where did you disappear to last night? Where did you sleep?"

Abigail responded pointedly, "Worry about yourself and your brothers and not my comings and goings." He continued to go after her. Finally, she scolded him, "Just give it a rest. I don't have to account my every step to you."

James and I threw rotten vegetables at each other. As he headed for the barn to sulk, I caught him on the cheek with a rotten tomato. Peace was momentarily restored when we found an old rope ring-toss set in the barn and played until a dispute ended our fun.

On my way to the kitchen for a drink, I stopped and watched as a couple of the men shoveled and refreshed the holes that took the posts for the volleyball net. They unwound the two-by-fours, a tangled net, guide ropes, and pegs that they found in the barn. It was a tedious process of setting up the net. Inside the kitchen, several women collaborated in making lunch—a cauldron of corn chowder, a tossed vegetable salad, and grilled cheese sandwiches. As the women slid and bumped past each other between the old-fashioned black soapstone sink and the wooden countertops on either side, I heard them quietly talking about the situation between Reverend Butler and Abigail, which seemed to be heading for trouble.

After lunch, we played volleyball. Three teams were fielded. There was a lot of lunging and swaggering going on among the boys and their fathers. Several participants hobbled off the court. One of the moms who had gone into town to pick up supplies for dinner drove by the volleyball game at the most inopportune time. A wild hit by one of the women bounced the ball under the chassis of the station wagon. And with a sound as sickening as that of our box turtle that had been crushed under the wheel of our neighbor's car, the ball burst. The match ended on that note as there were no more balls.

The exercise left the adults feeling contentious, vigorous, and thirsty. There was a rush to the liquid refreshments. Some of the adults were over by the far wall, where the wallpaper had been scorched and curled by the pipes of an old woodstove that was no longer there. They were engaged in a contest of endurance. The idea was to time how long each man could sit against the wall, posed as if on a chair that was not there, before muscle pain in the thighs forced surrender. Other games were introduced; other feats were performed. Abigail and Reverend Butler appeared from another one of their disappearances and joined in.

And there was the leg wresting, husband against wife. How strangely sweet and clarifying it was to see Abigail and Reverend Butler lying hip to hip, face to feet, while the circle of excited faces counted "One! Two! Three!" On the count of three, their inside legs, lifted on each count, were joined and a brief struggle ensued, brief as the mating of animals, and ended with a moment's exhausted repose side by side. James and I watched as Abigail and Reverend Butler continued their playfulness. Standing back-to-back and hooking arms at the elbows with Reverend Butler, Abigail showed everyone the way in which a woman can lift a man. One of the women sarcastically commented, "There seems to be no end to what bodies can do." This public display of affection between Abigail and Reverend Butler registered with everyone.

The children were fed and allowed to watch a little television. The adults ate and held Bible study. It was not well attended. Something had offended them. It was not difficult to guess what caused the tension and disruption. The kids packed themselves into their sleeping bags; most of the adults were not far behind. Abigail crept downstairs.

It rained that night. The purring of the rain, its caressing of the roof shingles, its leisurely debate with itself, drowned out the breathing and noises of the other kids. I fell asleep.

A bright, sunny morning arrived; an enclave of irritable adults congregated. Gossiping was rampant in the living room. It offered no consolation to anyone to see Reverend Butler massaging Abigail's neck while she sat on one of the chairs in the kitchen. He tried to get at her shoulder muscles with his thumb by going under the neck of her blouse a little. She groaned innocently, "Oh, that feels so good." This display probably pushed the limits for those who were not already outraged.

Everyone held hands in a circle as Reverend Butler prayed for a safe return home. He obtusely hinted at the allegations: "God does not abide gossip and stories appealing to some of our most base instincts." It took everyone the remainder of the morning to pack up and leave. We were the last. Reverend Butler and Abigail were very tender with each other. That weekend changed things. Our mother stopped going to church.

* * * * * * * * *

We continued the drive to the hospital in silence until Reverend Butler offered, "I've known Abigail since your first days in Washington. Our souls take comfort in each other. Secrets bind us. Early ones."

"Why don't you just speak in some foreign language? You'd make more sense."

"You were too young to know anything about your mother, or father for that matter, during her years in Arkansas. There were things she told me. She had trouble finding peace with herself."

"You dare to discount my childhood memories." I answered back.

Another gap of complete silence issued before he answered, "That is not what I meant. You are naïve to ...," he never completed his sentence. And silence ensued.

As soon as I parked the car, we hurriedly entered the hospital and went straight to my mother's bedside. I waved to my brothers as we passed, but the reverend moved through the waiting room as though they were invisible. His lips were moving in prayer as he laid his case at the foot of her bed and began to prepare for administering last communion. But before he began, Reverend Butler sat beside Abigail; he took her hand in his, kissed the center of her palm, closed her hand, and then quietly wept.

Finding his behavior odd and unbecoming, I walked over to the window with James who had entered the room. We looked out of the blinds toward nowhere, trying to make our presence disappear. Reverend Butler was a difficult man to warm up to—ice cold in the center, blizzard-like at the edges. My mother's friendship with him always seemed like a rejection of her sons. Then I heard him say, "They don't know what we went through, Abigail. They don't know how we got here."

The words surprised me as much as his tears. Here I was judging this gaunt reverend for his remoteness, yet I stood before my unconscious mother struggling with feelings I could not reach or touch. My mother had raised her sons to be tender, yet stoic. It cost her that portion of tears I should have shed for her. I turned back toward Reverend Butler, who was now preparing to administer the communion.

He lit candles and handed them to McNair. We were all there, James, Daniel, other members of the immediate family. As the reverend stepped closer to my mother, his words were winged and feathered as they drifted around us, "Peace be unto this house and unto all who dwell therein." He put a crucifix to my mother's mouth for her to kiss. He forgave Abigail all of her sins and, according to the faith, her immortal soul blazed like a newly formed coin. It was now pure white.

We watched Reverend Butler sprinkle holy water over her body and across her bed. "May the devils fear to approach this place, may the angels of peace be present therein, and may all wicked strife depart this house .... ."

I knew all of these words. I had heard them hundreds of times being administered by chaplains over soldiers in Vietnam jungles as I struggled to provide emergency medical attention to keep them alive or reduce their pain. The religion didn't matter; last rites were about the same. Reverend Butler was calm now, lost in the formalities of the sacrament. Lastly, he asked Jesus to take Abigail up in his loving arms.

After the communion ended, he kept a vigil for Abigail in the waiting room. Dr. Leyton came into the room and asked us to leave.

James and Daniel had been at the hospital for three days before I arrived. They were exhausted and knew dying was a full-time job. Our mother made a soft surrender to the night. James was there when she lapsed into her final coma. He told me her last words were an apology. His recollection was, "I did the best I could for you boys. I wish I had done better. I should've loved you more and needed you less."

During the month prior to the first hospitalization, James had made frequent trips from Cleveland to help Ann take care of Abigail. It played havoc with his hospital rotations. He bought her new nightgowns and a wig to wear when her hair fell out due to the chemotherapy. Daniel was given an extended leave from the air force base in Texas. James talked to me about that month and how unprepared he was for our mother's death. "She had hidden her illness so well from everyone. Her early symptoms were dismissed as small depressive episodes because of the nature of her separation from McNair. I was angry with Ann for awhile for not having been more aggressive in getting mother to a doctor.

"Daniel and I watched the quick process of her becoming a complete stranger, a woman devoid of energy and animation who never left her bed. Mother's eyes grew dull with painkillers. She would ask me to lie down with her for a nap and then be asleep before I could even respond. Her decline steepened its angle hourly. What had been an invisible process for so long began an accelerated pace. Then the terrible galloping began."

James recalled the occasional evening when she seemed better and they had long talks. "But she was a master of indirection," James complained. "There wasn't a query that she could not evade. The English language on her tongue became a smokescreen without her eyes changing expression in the least. I never got her to answer the questions I had stored up from childhood. I tried to milk her of that concealed trove of knowledge. During those rare times when the haze of pain would lift, everyone swarmed about her, desperate for a task to perform, a heroic deed to pull off in exchange for her life." James stopped for a moment quiet in his own thoughts.

He looked up and continued, "As a group we were useless, disquieted, and in the way. Home nursing care was helpful; the nurses were interchangeable, sweet, and efficient. Although family members wanted to hold her in their collective arms, and pass her around, there was a shyness about touch, a fear they would break something as the withering began to take its toll. It took enormous concentration just to look at mom prior to this final hospitalization. Lesions had formed on her gums and lips; her body no longer fought infections. She had given death all it could handle but her unyielding body had now been tested to its limit. Her naturally rosy complexion had jaundiced and something dark was moving close to her eyes. Her stillness began its silent walk into a coma."

I listened quietly not wanting to provoke an uncomfortable conversation about my absence from the family.

It took my mother twenty more hours to die, during which we hardly left her side. Nurses came and went, checking her vital signs and making her comfortable. Her heart rate wrote its signature across a graph paper as it beat steadily under the watchful gaze of nurses. Dr. Leyton delivered frequent reports in a dry, uninflected voice. There was no more optimism, no miracles in sight. Her breathing became an agonized, desperate noise. It was a ragged and hydraulic sound. For me, it became the only sound on earth. We spent those last hours kissing her frequently and telling her how deeply we loved her.

She died with her sons around her. When the undertaker came to take her body, her nightgown was wet from the unfamiliar tears of her three sons, estranged husband, two brothers, two sisters, her best friend Doretha, and Reverend Butler. The world seemed to stop when she stopped breathing. But the sun lit a fire on the horizon, the first sunrise for which Abigail would not be present in her brief forty-five years on this earth. In our own way, each of us had to come to terms with life's impassivity and cruelty. But now we faced a sunrise that was not only impersonal but one that was motherless as well.

I was not prepared to think of my mother as dead, let alone to see her buried. Everything else aside, the death of a forty-five year old woman had its own awful poignancy.

— Chapter Fifteen —

The day my mother was buried was an unseasonably warm, crisply lit November. With the remainder of the leaves having fallen from the trees, the contour of the rocky foothill landscape was now nakedly exposed by the sunlight, its joints and striations etched in the fine-hatched lines like an old engraving.

My brothers and I made the funeral arrangements. The mortuary service we used belonged to an old family friend, John Banks. The funeral parlor, once a home, was now divided into five viewing rooms. In the small reception area, a round wooden table with curved legs stood on the highly polished hardwood floor. Red velvet curtains hung on the windows—floor to ceiling—blocking out whatever light there was. A set of Queen Anne chairs covered in black and red brocade were lined up against the wall. Banks had several bodies that week.

Abigail was given the best accommodations in the large burgundy and pink main room—almost like a chapel with several rows of seating. The dense, well-worn, pale-green carpet deadened our footsteps. The unnatural coloring of the interior came to a violent head with the hothouse flowers arranged around her white coffin. The coffin, with handles of painted gold, rested on a platform draped with a deep purple curtain. It gave the impression the curtain might draw apart and reveal, like a magician's trick, a living Abigail underneath. I thought it all quite gaudy. Several guest books had been filled with those who had come a day earlier for viewing and paying their respects.

My brothers and I gathered early at Ann's to be picked up by a driver in one of Banks's Cadillacs. There was something undignified about waiting, wrapping our hearts in numbness and small needs, and milling around the living room watching the minutes ebb in the silver-faced clock, nervous for the proceedings to begin. We were all pressed around the window when the driver stopped the limousine out front. By the time the man had come up the walk and knocked on the door, we had scattered to the corners of the room as if a bomb of contagion had been dropped among us.

We stood at the door to Wright's Memorial Chapel to greet the mourners as they filed in. They came from Washington and the nearby towns of Cleveland, Pittsburgh, Newport News, Philadelphia, Omaha, Akron, and Buffalo. The mourners were rich and poor, black and white, and from all walks of life. They came in what seemed like a procession of twos: husbands and wives, pairs of arranged and rearranged relationships, and other couples. All were neatly dressed in dark colors. There were no wheelchairs, no walkers, no crutches, and no canes. Spry people around my mother's age, seemingly no less fit than she might have been before her illness.

I cornered James and inquired, "Why is the service being held at the black Methodist Chapel rather than the Adventist church?"

"It was a wish mom expressed to Daniel and me about a month ago when she had come to terms with dying. Her desire was to return to her family religious roots and honor Papa who had taken exception to her joining the Adventist faith," James explained.

I was not surprised that Papa had issues with our conversion and how the practice of that faith affected our lives.

The turnout for Abigail far exceeded what I'd imagined it would be; it certainly exceeded what she could have imagined. The first six or seven pews filled quickly, and people continued to stream in. When my brothers and I took our seats in the front row, I realized the church was almost full, two hundred people, maybe more, waiting for this natural human event to absorb their terror about the end of life. I had taken the hand of so many people, unable to acknowledge most of them by name, and said, "Thank you for coming. It means everything to the family that you are here." I must have repeated some version of that to a third of the mourners, among whom there were many people I had known since childhood.

Just as my brothers and I were about to mount the pulpit together, there was a slight commotion at the rear of the chapel. As the outside doors pushed open, a very feeble Arnetta entered, escorted by Margaret. She had been bedridden for weeks with a respiratory problem and no one expected her to make the trip from Virginia. In unison, the three of us walked down the center aisle to greet them and escort them to our seats. Arnetta, more demonstrative than Margaret, kissed each of us and said, "Your mother would have appreciated this grand entrance."

* * * * * * * * *

When Arnetta's husband died two years after we arrived in Washington, she closed her dance studio, sold her New York flat, and set out on an extravagant odyssey that took her around the world in a period of three years. So deeply did she associate her grief over losing her husband with the city of New York that she never returned there. We never learned the circumstances of his death. In spite of her sister Elizabeth's claim of infidelities, Arnetta loved her husband. We called him Uncle Billy. He had his own law practice and taught at New York University. I can recall seeing him only a few times and was left with the vague impression of something comfortable, something friendly about him.

Arnetta was the kind of woman who knew instinctively that extreme happiness could not be duplicated; she knew how to shut a door properly on the past. She visited us before leaving and promised to take us along as travel companions. We did not understand what she meant until postcards began to arrive. Hundreds of postcards chronicled those three years of relentless footloose travel that took her to thirty-two countries. With the exception of our father's letters, journals, and memorabilia from Europe during the war, Arnetta's postcards, written in her barely legible scrawl, became the first travel literature any of us ever read. In the right corner, the postcards bore the most luminous, wonderful stamps—sometimes landscapes from obscure countries. We especially loved the stamps we received from Africa. They sang with bright fruit, parrots preening in mango trees, mandrills scowling with fierce rainbow faces, elephants fording deep rivers, and a processional of gazelles crossing the plains below Mount Kilimanjaro.

Without knowing it, she transformed us into passionate stamp lovers, particularly James, as we struggled to decipher the hasty travelogues she wrote. Whenever she wrote letters she included a handful of coins from all the countries she had entered. We stored those coins, solid and exotic, in a canning jar. Our mother bought us a map of the world. We would spread the coins out on the linoleum floor and match each coin with its country by placing it on the map. It was as if we were all traveling with her, just as she promised.

Using a pale yellow crayon, we colored in each country on the map once she had set foot inside its borders. We grew fluent in the invocation of mysterious places named Zanzibar, the Belgian Congo, Mozambique, Singapore, and Cambodia. These names tasted like smoke in our mouths; they reverberated with echoes of the primitive and the obscure. As children, we considered Arnetta brave, prodigal, and lucky.

For three unstoppable years, her task was endless voyage, the discovery of uncommon things in uncommon places, and the study of herself in the text and footnotes of alien geographies. She admitted in letters to Abigail that she wanted to build up a reserve of scintillating memories for her old age. She traveled to be amazed and transformed into a woman she was not born to be. By rambling about, Arnetta discovered there were things to be learned on the tangents and extremities—much the way she had lived her life. She hovered over the margins; the wild side made all the difference.

Arnetta returned from her travels and took up residence in Newport News, Virginia, the place she had spent her childhood. She brought with her ten trunks full of the most marvelous, and useless, exotica. The house she purchased overflowed with much of the eccentric memorabilia that had struck her fancy—according to Papa who had visited her on numerous occasions. As he described it, her living room was filled with African masks and art, ceramic elephants from Thailand, and trinkets from every bazaar she had plundered in Asia. And with each item there was a story, a country, and a specific set of adventures. She could retrace her journeys by letting her eyes circle the room. She shared her secret with us, "Once you have traveled, the voyage never ends, but it is played out over and over again. The mind can never break off from the journey." She explained to us that she had done everything she wanted to do in her lifetime.

Arnetta accepted a position in Newport News, teaching music at a well-endowed prep school. During semester breaks and a couple of times during the summer, she visited us. She helped Abigail through many bouts of depression and, in some ways, saved her from herself. She attempted to help my mother rediscover that spry, gifted, beautiful young woman she had been when growing up in Tuskegee and during those summers in New York by illuminating the mordant, unglossed chronicles of the past. She tried unsuccessfully to get Abigail to take up the piano again and even offered to pay for lessons. Arnetta's importance to our life was at times vicarious, but always immeasurable.

* * * * * * * * *

James stepped forward to speak first. He began with something of the earnestness of a black preacher in both his stern bearing and ominous, hanging-judge voice. From behind the podium, he had only to say his name—"My name is CJ Duncan, James, the eldest son"—and stare silently at Abigail's coffin and then return his gaze to the congregation to cast his spell and invoke that realm of feeling associated with the moment.

"Thank you all for coming and for your prayers and kindness these past few weeks. My mother loved spirituals and one of her favorites was 'We've Come This Far by Faith.' She was partial to the rendition sung by the Mighty Clouds of Joy. When life seemed to be getting the best of us, the melody and the message of that spiritual filled our house and filled our lives. So often, that was all we had—faith and her extraordinary will and spirit. She made us believe all things were possible if we had faith in God and in ourselves. The first few words, 'We've come this far,' has special meaning. Most of you don't know that we arrived in this town in 1947 from the backwaters of the rural Arkansas Delta. You can't know the emotional distance we have had to travel from that fall of 1947 only to reach this end. So, today we look for a redeeming meaning, some justification for my mother having struggled during her time on this earth. And that redemption we find in her sons and all of you whose lives she touched and changed.

"I want to share with you an early childhood memory from Arkansas. One bright summer night, when we were very small and a humid air hung like moss over the Delta, my brothers and I couldn't sleep. Lander and I had summer colds and Daniel had heat rash. Our mother walked us down to our favorite spot on the river, where there was a small floating dock of sorts. We sat at the end stretching our legs trying to touch the water with our bare feet.

"She told us there was something she wanted us to see—something that would help us sleep. She pointed out toward the horizon to the east. It was growing dark on this long southern evening, and suddenly, at the exact point her finger indicated, the moon lifted a forehead of stunning gold above the horizon. It lifted straight out of light-intoxicated clouds that lay on the skyline. Behind us, the sun was setting and the river turned to flame in a quiet duet of gold. The new gold of the moon was astonishing and ascendant. The depleted gold of the sunset was extinguishing itself in its long, westward slide until the sun vanished. Its final signature was a ribbon of bouillon strung across the tops of water oaks. The moon then rose quickly like a bird from the water, from the trees, from the river, and climbed straight up. It shimmered with gold, then yellow, then pale yellow, pale silver, silver-bright, and then something miraculous, immaculate, and beyond silver, a color native only to Arkansas nights.

"We sat transfixed before the moon our mother had called forth from the waters. When the moon reached its deepest silver, an astonished wide-eyed Daniel, two years old at the time, coaxed our mother with a hug and refrain to 'Do it again, do it again.'

"From those early years, throughout my life, and even now, I marvel at this lovely woman, my mother, who could summon moons, banish suns to the west, and call forth a brand new sun the following morning from far beyond. She brought wonder, passion, imagination, and reverence for nature and God's miracles and gifts to raising us." James paused to collect himself, walked to the casket, kissed my mother on the cheek, and concluded, "Mother, I will see your beauty in every sunset and know you are keeping watch over us with each sunrise."

Daniel and I were left with the impossible task of complementing his tribute to our mother. I walked to the podium carrying our mother's cherished volume of poems—the oversized book with the floppy, leather binding that, when I was a young boy, always reminded me of a cocker spaniel. As I began reading several passages from Wordsworth's "Intimations of Immortality," I felt my mother's majesty and grandeur as never before:

"The Rainbow comes and goes,
And lovely is the Rose,
The moon doth with delight
Look round her when the heavens are bare;
Waters on a starry night
Are beautiful and fair;
The sunshine is a glorious birth;
But yet I know, where 'er I go,
That there hath passed away a glory from the earth.
Wordsworth's words never rang more true. *There has passed away a glory from the earth.*"

Saying those words stripped away my manly effort at sober, stoical self-control and laid bare a child's longing for the woman I would never see again. Our larger-than-life mother expressed herself so easily, so sweepingly. With just the powers of her beauty and imagination, she taught her sons to want to be extraordinary.

I wept uncomfortably with the most fundamental and copious of all emotions, reduced helplessly to everything I could not bear. Little did anyone realize that I was trying to bridge a distance of more than nine years in which not a single word had passed between us.

I could recite many lines from that poem; I had heard it so often from my mother. And yet, only with her lying in that coffin did I at last bother to hear them. I continued:

"What though the radiance was once so bright
Be now forever taken from my sight,
Though nothing can bring back the hour
Of splendour in the grass, of glory in the flower
We will grieve not, rather find strength in what remains
behind ....

"Wordsworth tells us to take strength from what Abigail has left behind. And in our sympathy, we must find soothing thoughts from her spirit and maintain a faith that allows us to look through her death.

"Allow me a few minutes longer to tell you a story about my mother, first told to me by my grandfather. It became my mother's story during the Christmas season, slightly revised to impart her message to her sons. I borrow it to help me memorialize a mother of extraordinary gifts. When she was a child, she developed a habit of concealing her gifts to her family. They were never under the tree on Christmas morning. However, she provided everyone with an elaborate map to help in the search for their present. Once she had hidden a pearl ring for her sister Margaret, a ring she had bought with the help of her aunt, but had hidden it too well. She had placed it in an abandoned bird's nest in a neighbor's backyard, framing it among stems and moss in the hollow of a tree. But her written directives were fuzzy and unsure; she could never lead her sister to that nest.

"She described that lost ring as the perfect, the most immaculate gift. A perfect gift, she would tell us, is always hidden too well. And so it is, she was the perfect gift to this world. Everything about her had puzzles, misdirection, feints, and pivots. Nothing was direct or straightforward. She could not break the lifelong habit of hiding things, particularly the gift of herself. My mother was remarkable. Nothing was ever lost to her. She transformed everything about herself into mysterious gardens of language, hiding her gifts behind a trellis of words and her heart-stopping beauty, making bouquets out of her losses and disappointments. And there were many.

"Most of you don't know that my mother studied voice and piano in New York and was gifted at both. My great aunt, a music teacher, once told me God had marked all the lines and spaces on a sheet of music with notes so perfect they praised all his creation with beauty. And my mother was good enough to play the music written by God. Most of us would be happy to have such talents. But Abigail's gifts even exceeded this.

"She was a remarkable poet. Many of her poems were published right under your nose in the Thursday section of the *Washington Reporter*. In 'About Town,' she used only her middle name of Louise. We shared in her love of these little games that she played with her gifts. All her poems were strong, melancholy, and beautiful, just like her. Much of my mother's journey through a difficult life is revealed in her poetry."

I made it to the coffin and looked at my mother's face for the last time. I spoke tenderly to her, but in a voice that could be heard throughout the church, "Sleep peacefully my precious mother. You are now free of all you had to endure—the impositions, the humiliations, the obstructions, and the wounds and the pain and the posturing and the shame—all the agonies of a brutal life. You are in a better place. You were too good for this world."

Everyone waited for Daniel to begin his tribute. For a moment there was nothing. Without a word, he returned to his seat. There was only the silence and the coffin and the emotional intoxication of the crowd.

Moments later, the choir director stood up, ascended the few steps, and moved to the left where the robed choir was waiting. Accompanied by the pianist, they sang a medley of my mother's favorite spirituals: "Oh Master Let Me Walk with Thee," "Blessed Assurance," "Savior like a Shepherd Lead Us," "His Eye is On the Sparrow," and "Just as I Am." Sometimes, you can't just listen to those spirituals; they pick you up and shake you. People clapped and sang along. By the end of it, we were all wrung out. Interspersed with the spirituals were popular songs my mother loved. It was an extraordinary celebration of her life. It was what she wanted. My brothers, Reverend Butler, Welcome, Fletcher, and I carried the coffin to the hearse.

We got into cars and drove through the uphill streets. The town seemed to hush around us; a woman came out on her porch with a baby in arms and waited there; a small boy stopped in the middle of throwing a ball to watch us go by. We passed between two granite pillars linked by an arch of wrought iron. The Washington Mountain Cemetery was beautiful at three in the afternoon. The nap of the nurtured green lawns sloped down somewhat parallel to the rays of the sun. Tombstones cast long, slate shadows. The procession moved in second gear up a crunching, blue gravel lane—its destination a meek, green canopy smelling of earth and ferns. The cars stopped; we all got out.

Beyond us, at a distance, stood a crescent sweep of black woods. The cemetery was high on the mountains between the town and the forest. A man on a power lawnmower rode between the worn teeth of tombstones near the far hedge. Swallows dipped and tossed themselves above a stone cottage, a crypt. The white coffin was gently rolled on casters from the hearse onto crimson straps that held it above the nearly rectangular grave. The small creaks and breaths of effort scratched on a pane of silence. Silence. A cough. The flowers had been moved here and were densely banked with the tent. Behind my feet, a neat mound of dirt topped with squares of sod waited to be replaced. The undertaker looked pleased, his job nearly done, gloved hands carefully poised. Silence.

"The Lord is my shepherd: therefore I lack nothing." The minister's robust voice sounded fragile outdoors. The distant buzzing of the power mower halted respectfully. My chest vibrated with excitement and strength. I wondered whether my mother had ascended to heaven. Caught in thoughts like that, I didn't hear anything until "… and bring us all to the heavenly kingdom; through thy Son, Jesus Christ, our Lord, Amen."

Several people whispered, "Amen."

That is how it was. I felt them all. Everyone had gathered here to give Abigail the energy to leap to heaven.

An electric switch was turned; the straps began to lower the casket into the grave and stopped. James came forward and made a cross of sand on the lid. Stray grains rolled one by one down the curved lid into the hole. Margaret and Ann threw crumpled petals. "Deal graciously, we pray thee, with all those who mourn, that, casting every care on thee ….

The straps whined again. Doretha at my side staggered. I held her arm and even through the cloth it felt hot. A small breath of wind made the canopy full and lift. The smell of flowers rose toward us "… and may the Lord bless you and keep you, now and forevermore. Amen."

I had doubted most people would accompany the body all the way to the grave. But our mother—even in death—had a flair for drawing out and sustaining pathos. This, I assumed, was why there were so many people crowded around as close as they could to what was to be Abigail's eternal home. As though eager to crawl in there and take her place, to offer themselves up as surrogates, as substitutes, as sacrificial offerings, if that would magically allow for the resumption of a life that had been as good as stolen from her. Everyone felt a grim serenity.

Daniel, however, was overcome with hysteria. A slow buildup at the chapel had him incapable of uttering a single word of tribute. Now, finally at the grave site, with all of us watching him, he fell apart. He helplessly flailed his arms in the air and began to wail. That wild sound of lamentation rose in intensity. When he saw James rushing toward him with arms outstretched, his face contorted, and in sheer childlike astonishment cried, "We're never going to see her again!"

A profusion of weeping cascaded through the cemetery. My mother's love had indentured us and leveled us. She left us hurt and powerless, on our knees, taking our time to say good-bye. The date on her headstone would read 1923–1968. How simple and direct those numbers are. And how little they connote of what went on in her life.

The minister closed his book. Ann's children, standing side by side, looked up and blinked away tears. Mourners moved into the sunshine. Rather than drifting away, they lingered. I saw McNair move along the path between the gravestones in the direction of the street. He was all but ignored with not even the most cursory of good-byes. His claim to a relationship with this family ended with our mother's death and he knew it. Personal invitations were being extended by family for the celebration of Abigail's life at the Methodist Fellowship Hall.

James and I moved several steps away from the open grave. Although I was crying silently, I looked up and the sky greeted me. The low clouds were pink, but up above, high in the dome, tails of cirrus still hung pale and pure. A strange strength sank down into me. It was as if I had been crawling in a cave and now, at last beyond the recession of crowding rocks, had seen a patch of light.

I turned, and James's face, numb with grief, blocked the light. James was distraught and not thinking the most generous of thoughts. Charitable thoughts were hard to come by that day from him. Rather than consoling, he unleashed what he had been hiding since my arrival, "What difference should mom's leaving make to you? You certainly didn't want to see her when she was here. Did you expect to have her around to hate forever and, in your own good time, you'd forgive her? You're here crying with the expectation of some conciliation. It's a foolish illusion for you to hold. You had your chance."

Heads snapped around at a voice so sudden and cruel. My face burned. I was breathless and gulping for emotional air. There were looks in my direction, horrified and blank with shock. I knew there would be no completion, no just and perfect consummation. But did it have to mean standing just feet from where the coffin rested in its freshly dug pit? The withering attack from my brother was timed to do great damage to the future of our relationship. It was just too much truth for James to keep concealed. My absence was one long, perverse, willfully arrogant defection James found not only difficult to reckon with, but impossible to forgive.

My embarrassment was savage. A suffocating sense of injustice blinded me. Looking back, it seems melodramatic, but I turned and ran. It was an impulse, all I could think to do among the stares.

Uphill exultantly, I dodged gravestones. Dandelions grew bright as butter among the graves. I heard James call my name. I felt him chasing me but did not turn to look. I cut diagonally through the stones across the grass toward the woods. The distance to the dark swelling of trees was greater than it seemed from the grave site. I arrived between the arms of the woods and aimed for the center of the crescent. Once inside, I was less sheltered than I expected. Turning, I could see through the leaves down to the graveyard where, beside the small green tent, the people I had left still clustered. James was halfway between them and me. I stopped running. Daniel joined James temporarily in the chase. James's narrow-set eyes concentrated on the woods. Daniel and others in dark clothes flashed mute signals toward the woods and turned away. Only James's gaze was steady. He was gathering energy to renew the chase.

I crouched and ran raggedly. My hands and face were scratched from plowing through the bushes and saplings that rimmed the woods. Deeper inside, there was more space. The pine trees smothered all other growth. Their brown needles muffled the rough earth with a slippery blanket; sunshine fell in narrow slots on this dead floor. The unseen late-afternoon sun baked the dark shingles of green above my head. It was dim, but hot like an attic. Dead, lower branches thrust at the level of my eyes. My hands and face felt hot where they were scratched. I turned to see if I had left the people behind. No one was following. In turning, I lost some sense of direction. But the tree trunks were at first in neat rows that carried me along between them, and I always walked against the slope of the land. If I walked far enough uphill, in time, I would reach the scenic drive that ran along the ridge. Only by going downhill would I be returned to the others.

My shins hurt from jarring uphill into pits and flat rocks that the needles concealed. I took off my black suit jacket and carried it in a twisted bundle. The light widened enough for me to see a nest of old tin cans and bottles sunken into the needles. I jacked my legs over the guard fence and straightened up. The asphalt scraped under my shoes. Chilly air stroked my shoulder blades. I had come out of the woods about a half mile from the cemetery entrance. The sun was gone; it was dusk.

As I walked, with my coat hanging over my shoulder on the hook of one finger, I decided to call Ann to let her know I was okay. Down the road a bit was the old Pinnacle Hotel. I went to the pay phone on the mustard colored wall near the registration desk and found Ann's number in the book. No one answered. They were probably still at the church gathering. Adding insult to injury, I had taken flight from my brother's tirade, gotten lost in the woods, and was now missing the final celebration for my mother.

I stood on the ridge at the edge of the parking lot. Washington spread out like a carpet; its flowerpot red going dusty. The lights were already turned on. The neon sunflower at Ferrero's Nursery on the outskirts of the city looked small as a daisy. As I started down the steps, I wondered, *What should I do about my relationship with James?*

I went down the mountainside on the flight of log stairs and through the park, where some people were still playing, and down Charlton Street. I put my coat back on and walked up Wheeler. By the time I reached Forrest Avenue, my head was clear about what happened at the cemetery. How is it that what makes you move is so simple; and the field you must move in is so crowded? The fact that I didn't know what to do about James made me feel infinitely small and the situation impossible to capture. Its smallness filled me like a vastness.

— Chapter Sixteen —

I decided to remain in Washington a couple of days longer to help sift through and dispose of my mother's possessions. The belongings she had brought back from Buffalo remained packed and stored in the shed by the side of the house. These included her beloved collection of 78s, some loose and others with album covers. We also came across class photos, reports cards, athletic medals, trophies, and certificates of academic achievement. There were costumes made for church plays and Halloween. Cigar boxes were filled with Valentines wrapped with faded crepe paper and studded with construction paper hearts and cut-up doilies. Yearbooks and yellowed newspaper clippings were mixed together. Dozens of Big Chief writing tablets held unfinished poems. Bags of useless things we made for our mother, from misshaped ceramic plates and vases to potholders in insipid color combinations, had been kept. Satchels from our paper routes, toys we loved as boys brought back memories. There were boxes of clothes that never made it to the Salvation Army or rummage sales and crates of books. The old Singer sewing machine and every keepsake, relic, and reminder of our childhood seemed to be stored in the shed. Abigail had refused offers to help sort through the boxes and never quite garnered the emotional or physical energy to wade into her recent past.

For a day, we sat together renewing the fragile, tenuous bonds that were both the conundrum and the glory of facing the world as brothers. Nothing was said about the graveside confrontation. I was puzzled, but decided to ignore it.

We interspersed our difficult project with the telling and retelling the stories of life as a family. We talked about how we arrived at this point in time and what benedictions and grievances we carried from the Delta and Washington. Each of us played an indisputable and unchangeable role in our family's melodrama. We recognized we had survived a spectacularly rocky childhood and thus carried a portion of the inevitable emotional baggage.

The stack of old catalogues contributed to our recollections. The major part of our Christmas every year came from the one-hundred-dollar credit my mother had at Sears and Roebuck. She had gone down to their credit office and told them her three boys would not have a Christmas if they did not grant her a time-payment arrangement. Without a credit application process, they extended her the one hundred dollars. It took only one phone call to verify her employment as a day maid for the wealthiest family in town. That credit she was granted was used twice a year: for Easter outfits and Christmas presents for us boys.

Every August, we received the latest edition of the Sears and Roebuck catalogue. Few events were more momentous. It came in a brown wrapper and was mailed from Chicago. Our mother required that it be kept at the kitchen table, next to the radio and the family Bible. My brothers and I scrutinized and dwelt on the important sections—toys and sporting goods. I remember scuffling with them over who would have first dibs on the Christmas supplement that came in October, which gave us time to write down our Christmas wishes.

We pondered for hours, for days, about our toy selection. Daniel thought Sears and Roebuck had some special relationship with Santa Claus. Everything in the catalogue seemed to exceed our allocation. Several years, James talked me into combining our portion of the credit for things like erector sets, wagons, scooters, and a bicycle we could share. We changed our mind dozens of times before the order had to be in to arrive before Christmas. The excitement for James and me resided in what arrived. An Out of Stock notice often brought tears. For Daniel, there was a determined effort to find ways to make sure he did not lose the wonder, magic, and sentimentality of his childhood. Hope and so many intangibles of the heart had disappeared from my mother's life; she was desperate to see it remained in our home. Christmas was a test of this. James and I devoted most of our Christmas tips from our paper routes in futile attempts to overcome our mother's gloom and melancholy.

The Salvation Army and Thrift Store distributed a box of candy, a piece of fruit, and a toy each Christmas that we came to depend on receiving. My brother's and I did a lot of wishing and pressing our faces against store windows. Our imagination carried us great distances.

James came across a box filled with dozens of forgotten, broken games—Parcheesi, Monopoly, Chinese Checkers; games of real estate speculation, of international diplomacy and war; games of crime detection; games with spinners, dice, lettered tiles, cardboard characters, and plastic battleships. We found games bought in five-and-dime stores, through catalogues, and department stores; received from charities, like the Salvation Army; and acquired as gifts from Christmases past. There were games enjoyed on an afternoon of a birthday and for a few afternoons thereafter, and then allowed, shy of one or two pieces, to drift into our closet and storage shed. The games presented a forceful semblance of value. Given a chance, the springs of their miniature launchers would still react and the logic of their instruction would still generate suspense.

"What shall we do with these games?" James asked in a tone of agony.

A sad wealth of abandoned playthings silently groping with us for the particular happy day connected to it. Our lives had touched these tokens and counters once; excitement had flowed along the paths of these stylized landscapes. But the day was long gone, and scarcely a memory remained.

"Toss them, or give them to the Salvation Army," Daniel suggested at just the moment he had finished winding up a tin Donald Duck. We all laughed as it responded with an angry clack of its bill and a few stiff strokes on its drum.

The sight of two wooden tennis rackets my mother had salvaged from the Fitch garbage quickened in me a memory that surfaced after long suppression. When I was nine or ten, my mother put shorts on her long, lean, athletic legs and walked with me to the courts on the corner of North College and Wheeling that belonged to W&J. She opened the latched door to the eight courts fenced in by heavy galvanized wire. Neither of us had ever played. It was frustrating that the balls bopped into the braided net or blooped through the air out of reach. I was embarrassed by her bare-legged, attention-drawing figure. Her face became redder as her clumsy efforts continued. Cars and foot traffic passed close enough for people to stare at us, this little boy and grown woman, trying to pat an uncooperative ball back and forth. Upon reflection, her purpose was to help me gain a skill I might use in life. In fact, I went on to play a lot of tennis around East Washington. But the game had always been tainted for me by that embarrassing memory, the public struggle with my mother. There had been a pathetic impotence to the fuzzy ball as we hit the net or the fencing with a sad, reverberating thud. Mother and son seemed so lost. The two of us, at the far end of the campus, were linked in a common ordeal that was characteristic of our life together.

Sorting through our past, we told every story we could remember about our early childhood and youth. We had been stimulated, provoked, and seduced by the residues, remains, and tokens that we found in the shed. We tried to assess the damage and strength we brought to our adult lives being raised by Abigail.

We came across a box of my mother's shoes piled indiscriminately on top of each other. I reminisced about the miles we put on our shoes aided by pieces of cardboard in the soles that helped cover the holes and tided us over from one rummage sale to the next. I always found the best shoes were in the smaller sizes and endured the discomfort for a better selection. Sometimes, I would forget about the holes and look up to find kids in my class staring at the soles of my shoes laughing.

The cruelty of those kids began on the day my brother and I became the first black children to enter the East Washington Grade School. Parents hung around the entrance to see if the rumor was actually true that they were about to get their first "colored" students. We had been seen at the school with our mother on two previous occasions, but had been repelled by the words of the principal, Paul Varnum, "Colored children go to the Third or Sixth Ward School. You don't belong in this district."

My mother was relentless in turning the fluke of annexation that placed our house in East Washington borough into what she described as "the ticket to our future." Nearly every graduate from the East Washington system went to a four-year college. The curriculum beginning in the early grades was college prep. There was no such thing as "general studies." Papa was brought into the skirmish and pushed with a deft hand in all the right political places and helped to obtain a reluctant admission.

That solemn walk toward the three hundred white students who gathered in the halls and silently watched us approach had my stomach doing flip-flops. I noticed two sheriff cars parked beside the entrance. The atmosphere of the school that day, and many after that, was estranged, dangerous, and tense. The halls were magnetized like sea air before a hurricane. Hatred prowled the rooms and hallways. The word *nigger* appeared in angry, hastily applied graffiti in our homerooms until the teachers, nervous and unstrung, entered and expunged the word from sight with the birdlike skittering of the eraser. I chose the last seat by the window. The seats around me were empty, a forbidden zone no white student would enter.

Rumors circulated that we would not be there long. My mother carefully instructed us to not respond to any provocations and keep our emotions and feelings in tow. I was petrified when James told me at lunch not to let anyone catch me alone. He had heard some middle school kids whispering along the breezeway about a plan to get one of us alone on the playground behind the school.

Most of the kids tried to just ignore our existence, to go their own way, and to navigate through the tainted electorate of that aroused school population. Others had to prove they could talk *nigger* talk with the best of them and had a mental file of *nigger* jokes to entertain their contemporaries should their loyalty ever be questioned. At this tender, formative school age, the racism issued forth from a passionate need to conform rather than any serious credo or system of belief. Many of my white contemporaries could hate with ardor—but only if they were perfectly sure their hatred echoed the sentiments of the majority. Others had just the beginnings of moral courage to tap into but to do so was far too dangerous for most. We were probably the first contact most of the kids had with anyone of color.

In spite of our collective efforts to escape poverty, it was always nearby. Disregarding our mother's strict rules and code of conduct for not accepting anything we did not earn or pay for, we were ceaselessly foraging—coal for the stove, pieces of ice for the icebox, or anything that we could turn into money. It seemed scraping for food kept us constantly in lines—for government surplus, Salvation Army and church basement give-a-ways. Sometimes, we were reduced to looking in dumpsters behind Woolworth's for discarded candy bars that had exceeded their shelf life. No one told us they might contain eggs or actual worms that could find their way into our upper intestines.

At times, we had pinworms so severe that not only were they in our bowel movements, but they also came up into our throats and caused us to choke as we tried to pull them out. In one of our rare visits to the doctor, he explained it this way: The worm lives in your large intestines. The female worm, loaded with eggs, migrates down your intestine, through your rectum, and out of your anus, where it lays its eggs. The fact the worm is a nocturnal creature, laying its eggs at night in and around the anus is the reason why you're kept awake by the intense itching. The worm then heads back into your intestine and continues a life that could last for six to eight weeks.

Aside from having to drink a very bitter liquid, we had to suffer the indignities of almost nightly enemas. Daniel had the worst time of it because he sucked two fingers all the time, the same fingers he used to scratch himself, and thus prolonged the worm's lifecycle. Even though we knew about the possibility of worms, it didn't stop our foraging.

We had severe eczema outbreaks throughout our childhood that produced scaly red patches on our scalp, loss of large areas of hair, and deep ulcerative, inflamed lesions. As a finishing touch to our general appearance, we had circular patches or discoloration on our faces that were about the size of quarters. The condition was referred to as ringworm. Aside from our outward appearance, we had whopping cough nearly every year, coughing sometimes eight or ten times in one breath to a point of gagging and vomiting. Without basic immunizations, we were not spared measles, rubella, mumps, and diphtheria.

The worst of the medical crises was visited upon James at the age of fourteen. Shortly after Halloween, he had a cough and an accompanying sore throat. At that time, I also had a cough. But after all, what was a cough or sore throat? We all had them many times. In winter, we passed them around like sweets. Enough coughing or complaining about an ailment meant no school—when it was Daniel or me doing the whining and fretting. But James pleaded to the nurse, "Please don't send me home. I'm going to be okay, I promise. I'll just sit in the back of the room and put my head down on the desk for awhile."

For days, there was a dry, raspy cough that agitated his sore throat, gripped it, and then let it go. Then vomiting began to accompany the coughing. We all had vomiting spells—so we knew the drill to get the bucket. "Something's wrong," I warned my mother. James's odd look and the rasping breaths he was making worried me.

Touching his forehead, she said, "It's just a sore throat." She dismissively added, "He's warm, but not hot—whatever's going on will pass in time." I resented her nonchalance.

We had no family doctor or health care provider; we did not seek medical intervention from public programs, not even free immunizations. The most serious obstacle to receiving simple basic care came from our mother who clung tenaciously to her stubborn rules about not accepting anything that we didn't earn, barter, or pay for. Home remedies brought with her from the Arkansas Delta were primitive and equally limiting with the likes of sardines and turpentine, herbs boiled down to syrup, roots and teas, and bark.

Each week, James's frightening downward spiral continued. By late November, James was suffering from a multitude of symptoms: swollen and tender knees and ankles; vomiting long streaks of bright green bile and mucous; a rash of small, red dots just under the skin, from sternum to groin and an angry range of welts across his back; constant exhaustion; and blood in his urine. He complained his heart was racing so fast he thought it would pop out of his chest.

My mother was in a dark spiral of her own. A deeper depression than we had seen before had its grip on her. She was incapable of attending to her own needs; James was all but forgotten by her. His suffering intensified. Finally, a whimpering James pleaded with me, "Take me to Dr. Wade's house." I pulled him in our wagon. When we arrived, James was shivering, his shallow breathing was coming in shudders, and he could barely keep his eyes open.

Dr. Wade had an alarmed scowl on his face as he examined James in the small office adjoining his study. James didn't have the strength to lift his arms to get his shirt off. Dr. Wade saw the scattered red marks that looked as if a bird had walked along the short length of his spine. He pulled out his stethoscope and listened to James's breathing and heart sounds; he checked other vital signs. After pressing James's finger, until the flesh under the nail turned white, and counting how long it took for it to flush pink again, he turned in my direction and said, "He's not getting enough oxygen." Dr. Wade bolted from the room into his study and called for an ambulance.

We overheard and when he returned James feebly protested, "Our mother will be angry, we can't afford this."

He tried to pacify James, "You're very sick, and we have to get you to a hospital right away." Not one to coddle, he continued, "I'm sure you have an acute case of rheumatic fever. The diagnosis will be confirmed at the hospital."

"He'll be alright?" I wanted to know. "It's just a fever, right?"

There was no answer, which increased my worry to a point of near panic. A barrage of questions about James's symptoms came my way as though James was not present. Of particular interest was the strep throat. When he learned how long James had been suffering, he became furious.

James was trembling. I held his hand as we waited for the ambulance.

"Where are they going to take me?" James asked in almost a whisper.

"Washington Hospital. I'll personally see to your admittance," Dr. Wade informed him. "And don't worry about your mother or the costs."

A medical bill that had no chance of being paid was of less concern than his fears about Washington Hospital. Several months earlier, we talked Mr. Birch into hiring us to help him around his funeral home. Birch's Funeral Home catered to the Negro Washington community. Each body that came to Birch's had a medical examiner's report and a story about the cause of death. We heard far too many scary accounts in his embalming room involving unnecessary deaths at Washington Hospital due to infections and surgical mishaps. What stuck with us were Mr. Birch's comments about blacks not coming out of Washington Hospital alive. While it might have represented a flippant observation to him, we interpreted it as deadly serious.

Dr. Wade and I rode in the ambulance with James. An oxygen mask was put over his face. Dr. Wade peered at James on the stretcher and observed that the whites of his eyes were bright red and the fingers on both hands looked scorched.

In the emergency room, the ambulance technicians slid him onto a bed. A covey of nurses gathered around him, dressed him in a threadbare hospital gown, and inserted an IV into his left hand.

I hovered around the examination room. After the emergency room doctors finished examining James, I eavesdropped on the conversation they had with Dr. Wade. I listened carefully because I knew this was a test. It was the first of a score of explanations we would be given over the next days and weeks. As I listened, I thought, *this is what growing up is.* What I learned was more than I ever wanted to know about things I wish I'd never heard of.

They talked about tests to confirm their near certainty that a streptococcal infection had run rampant and triggered James's immune system to attack his body's own tissue and cause an inflammation of his heart. Dr. Wade offered his verdict, "It's rheumatic heart disease. Now, what's left to determine is how much damage there is to the opening and closing of the valves."

I was expelled from the trauma area and escorted to the waiting room. Dr. Wade took care of James's admission at the business office and joined me. I had to sit through an onslaught of disparagement of my mother for what he called neglect that bordered on child endangerment and abuse.

"If she had just had him treated for the strep throat with penicillin, we wouldn't be here today. Why did she let it go so long? Do you have any idea how much James has suffered at the hands of her neglect—the fever, abdominal pain, swelling, rash, vomiting? What's worse, she has caused your brother to have permanent damage and a lifetime of compromise with severe heart disease that will eventually lead to heart failure. This is not the first time. I have watched you boys endure unnecessary hardship and live by the seat of your pants. Your childhood isn't supposed to be this hard. I'm contemplating reporting your mother to County Social Services."

I was not overwhelmed by Dr. Wade's barrage. I had heard this all before, only in different contexts. And, my response was the same—I defended my mother against such accusations.

"I don't mean any disrespect, and I know you mean well, but I will not listen to your harsh words and threats against my mother," I began. "We've had sore throats, coughs, vomiting, rashes, and much worse and have gotten through it. Besides, don't you need a prescription for penicillin? We're not on welfare and we pay our own way. There's no money for doctors or medicine. Some doctors in this town won't even see Negroes. It's easy for you to judge my mother from the life that you have. She's doing the best she can to raise three boys alone. Give her some credit. If you want to do something, help my brother. He needs you."

Dr. Wade disappeared and returned a couple of anxious hours later in the company of a dry, middle-aged doctor who spoke in an imperturbable Texan wake-me-up-when-something-interesting-happens tone. He picked up on Dr. Wade's mantra, "Your brother is very ill. He has rheumatic heart disease. Dr. Wade will tell you what that means. We have moved him to intensive care. I've given him something to help him sleep."

As they were about to walk away, my mother arrived. Mrs. Fitch was with her, which no doubt had something to do with the extreme courtesy Dr. Wade extended to Abigail.

The diagnosis was repeated. When they got to the part about inflammation around the heart, evidence of gastrointestinal bleeding, mitral valve stenosis, and heart damage, my mother collapsed in a heap. Attendants had to be called, and she was placed in one of the examination rooms. I wondered if my mother had staged another one of her dramas.

When we finally reached intensive care, James was sleeping. He was hooked up to monitors; IVs and tubes poked out from everywhere. James's condition dramatized how far out on the edge our poverty had placed us. He was in intensive care for nearly a week fighting the acute phase of the disease with penicillin, erythromycin, corticosteroids, and anti-inflammatory drugs.

When James was finally ready to be released to the ward, Dr. Wade arranged for a private room. Hospital life itself, the details of it, made James happy. The taut, white bed had hand controls that lifted and bent the mattress in a number of comfortable ways. A television set had been mounted high on the wall opposite him and was obedient to a panel of buttons nestled in his palm like an innocent gun. Effortlessly, he flicked his way back and forth among news programs, cartoons, mid-morning quiz shows, afternoon soap operas, and the evening lineup: *Gunsmoke, Paladin, The Lone Ranger,* and *The Invisible Man.*

I showed up every day. Sometimes, James pressed the off button on the little control, used another button to adjust the tilt of his bed, and fell asleep as simply as an infant. I usually stayed awhile longer, turned the television back on, and covered James with blankets, being careful not to disturb the IV tube in his left hand.

Near the end of the first week, James was instructed to get up and walk a little each day. Walking meant pushing the spindly, rattling IV pole along with him. He always waited to take his walks until I was there. There was a certain jaunty knack to it. He eased the wheels over the raised metal sills here and there in the linoleum corridor and placed his left hand at the balance point, swinging it out of the way of another patient promenading with his own gangling chrome partner. It was a sport for us. From observing other patients, I learned the trick of removing the IV bag and threading it through his bathrobe sleeve and reshaping it—so that he could close his bathrobe.

James was very weak. His first steps, in the moss-green spongy slippers the hospital provided, were timid and brittle, but as the days passed, the duration of his walks increased. He found amusement in my self-appointed coaching, "Let's get to the end of the hall, by those windows in the waiting room." On another day, we made it around the corner and past a snack bar where I purchased a candy bar to share. We went farther to an elevator bank and a carpeted lounge where pregnant women and young husbands held hands. The attendants at various desks in the halls came to know us and nodded and cheered James on as we passed. As his handling of the IV pole increased, so did his immodesty.

Two weeks passed before James was discharged. Follow-up treatment required another five weeks of strict bed rest involving daily doses of microsulfon, weekly injections of penicillin, and intensive nursing care. This phase of James's recovery was spent as a guest at Dr. Wade's home. Over my mother's objections, Dr. Wade paid the hospital bill and flatly refused any attempted payment arrangements.

What happened to that guardian angel believed to watch over children? Dr. Wade came along a little late in our childhood, but his presence helped ease us into adolescence. It took James months to recuperate. He remained underweight, suffered abdominal pain, and experienced a loss of appetite. His physical health was never the same with the irreversible damage to the valves of his heart.

A bond developed between James and Dr. Wade that I envied. As Thornton Wilder said, "I am convinced that, except in a few extraordinary cases, one form or another of a childhood filled with neglect and unhappiness is essential to the formation of exceptional gifts." I am convinced that James's gift was becoming a heart surgeon.

* * * * * * * * *

Our mother's complexity continued to surprise us as we grew older. We took turns trying to describe her. Glib, tossed-off sentences proved to be inadequate.

James caught me off guard with his self-deprecating participation, which at times had the texture of some kind of act of sanctification and unburdening. It was awkward, detached, and analytical. "I'm a cold man. It's difficult for me to let anyone get close. Even Rebecca, that's the girl down in North Carolina, complains I'm standoffish."

I grimaced when Daniel seized on this rare opportunity, "I've known people who almost suffered from frostbite after being around you for awhile."

I was beginning to grow weary of Daniel's cynical repartee. When I asked about beautiful memories, he responded, "Don't know. Heard of 'em. Just never had one."

We were getting a lot of that from him. I jumped at the opportunity to gently chide him, "Little brother, give it a rest. Your sarcasm and contempt is getting a bit old." Daniel had not changed. He had a most difficult personality to try to grasp. The resentments were all too easy to understand, but to grapple with the whining and sulking, which began before he was old enough to go off to first grade, and the protesting against anything in the name of authority, which started soon after despite all attempts at propitiation, solidified over the years into his core.

He was still clever, had a quick mind, and spoke with a sharp tongue. Because of his unshakable enmity and anger, he made himself into whatever anyone in authority said he wasn't. More sadly, and to the point, he made himself into whatever he wasn't. Growing up with Daniel meant there was a constant tension close by. He worked hard to keep his life a perpetual challenge.

James continued, "I don't want to be this way. But even when I'm most aware of it, I'm helpless to do anything about it."

Daniel would not relent entirely, "You probably think love is just another thing that has to be learned. This isn't something from one of your anatomy texts. If it could be divided into parts, numbered, and named, I have no doubt you would have mastered it."

"What I am getting at is that I don't think we were taught it," James responded. "I think mom once knew it, but it got lost somewhere and made her instruction to us flawed."

James's comment made me think about the young woman who brought trouble and misery to the art of loving. Love had to cross the threshold of a burning house where so many memories died in a fire set by the KKK. Love had to tiptoe beneath the heartache of a stillborn daughter and the corpse of her husband. What did love feel like when its hands were bloodstained in the strands of time?

Daniel became silent. James stared at him and said in a wry, sardonic demeanor, "Maybe you got it. I didn't." After a brief pause, hoping for a return of fire from Daniel that never came, James mused, "Everyone talks about love all the time. It's like the weather. But how does someone learn to do it? How do I unlock those pipes and jets where it lies in the deepest part of me? No one taught me the steps to that dance." Anguish accompanied James's words.

I stepped into the void of silence and tried to offer some comfort, "It's something that doesn't take to worry very well." James had this habit of embracing pessimism that drove us all crazy. On the most perfect days—for us that didn't entail much—my mother would quietly say to Daniel and me, "Don't fret. James will find something to worry about."

Wanting to offer James more, I said, "Let love be. Don't handle it too much. It'll find its own way in its own time."

"It doesn't work that way for me," James answered.

Daniel chimed in, "Love any way you can, James. You need a definition for it, nine or ten words you can repeat over and over that sum it up. You like it when you've got procedures to follow. Well, here's a news flash for you: love is about action. It isn't about talk and never has been. Growing up together, you've shown plenty of love to us. You've always been there for our mom."

I was surprised and impressed with Daniel's sudden sensitivity. "What about Rebecca? You said something about heading toward the altar."

"That was all talk, Lander, wishful thinking. She says she loves me, but I'll do something to screw it up."

"That doesn't sound like you," Daniel insisted. At that point, James let the conversation die and we made no attempts to resurrect it.

And that's the way our conversation went all day—serious at times, melancholy at others. The laughter was frequent, but now and then had a cutting and bitter edge. A soft fire of friendship burned that seemed capable of being extinguished with the slightest provocation.

As we grew up in Washington, some invisible river ran through us, marking off separate realms of the spirit that rendered our brotherhood both inscrutable and promissory. People always made the mistake of thinking we were closer than we really were. James and Daniel resembled each other in some ill-made, thoughtless way, like cheap copies. I was the aberration. In most things, we related to the world in opposing styles.

Our life had been dangerous and harmful, yet all three of us found it somehow enabling. It had produced somewhat strange children. Our existence had been the breeding ground of eccentricities, beauty, and an ineffable resiliency. Growing up had been unrelentingly harsh. We endured the long years of watching our world corrode around the edges and our mother growing weary of even faking the art of mothering. We all agreed that we had been born to a difficult mother and could draw passionate indictments against her. But I think we began to forgive her for being exactly what she was meant to be, given the brutality and treachery of her experiences.

But there were huge, unbridgeable gaps in our memories of our father and life in the Arkansas Delta. Repression was both a great theme and a burden of our lives. We all had serious demons within us who were ruthless censors. They effaced the Arkansas Delta past and replaced it with the white, baffled noise of forgetfulness. We never broke our vow of silence about the Ku Klux Klan, the devastation, destruction, and death they brought to our lives and interior existence.

We had cleared out the shed and anything of value was given to Ann. Everything was boxed and labeled properly and left in the attic. It was agreed that James would take possession of the library of memorabilia when his residency was completed.

We convened the following morning, with little of the previous day's enthusiasm, having seriously misjudged the toll this final chore would usurp from our overwrought and depleted eagerness. Ann helped us dispose of Abigail's clothes. A woman's shelter in Pittsburgh would pick up the boxes. Understandably, Ann said, "I don't want to see anyone around Washington in my sister's clothes." We began to empty the contents of my mother's dresser. In the top drawer was the overstuffed combination album and scrapbook that contained photographs, newspaper clippings, and letters—most of them from Arkansas.

For all the times Abigail had opened and closed the album she loved so much, the two brass pins that attached the front and back covers had bent and then broke, causing most of the book's black construction paper pages to loosen and detach. My mother had made no attempt to restore the loose pages to their proper chronological order. The result was a book of anachronisms: snapshots from the forties and fifties opposite turn-of-the century studio portraits; time shuffled up and bolted. Having survived our exodus from the Delta, during our first few years in Washington, the album was a constant evening companion to my mother. As time passed, the scrapbook slowly disappeared from her lap.

We took the album out to the living room and began to leaf through its contents. Tucked in the inside front cover were pictures of our father that had been cut from folded newsprint, now stained brown with age and as light and brittle as dead skin. Papa, the stern-faced paragon of accomplishment, was the subject of a few dozen sepia-tinted photographs. As we flipped through the pages and made the Bryant family a jerking, imperfect movie, my mother was the star of the album. In one picture, she's one in a line of her dour-faced brothers and sisters posed in front of the campus rectory. In another photograph, at nine or ten, she stands beside her lanky father on the front porch of the Tuskegee house wearing a sack-like dress and a sober look that matches Papa's.

Our eyes rested on one photograph that we recognized from our mother's repeated story about it. Like so many of our recollections of events represented by the photographs, they were fragments—sounds and sensations that had more to do with my mother's retelling of a story than anything stored in our brain.

CJ had taken the picture just a couple of months prior to that September night of 1947 down by the river dock. James and I were smiling at the camera and both of us had our arms draped around Daniel's shoulders. Daniel was laughing and staring up at James with the pure, uncomplicated affection for a big brother. Behind us, past the dock and the marsh, small and barely visible, my mother was waving at my father from the backyard. If any of us knew what that September night would bring, we would not have been smiling. But the photograph stopped time, and those three smiling Duncan boys would stand on that riverbank forever holding one another close in a bond of frail, but imperishable love.

Next was the picture of two young people in front of a brick stoop. The extravagantly beautiful young woman wore a large hat and a long summer dress. The tall, young man, looked confident in his full-dress army uniform with cap, leather bandoleer, leather gloves, and high sleek leather boots. This was one of my favorite photographs. My father was a handsome, young fellow, especially in that outfit. Shaded by the hat, our mother looked white. They were so attractive; they looked like the children of royalty. They shone with a radiant health. My father was hard and muscled and a soldier; my mother's generous beauty was as voluptuous and lush as a field of flowers in the rain.

Whenever I saw that picture, I shamefully wondered about the joy they must have taken in each other's bodies, the fires and passions that must have lit the way to the conception of three boys. The pictures, all of them, broke my heart. In the photographs, like most children, we always smiled and my parents were laughing. All the images pasted to that album spoke a fluid, happy language of an extraordinary man and woman who produced a line of children—sleek, shining with vigor, robust, green, and hard to hold back. *What a lovely, wonderful family we were*, I thought as I studied the photographs that framed the flood tide of egregious lying.

Daniel's favorite photograph of our father, a faded black-and-white one, occupied a separate page in the album. It was a snapshot, more than likely taken with a Brownie box camera before a boxing match, of Lieutenant CJ Duncan as a middleweight participant on the army base special services boxing team.

An inspection of the photograph showed CJ's athletic, lean, and muscular physique with handsomely carved features and his signature Clark Gable mustache. With an intense glare, he had the unwavering gaze of the prowling carnivore; everything eradicated but the appetite for victory. The look is level, issuing straight out of him like a command, even while his chin is steeply tucked into the shoulder. His boxing gloves are at the ready in the classic position, out in front, and each looks as large in circumference as his face. One gets the subliminal sense of someone with three heads. *With love from the Champ* was inscribed in faint blue ink across the back of the picture.

This photograph provoked a poignant admission from Daniel, "I have a notion that sometimes I see him—our father. The last time was six months ago in a supermarket. There he was—as I picture him in my mind—leaning on his shopping cart. He smiled at me with such a jovial recognition. And all I did was stretch my mouth impersonally, as at a stranger, and kept on going toward the checkout. Once I was in the parking lot, I made an excuse to myself—to myself, mind you—that I had forgotten something, and I hurried back into the store. I went up and down the aisle, looking. But in just that time, he was gone. There was the bare chance, though that he was still there; I kept going up and down the aisles. I found myself going in one direction and then in another, looking into faces beseeching them to tell me where I could find my dad. I finally convinced myself that whoever that was, it was not my father who had left me behind again."

Tears fell from Daniel's eyes as he added, "I feel humiliated for telling you this. Am I crazy?"

"Well, join the club," James chimed in. "I've seen him at airports, church, on a street corner."

I added my list of sightings. We shared a feeling about the history of our father and had not found closure. The feeling was in our voices when we said his name on rare occasions. His story was a horrible treasure to us, something we could claim that no one else could, a distinction that we would never let go.

The photograph album suddenly took on the semblance of a scrapbook of letters and greeting cards from her family and friends. Arnetta wrote some of the most delicate and graceful letters. One of our favorites was about how to raise us:

May 1, 1946

Dear Abigail,

There are some things that aunts can teach children who become mothers. Teach your boys these things and teach them well. Teach them the quiet verbs of kindness, to live beyond themselves. Urge them toward excellence, drive them toward gentleness, pull them deep into yourself, and pull them upward toward manhood, but softly like an angel arranging clouds. Let your spirit move through them softly, as your spirit has always moved through me. Teach them what you know the best.

The letter was torn carefully at this point as if by design and ended abruptly.

Three hours later, we thought we had come to the end of the dizzying, overwhelming collection of the past. But in the pocket of a partially torn back cover, there were a half-dozen letters from CJ, written when he was in the midst of the war. What a find! The existence of these letters had escaped us and was never brought to our attention after we left Arkansas. James placed the letters in chronological order and passed them around.

Another hour passed and we hardly uttered a complete sentence, captured by the contents of CJ's letters. As we read and reread them, it was as though the winds of time blew his words toward us in a final gesture of an exquisite sensibility, telling us to remember him. I was surprised by the peace those letters brought me.

It was now midafternoon and our rescheduled flights gave us only another couple of hours before we needed to head to Pittsburgh. We lost track of time and were now rushed. Ann would finish the dressers and store anything she deemed of sentimental value in the attic.

When we returned the scrapbook to the bedroom, the white Bible on the night table, that Papa had given Abigail as a wedding gift, caught my attention. As I picked it up, a sprinkling of mementos and flowers fell out in tough, withered petals like lost gloves of elves.

In springtime, my mother would wear gardenias in her hair, a habit she inherited from her mother and brought with her from the Delta. By our second year in Washington, my mother had thriving gardenias and rosebushes. She would wear a flower as though it was a piece of white jewelry stolen from a king's greenhouse. When the gardenias exhausted themselves on the bush and the bruised flowers lay on the ground, haunting the air with their sweet decay, we knew the roses would not be far behind. We could annotate the spring and summer days by the flowers in our mother's hair. And it was from this innocent and charming habit that I learned yet another unforgettable lesson about the disfiguring cruelty of bigotry and racism in that little town.

Abigail always wore her gardenias when she shopped. Though she seldom bought much, she loved the rituals and courtesies of shopping in a small town—the pleasantries exchanged over counters, the cheerful gossip of shopkeepers, and the streets alive with commerce. She had Wednesdays off from her domestic job at the Fitch's and that became her shopping day—with me in lockstep behind her. She dressed carefully on those days. Walking down Main Street, Abigail had to be one of the prettiest, most exotic women in Washington—and she knew it. It was a joy to watch her walk, to see the eyes of men attendant and respectful as she approached. The eyes of women, black and white, registered something else when she passed. I watched the women withhold approval as my mother made her way past storefronts, pausing briefly to admire her reflection in the window and to note the stir she made in her lovely passage. She moved with a flawless coherence of instinct, but she moved with beauty alone. With a gardenia in her hair and her makeup artfully applied, she entered Gertrude's dress shop. Wearing makeup was forbidden of Adventist women, but on Wednesdays,

Abigail took a day off from these prohibitions. This was consistent with the way she pursued our new faith.

Abigail said good morning to Mrs. Adams and her sales staff, who were all congregated near the counter. The women returned her greeting politely. Tommie Adams, the son of the dress shop owner was one of my schoolmates, so I would say hello or nod my head in greeting. I remember one particular day when my mother selected a dress she could not afford from the rack and went to the dressing room in the back of the store to try it on.

I stood near the dressing room and heard Mrs. Adams say to one of the women, "I wouldn't be surprised if that woman came in here with a rose hanging out of her mouth, snapping her fingers like a flamenco dancer. She's one of the colored maids who works for the Fitch's and tries to pass as white. I should enforce our policy of not allowing coloreds to try on clothes, but I give her some slack because the boy with her goes to the same school as my Tommie. I don't know why they even let that colored family attend our school. Did you see her nails? They are deplorable; I'm sure she's got her hands in cleaning solutions all day."

I didn't know whether Mrs. Adams intended my mother to hear her—I hoped not. My mother pulled the curtain open, smiled, and put her fingers to her lips. Then she turned back to look at herself in the mirror. She reached up and took the gardenia from her hair and tossed it into the wastepaper basket. Then she studied her nails. She stayed in the dressing room another few minutes pretending to make up her mind about buying the dress she could never afford. We never saw her adorn her glorious hair with a single blossom again. I missed those gardenias and the sweet scent that she carried with her that attracted bees and worshipful sons. I cannot smell a gardenia without thinking of my mother, and I cannot think of a woman's fingernails without hating Mrs. Adams for stealing the flowers from my mother's hair.

I opened the Bible to the glossy pages between the Old and New Testament to see my name inscribed on the family tree and found an unaddressed envelope. I took the letter out carefully, feeling a bit unsure. My brothers had taken up positions on either side of me. The sheets of paper had been folded in thirds. I did not have to be told to read it aloud; their quizzical expressions spoke for them. As I unfolded the pages, it was immediately obvious the letter had been written in starts and stops. It was not dated. I stumbled over words in the first couple of sentences, trying to become accustomed to the idiosyncrasies of my mother's scribbled hand.

Dear Doe,

I hope you can make sense out of my scribbling. The chemo seems to be doing no good in even slowing things down and unless by some miracle I go into remission, I have only a few weeks left to my life. Your expected visit at the end of the month might come too late for what I need to discuss with you.

Our lives have been so interwoven since the age of fifteen when we were both pregnant and our husbands were thousands of miles away on some army base preparing to go to war. We were just frightened girls clinging to each other for strength to survive in a godforsaken place like the Arkansas Delta that bred hardship and calamity. Our deep friendship and sisterhood have been like an open book, sharing the pages of our lives, including our most intimate secrets. You have never judged me or been critical of my life, so I don't know why I've waited so long to solicit your advice. Deathbeds have always been known to produce some dramatic confessions— and mine is a doozey. My pen always gets stuck here because writing it down makes it more real. I've never told Lander that CJ isn't his father. You were wary of that white well-driller, Lucas, the first time he came to the farm. Right from Lander's birth, there's been no mistaking the resemblance. The last time I saw Lander, nine years ago, he was the image of Lucas. CJ had to know something. It broke my heart to watch the way he mistreated Lander and the affection and attention he heaped on James and Daniel—I know you saw it too. You and I were the only ones who knew he was a full-term baby. Everyone thought he was premature, coinciding with my trip to Fort Huachuca. Thank God, he was so small. I was so ashamed and afraid. Maybe this disease is God's way of dealing out his ultimate punishment. I thought he was finished when he took CJ from us. He has tested me and I have shown him my faith and atonement. Aside from you and the good Lord, I have shared this with my pastor, Reverend Butler.

I come to you this last time for your wisdom. I am afraid that taking this secret to my grave without telling Lander will not let me rest in peace. But the consequences of such a revelation might do more harm than good. I've asked James to find him.

The letter ended with the same abruptness that we felt from the impact of what we had just learned. For several minutes, I just sat there, expressionless, profoundly dumbstruck by the revelation. My first instinct was affront and anger. I was afraid my somber demeanor would give way to an eruption of emotion with the severity of one who is bereft beyond redemption.

Unlike Daniel, for whom the English language was an instrument of disharmony, bedlam, and obfuscation, it was one of clarity, calm, and equanimity for me. But I was emotionally high-strung and tender. Words spoken in innocence by anyone in the family could take on a worrisome significance to me. Conversations had the possibility of easily puncturing me. The slightest change of emphasis or shift of intonation could cause hurt feelings or even tears. It was not always easy to gain access to those stationary realms where I felt safe. My emotional equilibrium was movable and often adrift.

Rather than an outburst, seemingly glued to the edge of her bed, I asked no one in particular, "I'm not a Duncan? I'm the progeny of some white man I don't even know? Can this be true?" I read the letter again slowly and began to sob like a little boy who had something precious taken from him.

Suddenly, I was aware that James and Daniel, dumbfounded, looked at me differently. At that moment, it was impossible not to see the total absence of a resemblance to me. It registered and registered quickly, in rapid increments, as with a distant star seen through a lens that you've steadily magnified to the correct intensity. What I saw, when at long last I did see—all the way to my mother's secret—was the facial resemblance of a white man.

Growing up, I never took seriously my remarkable physical disparity from my brothers. My mother always answered that I was a "throwback" to someone on her father's side. In general, questions about us light-skinned Duncans—blacks, to be sure, but in the words of one tolerant mother of a school friend of mine, "people of a very pleasing shade, rather like eggnog"—were answered by stories about our genealogy and how intermingled with whites we were. Of course, there was the stark reality of having a great-grandfather who was white. But the more interesting stories came from Papa's side of the family, the cornerstone of which was a settlement of *colored* people, many nearly

271

white, including a great-great-grandmother. In some way, everyone was related to everyone else. The way we heard it, was the way Papa used to explain it to Abigail when she was a girl. Beginning with "way, way back" and simplifying and condensing as best he could, he passed on all the lore he had ever heard.

My brothers and I took great interest in the maze of family history. We loved our mother's stories about our ancestry. When she used the word pedigree, it made our kinship and our light complexion something that gave us a special identity worthy of respect.

The elaborate clockwork of her secret, the beautiful collaboration of her deceit that kept it hidden until now overwhelmed me. I felt blindsided by the uncontrollability of something and the provisional nature of everything—the present moment, the common lot, the current mood, and the skeletons falling out of family closets.

I couldn't imagine anything that could have made my mother more of a mystery to me than the unmasking of this secret. Now that I knew this, which seemed like everything, it was as though I knew nothing. The letter not only failed to unify my idea of her, but she became an unknown person who lacked cohesion. In what proportion, to what degree, had her secret determined her daily life, permeated her everyday thinking, and affected her relationship with me? Did our father know—but choose to find denial, sublimation, and anger a more suitable refuge to hide his pain? It would have been difficult to ignore my obvious distinctness.

Did my mother's secret transform over the years from being a smoldering secret to being a composed secret to being a forgotten secret of no importance? Was that the reason for the intermittent episodes of severe depression? At one moment, was it a secret that took her away from us, and, at other times, was she able to bury it somewhere and crawl back to reality?

By the time we had grown up, had the secret become merely a pigment barely tinting the coloration of my mother's total being? Or was the totality of her being nothing but a vestige in the shoreless sea of a lifelong secret? I assume, yes, and at a certain point the balance shifted toward the new life in Washington. The life in Little Rock receded. But did she ever completely get over the fear that she was going to be found out? The only person aside from Doretha who knew her secret was Revered Butler. Why him? As it is a human thing to have a secret, it is also a human thing, sooner or later, to reveal it. But Abigail was different.

Our mother loved secrets. From the day we arrived in Washington, and having to maintain the circumstances of our exodus from Little Rock, there were always little secrets with her. She never let anyone in on her secrets or what was going on in her head. Others always opened up to her about themselves. But that wasn't the power or the pleasure for her. The power and the pleasure were to be found in the opposite by not revealing her true self. When she let a secret out, she let it out in other ways. Her sons, her music, her poetry, and her beauty spoke her secrets.

I thought back to that puzzling conversation with Reverend Butler during the ride to the hospital when he had said, "Secrets bind us. Early ones. You were too young to know anything about your mother or father for that matter during their years in Arkansas. There were things she told me. She had trouble finding peace with herself."

She had entrusted her secret to Reverend Butler. It tied into the pact that I, as well as my brothers, sensed was between them. They had a mutual recognition that there was no clean way out, no way to reveal this secret to me. Maybe that pact froze everything in time. People age. Nations age. Problems age. Sometimes they age right out of existence. But her secret froze right there with Reverend Butler—at least until she approached death.

Why didn't she just mail that letter to Doretha? A part of me wanted to believe she placed that letter in the Bible to be found by us. It was a confession. The placement of the letter where the family tree was recorded gave a poetic, if not cruel, impression of not knowing where to place me in the order of things.

My restraint finally collapsed. The way I careened around that bedroom made me think of those familiar chickens that keep on going after having been beheaded. My identity had been lopped off; I became emotionally amputated and was spinning out of control. I got up off the bed, sat down, and got up again. I roamed round and round the room, speaking loudly and in a rush. My ranting was filled with charges, denials, gross and deliberate misinterpretations of the letter, and a pervasive sense of unreality. I uttered my random thoughts, "There is something awful about withholding something so crucial to what a person is …. It was my birthright to know my real father …. I was born recognizably white. Why didn't she just admit it? … Should I hate mother for never telling me? I had the right to know and hear it from her …. There will always be a lie at the foundation of my relationship with her, a terrible lie." I felt lopsided and distorted from the toxic affect of all the emotion coursing through me. There was nothing that could be said to ease my suffering.

It had long passed the time to leave. I was clearly unhinged, and James and Daniel offered to take me to the airport. Although it was cutting it close, I asked James to detour crosstown to the cemetery. We parked on the street and walked through the gates together to our mother's grave site. We stood beside the uneven mound of earth roughly heaped over her coffin. The bells of the college rang clearly through the shimmering light and the cool damp air. I tried to think of something to say, a summing up, but I could think of nothing.

The sun, red and enormous, began to sink into the western sky. Simultaneously, the moon began to rise on the other side of the hills with its own glorious shade of red, coming up out of the trees like a russet firebird. The sun and moon seemed to acknowledge each other as they moved in both opposition and concordance in a breathtaking dance of light. As we watched it, I thought I would cry. We remembered her story—pointing to the sun and then turning to look at the rising moon, calling to the sun and then to the moon.

"I'm going to make it," I said. Then, looking at the sun and the moon again, added, "It all comes back. It's all a circle." I turned around, and facing the moon, which was higher now and silvery, raised my arms into the air. I cried out in a brittle yet defiant voice, "Oh, mother, do it again." I said it as a prayer, a regret.

Turning to James, I said, "I'm so sorry for everything. For being gone so long."

"It's all right Lander. We've made it back to each other. We've got lots of time to try our hand at restoring the ruins."

We embraced, no promises were made. James, Daniel, and I joined hands, lowered our heads, and repeated the watchword: "May the Lord watch between me and thee, while we are absent one from another. Amen."

As we walked away, I knew that I would have to deal with the deep fear that the broken link of progeny would haunt the remainder of my life. I was afraid that one of the consequences of having loved my mother so fully, of having been estranged from her at the time of her death, and of her leaving behind such a damning and destructive secret would never let me be.